Blue Spell

John Harvey

BLUE SPELL

john@johnharvey.net

Published 2021 by On-site Creative
OnsiteCreative.ca

ISBN: 9781777720032

FOR MICHELLE. ALWAYS.

.

Chapter 1

Jack Scatter balanced at the edge of the two-story roof, practicing magic.

A yellow tennis ball hovered beyond his reach. It was an ordinary ball, one he'd used on his school's courts many times. He moved the wand's tip in a circle to set the ball spinning. The gesture was unnecessary—his thoughts controlled the movement—but the motion helped him picture the invisible energy field.

He released the ball and let it drop twenty feet. Just before it hit the gravel, he flicked the wand, directing a beam of energy to bounce it back to its original height. He stretched out to snatch it, overreached, slipped, and fell.

"*JACK*," his father warned, too late.

Jack flung his arms forward. The tennis ball shot into the sky and he froze at an impossible angle, leaning over open air with his feet glued to the weathered concrete parapet.

"*Hold on.*" Victor scrambled onto the roof through the hatchway.

Jack hung motionless, as if gravity didn't apply to him. *I must have redirected the field instinctively*; a surprising and fortunate discovery. "I'm okay."

With his heart pounding, he concentrated on tilting himself upright. He imagined the energy field as a rising wind, pushing him from below. The movement was disorienting, but the world slowly rotated back to normal.

Victor grasped his shoulder, pulled him down onto the flat roof, and spun him around. "Your mother would've had a heart attack if she'd seen that." His grip, hardened by decades of labor, was firm but not painful.

Jack met his father's eyes and saw concern, not anger. "Sorry. I slipped."

"I saw." Victor's expression softened. "And you shouldn't be playing with that where someone can see you."

Jack tucked the wand into his jacket pocket and gestured at the two dozen neighboring structures. "There's no one here anymore. There hasn't been for weeks."

Victor considered the abandoned warehouses and garages a mile from town, and didn't argue. "Can you see the drone?"

"Not yet." Jack picked up the binoculars. "It's really late this time."

"They may not have sent it if they saw the storm coming."

"Maybe. I've never seen one like it, either." It had formed so quickly. Towering clouds lined the entire eastern horizon, but the sun was setting behind them in a clear sky. The missing drone should have been easy to spot against that backdrop, yet there was no sign of it.

Two months ago, locating the drone would have taken only a few taps on his phone. But then Pieter Reynard—well, actually Jack himself—had partially fulfilled a centuries-old prophecy by Sir Isaac Newton to bring about the apocalypse. The world didn't end as Newton predicted, but Jack had wiped out the portal network and most of the services people took for granted.

Portals—tiny wormholes through which power and data flowed—had been part of modern life for decades. There was no longer an internet, no phones or text messaging, and limited electricity. He'd destroyed the portal crystals to save Cirrus, the world-sized space station he lived on, and unintentionally isolated it from Earth. Likewise, his hometown of Fairview felt more cut-off than ever.

The roof they stood on covered the family's workshop. *Before Newton*—the time before the loss of the network—their business had been drone-maintenance and repair. The self-guided aircraft were essential to the small farming community, and the warehouse below was once filled with them. The few it contained now are lifeless.

Jack was about to give up for the night when fading sunlight reflected off a shiny surface traversing an angry black cloud. "Finally. Uh … that's not right."

"What do you see?"

Jack passed the binoculars to his father. "Look how fast it's coming." Ahead of the drone, which was still miles away, the treetops lashed chaotically.

Victor glanced at the collection of objects Jack had been practicing with: more balls, a folding chair, books, assorted tools. "We have to clean this up. Now."

The windstorm approached with a roar as they scurried around the roof, gathering and throwing items through the open hatch without looking. Like a vast, invisible river, it ushered a wave of frenzied motion across the yellow-green fields of canola. When the cold front hit the workshop, it pushed Jack backwards, causing him to lose his footing again.

Victor, Jack's height but thirty pounds heavier, helped him stand. "That blasted drone is trying to land."

Jack shielded his eyes from flying debris and looked up. The six-foot wide aircraft had slowed and tilted sharply into the howling wind. Before Newton, a drone would have linked to sensors on the ground and compensated for the gusts, or just waited until the storm passed. But this one was following its limited programming and struggling to stay upright as it descended.

He drew the wand. "It's going to need help."

Victor retreated to the warehouse to give the drone a clear landing zone. "Can you reach it from here?"

Rain fell as Jack sheltered in the hatchway, then turned and focused on the flying courier. "It's about sixty feet up. That's near my limit." He concentrated, sensing the drone's mass and inertia through the wand.

Ethan Marke, Jack's cousin, had dubbed the device a magic wand, although it was really a cylindrical portal crystal encased in a metal tube. The name stuck because, well, what else could it be? Jack had learned to move objects, produce water, fire, light, even unlock doors. To an observer, it would appear to be magic, and Ethan had been pestering him for details about it for weeks.

Jack started with a gentle downward pressure, then gripped the sinking drone more firmly. The machine fought, spun, and nearly flipped over once. But as it dipped near the landing pad, the action of its rotors became irrelevant—Jack's control was absolute; he could move it wherever he wanted.

"I got it." The drone's motors shut off as soon as its landing struts touched the rain-slicked surface.

When it was safe, he and Victor dashed onto the roof to tie the aircraft to three anchor bolts. Jack retrieved a handful of papers from the small cargo hold and tucked them into his jacket pocket to keep them dry. Even though there'd been no real trouble in Fairview since the breakdown, Victor removed the drone's power cell.

By the time they finished, the sun had set and the shower had become a downpour. Victor closed the roof hatch and joined Jack in the nearly empty warehouse. He shook water from his thinning hair. "We're already soaked. There's no point waiting for it to stop."

Lightning flashed as they ran, revealing Fairview's squat, pyramid-like profile. Their home was a two-story townhouse on the outskirts, but most of the town's five thousand residents lived in increasingly taller towers clustered within a single square mile.

The sudden storm was unlike any Jack had experienced; Cirrus' weather-control systems must have failed. An unseasonably cold wind pelted them with falling branches as they fought their way up the tree-lined street. It was raining even harder when they jogged up the steps to their front door.

- - - - -

Jack's mother, Emily, sat at the kitchen table and read the letter from her father, Holden. "Dad wants us to come tomorrow." She passed the page to Victor.

"Why?" Jack asked as he toweled off his wet hair. "Didn't he originally say next week?"

"Apparently, Niels thinks his fusion generator is failing and wants your father's help to complete the solar farm."

"Is that something he *remembers* or something he *knows*?"

Victor scratched his stubbly beard: a recent acquisition that had more to do with rolling blackouts than fashion. "With Niels, it's best to assume there's no difference. If he says something is going to happen, it will."

Niels, an accomplished engineer, was also a *Traveller*: someone who could *remember* things that hadn't happened yet. He'd warned of turmoil across Cirrus in the months ahead and invited Jack's family to join him and a dozen others in Icarus to ride out the worst of it. Jack's parents had been preparing for the trip for weeks.

Emily rested her chin heavily on her palm. "Are you okay with leaving your friends behind?"

"Yeah," Jack said, "it's fine. Ethan will be there. And I'm bored without school anyway." Saying this, he realized why his mother seemed so tired; his parents must feel the same without their jobs. He'd kept himself busy searching the fields and forests for crashed drones, but they didn't have even that distraction. And he was running out of drones to recover, having to walk farther from town each day. Last month he'd celebrated his sixteenth birthday trolling the bottom of the lake for salvage. "But Icarus is hardly more than a wilderness camp. We'll be roughing it. When do we leave?"

"First thing in the morning," Victor said. "So no one sees that we've still got a working vehicle."

"There's something else in the envelope." Jack removed another slip of paper and recognized Niels' shaky handwriting. "It's a map." He flipped the page around to position north at the top. "Niels sent directions for getting to Icarus."

"Good. I wasn't looking forward to finding it by memory."

"I could find it again. Ethan and I found the lake in the dark."

"We are *not* going over the Spine where you did," Emily said. "With this weather, it's probably buried in snow. We'll follow the highway."

"What's this mean?" Jack pointed to a caption on the map: *Here be dragons*.

Victor chuckled. "It's an expression that was used on maps centuries ago. It meant the area beyond was unexplored, that no one knew what to expect. That's got to be Niels' way of saying not to go off-road or we'll get lost."

- - - - -

There was another letter in that day's delivery: from Sarah Rogers. Jack brought it to his tiny second-floor bedroom.

He was surprised by how much he missed her. Although they'd known each other most of their lives, they'd spent only a few days together in August. Before that, they'd only ever met online. Now, limited to sending letters, he was frustrated by how difficult it was to communicate.

Sarah was a natural letter writer. While Jack struggled to create even the briefest note, hers were long and detailed. Their correspondence ran on a six-day cycle, the time the drone took to fly a circuit between Caerton, Port Isaac, Fairview and Icarus. Her two-page letter described events in Caerton and how life there was becoming depressingly boring. With no computers, there was no school, and the only jobs were those in the greenhouses.

Her closing line: *See you soon*, made him smile. She'd been dropping hints about meeting for several weeks, which was both maddening and intriguing. *Is that something she remembers?* Or was she making a subtle suggestion so he'd find a way to make it happen?

Sarah, like Pieter Reynard, was also a Traveller, although neither was as talented as Niels. Before Newton, conventional wisdom said that Travellers must pass through a large wormhole to connect to their future memories. Now, *After Newton*, that wasn't so clear.

Niels, possibly the most gifted Traveller ever, had made accurate predictions leading up to Newton, but hadn't left his private island for decades. Things Sarah wrote about in her letters had come true, but even she wasn't sure she hadn't just worked them out logically. The world had changed so much that it was unlikely she'd ever *travel* again.

Jack faced the window as lighting illuminated the cluster of workshops a mile away, across the canola field. The storm was worsening as it settled in, but his mood was lifting. His chance of reuniting with Sarah had just improved; Icarus was on the other side of the Spine, hundreds of miles closer to Caerton.

Chapter 2

Fifty-two hadn't sounded so bad when Sarah started, but each level in the Magnolia occupied two floors and she'd had to stop several times to rest during the grueling climb. Even so, after nearly two thousand steps, she entered the atrium on the fifty-second level with time to spare.

She hadn't encountered any of the Magnolia's residents in the lobby or stairwell. To conserve power, the elevators only ran every second hour. Soon, the tower's inhabitants would emerge from their dwellings to take advantage of another brief window of easy access.

Pre-Newton, the interior garden was a pleasant spot for visitors to rest: verdant, fragrant, and brightly lit by floor-to-ceiling windows at each end of the building, with park benches scattered throughout. But now, strangers were considered suspicious, and someone might see her. Second-floor windows on the inner apartments, once hidden behind branches, opened onto a thinning canopy of brown and curling leaves.

She hurried past a dozen closed doors to the short corridor that connected the atrium to a parallel hallway and an outer strip of apartments. The address she wanted was straight ahead, at the intersection. Like the atrium, windows flanking each end of the long hallway allowed sunlight to make up for the lack of interior lighting.

Six weeks ago, Holden had sent a key in the mail drone—not for her to use—for his Caerton apartment. She was meant to hold on to it until Detective Priya Singh came to collect it. That turned out to be unnecessary; Priya had found a spare in Holden's house in Washington.

Following the same schedule as the elevators, Holden's apartment was without power and gloomy when Sarah entered. She slipped off her shoes and crept into the living room.

Two bedrooms overlooked the main level. Their doors were open. Below the balcony, the door to Holden's workshop was ajar. The kitchen and living room were clean, as if the elderly man was still living there, but most of the books had been removed from the tall shelves that flanked the electric fireplace.

A flash of lightning illuminated the painting above the hearth. Still slightly out of breath, she gasped at the sight. *There it is.* Although she didn't appreciate the abstract landscape, it was easily the most valuable artwork in the city.

Hidden in plain sight, Holden's portal could create a passage to Earth with the press of a button. More importantly, the device had the ability to connect her consciousness across time. She'd *travelled* through it several times already and received future memories that had come true.

What's the harm in a quick trip to Earth? She leaned closer to the frame, searching for the five inconspicuous squares. Disguised as wood inlays in a geometric border, a gentle tap would trigger a color change to show how much charge the portal's crystal matrix held. *I should at least check that it's still working.* She reached out to touch the frame and heard a soft footfall.

Without hesitation, Sarah twisted and struck out with her heel, but the person sneaking up behind her ducked it easily.

"I'm regretting teaching you that move."

"*Priya.*" Sarah's defensive posture vanished and she rushed in for a hug. "You scared me."

"You should be scared. What if I'd been a looter?" Priya, a third-level black belt, leaned past Sarah to check that the hallway was empty. She'd arrived by portal and hidden in the workshop when she heard Sarah. "What are you doing here?"

"I came to see you."

"Who told you I … never mind." There was no point questioning a Traveller.

"You're moving the portal today, aren't you?"

"The storage lockers in my building have power outlets. It'll be a secure place to keep it charged."

"We could store it at my place. It'd be easier for me to pass messages."

"This is still a police investigation. Any messages I need to pass are not for your ears. Besides, I don't think you could resist the temptation of using it."

"But wouldn't that be a good thing? You could tell me where you're looking for Pieter Reynard, and I could remember if that's the place you'll eventually find him."

"We both know it doesn't work that way. Travellers can't fixate on something without their imagination taking over. But now that you're here, I can use your help."

"With the investigation?"

"No, Miss Amazon." Priya handed Sarah a socket driver and pointed at Holden's portal frame. "I can't reach the upper bolts."

The power came back on shortly after Sarah started working, but it took most of the hour to swap the Art Deco frame. Thirty inches on a side, the square, metal-backed wooden frame weighed twenty pounds. The portal crystal itself was only twenty-four inches wide—a tight fit for some Travellers, but large enough to diagonally pass the replacement frame from Earth.

While Sarah hung the new frame, Priya lay the original on the kitchen counter and followed Holden's detailed instructions to remove the landscape print from behind the crystal. What had appeared to be an oil painting on canvas was really a printed plastic film, thinner than paper. Once removed, the polished metal surface under the diamond sheet reflected her image as an ordinary mirror.

Priya handed the print to Sarah to install in the second frame while she adjusted the gap between the square crystal and the metal backing.

"A quarter turn each," Priya recited as she slowly rotated the screwdriver. Holden had stressed that each of the thirty-six screws was to be turned *exactly* that amount, then repeated sixteen times in a pattern that spread the pressure evenly across the crystal.

After turning the final screw, Priya checked on Sarah's

progress. "That's upside-down."

Sarah stood back for a better view of the painting. She tilted her head. "Are you sure?"

Priya rolled her eyes. "It doesn't matter."

"Your apartment is five miles from here. How will you carry the frame?"

Priya tapped the hidden switch, vanishing the sheet of diamond and creating a wormhole to her rented accommodations in Olympia. She reached through and lifted a set of foam-padded aluminum tubes. "Davis uses these to carry a surfboard on his motorbike. How much time do we have?"

Sarah turned the hot water tap. Without communications, the building's management needed a way to prevent residents from being trapped in elevators. They'd decided on shutting off the hot water as a signal that they'd be cutting the power soon. She ran her fingers through the clear stream that poured into the sink.

"It's still warm. We should have at least five minutes."

As expected, the building's residents remained active as long as electricity flowed. Priya and Sarah crowded into a full car and rode to the basement. The mirror they carried earned them some unusual looks, but no one questioned them when they recognized the UN Police logo on Priya's jacket.

In Caerton, bicycles had always been the preferred means of transportation. Pre-Newton, the city's underground freeway thronged with hundreds of thousands of commuters. But that was when people had jobs and somewhere to go, and bikes had power for their electric motors. Now, with only skylights to illuminate the tunnels, Priya and Sarah had their pick of hundreds of abandoned bicycles in the Magnolia's garage.

Priya mounted the surfboard rack on a free bike, strapped the mirror to it with elastic cords, then rolled out of the garage towards the on-ramp.

Sarah knew the way to Priya's apartment and so pedaled beside her, keeping the mirrored surface between them. With only a few hundred riders on each block, the freeway was far from crowded. But with the storm raging above, the tunnels were gloomy and they couldn't risk a collision—a four-square-foot diamond sheet was not indestructible.

At the underground entrance to her building, Priya dismounted and unlocked the door at the end of a short, yellow corridor. Sarah held it open so she could push her bike into the garage, but Priya scuttled backwards saying, "*Quick, close the door.*"

Sarah let it swing shut. "What's wrong?"

"It's Davis." Priya crouched and activated the portal. "He can't know I'm here." She dove headfirst through the wormhole, twanging the elastic cords that secured the frame.

"Why not?" Sarah leaned over, listening to the clamor as Priya struggled to right herself. "You work together."

"Later. Move the frame against the wall."

Sarah swerved the bike and tipped it against the concrete wall seconds before a stocky man wearing the same blue jacket as Priya burst through the door.

Davis, not expecting a bike in the hall, stumbled around it and hurried to the end of the painted corridor. He scanned the crowd of riders, but there were far too many people moving to spot an individual. After only a few seconds, he gave up and confronted Sarah.

"Did you see a woman come out this door wearing a blue jacket?" He pulled the fabric straight to display the UN logo. "Like mine?"

"Sorry." Sarah peered over Davis' shoulder, as if she might have missed someone. "I wasn't paying attention."

Davis stood for a moment, looking puzzled. He glanced at the square frame mounted on the bike and seemed about to question it, then shook his head and returned to the garage.

Sarah stooped towards the mirror after the door closed. "He's gone. Why can't he know you're here?"

"If he knew there was a way to get back to Earth, he'd insist on using it. Then everyone would find out, and that would lead

Pieter to Holden's—"

Sarah coughed loudly as Davis pushed the door open.

"Hi." She smiled and shuffled to place herself between Davis and the mirror, but the man leaned over for a better look.

"I have a set of racks just like that. I didn't know you could get them here."

Sarah glanced down. A faint rectangle of light shone against the yellow wall—Priya's room was brighter than the corridor.

"Uh, my mother brought them from Earth."

"Huh." Davis nodded, perhaps wondering why an immigrant had used so much of their limited cargo space for such an unusual item. He shook his head again and closed the door.

"Are all UN officers so … uh … not tall?" Sarah asked when she and Priya were alone. At five-seven, she'd been looking down into Davis' eyes.

"I'm five-three. I'm not short."

Sarah decided that silence was the best response.

"Davis is on the short side, but our other partner, Katherine, is taller than you. Anyway, we can't move the frame inside now. I'll try another day. Just take it back to Holden's building and open the portal when you get to the garage. I'll help you carry it upstairs."

The light against the wall disappeared.

- - - - -

Priya scanned the room. "This isn't Holden's apartment."

Sarah, sitting cross-legged on her bedroom floor in front of the open portal, gestured defensively. "No, it's my place. But just hear me out. This will be a lot easier. We … I mean, you, won't have to climb all those steps at the Magnolia. My mother works four days a week, and this is actually closer to—"

Priya, also sitting cross-legged on her own carpeted floor, hung her head with an exasperated sigh and raised a hand for Sarah to stop. "Okay, okay. It's fine. Just give me your mother's work schedule and keep the frame out of sight until I have time to try again. And no *travelling*."

"I won't." Sarah began writing her mother's timetable on a scrap of paper.

"I'll know if you do. I've moved the Earth-side frame to my place in Olympia." She leaned forward and met Sarah's eyes. "I'll know if you've been there."

Sarah handed the slip to Priya. "I won't use it. Honest."

"Good, because I'm serious. I know you must want to see if you can make more predictions, but if Pieter Reynard survived Newton, he's looking for this portal. He must suspect that I have it. If he finds *it*, he finds *you*."

Chapter 3

Jack pushed the keyboard away. "I should fill the cargo hold with garbage and send it back. This code makes no sense."

"I'm sure Ethan did the best he could," Emily said.

"Yeah, but I can't figure it out. I'm just gonna delete the whole Port Isaac section."

"Will that work?"

"It's not ideal. The drone will reset back to Caerton first, but it'll end up in Icarus and he can fix it there."

Jack knew enough to work with what Ethan had created, but had little programming experience. His own talent was with mechanical devices; he could *see* how they worked inside. Until recently, he'd thought that was his imagination. Then, during Newton, he'd learned that his skill came from a lifelong interaction with the energy field present in all wormholes, which gave him a sonar-like sense of the internal structure of machines.

Considering what little technology remained, the cousins had done a remarkable job. Jack had rebuilt enough drones for mail service for every city in the sector, and Ethan had devised a way to make them follow the major roads. The families' courier had been flying its sixteen-hundred-mile route for two months without a glitch.

"I've got everything I need." Victor loaded the last of his tools into Dave, a self-driving, open-sided all-terrain vehicle designed for recovering crashed drones. Dave—short for *D*rone *A*ssist *Ve*hicle—had only two seats; Jack would have to squeeze his narrow frame into the cargo bed along with the family's personal effects.

"I'm almost done too." Jack scampered up the ladder to the roof, connected the reprogrammed navigation module, and placed a letter to Sarah in the drone's cargo box. He studied the pre-dawn clouds as the aircraft lifted into a brisk headwind with an energetic buzz. As he lowered himself through the hatchway, he said, "We're going to pass the drone."

"It'll catch up to us eventually." The aircraft's destination lay far to the north, but both vehicles would start off following the highway to the east.

"Will you be okay back there?" Emily asked as Jack wriggled his way into the cargo box. "We could stop at the house for a pillow."

"I'll be fine." Jack and his father had made more room by removing Dave's robotic arm, but it was still a tight fit. "Besides, I thought we carried our stuff here so we wouldn't be seen."

Victor was turning out of the alley when the lights in the neighboring buildings went out. "That's the fourth blackout this week." He pressed the accelerator and Dave sped away from the shop. Its electricity came through a portal connection on Icarus Island.

"Do you think Niels foresaw this?" Jack asked as they rolled away from the darkened town. While most of the sector struggled with rolling blackouts, Icarus had power to spare. "His fusion reactor must have cost millions. It would've been so much simpler to use portals, or even a standard fuel cell, to provide energy to the island."

"That seems unlikely," Emily said. "He would have made that decision decades ago."

"I guess." Jack pulled his collar to shield his neck from the wind as he considered stories he'd heard about Travellers. "But we'd be walking right now if he hadn't."

- - - - -

After many hours of driving, Jack was relieved to see the roadside cairn, the one Niels said marked the final turn. Not only was he cramped and sore, he was freezing. Even though they'd taken the lower-elevation central pass over the Spine—the world-spanning mountain range that divided Cirrus—the family still encountered sleet and hail. The pile of stones pointed to a break in the trees and the rough forest track that led to the perfectly round lake.

"What's all this?" Victor asked as he drove onto the beach. "There were only shacks here last time."

The rocky shoreline had become a construction yard. There was a portable sawmill, piles of lumber, spools of wire, and stacks of plastic tubing. The sounds of saws and other tools resonated through the trees. He parked next to a group of compact vehicles similar to Dave.

Jack tumbled out of the cargo bed, stretching limbs that had been cramped in awkward positions for too long. "Niels said they were planning to build a fishing lodge. It looks like they finally did."

Anders and four younger men were taking advantage of the break in the rain to finish installing shingles on a two-story timber structure above the high-water line. He raised his hammer in greeting when Jack looked his way. The smell of fresh bread wafted from the building to the lake.

"That'll make life easier," Victor said. "Our tents are fine for sleeping in, but I wasn't looking forward to cooking outdoors."

"There's Natalya." Emily waved to Anders' wife, a tall, older woman waving from the broad deck that wrapped around the lodge's second floor. "She looks happy."

Victor and Emily climbed to the lodge on steps built from dry-stacked stones, and Jack followed as soon as he was able. Natalya met them halfway, greeting them like family. Her apron carried the perfume of baking. Jack's stomach grumbled; he'd enjoyed her cooking on his previous visits.

"Come," Natalya said in her strong Russian accent. "I'll introduce you to everyone." She led them along a gravel path that curved around the lodge. Dense trees made it impossible to see behind the wooden building until they entered a football field-sized clearing, lined with twenty-eight cabins of various sizes. "Welcome home." Her voice held warmth and pride.

"Home?" Emily sounded confused.

"Niels hoped to have the roof on your cabin before you

arrived, but yesterday's storm forced us to stop working."

"Our … cabin?" Victor grinned, taking in the scene.

"If you want it." Natalya offered a door key. "Niels included your family in his plans."

The cabins nearest the lodge were complete. At the far end, an automated fabricating machine was busy printing the walls of a new structure.

There were also people—lots of people. A group of twenty men and women were operating machinery around the village while young children played near the forest's edge. Jack recognized several of the adults as Niels' friends and assumed the rest were their families.

"It's lovely." Emily glanced at Victor. "But it … we'll have to discuss it." She smacked Victor on the leg, prompting him to speak.

Victor's grin vanished and he adopted a more serious expression, though he'd already taken the key. "Uh, yeah. We'll have to discuss it."

"What's to discuss?" Anders came around the corner, wiping dirt on his trousers before extending a giant, calloused hand to Victor. "This is your home now." He released Victor's hand, then enveloped Emily in a bear hug that lifted her off her feet. The bottom of his bushy white beard cleared the top of her head by several inches.

There wouldn't be much discussion; even the smallest *cabins* were as large as their tiny home in Fairview. And no one argued with Anders. He was seventy-one years old and wouldn't hurt a fly, but he was also nearly seven feet tall and powerfully built. Emily laughed nervously when Anders set her down.

"Jack," Natalya said, "your parents will have to use the spare bedroom in your grandfather's cabin for a few days. You can drop your bags in the bunk room." She pointed to the lodge's lower level.

As she led his parents away, Jack stepped through a set of glass-paneled doors under the deck and entered a wood-paneled room furnished with six overstuffed chairs, three couches, and a wide stone fireplace. A stairwell leading up to the main level was straight ahead. To the right, six numbered doors led to private suites, set up like hotel rooms.

The common room was empty, and there were only two doors in the left wall. A sign above one read 'Men'. Jack assumed this was one of the bunk rooms.

"Hey, Jack. You made it." Ethan had been sitting on a bed across from another young man and spotted Jack the moment he entered. "Sorry, I took the last lower bunk."

"That's okay." Jack surveyed the room. Four bunk beds lined the outer log wall. There was a second identical row against the inner wall. *Sixteen*, he thought, and gripped the door frame so tightly his knuckles turned white.

"Take it easy, Buddy." Ethan placed a supportive hand on Jack's shoulder. "There are no phones here."

Jack's old habit of counting how many people would be near had kicked in automatically. But the anxiety that caused him to avoid crowds was never created by people. Instead, it was feedback from the emotion detectors embedded in their phones— a *Before-Newton* ailment.

He released the door frame and threw his bags on the bunk above Ethan's, then breathed deeply. "So, this is home, is it?"

The young man Ethan had been speaking with before Jack entered stood and extended his hand. Ethan, six-feet tall with an athletic build, looked like a child compared to the tall blond. "Hi, I'm Marten. You're Ethan's cousin, right?"

Ethan stepped aside as the two shook hands. "Don't know if you knew this already, but everyone here is related to one of Niels' friends. Most of them only left Earth this year."

Marten's kinship with Anders was obvious. He was a couple of years older than Jack, had Ander's height and broad shoulders, but lacked the bulk that would come with age.

"How long have you been here?" Jack asked.

"We came from Caerton shortly after Newton. And it turns

out that we landed on Cirrus the same day as Ethan. The rumor is that Niels pulled strings to make sure we got off Earth in time. But that can't be true; no one could have guessed the prophecy would really happen."

Jack gave Ethan a wary glance. The cousins were members of the small group who knew that Niels had made billions predicting lottery numbers on Earth. He'd used the money to build Icarus Island.

"No, you're right," Ethan said as he sidled past Marten. "That's, uh … I'm gonna take Jack and show him where Grandpa's cabin is."

"Okay. I'll see you later. My shift on the fabricator starts soon anyway."

Besides hiding what he knew about Niels, Jack got the impression that Ethan wanted privacy. He also had a good idea what his cousin wanted to talk about. He stepped backwards out of the room.

Ethan grabbed Jack's elbow. "Watch your step."

Jack glanced behind but there was nothing there. Not until a petite girl with jet black hair emerged from the neighboring bunk room. "*Jada*. What are you doing here?"

"I could ask you the same thing, you know." Jada pulled on a black jacket, covering the colorful tattoos on her arms. "Except I already heard you were coming. My parents are Suresh and Cara."

"I didn't know that." Jack had known Jada—one of Sarah's friends from Caerton—since first grade. However, there were only a handful of students his age in Fairview, so school for him was a remote video connection and he'd never met his classmates in person. "I met Suresh in August, but I didn't know his last name was the same as yours."

"Well, we can't all be as famous as you."

"Famous?" If Marten had noticed that Ethan's warning to Jack came two seconds before Jada appeared, then he'd forgotten it when he overheard the comment. "How are you famous?"

"Uh …" Jack stammered, wondering how much Sarah had told Jada.

She gestured dismissively. "It's an inside-joke."

"Hey," Ethan interrupted. "Jack and I are gonna run and have a look around before someone puts us to work. We'll see you guys later." He shoved Jack's shoulder to get him moving.

"What's going on?" Jack asked as they hiked along a footpath in front of the cabins. "I notice you can still see two seconds into the future."

"Uh huh." Ethan responded as if his extraordinary talent were trivial. "This one is Grandpa's."

If Jack had been forced to guess which of the many cabins belonged to Holden, he'd have picked the one Ethan indicated. Structurally, it was identical to its neighbors, but there were two empty mugs on the porch floor, beside a wooden chair, and a third on the railing. Holden loved tea of all varieties and could usually be found with a cup. It wasn't unusual for him to dirty every mug he owned before finally washing them so he could brew another cup.

Ethan swerved off the path. But instead of walking to the front door, went around the side of the building and motioned for Jack to follow. He led the way through the dense woods until they came to a dirt trail, then angled towards the lake. "What did you find out?" he asked eagerly.

"Not much. Marten is related to Anders. Jada's dad is old enough to be her grandfather."

Ethan gave Jack a disgruntled look. "You know what I mean."

Jack laughed; he found so few opportunities to tease Ethan. It was fun to get the upper hand once in a while. He feigned enlightenment. "*Oh*, you mean the wand."

Ethan gave him another dirty look. Then his enthusiasm returned as they arrived at the rocky shore. "So, let's see it. What can you do with it?"

Jack looked around to be sure no one was near. Jada's furtive response to Marten said that not everyone in the village knew about his talent, and he thought it best to keep it quiet for now. He pulled the wand from his pocket and pointed it away.

"*Blowtorch*."

A foot-long flame erupted from the smooth tip of the rod. It lasted for only a second before snapping off as quickly as it had appeared.

Ethan laughed. "That is *so* cool. Can I try?"

"Sure, but let's start with something safer."

Jack pointed the wand at the ground. A smooth, cookie-shaped stone lifted. He positioned it above the wand's tip and kept it hovering as they walked.

"Skip." He flicked the wand toward the lake. The stone shot off and skipped across the water.

Ethan laughed again. "Let me try."

Jack handed him the wand. "It's not like Niels' tractor beam; there's no button." He and Ethan had experimented with Niels' invention in August. "You have to *feel* the energy field."

Ethan selected a stone and moved the wand's tip in a circle, jabbed the wand at the stone, even prodded the stone, but it refused to move. "What do you mean by *feel* it? What does it feel like?"

"It's … it's just there. It's like when you bring one magnet near another. Except that this doesn't actually push or pull, and it works much farther away."

"I don't feel anything at all. C'mon, skip," he commanded the stone with a flick of the wand.

The stone lurched and bounced against its neighbor.

"*Did you do that?*" Ethan asked. "Or did I?"

"I'm not sure. When you said 'skip', I couldn't help but remember that's what *I* said, but I wasn't *trying* to move the rock."

Ethan pointed the wand again. "Skip." Nothing happened. "Skip." He tried a few more times. Nothing.

"Try flicking it the way I did." Jack mimed the motion.

Ethan copied Jack's movement. "Skip." The stone rolled over. He stared at Jack suspiciously. "That wasn't you?"

"No, honest. I'm not doing it. Look, I'll turn my back so I can't see which rock you're moving."

With his back to Ethan, Jack waited while his cousin repeated the command and motion. There was a clatter of rocks each time. Then Ethan said, "Jump." Nothing. "Jump." He repeated it while flicking the wand. Still nothing. "Okay, then. Skip." The rock tumbled again.

Jack turned around, unsure what was happening, and found Ethan beaming.

"You know what this is?"

Jack shook his head. "Not really."

"You've created a magic spell. For skipping rocks."

"*What?* There's no such thing as magic. It's some sort of energy field."

"An energy field that responds only to words and movements? Sounds like magic to me. Show me another spell." He pushed the wand into Jack's hand then snatched it back. "No, wait." He pointed it at the ground and shouted, "*Blowtorch.*"

Apparently, enthusiasm changed the way a spell worked because Ethan's flame was a foot longer than Jack's had been. He whooped as the intense blue tip played across the stones.

"Stop that." Jack seized the wand. "And I don't know any spells, if that's what you want to call them. It took a month of practice to figure out how to control it well enough to skip a rock." He pointed with his chin over Ethan's shoulder. "Besides, we've got company now." Natalya was walking their direction.

"Okay." Ethan blocked Natalya's view while Jack tucked the wand away. "But we *are* trying this again later."

Chapter 4

"Jack," Natalya said, "your grandfather is looking for you." She handed him a package. "Could you take this to the island for Niels? And Ethan, your father wants your help with the pumps."

"Thank you." Jack was surprised. He'd hoped to talk to his grandfather soon, but if Holden was waiting, it might mean he had something to say about the wand. He subconsciously patted his jacket pocket to confirm it was still there.

Holden Marke and his mentor, Niels, had been testing portal crystals for months. They'd learned that a wormhole's energy field responded to subconscious thought—something not easily measured—and that Jack possessed far greater control over it than anyone else. Niels had decided that Jack should have his own crystal to experiment with and built the wand from one of the crystal rods Holden sent to Cirrus before Newton.

At the pier, Jack met Suresh, returning from the island. The man had changed little since Jack's first visit to Icarus in August, other than his perfectly trimmed, salt-and-pepper beard seemed even thicker.

"Hello, Jack. Are you going over?"

"Yes, sir. Grandpa wants to see me."

Suresh handed Jack the rope for the boat he'd just climbed out of, a carbon fiber skiff with an electric outboard motor. "Have you piloted a boat before?"

Jack's face grew warm. "Once." He recognized the boat as the one he and Ethan had *borrowed* in the middle of the night to escape from Anders.

"Ah, yes. I forgot about that." Suresh passed his lifejacket to Jack. "Just steer for those birch trees."

The bright white trunks stood out clearly against the darker pines, three miles distant. Jack thanked Suresh and set off. A light rain was falling but the wind was weaker than it had been all day;

the water was only choppy.

Here it comes, Jack thought when he reached the mid-point of the crossing. A calm settled on him, as it had on previous visits, at the same distance from the island. It wasn't his imagination, either. He'd experienced the same sensation on the Vault: the mountain pass he and Ethan crossed over the Spine. There was definitely a threshold between these places and the rest of the world. But how could he discuss something no one else sensed? *Hey, what's up with that invisible mood-wall around the island?*

The feeling didn't pass but settled into familiarity, so he kept the skiff's nose pointed at the birches and eventually found the dock. It wasn't deliberately camouflaged, but the dense trees prevented him from recognizing it until he was less than a hundred yards away.

Jack tied up the boat, then made the brief climb to the log cabin nestled in the trees. He stopped at the front door and knocked. There was no reply but he heard distant laughter, so he let himself in. The cabin's main room—an open plan containing a well-equipped kitchen, living room, dining room, and office—was empty, but a steel door at the building's far end was ajar.

"*Smoke test*," Holden hollered from the workshop. There was a loud pop followed by boisterous shouting.

Jack dropped Natalya's package on the dining table and followed the noise. He pushed open the heavy door.

The windowless, but brilliantly lit workshop, was an even greater contrast to the cabin's rustic exterior than its modern kitchen. Banks of sophisticated computers and fabricating machines lined the walls under chalkboards covered in bewildering equations and diagrams.

Niels sat at one end of a metal-topped worktable in the center of the room. Holden was at the other, with two empty mugs. He was wearing a leather apron over a vibrant orange Hawaiian shirt, and Niels was protected by a stained and singed lab coat.

"Come in, Jack," Niels called. "It's good to see you again."

"Smoke test?"

"If the equipment smokes when you test it, it fails." Both he and Holden burst into laughter.

A cloud of bluish smoke hovered near the ceiling, and Jack couldn't help but join the laughter. He'd always thought of his grandfather as a very serious person, but here he was acting like Ethan after pulling a prank. Niels, a man well into his nineties, giggled like a schoolboy.

"What went wrong?" Jack recognized a tractor beam generator from his first trip, though the flashlight-sized cylinder now bore the scars of many failed experiments.

"Oh, we didn't expect that one to work." Niels dismissed the smoke as if it meant nothing. He flipped a switch on the side of the workbench, starting an overhead fan. "We're trying to shed light on the inertia problem."

"What's …" Jack coughed and waved a wisp of smoke away from his face. "What's the inertia problem?"

"Do you have the device with you?" Holden asked.

Jack took out his wand. He didn't want to admit that he hadn't been without it since his grandfather sent it, that he'd been practicing with it almost constantly, or that he and Ethan were now calling it a magic wand.

Holden indicated two piles of metal bars on the table. "Try moving those stacks."

Jack pointed the wand. The nearest stack lifted and hovered a hand's width above the scratched and dinged tabletop until he set it down. The second pile, the same height as the first, rose after a moment's hesitation and bobbed several times before stabilizing. Then, instead of lowering it, Jack made it rotate and drift to the other end of the table.

"How heavy would you say those are?" Holden asked.

"I think the first stack is aluminum. Maybe five pounds? But the second must be steel. Twenty pounds?"

Niels nodded. "About that. But what is the difference for you, physically? Is there feedback? When you pull something towards you, do you feel the device being pulled away from you?"

26

"The wa … the device seems to know how much energy it needs on its own. I'm just sort of, uh, holding it together. I can sense the difference in mass, but the device doesn't move. You're saying it should?" Jack set the wand on the workbench and concentrated. The pile of steel weights scraped across the table, but the smaller rod remained motionless.

"That's a *perfect* example." Niels flipped a switch on the tractor beam. The cylinder, much lighter than the weights, slid steadily until it hit the metal stack.

"I get it." Jack had learned Newton's Third Law in school. "The inertia problem is about where the equal and opposite reaction is happening? If I lift something that weighs twenty pounds, something else needs to push back with the same force."

"That's right. What do you think that *something* is?"

Until now, Jack had taken for granted the energy field that flowed through portals. As with his talent for understanding mechanical devices, it hadn't occurred to him to question where it came from. Remembering what he'd learned in school, he suggested his own theory. "The energy is coming from the field that binds dark matter to Cirrus?"

Niels nodded and gestured broadly. "The dark matter isn't confined to a ball in the middle of the ring. It surrounds us. If we could build detectors sensitive enough, we might see ripples through it each time the tractor beam is used."

Jack understood 'see' to be a metaphor. Unlike smaller, rotating space stations, Cirrus used artificial gravity and its habitable surface was under a transparent roof on the ring's outer face. "But how am I controlling it?"

"Well, let's consider what we know." Niels picked up Jack's wand and spun it in his still-nimble fingers. "First, Travellers have been proven to have a memory of future events. This was always assumed to be a wormhole-derived connection to their own consciousness, something we still know very little about.

"Second, there are ways to read brain activity from a distance; the automatic emoji selectors in phones are the best example.

There are even methods to remotely influence a person's thoughts by stimulating parts of the brain; the motivators used for training animals work that way.

"We …" Niels indicated himself and Holden, "now believe that what you're really doing is interacting with a computer—an Artificial Intelligence—through the wormhole. This hypothetical AI reads your thoughts and uses a device similar to our tractor beam to manipulate the energy field."

"That's …" The idea was absurd. But then Jack had never believed that his ability to control the energy field was unique; it was a skill anyone could learn with enough practice. "I've never heard of a computer like that. Where is it? Why wasn't it destroyed during Newton?"

"That's the other problem," Holden said. "Right now, we don't have the technology to interpret thoughts so accurately. So, the portals must create a wormhole to a time where that *is* possible."

The first thing that jumped into Jack's mind was the word *paradox*. "But that's time travel. Couldn't it just be a more advanced computer that exists now? Maybe at the Mars colony, or the Earth's moon? What about Dawn?"

"It might be years before the first portal crystals reach Dawn," Niels reminded him. "And it's unlikely that the colonies have more advanced technology than Earth does."

"Also," Holden said, "the colonies' crystals were created on Earth. We can only assume that most were destroyed during Newton."

"If all this is true," Jack said, "then what does it say about Travellers? If I'm interacting with a computer in the future, are they as well?"

"That's another reason we think the computer is from a different time," Niels said. "Human consciousness is as deep a mystery as anything in the universe. It's much easier to accept that—like emotion detectors—the AI is playing my recorded thoughts back to me, but at an earlier time."

"But why can Travellers only see things related to themselves? Shouldn't they know what the AI knows? Or shouldn't they remember things like … like lottery numbers?"

"Eventually, it might become normal for everyone to store their memories digitally. This personal experience limitation might be a security feature, designed to protect everyone's privacy. As for lottery numbers …" Niels failed to disguise a smile as he stroked his chin. "Our current AIs are self-learning and have ethical algorithms. This hypothetical computer would be far more sophisticated, but mistakes could happen as the system learned."

"Perhaps the owner of the recording decides," Holden said. "Think of your memory of the power cell my brother left for you. Was it your memory or his?"

Jack's head swam with conflicting thoughts. He was a *lucid dreamer*, meaning he knew when he was having a dream and could control it. For most of his life, he'd had a recurring dream of Uncle Carl that turned out to be an aspect of the *Traveller Effect*, which had led him to find a power cell Carl hid in the Spine. The dream had always been from Jack's own perspective, but Holden had once explained how the brain couldn't tell the difference between a Traveller's visions and imagination. That meant it didn't matter whose eyes Jack *thought* he was seeing through. It came down to how his mind presented those images. He could only offer a shrug in response to the question.

Niels returned Jack's wand and his expression became more solemn. "How are you feeling these days? Post-Newton?"

Jack glanced at his grandfather before lowering his gaze. "I'm … now that there are no more phones, I'm not so anxious around crowds. I don't get stressed out as easily." He met Niels' eyes, sensing that the question was more important than it seemed. "I don't hear voices anymore, but I worry that I will because I sometimes still know what people are feeling."

Niels was about to answer, but Holden interrupted in a reassuring tone. "That may just be natural empathy. You were affected by the emotion detectors in phones for so long that you probably learned how to read expressions better than most."

"Maybe." *I hope it's that simple.* "But when life gets back to normal, people will want phones and I'll be overwhelmed again."

Niels sighed. "I wish I could tell you that it will get better. But things will change. Soon. You understand the source of the anxiety now. Embrace it. Make it a strength, not a weakness."

- - - - -

The two men argued theories about the crystals and the AI for the rest of the afternoon. Jack could only follow them in the most general terms. Once they got into the finer details, the discussion was way over his head.

Holden stood. "Well, that does it for now. I'm looking forward to seeing the rest of my family. Will you join us for dinner this evening?"

"No, thank you." Niels rose, with difficulty, and supported himself against the table. Jack was surprised at how unsteady the man had become; he'd been seated on an aluminum walker this whole time. He'd also lost a lot of weight since August. "There are still some things I want to work out," he said as he shuffled to his desk, "and I find it easier to put my mind to them when I'm alone." He added a line to a handwritten list and then handed to slip to Holden. "Can you give this to Terrance? I need him to pick up supplies in Caerton tomorrow."

Jack already knew that Niels wasn't coming to the lodge; the package he'd brought from Natalya was warm and smelled of chicken. Niels hadn't left the island in decades, and now his friends in the village were preparing meals for him. Jack was sure his grandfather knew this, but that it was polite to ask.

There was something else Jack knew. Every person who passes through a portal experiences déjà vu on their first trip. Travellers have it after every passage. Having travelled to Cirrus as an infant, Jack didn't remember the first event, but he'd felt something similar in the minutes before Newton when Pieter lied. *Déjà senti*—the sense of having already *felt* the same thing—passed more quickly than déjà vu, but was as profound. And he'd just felt it again.

Niels wasn't lying outright, and there were no phones and therefore no emotion detectors nearby, but Jack was certain that Niels had withheld something very important.

Chapter 5

The explosion sent ripples across the lake as Jack piloted the boat towards the village. He ducked instinctively. "What was that?" A narrow column of smoke shot into the sky from a shed near the wharf.

"It's fine," Holden said. "It sounds worse than it is. The same thing happened last night. The island's fusion reactor is becoming unstable and overloading the portals on this side."

"I don't hear the saws anymore."

"The reactor will have shut itself down as a precaution. Niels will restart it in a few minutes."

A group of people ran towards the shed with shovels and fire extinguishers, but there was no visible flame, and the plume of smoke had dissipated so rapidly that it must have been mostly dust. Ethan and his father, Nathan, were waiting on the short wooden pier the villagers had added to the original stone jetty. They didn't seem concerned, so Jack picked up an oar and paddled the rest of the way to the dock.

"Let me help you up, Dad." Nathan steadied Holden while Ethan tied the boat to a cleat. "Hello, Jack," he added. "I'll take Dad's bag."

Jack couldn't help but grin at how much Uncle Nathan resembled Ethan. Both father and son kept their dark hair cropped short and could pass for twins, if not for the age difference. That and the fact that years of martial arts training had broadened Ethan's shoulders while decades of working as a desk-jockey had rounded Nathan's.

Suresh stopped Anders as he left the shed. "We can't wait any longer. Let's get everyone together in the lodge tonight."

- - - - -

As the villagers returned to work, Ethan pulled Jack aside. "What did Grandpa say about the magic wand? And did he

32

mention my two-second warning?"

"For starters, it's not magic." Jack explained what Niels and their grandfather had learned, and how there was nothing supernatural about the cousins' unusual talents. "It's all being done through a link to a computer system somewhere in the future."

Ethan looked as skeptical as Jack had felt. "But for that to be true, it would have to record everything I think, all the time. If it does that for every person, it'd be big as a planet. Sarah sees things weeks ahead. Niels knew what was going to happen decades ago."

"Maybe it records everything but only keeps the important things. Sarah and Niels' memories are more like things written in a journal, but yours are of your own actions on a two-second loop, and they're far more detailed. Maybe it stores actions and events differently. Can you predict what someone is about to say?"

"No, you're right. I've tried that; it's only actions. But doesn't this also mean that time travel is possible?"

"In a *very* limited way. Grandpa thinks it's possible to send a tiny amount of energy from the future through a wormhole—just the signals that read or shape brain activity."

"Hold on, that makes no sense." Ethan pulled a coin from his pocket, flipped it, and caught it on his wrist. "Why can I still predict a coin toss? I don't have a portal anymore. They were all destroyed during Newton. Wouldn't that break the link?" He uncovered the coin and seemed satisfied that he'd called it correctly.

Ethan's ability to foresee events two seconds before they happened had been crucial to their success, and survival, during Newton. That talent had manifested after he passed through Holden's portal, and no one knew if it would last.

"Niels thinks it was Newton itself that created the connection," Jack said, "and that *I* somehow merged crystals from the future when they were in resonance. Yeah, I know, you don't have to say it. It's a paradox. And you *do* have a portal. It's in your hand."

Ethan held out his 'lucky coin'. It wasn't money, but a wafer-thin portal crystal bonded to a gold-plated substrate. The quarter-sized disc resembled a gold coin with a dime-sized gem embedded on one side and an electronic circuit etched on the other. "It's active?"

"Well, it is and it isn't. Hold it steady, I want to try something."

Ethan held the coin flat with the crystal facing upwards. "What are you gonna do?"

Jack tapped the coin and said, "Fire." A two-inch flame sprouted from the gem.

Ethan recovered quickly from the surprise and laughed as he held the burning disc. "You mean I've had the ability to use this all along?"

"Sort of. Grandpa sent it to you because he wanted to test a theory; that the connection exists even if the portal is dormant. Apparently, he's right. The crystal in your coin is a slice from the end of my wand. I don't think you could have created a flame, but it's what powers your two-second foresight." Ethan's expression turned sheepish. "What's wrong?"

"I thought my talent was permanent; something caused by using Grandpa's portal." Ethan chuckled nervously. "I've been juggling knives."

"Are you serious? When did you start that?"

"Last month." He reached under his jacket and produced a set of three wicked-looking daggers. "I've been relying on my two-second warning to stay safe. I haven't always had the coin with me."

"Then I guess you'll want to be careful not to lose it."

- - - - -

Later that night, Jack sat at the back of the wood-paneled dining room in the lodge with Ethan. He scanned the crowd. "Have you seen Terrance?"

"No, why?"

"He's going to Caerton tomorrow to get supplies for Niels. I thought he might need help."

Ethan grinned. "Yeah, I'm sure that's your only reason."

"*What?*"

Ethan didn't answer because Jada and Marten were approaching. They took chairs next to the cousins and spun them to face Suresh, who addressed the group of more than forty villagers.

"Niels believes his fusion generator is about to fail. It's too small to support a village as large as Icarus has become. Our solar farm is nearly complete and will produce more power than we require, but we'll need batteries before we can turn it on."

Marten raised his hand. "I thought Niels had the equipment to grow portal crystals. Can't we use them to buy power from Caerton at night and sell our excess back during the day?"

Suresh shook his head. "It takes months to grow a crystal, and Caerton's main fusion plant is already running at reduced capacity. Also, those buildings that have their own plants aren't connected to the grid, so there's no distribution network there."

"And even if we could produce crystals to connect them," Anders said, "it's not a question of buying and selling. Many people are still hoping for a recovery, but Niels says that won't happen."

A chorus of anxious voices spread through the room.

Ethan whispered, "I thought Niels didn't have a portal to *travel* through."

"He doesn't," Jack said. "But I don't think he needs one. You're still getting a two-second warning from your coin. That must mean Travellers only have to be *near* a wormhole, not pass through one."

"Does that mean the things Sarah predicted will come true?"

"It might." She had written, 'See you soon'. *How soon?*

Suresh continued with his proposal. "I worked on the high-speed trains before Newton. Each coach had enough batteries to get it to the nearest port city if the fusion generator needed a cool-down period. Before I left Caerton, I helped dismantle one and move its batteries to the hospital. They're far too large for use in a road vehicle, so most coaches are still sitting in the station, untouched. But Caerton won't give up the batteries and I don't expect others cities will either. However, we've recently learned that at least one coach ended up at a maintenance depot in the sector wall, east of here. It took the passengers several days to walk to the closest town."

"How does that help us?" Ethan asked Jack. The rest of the group seemed to grasp the significance of Suresh's remarks and were discussing it among themselves.

"The sector walls aren't just for weather control. There are train tunnels up there too. That's how they cross between rims." Cirrus' rims—eight-mile vertical walls over seventeen-thousand miles in circumference—were connected by eight-hundred-mile long mountainous berms that divided the ring into twelve sectors. "The maintenance depots must be far from any city. No one will have claimed the batteries yet."

At that moment, the lights flickered and dimmed. As one, the entire room held their breath, waiting for another explosion. But the episode passed and the group's voices rose as the lights returned to normal. Suresh motioned for silence.

"We can take the few vehicles we have and retrieve enough batteries to power our village."

Anders stood and spoke to the room. "We need a few volunteers." Jack's father was one of the first to raise his hand. "Actually, Victor, we want yours and Emily's technical skills here to get the solar farm ready. The extraction will mostly be labor." Anders pointed to Jack's group, none of whom had raised their hands. "Thank you, that's four. Now we just need a few qualified mechanics."

There goes my trip to Caerton.

Jack wasn't upset at being volunteered; he'd have wanted to go if he hadn't been making other plans, but he was miffed that Anders didn't consider him a qualified mechanic. After all, he'd worked on drones, vehicles, and farm machinery around Fairview for years.

Anders accepted two more men and one woman and told them where to meet in the morning. Jack, Ethan, and Marten returned to the common room on the lower level.

Ethan dropped into a chair by the fireplace. "Maybe we can take a side trip to Caerton and you can visit Sarah."

"Who's Sarah?" Marten asked.

"His girlfriend."

Jack responded without thinking. "She's not my girlfriend."

"Uh, yeah." Ethan grinned. "She kind of is."

Jack opened his mouth to respond but hesitated. Although they'd only spent a few days together in August, they'd known each other for years. And since Newton, he'd taken every opportunity to correspond with her and she with him.

"Well, maybe." He felt his cheeks flush and was glad for the dim light.

Chapter 6

"I'll do my part," Jada snapped. "You do yours."

"What's going on?" Jack whispered as he hopped into one of the five waiting vehicles.

Ethan failed to hide a smirk. "Marten asked Jada if she was up to the task."

"Ooh." Jack winced. "Bad move."

Jada had taken the passenger seat next to Marten in another car. At five-foot-two, she was the smallest person in the group but had been doing her part for two months, clearing land for farming on a plot beyond the cabins. Her hands were as calloused as anyone's, and Jack knew her well enough that he'd have been shocked if she hadn't shown up that morning. He also knew that she could carry a grudge for days; Marten would have to watch his back.

Marten, who towered over Jada when standing, backed off. Anders watched the scene with amusement, then signaled his grandson to come sit beside him. Suresh took Marten's place.

Ethan would drive Dave, even though Jack had more experience on the road. During their escape from Fairview, Ethan had proven his talent for high-speed driving. That wouldn't be necessary today but the arrangement felt natural now. Also, Ethan's two-second foresight gave him a significant advantage in the event of an emergency.

"Did you …" Jack was about to ask if Ethan remembered to bring his coin when he spotted a cord around his cousin's neck. His talent for sensing nearby portals confirmed that it was under Ethan's shirt. "Never mind."

- - - - -

The group set out following the same unmarked shortcut Jack and Ethan had taken months ago, one that exited the woods northeast of the lake. Jack recognized the pitch-black crag that marked the final turn before an open, grassy field.

After crossing the meadow, he looked back to make sure Jada and Suresh, in the last car, were keeping up. The trees had swallowed the narrow dirt track and the resilient grass was already rebounding, erasing signs of their passage. It would be impossible for a stranger to locate Icarus without a map.

It took another three hours to reach the sector wall. They'd driven both gravel and paved roads, climbed and descended the steep, eastern pass over the Spine, and encountered rain and snow but no other vehicles.

Anders signaled everyone to stop at the base of the slope, then grunted with the effort of extracting himself from the compact vehicle. He stretched his massive frame, saying, "These seats are too small."

"Every seat is too small for you." Suresh slapped his friend on the back. "But we're almost there. We should reach the tunnel in half an hour."

"I didn't see a single grain carrier," Jack said.

Suresh shook his head sadly. "There are no large power cells anymore."

Jack felt a pang of guilt, thinking of their own vehicles. The power modules they used were not big enough for tractor-trailers, combine harvesters, or other large vehicles, but he couldn't help worrying that they could be put to better use. Before Newton, Cirrus provided a quarter of Earth's food.

Suresh noticed his discomfort. "Our mission will benefit everyone, eventually. As soon as we're self-sufficient, we'll return for more batteries and adapt them for other uses."

Jack accepted this as true; they already had more solar panels in Icarus than they needed. The batteries would not only provide the village with continuous power, they'd help produce more panels for others. As far as he knew, Icarus was the only place in the sector with the equipment to build solar panels—another example of Niels' foresight.

Suresh took the lead after Anders worked out the kinks in his back. As they climbed through a series of switchbacks, the dense forest gave way to grasses and lichens, and the fog lifted, giving Ethan his first ground-level view of the wall.

"This is not what I expected." On their left, several miles distant, the steep, nearly black cliffs of the Spine merged into the brighter, more gently sloped wall. Straight ahead and for as far to the right as he could see, deep runnels, etched in the meager soil, flowed with muddy water. He'd seen the wall from space a few months ago and thought it was solid rock. "It looks like a pile of gravel."

"That's pretty much what it is," Jack said, "except it's four miles tall."

"That's taller than Mount Rainier." Ethan had lived in Seattle before coming to Cirrus. "How does it stay together?"

"Remember what Anders said about how Terrance got caught trying to spell his name in nickel under a sector wall? As I understand it, most of it should have fused during bombardment, but the top layer might have stayed cool."

Cirrus' twelve sector walls, built layer upon layer from marble-sized stones dropped from space, buried even the tallest points of the Spine. The gravelly debris, leftover from mining the asteroid belt, was free of metals except for that misdirected by Terrance and other members of the orbital construction team.

"Where is Terrance, anyway?" Ethan asked. "I didn't see him this morning."

"Maybe he stayed in Caerton, running errands for Niels."

After half an hour of crawling over muddy switchbacks, Suresh stopped before a large concrete shed just above the tree line. He and Anders got out of their vehicles and cranked open a set of heavy metal doors, revealing a semi-circular tunnel twelve feet high and twenty wide.

Speeding along the smooth gray passage was a surreal experience. They were only doing forty miles per hour, but with so little visual reference, it felt like hundreds. A large number painted on the wall every mile reported the distance to the elevator. The last mile was marked every hundred feet, and large signs warned them to slow at the very end.

Ethan's tires chirped on the smooth concrete as he swung Dave into a parking spot at the end of the tunnel. "Well, this is disappointing. I was expecting some sort of high-tech control room."

The tunnel ended in a warehouse with a coffered dome ceiling. The shelves lining the walls held only a few basic tools, and a compact forklift was parked next to one of two elevators at the far end of the round room. Isabel, an experienced mechanic, checked it for power.

"Dead." She tossed the inactive power cell into a trash can.

Suresh started handing out flashlights. "Please remove the power cells from your vehicles. We'll need them to run the elevator and equipment in the maintenance depot."

Jack briefly thought of using his wand to create a light bright enough for the entire room. He was certain that his grandfather or Niels had described the device to Anders and Suresh, but he didn't know about the rest of the village. Regardless, he located and disconnected the thumb-sized cylinder before Suresh got to him with a flashlight.

The elevators were large enough to drive one of their vehicles onboard, but then there wouldn't be room for passengers. They also had fold-down seats mounted on the side walls. Jack followed Suresh's example and lowered a seat, realizing that this would not be a quick ride.

Henri, another mechanic, installed a power cell and the elevator's lights came on. Suresh sealed the doors, pressed a button on the control panel, and everyone fell out of their seats.

Suresh, hanging on to a grab bar, struggled to hold back laughter. "I am *so* sorry. I forgot to tell you that the shaft isn't vertical. We're not just going up four miles, we're going the same distance sideways."

The car's diagonal movement had caught its passengers off guard. Ethan, seated in a corner next to the door and supported by the wall, smirked as Jack reclaimed his seat. Jada, seated across from Ethan in the other corner, seemed pleased that Marten had also fallen.

"Why didn't you see that coming?" Jack whispered.

Ethan wore a mischievous grin. "Maybe because I wasn't going to fall no matter what."

"Why don't I believe you? You knew, didn't you?"

Ethan chuckled but didn't answer.

Chapter 7

Sarah eyed Holden's frame. She'd covered it with a blanket but the fabric had slipped, exposing a corner of polished wood. Now it lurked on the floor next to her easel; teasing, inviting.

For an entire day … *No. A day and a half*, she congratulated herself, she'd resisted the temptation of opening it.

She turned her attention to the window, considering the storm that had begun two days ago and still punished the city with an occasional downburst. The rain wasn't so bad, but the cold that came with it was. Her block of townhouses had been allocated power for just two hours a day: the first at 4:00am, and the second twelve hours later. Without a clock, she guessed it was still several hours before they'd be able to reheat their home.

I'll bet Priya's place is warm. Sarah slipped off her bed and scooted over to the frame. *Even if her neighborhood is in a blackout right now, it should be warmer in Olympia than it is here.*

She pulled the blanket aside, baring the entire mirrored surface. *I won't go through. I'll just open it for some warm air. Priya can't complain about that. And she's probably at work anyway.* She hovered her finger over the switch. *But what if she's home?*

A cold gust rattled the window, creating inspiration. Sarah leaned back and dug into the bottom drawer of her dresser, found a scarf, and wrapped it around her neck. Just in case, she practiced a shiver before tapping the control.

Bright sunlight speared through gaps at the top and sides of the frame. Before leaving, Priya had pinned the device against her bedroom wall. There was no way Sarah could reposition the boxes behind it from her side, but the narrow openings let through plenty of warm air.

Although she couldn't pass through the wormhole and create more future memories, just knowing the frame was near eased the frustration she'd been feeling. And as long as she didn't make an appearance on Earth where Pieter might see her, she was safe, too.

Pieter can't find me. And he's probably colder than I am, brooding in his penthouse with its windows smashed out. He's … Now where did that thought come from?

Sarah had just pictured Pieter's downtown office with one of its floor-to-ceiling windows missing. But she'd seen it from the fifty-second level atrium of the Magnolia yesterday and it looked fine. She stood and crossed to her window. If she leaned against the casing, she could just see the tip of his needle-like office tower poking higher than every other building in the city.

Had it been sunny, and had she been using binoculars, she might have been able to make out the penthouse windows. But the rain tinted everything a uniform gray, and the pinnacle was nearly invisible against the background clouds.

Was that a memory? But she hadn't passed through the wormhole. *That's not how it's supposed to work.* But then, Holden's portal was unlike any other. *Who's to say how it should work?*

She knelt before the frame and concentrated on the opening. There was no sound; Priya wasn't home, and the sunlight was flickering, shining through trees in her backyard. The dancing pattern made the wooden frame resemble a fireplace. *Except the fire should be in the center, not surrounding the hearth like it did when Jack and Pieter …*

Sarah gasped and fell back. There it was again. Jack and Pieter were—*would be*—surrounded by flames. It felt so real, but was the memory valid? And if so, how to warn him? The only person who might be able to arrange a ride to Icarus was Priya, and she'd want a good reason.

I can't wait. Sarah fetched a jacket from her closet. She'd have to go downtown to see Pieter's tower for herself. If one of its windows was missing, her friends were in danger.

Assuming she'd return long before her mother got home from work, she didn't write a note before dashing out the townhouse's back door.

The streets were slick even though the last shower had ended an hour ago. Sarah swerved her bicycle around puddles on the way to the freeway entrance. Underground, the multi-level tunnel was as deserted as the road above, so she decided to risk using the Magnolia's elevators. Even if she were seen, it wouldn't be a problem unless someone rode to the same floor. Luckily, the only two residents she met exited at level thirty-nine, leaving her the car to herself. The atrium was empty on Holden's floor, and she walked to his apartment without an encounter.

Inside, she glanced at the framed painting over the fireplace as she crossed the living room. If Pieter had somehow returned to Cirrus, Priya assumed he'd come for the frame, but it was untouched. *Maybe I just imagined everything.* She leaned against the window, her heart pounding in anticipation of what she'd see. *Is that …?*

She couldn't be sure. From this angle, its mirrored surface melded into the gray background. She'd have to go there to check.

The power will be turned off soon. I've got to hurry. She dashed into the hall, opened the door, and ran straight into Terrance.

"Oof," Terrance grunted as he stumbled into the wall.

Sarah clutched the door frame to steady herself. "What are *you* doing here?"

Terrance, caught off guard, was dumbstruck at first. But then he straightened his jacket and looked over Sarah's shoulder. "Ah, this must be Holden's place."

"Did your boss send you to spy on me?"

"What? No. I'm just in town getting supplies for him."

She crossed her arms. "Do you always shop at Holden's apartment?"

"No, of course not. I … I thought I'd check in and make sure looters hadn't been here."

"It wouldn't matter. Priya moved the portal yesterday."

"She did?" Terrance's surprise was genuine. "I see. Well, my work here is done, then." He turned and strode to the elevator.

Sarah trailed behind him. "I don't believe you." Terrance kept his face angled away from her after pressing the elevator button.

"You knew that was his apartment."

He laughed. "I've never been here before."

The elevator door opened and an elderly woman gushed, "*Terry*. Back so soon?" She seemed delighted to see him. And despite the city being mid-apocalypse and suffering its worst storm ever, she was wearing more jewelry than Sarah had ever seen on one person. But the teacup-sized dog resting in the crook of her arm was the real indicator of the woman's wealth.

Without missing a beat, Terrance said, "Mrs. Susskind, what a surprise." He was pouring on the charm as thick as syrup. "I'm just passing through."

Sarah grinned and extended a hand to the plump woman. "Hi, I'm Sarah. *Terry* and I were visiting my uncle. He didn't tell me he knew anyone else in the building."

"Oh, I've known Terry for years." The woman tittered. "He always brings me little gifts, and I don't know *where* he finds them. Just last week he brought me a dozen fresh strawberries. And that was four days after the markets said they'd run out."

"Is that so?" Sarah stared at Terrance, whose confident smile was twitching.

Mrs. Susskind nattered about the challenges of caring for Buttons, her diminutive dog, as the car descended. Terrance was sympathetic and promised to bring more doggie treats on his next visit. He and Sarah got out at the ground level and Mrs. Susskind continued to the basement.

When the elevator doors closed, Sarah said in a harsh whisper, "You've been using Holden's portal to smuggle from Earth."

"Nonsense. I know Mrs. Susskind from the salon." He headed for the street. "As I said, I've never been here before."

"Hey, Terrance." A well-dressed man waved as he entered the lobby. "Any chance you can get me another bottle of that Pinot?"

"I'll … I'll see what I can do."

"Thanks, man."

"Fine," Terrance said, when the man was out of hearing range. "I may have taken advantage of Holden's frequent absences to earn some extra cash."

"Does that mean you've travelled to Earth?"

"*Me*? No thanks. I value my sanity too much. I have packages dropped at his back door, and I programmed his cleaning-bot to pass them through the wormhole."

"Well, Priya moved the other frame from his house too. So that's the end of your side-business."

Unlike a conventional portal, Holden's created no flux and was undetectable. Before Newton, Terrance would have been imprisoned if he'd been caught. Now, using possibly the only link between Cirrus and Earth, anything he shipped would be extremely valuable.

He stopped on the sidewalk under the awning and stroked his chin. "Do you know where she took it?"

"No chance. Get your illegal goods somewhere else."

He sighed, then his eyes narrowed. "What were *you* doing in his apartment?"

Sarah glared at him, but knew that he was aware of her Traveller talent. "I had a memory of Pieter. I need to know if it was real."

"But if Priya's taken the portal, you can't use it for confirmation."

"I don't need it. I remembered a smashed a window in his office. I thought I could check from Holden's but the angle's wrong. So I'm going to climb up and see for myself."

"Have you seen that building recently?"

"No, why?"

Terrance shook his head. "Follow me." He pulled his collar up against the wind and led Sarah three block to the base of Pieter's tower. The street outside the building was strewn with smashed furniture and granules of safety glass. There was hardly an intact pane below the thirtieth floor. "People have been taking their frustrations out on Pieter for months. If the building's power plant were working, they'd have looted every floor."

"I'm still going up." She marched to the broken lobby doors.

Terrance didn't move, and his expression was smug. "Finding a smashed window won't prove it was Pieter. Are you sure it was him? Did you *see* him in your memory?"

Sarah turned but kept walking backwards. "Who else could it have been?"

He spread his arms to encompass the city. "Anyone. Nothing's important enough to venture into the lion's den."

"I had a second memory. Pieter was with Jack. If the window's gone, then it means he's back on Cirrus."

Terrance's grin vanished. "Your concern for your friends is admirable; there's nothing I wouldn't do for some of mine. But he's in good hands. He's on an errand right now with Anders, Suresh, and a few others from the village."

Sarah didn't stop. "I have to know." She stepped over a mound of twisted steel.

Terrance sighed and followed. "Look, I owe you for what you did in August. Let me—"

"Yeah, you *do* owe me." Terrance and Niels had convinced her to break into one of Pieter's businesses and steal an encrypted access card. "So stay out of my way."

Terrance raised an open palm. "As I was saying, let me go up *instead*. I'll let you know what I find. Deal?"

At that moment, a ceiling panel dropped and crumbled on the tiles behind Sarah. She flinched, then studied the stairwell at the back of the lobby. It was littered with glass, wire, and steel. "When?"

"It's a long climb, and it'll take just as long to get down. Go home. Come back in three hours."

Sarah waited until Terrance reached the second floor before she left the lobby. But she didn't go home. Instead, she shielded her eyes against the driving rain and hurried back to the Magnolia. *Maybe I can see the windows more clearly from the roof.*

Pieter's tower was the tallest in the city, but the Magnolia was only five hundred feet shorter. Its rooftop café, run by Jada's parents, was the next best option for seeing the window herself.

And it would be empty too. With limited power and access, business had dried up and Jada's family had moved to Icarus.

In the lobby, Sarah found she'd missed the last elevator. *It'll be an hour before power is restored, and then it'll be packed for the first half hour.* She considered the stairs. She and Jada had done the climb once. It wasn't fun. *No matter what I do, I'll get there at the same time.* But she couldn't just stand and worry. She tightened her shoe laces and started climbing.

Four thousand steps later, she pushed the glass door and stepped onto the open-air deck. This time, the frigid wind that greeted her was refreshing. She glanced at her tired reflection in the rain-streaked windows as she crossed to the opposite corner of the building. The dozens of tables she'd normally have to weave between had been shifted to one side, and all the chairs were stacked neatly in a corner. There was no sign of the colorful umbrellas that once sheltered diners.

Sarah faltered as she approached the railing. The rain had lessened, leaving her with a clear view of the two-story penthouse.

It's gone. One of the mirrored panes was missing—just as she'd remembered. *There's even a chair. It's true. Pieter is—*

But the chair was empty, and Terrance's words troubled her. He'd insisted that finding the glass missing wouldn't prove anything, and maybe he was right. After all, she hadn't actually *seen* Pieter in the chair, hadn't even recalled it until a moment ago. Mostly, she'd gotten the impression of someone brooding and knew that her imagination could have created the chair to fit the memory.

A shadow approached the window. Sarah held her breath. *It's him.*

But it wasn't Pieter who stepped into the light. Terrance seized the window frame, shook it to test its strength, then leaned forward to survey the street below. After a moment, he backstepped and sat in the leather chair.

Sarah couldn't see his expression at this distance, but when he leaned back, stretched out his legs, and clasped his hands behind his head, she knew it was smug.

"Fine," she shouted. "You were right. But that doesn't mean—
"

Terrance sat up, then leaned over to pick something off the floor. The object was far too small for Sarah to identify, but he raised it to the sky in one hand as if looking through it. Then he leaned forward with his elbows resting on his knees and stared at the object in cupped hands. Whatever he'd found, it held his attention fully. His posture was absorbed, pensive, almost—

Brooding. Sarah gasped. It wasn't Pieter she'd recalled, but Terrance. That meant her second memory was also true; Jack would meet Pieter somewhere there was a fire.

She turned and sprinted for the elevator, but its button didn't light when she jabbed it. Swearing loudly, she slammed her foot into the door; the power was out off-schedule and there was no telling how long the failure would last. Worse, she hadn't asked Terrance about the errand Jack was on, and had no idea where to tell Priya to find him. That left her with just one option: send the mail drone to Icarus with a warning.

She ran for the stairs.

Chapter 8

A red light flashed on the elevator's control panel and pressurized air hissed through a silver valve over Jack's head.

Suresh handed out oxygen masks. "This is only a precaution. We've reached the halfway point. From here on, pressure will be maintained at seventy kilopascals. That's the same as two miles above sea level." He showed everyone how to fit the masks and use the compact air tanks. "We shouldn't need these, but keep them with you at all times."

"Feel that?" Ethan asked.

"The gravity you mean?" Jack hefted his flashlight, noting how light it was. "Yeah, it's starting."

Jack hadn't been on a train in years, but recalled the floating sensation from the ride up to the tunnels. Unlike natural gravity, Cirrus' artificial field decayed a few miles from the core. It felt as if the elevator was slowing, but they'd just passed the elevation where the gradual decline became obvious.

Ethan stood and jumped for the ceiling. At twelve feet, it was still out of his reach, but his hang time improved as they approached the summit. By the time they reached four miles, the apparent gravity was equal to one-half gee.

Jada was also competing for height in a good-natured contest with Marten. Apparently, seeing him tumble from his seat was enough to appease her anger over his earlier remark. Marten's fingers nearly brushed the ceiling, but Jada seemed almost to fly as she tucked her legs at the top of her leap.

"Take your seats, please," Anders said, "and have your oxygen ready."

The elevator slowed to a crawl, shuffled sideways, and docked with a muted thump. Suresh checked the display. "Sixty-four kilopascals. After two months without power, I'm not surprised." He unsealed a valve next to the door to allow the air pressure to equalize. "It's cold too. Ten degrees."

He opened the doors to reveal a two-story, unlit foyer, the length and width of a single-car garage. Straight ahead, a four-inch-thick transparent wall separated the room from the main airlock. An upward-sliding glass panel took up most of that wall next to a normal sized glass door. Forklift tire tracks running from the elevator ended at steel doors on the airlock's far side, which provided access to the train yard.

Jada pointed at doors on the sides of the room. "Where do these go?"

Suresh tapped the door he was standing by. "Workshop." He indicated another directly above, at the top of a metal staircase. "Control room. And the one on the opposite wall leads to the observation tower."

"How far below the surface are we?" Ethan asked.

"Five hundred feet. If we have time, you can walk up to the tower later. I don't recommend going outside though, it may be snowing."

Jack approached the workshop door and shone his flashlight through the window. *The cold isn't our only concern.* Several pressure suits hung on the wall.

Suresh climbed the stairs to the control room and used the mechanical crank to crack the door seal. "Bring your power cells upstairs so we can turn on the lights."

Jack followed the group upstairs and joined them at the curved outer wall, where floor-to-ceiling windows overlooked the maintenance bay. Isabel opened a panel in the side wall and started connecting power cells. With each connection, equipment in the control room came to life amid a chorus of clicks, beeps, and hums. The ceiling panels cast enough light through the broad windows to reveal six sets of parallel levitation tracks in the adjoining bay.

Ethan leaned against the glass for a better look at the tracks sixteen feet below. "It looks like a subway station on Earth."

"The yard," Suresh described the facility outside the window, "extends a quarter mile to each side. There may be maintenance coaches in there, but we'll take the batteries from the passenger coach instead. We'll work in two-hour shifts: four workers on the floor, two spotters, and two in the control room. One person stays in the airlock in a pressure suit. Clear?"

Marten raised his hand. "Why does only one person get to wear a suit?"

"*Have* to, not *get* to. They're too bulky to work in. If there was a leak to the outside, through the elevator shaft or a crack in the wall, the air pressure would drop to fifty kilopascals. That's the same as base camp on Mt. Everest. You don't need a suit for that, but the worst-case scenario is a leak to the tunnels and total vacuum. The bay is so large that it would take minutes to lose the air, but somebody has to be ready to work the airlock in an emergency."

Suresh reviewed safety procedures for several more minutes, then paired Jack and Ethan together as spotters for the first shift.

Passenger coaches could be connected in a train or run on their own. In this case, the single coach had coasted three hundred yards to the right of entrance, far beyond the reach of the control room lights. Jack took a position outside the airlock door while Ethan watched over the worksite. Their job was to use flashlights to signal for help or to run and pass messages as required.

A metallic clink echoed thinly from the complete darkness to his left. Then another. Jack swung his flashlight but the beam faded beyond the control room. Jada, at her elevated window post, leaned to see what he was looking at. After a few seconds, she turned back to him and shrugged silently.

I could light up the far end of the tunnel with my wand, but that'd be an uncomfortable conversation. It's probably just something changing temperature.

Eventually, lights from the worksite bobbed towards him; the first team was returning with a pair of batteries on a cart built for that purpose. Jack thought he heard another distant noise as he waited for Marten to open the airlock doors, but with everyone talking he couldn't be sure.

Now it was Jack and Ethan's turn to work on the coach. At sea level, in a warm, brightly lit room, they could have completed the extraction in twenty minutes. The cells from their vehicles powered the emergency lights and tools, but did nothing to offset the cold or reduced air pressure. Two hours later, exhausted, they slung the second set of batteries onto the cart.

Each battery massed two hundred pounds. Thankfully, in the reduced gravity at high elevation, the apparent weight was only half of that. Even so, they were bulky and awkward to handle. The team's goal for the day was just ten of the large cubes.

Jack and Ethan took their next shift in the control room, where Suresh had reluctantly agreed to leave the door open. After several hours, air rising from the elevator's heater had warmed the room to be almost comfortable to wait in without a coat.

Each shift passed without incident. It was early evening before the entire group gathered in the control room after having loaded all ten cells into the elevator.

"We have enough for the village," Suresh said, "but we should know if more are available. Can someone walk to the other end and count coaches, please?"

Ethan raised his hand. "Jack and I will go. We're both warm now."

Jack understood Ethan's eagerness. From the time he'd found that he could control Jack's wand, they'd never been away from anyone else to try again.

Marten, who had just been acting as a spotter, agreed to wait outside the airlock again.

"Do you have another spell I can try?" Ethan asked when they were out of hearing range.

Jack pulled out the wand, pointed it in the direction they were walking, and concentrated for a moment. A modest red light projected from the tip. He covered it with his hand so Marten wouldn't see it. "How about that one?"

"Wait, what did you do? You didn't say anything."

"I don't need to. All I do is find the right crystal and open the wormhole. The point is to see if you can do the same thing."

"What do you mean, 'find the right crystal'?" Ethan accepted the wand from Jack. The red light stayed on.

"I don't know how else to explain it. Those crystals that were entangled during Newton but not destroyed; they're still out there. Once I know where they are, I can find them again easily. Maybe if I hold it open while you think about it, you can make the same connection."

"All right, then tell me what I should be thinking."

They'd come to the end of the track. Three wheeled cargo trailers were lined up end-to-end. Jack shuffled in between a pair and motioned for Ethan to follow so no one would see the light.

"It's only there at night. The rest of the time it's sunlight. It must be a place outdoors that still has power. And it's usually windy."

"If it has constant power, then it's probably on Earth. We have towers near airports with red lights on them. Maybe it's one of those."

"So, picture that, then. I'll close the link and you try to open it. Ready?"

The light went out. After ten seconds of darkness, Ethan said, "I've got nothing."

"Keep trying. I'll go count the coaches."

While Ethan tried activating the wand, Jack wandered around, shining his flashlight on nearby equipment. Most of what he found were cargo trailers that took their power from a towing coach, or wheeled service vehicles that could never leave the depot. There was only a single levitation-enabled coach resting on a track several lanes away from the trailers.

"Found one," Jack called. "The door's open." He climbed into the coach.

Ethan had given up on the wand and joined Jack. "It's different. It must be for maintenance."

The service coach was the same size as a regular one, but

contained only a dozen seats. Tools, workbenches, and other equipment filled the rest of the space. At the front, a panel rested on the floor below a bundle of exposed wires.

"Why take the dashboard apart?" Jack asked.

"No idea. Anyway, we should head back. The wand isn't working for me. Maybe it needs to be a word, like '*skip*'."

"Then let's try something different." Jack took the wand and stepped into the gap between the trailers. He pointed at a red tool cart against the wall and raised the wand with his palm facing upward. "Lift."

The cart mirrored his action, rising smoothly off the ground. He lowered it and handed the wand to Ethan. "Even before I move something, there's a sort of feedback that lets me feel the shape of it. This time I'll leave the wormhole open so that the field is already there, and you try it with the word and the motion."

Ethan pointed the wand at the cart.

"Can you feel anything?" Jack asked.

"Nothing." He copied Jack's movement. "Lift." No movement. "Here, hold this." He slipped a cord over his head and passed his lucky coin to Jack. "Maybe it's interfering." He pointed the wand again. "Lift."

Still nothing.

"Let me try once more." He shook out the tension in his shoulders and arms and assumed a relaxed posture. With a slow and deliberate motion, Ethan raised and pointed the wand. Holding his chin high, he enunciated clearly, "LIFT."

Absolute stillness.

"Arrgh. *Lift, damn it.*" He shook the wand and the cart trembled. "Hey, wait. I'm getting something. I … *GET DOWN*." He threw his shoulder into Jack and sent him flying.

Jack slammed into the side of a trailer. As he fell, something passed through his hair and exploded against the metal chassis. Ethan, off balance, fell on top of Jack, causing him to drop the flashlight, which rolled under the vehicle. Ethan dropped the wand and it bounced out of reach.

Someone stepped towards them from the darkness.

Jack tried to stand but Ethan's own struggling kept him pinned to the ground. From that position, and with the solitary light coming from under the trailer, he could see only the man's legs and a sturdy metal pipe hanging from one hand.

"An interesting toy you've got there, Jack."

Pieter Reynard reached down to pick up the wand.

Chapter 9

With Ethan's help, Jack staggered to his feet and backed away from Pieter. The last time he'd seen Pieter, the tall, broad-shouldered businessman had been carrying a pistol.

"I was expecting company," Pieter said casually, "but I didn't know you were joining the party, Jack." He spun the wand in his hand, examining it. "I also didn't expect a welcoming gift. How does it work?" He tossed the pipe and pointed the polished cylinder at them.

Ethan seized Jack's arm and pulled him to the side. Too late, they were caught in the field streaming from the wand. The blast threw Jack backwards into the wall with enough force to drive the air from his lungs. Ethan landed on the ground poorly and cried out in pain. The tool cart tumbled onto the tracks.

"Oh, I see." Pieter chuckled. "Very clever. How is it powered, I wonder? No matter. I'll have plenty of time to work that out once I take care of the other Traveller."

He pointed the wand again and the energy surged. This time, Pieter didn't hit them with a single blast. He kept the pressure on, crushing the cousins against the wall.

The other Traveller. Jack gasped for air. *He's going after Sarah.*

Through the pain, he met Pieter's eyes. There was nothing there but cold indifference, and he realized he had a more immediate problem.

Pieter's going to kill us.

Jack couldn't breathe. His consciousness was slipping away. It wasn't just the lack of oxygen; the field also acted within his body. A pins-and-needles sensation spread through his limbs as Pieter discovered how to increase the force. He had only moments to fight back.

He could sense the wand's portal crystal but was too far away to compete with Pieter. Ethan struggled to move against Jack's leg, then grimaced and clutched his injured ribs.

The coin.

When Ethan's hand went to his shirt, Jack remembered he was still holding the lucky coin. He angled it away from his body, and with the little air remaining in his lungs groaned, "*Shield*."

The energy field rebounded at Pieter, throwing him off his feet. He landed roughly between the two trailers and dropped the wand.

While Pieter got to his feet, Jack caught his breath and recovered his senses. He'd pushed the coin's crystal to its limit, risked shattering it with that brief, intense pulse. Pieter stooped to recover the wand. Jack knew he couldn't defend himself for long against the larger crystal. He had to gamble.

Pieter was just aiming the wand when Jack pointed the coin at a trailer, shouted '*Crush*', and waved his hand towards Pieter.

A screech of metal-on-metal echoed around the maintenance bay as Jack dragged the fallen tool cart against the trailer. As hoped, Pieter assumed he was about to be squashed and dove backwards out of the gap, then ran away, limping heavily.

Ethan tried to stand, then groaned and collapsed. Jack rubbed the back of his head and felt a bump growing where he'd hit the wall.

"Anything broken?" Jack asked as he helped Ethan stand.

"No." Ethan prodded his ribs gingerly. "But I felt something pop. Where's Pieter? How did he get back to Cirrus?"

Jack picked up the flashlight and shone it through the space between the trailers. "The maintenance coach. It's gone."

"Can he get into the tunnels without power?"

"I don't think so. But he'll reach the elevator in seconds. He said 'take care of the other Traveller'. *He's going after Sarah.*"

Jack started running. He'd gone only a few steps when Marten shouted. A rectangle of light from the airlock door illuminated the tracks, but a half mile was too far for Jack to see what was happening. Seconds later, the floor shook. A loud boom rang through the bay, followed by a deafening howl.

"He's breached the tunnel," Ethan yelled.

A second, muted boom echoed the first, and the light from the airlock faded.

Ethan overtook Jack and reached Marten first. He was just getting up as they approached. A crimson rash covered the side of his face where he'd slid across the concrete.

Jack's ears popped. "We're losing pressure. Get in the airlock."

While Ethan sealed the door, Marten pressed his hand to his face. It wasn't bleeding much, but he'd be sore for a while. "A coach sped past on the far side of the bay. I came out to look for you guys and then I was thrown into the air."

Ethan placed his hand against the glass wall that faced the foyer. "What happened to the window?" A layer of frost covered the opposite side, rendering it opaque.

"He must have broken the seal to the elevator shaft too. It got cold really fast in there."

"The control room door was open. *They don't have any air.*"

Jack blocked Ethan from rushing the door. "It's okay. The pressure in the shaft is equal to four miles. They'll be fine." *I hope.*

Marten cranked open the glass door, causing air to whistle through the gap as the pressure balanced, then sealed it again after Jack and Ethan hurried to the elevator. Their flashlights revealed an empty space where the elevator car should have been. Somehow, Pieter had bypassed the safety systems and departed with their batteries.

Jack passed the flashlight to Ethan, along with his lucky coin, to free his hands for operating the manual door crank. Ethan dashed upstairs to the control room—or tried to anyway. After running a half mile in reduced air pressure, the even lower pressure in the foyer affected him at once. He plodded the final steps.

By the time Jack and Marten sealed the doors and climbed the stairs, Ethan was attending to the fallen. The sudden drop in pressure hadn't been enough to cause serious injury, but half the group was knocked off their feet or lost their balance as their ears tried to cope with the rapid decompression.

Marten ran to help Anders. "Are you okay?"

Anders responded first with a string of dry coughs. "I'll be fine. Remember, I've been on the inner-surface of the ring. That was much colder and the gravity was two-gee. This is no worse."

Marten helped his grandfather into a chair. "You were a lot younger then."

Suresh struggled into his own seat. "What happened out there?"

Jack slumped against a console, out of breath from working on the elevator. "It was Pieter Reynard."

Marten asked, "Who?" Suresh said, "I thought he was on Earth."

"We did too. He attacked us at the end of the yard. Now we have to stop him. He's going to Caerton, to find Sarah."

"We've still got the second elevator," Suresh said. "How long to get it running?"

Isabel held up gloved hands as she headed for the stairs. "In this cold, it'll be a while."

"There are heaters in the suits. That will help."

Pressure suits hung on hooks at the back of the control room, but there weren't enough for everybody and definitely not one to fit Anders, who appeared pale and was still coughing. Jack knew what he had to do.

"Ethan, can I see your coin again?"

Ethan held out the coin, letting it rest on his palm. Jack concentrated for a moment, then air shrilled through the open portal, accompanied by a bright yellow light.

Jack watched everyone's expressions. He already knew about Suresh and Anders, and wasn't surprised that Jada understood his ability to access other portals—Sarah must have told her. Marten's reaction spoke for the rest of them.

"*What the* … What is that?"

Jack shifted uneasily. "It's difficult to explain. Let's wait until there's more air in here."

Ethan bounced the coin between hands. "This is getting kinda warm, Jack. *Ow*." He dropped it on the table.

"Sorry. That one's in a desert."

Chapter 10

Warm desert air hissed from the coin until the pressure equalized. When he was breathing easier, and Anders had stopped coughing, Jack explained.

That the coin's crystal was a portal to another crystal in a desert was a simple thing for everyone to accept. That Jack could open a wormhole to *any* other crystal was harder. He tried describing in simple terms how the device manipulated dark matter and its associated energy field.

Marten, who'd been dabbing his face to see if it had stopped bleeding, said, "It's magic."

"*See,*" Ethan said. "I told you."

"No, it's not. It's just a wormhole connection to an AI somewhere in the future that has the technology to manipulate dark energy." That brought blank expressions from everyone.

Jada stood in the doorway overlooking the foyer and jabbed a finger towards the elevator. "It doesn't make a difference if it's magic or not. What matters is stopping Pieter before he gets to Sarah."

The air rising from Ethan's coin had warmed the control room, but the elevator was a floor below and near freezing. Isabel overheard Jada's comment and shouted, "I'm almost done. The original module had already been removed."

"Who is Pieter Reynard?" Marten asked again. "Can he do magic too?"

"It's not … He stole my portal crystal. And yes, he can use it to move objects." Jack caught Marten applying a cloth to his wound. "And people. Sorry."

"Pieter is the one who was responsible for Newton," Jada said. "He destroyed all the portals to make it look like a terrorist attack on the eve of Newton's prophecy. Jack and Ethan were there and tried to stop him."

"Sarah too," Jack said.

"How could one man destroy nearly every crystal in the world?" Marten asked.

"It's complicated. Portal crystals are identical right down to the number of atoms, and their wormholes share a common space. Pieter made them vibrate in tune and shatter. He only needed thousands of crystals—one from every production lot—to affect billions."

The lights in the elevator came to life and Isabel stood, holding the doors open. "Done. We can go now."

- - - - -

The descent seemed to take forever. The elevator traveled at a constant speed and would take just as long going down as it had going up, but Jack kept reading the elevation anyway. His worries increased with the rise in apparent gravity.

"How did Pieter get up there?"

"Don't you mean how did he get back to Cirrus?" Ethan replied.

"That too. But the elevator needed one of our power cells. The one Pieter came up on would have needed one of his. Why did he remove it after he got there?"

"The maintenance coach? He'd have needed power to move that."

"That's true. But he only used that to escape. He said he was expecting us. He shouldn't have *needed* to escape."

Jada clapped her hands in front of their faces. "Let's focus on what's important. You said you can connect to any crystal. Can you find one near Sarah and warn her?"

"It's not that simple," Jack said. "They're not laid out in geographical order. And even if I somehow found a crystal that survived Newton, there's still no way to communicate. It'd be like shouting through the eye of a needle."

"We'll be down in a minute," Suresh said. "Help me tip the table in front of the doors."

Though Pieter would almost certainly be gone, Suresh

worried that he might have a firearm. He'd had the foresight to move a large metal-topped table from the workroom into the elevator for them to hide behind.

"Could you have crushed him between the trailers?" Ethan asked quietly as the others worked.

Jack stared at the floor. "The coin's crystal would have shattered from the effort, but not before setting the trailer rolling."

"You should have done it." Ethan clenched his coin in a fist through his shirt. "*I* would have."

- - - - -

"Lights out," Suresh said as the elevator slowed. Isabel killed the lights.

Ethan draped his lucky coin over the table's edge on its cord. Jack had no idea how effective the *Shield Spell*—as Ethan called it— would be against bullets. He was relying on the metal sheet for protection, but agreed that he should be able to prevent Pieter from moving the table itself.

The elevator stopped. The door opened onto the darkened warehouse.

"Give us a light," Anders whispered from a corner of the elevator.

Marten, Ethan. and Jada tossed their flashlights. They skittered across the smooth concrete floor.

Anders bobbed his head for a look. "Clear."

Henri did the same, looking the other direction. "Clear this side too."

Jack sensed no crystals nearby. "And there's no portal in the other elevator."

Suresh had worried that Pieter might lay in wait in the second car where he couldn't be seen. Jack reassured him that he could sense his wand at that range.

Anders leaned out of the elevator. "One of our trucks is gone."

"We'll have to leave one set of batteries." Suresh gestured to the pile. "Start loading the rest."

"*No.*" Jada sprang from the elevator. "We have to go. *Now.*

Sarah's in danger."

Suresh raised his hands to calm his daughter. "We must replace our vehicle's power cells first. We can load the batteries at the same time."

"How far can you control the wand from?" Ethan asked as the lights came on.

"I can sense it from over fifty feet, but I need to be really close to use it."

"Can you open a wormhole remotely? Will that tell you where he is?"

"I don't know. Give me your coin."

Before Newton, every portal crystal was entangled only with the other member of its pair. Jack had learned—through the AI link that brought memories to Travellers—to visualize wormholes as a thread linking those crystals. To access fresh air, he'd imagined rerouting the coin's portal to the one in the desert, and the AI took care of the rest. But to achieve his goal of destroying the network, Pieter's machine had woven billions of those threads into a fabric that Jack now envisioned as a gem-encrusted landscape of peaks and valleys.

He'd spent hundreds of hours surveying that virtual terrain, and knew how to link the crystal in his wand to any other, but hadn't thought of trying a reverse connection. While the others loaded batteries, he found a quiet spot to sit and concentrate.

If the connections were enabled through an advanced AI, then it made sense to Jack that there was an addressing scheme—like an internet for portals. He thought of them as being clustered in *neighborhoods*, organized by similar traits, but knew the relationship was more complex; like a four-dimensional Venn diagram joining function, location, size and other factors. He most often found portals by thinking about the environment they worked in.

None of that mattered. At once, Jack found what he was looking for. "Got it."

"That was fast," Ethan said.

"Yeah, a lot easier than I expected." Like a bright light in the darkness, his wand crystal stood apart from the rest. He opened the wormhole without caution and got an impression of the wand lying on the missing vehicle's seat; it was dark and there was a sense of movement, of bouncing. "He's already outside." The access tunnel's floor was smooth, the road descending to the highway was rough.

Now that he'd found the wand, he tried sensing the environment again to get a better idea of where Pieter was. He *listened*—although that was an inadequate description of the sense. He *reached*—another deficient term. He felt—

A wave of anxiety crashed over him, far worse than any he'd experienced from emotion detectors. The feedback was intense, dark, and ruthless. And there was something more: recognition.

[I know you.]

Jack recoiled. *Pieter?*

[Jack?]

"*NO*." Panicking, Jack fled through the wormhole, felt Pieter's thoughts pursuing.

[I see you.]

"*STOP*." He slammed the link closed and opened his eyes.

Everyone was staring at him. Marten was sitting on the ground, holding his bleeding nose. Jada was kneeling next to him, looking very concerned.

"You created a shield," Ethan said. Marten had been standing too near.

"Sorry. It was Pieter. He saw me."

"Saw you?"

"I'll explain later. We need to go *now*. He's thinking of murder."

Chapter 11

The return trip through the tunnel passed in a blur for Jack as he struggled to think of a way to warn Sarah. Past experiments had proven he couldn't manipulate the energy field beyond the wormhole. But if something was already passing through that opening, such as water or light, he could affect its flow up to the threshold. That meant it might be possible to signal her somehow, but finding a crystal near her was an impossible task.

The twisting road through the forest was as muddy as it had been on the way up. Ethan, driving Dave, passed Suresh and gained a big lead on the other vehicles, but it made no difference—Anders had ordered them to regroup at the highway.

Jada, riding in the second vehicle to reach the intersection, pointed into the sky. "What's that?" A wispy, violet cloud shimmered and waved like a tattered flag, miles above the wall.

"There's a hole in the roof," Suresh said. "The atmosphere is escaping and ionizing. That explains the extreme weather of the last few days."

"It also explains how Pieter got to Cirrus," Jack said. "He must have crashed a shuttle through the roof and landed by the observation tower."

"Isn't it supposed to seal by itself?" Ethan asked.

Suresh considered the stream of gas venting into space. "It depends on how large the tear is. For a hole large enough for a spacecraft? It could take days."

- - - - -

Caerton was a four-hour drive from the maintenance tunnel; plenty of time for Jack to suffer through cycles of worrying for Sarah, reassuring himself that everything would be all right, and blaming himself for not stopping Pieter. After two hours of this, Ethan interrupted, dragging Jack's thoughts back to the present.

"How did you know what Pieter was thinking? Does your

talent allow you to read minds?"

"No, nothing like that. Remember, it's just an AI recording our thoughts and playing them back. You've got two seconds, Sarah gets weeks."

"What about you?"

"I've been thinking about that. It's as if my link works only in real-time. Which sort of makes sense; moving an object accurately would be almost impossible from memory."

"So how does that let you know what he's thinking?"

"I don't know. Pieter seems to remember things months, maybe years in the future. But he can also manipulate the energy field." Jack didn't enjoy imagining that he and Pieter had anything in common. "Somehow, the AI allowed us to share memories."

"Does that mean he can also link to another portal? Can he read your thoughts?"

"I hope not. Connecting to the AI isn't difficult. You do it all the time—that's how you get your two-second warning. But linking to another portal is different. I can't locate a specific crystal."

"Then how did you find the one in the desert so quickly?"

"I found that one last month. I know where it is virtually, but I have no idea where it exists in the real world."

A loud buzzing noise passed overhead, causing Ethan to instinctively tap the brakes. "Was that … was that our mail drone?"

Jack spun around, catching a glimpse of the aircraft receding in the moonlight. "It had to be."

"Why is she sending it at night?"

There were only two possibilities, neither of them good. "Either she knew she wouldn't be there in the morning, or there's trouble."

- - - - -

The group encountered light rain as they neared Caerton. It made little difference to their progress and did nothing to improve their mood. Unless he ran into problems, Pieter had reached the city twenty minutes ago. Jack couldn't be sure when Sarah had sent the drone, but guessed it was at least an hour before that.

They approached the city from the south. Columns of lighted windows defined the skyline, but there were significant gaps where darkened towers stood. The rumors reaching Icarus told of residents climbing hundreds of steps each day, clinging to the hope that power would be restored soon. What they didn't know was that all fusion generators, even tiny ones that powered a single building, had been built on Earth; that technology did not exist on Cirrus.

Though it pained him to delay, Jack gestured for Ethan to pull over as they crossed the bridge into the city. "Let Suresh pass. Jada knows the streets better than I do."

Ethan slowed and waved Suresh past. At this late hour, and with a bit of rain, the surface streets were empty. Jada directed them on a course that passed through the very center of downtown, along boulevards of unkempt flower beds and thirsty trees.

"Grandpa's building still has power," Ethan said as they sped past the Magnolia, one of the city's taller buildings.

They'd seen no sign of Pieter. Had he gone straight for Sarah, Jack wondered, or had he reconnected with his private security? He'd had months to plan his return and was surely prepared, but had he even been able to communicate with anyone on Cirrus? If so, they could be racing into a trap.

The convoy slid to a stop in front of a block of tall, narrow townhouses. Jack was halfway out of his seat when Ethan dragged him back. Two seconds later, Sarah and her mother burst through the door of their home and ran to the street. They were already packed, and Sarah was carrying a large square frame: Holden's portal.

The recovery team had started the day with nine passengers and five vehicles. Only one of the four remaining had two rows of seats, and Sarah pointed her mother to the last free spot behind Suresh. Then she threw her bag onto Dave's overhead rack and clambered into the cargo box, squeezing herself and the portal frame between the batteries. Ethan spun Dave's tires as he sped away. The entire stop had taken less than ten seconds.

Jack would have hugged her if he could; her smile drove his anxiety away. And she'd cut her chestnut hair to shoulder-length recently. It suited her, made her seem more confident. Not that she needed more confidence. In the lead-up to Newton, she'd travelled alone to Earth to rescue Detective Singh, who had in turn rescued Jack's family.

"Are you all right?" he asked as she settled into a comfortable position.

"I'm fine. I knew you were coming and that we had to leave. Pieter is back, isn't he?"

"Why was Grandpa's portal at your house?" Ethan asked. "Not that I'm complaining; since you used it to find out about Pieter."

"Priya moved it from his apartment. And actually, I haven't used it. Not really. I only opened it. That's when I worked out that I was around the drone every other time I predicted the future. Travellers don't need to pass *through* a portal to remember their futures, we just have to be *near* one."

"We only figured that out ourselves yesterday," Jack said.

- - - - -

Suresh led the group to the highway and kept to the pavement instead of taking the more direct route along the narrower grain roads. After months without maintenance, potholes cratered the gravel surface, and the rain made it impossible to tell the shallow ones from those which could ruin a wheel.

They approached the forest from the southeast, on a path neither Jack nor Ethan had used before. Like the trail near the black crag, the shortcut was unmarked. Anders slowed several times and even drove into the wrong meadow once before finding the track.

Ethan had just cleared the shallow ditch between the road and the trees when Jack noticed a dull red glow in the sky. *Forest fire?*

No. There had been rain but no lightning since yesterday. He glanced at Sarah. Her expression was troubled. She knew.

"What is it?" Jack asked.

Tears formed in her eyes. "Something awful."

"*Faster,*" he shouted, but Ethan had already slammed the accelerator and was passing Anders.

The narrow road twisted through a dark pine forest. With Ethan's two-second warning, it may as well have been a race track. At the head of the convoy, he took blind corners at their optimum speed. The others only had to follow Dave's tail lights.

"Is that on the island or near the village?" Ethan asked.

They were angling toward the lake but were still too far away to say for sure where the fire was. Ethan's question was answered a second later; a brilliant blue flash lit the sky and all the vehicles lost power at the same moment.

"The fusion generator," Jack exclaimed as they coasted to a stop.

In that instant, he understood his mistake. Sarah wasn't the *Other Traveller*. It was Niels. Jack jumped from the truck and ran. Sarah and Ethan followed automatically.

It took only a few minutes to clear the forest and reach the shore. The blaze cast an orange glow across the water, towards the village, but the cabin was still hidden around the curve of the island. By the time they got close enough to see it directly, Niels' home was engulfed in flames.

"There are boats in the water," Jack said. But he and his friends had no choice except to continue running to the village, still four miles away. Occasional flashes of white and blue illuminated the road, creating silent, flickering stripes through the trees.

When they arrived, exhausted, they found there were no boats left. Everyone who hadn't gone to the island was awake and gathered on the shore in front of the lodge. Thankfully, Holden was among them.

"Where's Niels?" Jack asked, catching his breath.

"No one has returned from the island yet," Emily said. "We don't know what happened."

"It was *Pieter*." Jack spat the name. "He's back on Cirrus." A mix of gasps and wails answered his announcement.

Natalya checked the road behind Jack. "Where are the others? Is everyone all right?"

"They're fine," Ethan said. "They'll be here soon."

Jack focused on the island. The fire was still burning but the firefighters had stopped it from spreading. Suresh and the others arrived as a group several minutes later, but without a boat they were as helpless as everyone else.

Hours passed before Jack spotted the first boats coming from the island. The clouds had disappeared and the sky was brightening. Even from halfway across the lake, he could see it in their weary posture, in the tired and painful way they rowed.

He didn't need to hear it from them to know that Niels was dead.

Chapter 12

"This experiment will reveal the energy field's true nature," Niels said. "Jack, you're the only one who can sense the field, so I'm relying on you to make sure it doesn't get out of hand."

Jack gripped his wand firmly. "I'm ready."

Niels, wearing a pristine white lab coat, threw a switch and bright light spilled from a portal large enough for a man to crawl through. He adjusted the controls, causing the light to waver and cast animated shadows on the workshop's far wall.

Jack smelled smoke. He shouted a warning but no sound came from his mouth. The light grew brighter, forcing him to squint. He waved his arms to get Niels' attention.

Niels finally noticed that something was wrong. "It's out of control. Shut it down."

Jack raised an empty hand. "My wand." He scanned the floor frantically but found nothing. "It's gone."

The light grew even brighter. "*Jack!*" Niels tried to stand. His arms shook as he pushed himself up from his walker. "*Stop him.*"

"I'm sorry. I've lost it."

Niels faded into a white fog blossoming from the portal. "It's up to you now."

"*No. I can't.*" Jack raised his hands to shield his eyes and awoke with intense sunlight shining in his face.

It was late morning and the sun had finally moved into a position to light the bunk room. Flickering shadows created by overhanging branches mirrored the movements in his dream. He rolled away from the window but didn't get out of bed.

There was no one else in the men's bunk room, and the neighboring common room was silent too. Muffled machinery noises filtered in from outdoors but they didn't compare to the racket of earlier days when the entire village was a construction zone.

Jack had slept restlessly in his clothes. He hopped off his bunk and headed outside. A few children played in the field between the cabins, but the village appeared otherwise deserted.

A rhythmic banging from beyond the trees caught his attention. He followed the noise to the village's newly constructed barn. Several women were finishing the assembly of grain storage bins at the edge of a field. Emily, with her sleeves rolled up, was leaning into the tractor's engine compartment.

"Where is everyone?" Jack asked.

"Most are at the solar farm. Your father has gone with the others to fetch the trucks and batteries."

"I could have helped with that," Jack said, knowing that his heart wasn't in it.

"You needed sleep. Ethan and Sarah are at the dock. There's food upstairs if you want it."

"Not hungry." He turned around and made his way to the lake.

Sarah and Ethan were sitting quietly at the end of the pier, their legs dangling over the water. Without a word, Jack sat next to them. They glanced at him, accepting his presence silently. Sarah had been crying. Ethan's face showed only anger. Jack wasn't sure what he felt.

He hadn't known Niels all that well, had only spent a few days in his company, but had both liked and respected the man. He'd never lost anyone close before and didn't know if his feelings were normal or if he was numbed by the injustice of the situation; that someone as cruel as Pieter Reynard had inflicted such an injury on him, on the entire community, and gotten away with it. How many years would pass before a proper police force returned to Cirrus to bring him to justice?

Jack stood. "I'm going to the island." He trudged away without waiting for a response. Sarah and Ethan followed and joined him in the canoe.

Once they were away from the dock, Jack was glad he'd taken the front where his friends couldn't see his face. He wanted to scream, to reclaim his wand and direct its entire force at Pieter, to tear him apart. Instead, he held back his tears and directed his energy into the paddle, pushing as hard as he could. Ethan and Sarah did the same.

His rage subsided as the boat approached the island. Even if the mysterious threshold in the middle of the lake hadn't influenced him, the island had always been a place of calm; the spot where he and Ethan first met Niels, and where he'd found many answers. Now he didn't know what to expect. They were close enough to see the cabin's remains. The only part still standing was its stone chimney.

Many boats floated near the simple wooden pier; more than it had been designed for. The villagers who weren't at the solar farm or retrieving the vehicles had come over to help in whatever way they could. Jack pushed two craft apart to create a path, then tied up the canoe once Ethan and Sarah were on dry ground.

Tools and machinery recovered from Niels' workshop lined the steep trail to the cabin. The villagers had collected whatever they could salvage. Jack felt no emotion, only recognized the practicality of the task. *Niels would have wanted that.*

A series of groans and cracks drew Jack's attention. The cleanup crew were toppling a large, badly charred spruce tree that stood next to the ruin. It crashed through smaller, similarly burned trees and raised a cloud of ash.

With the site made safe, the workers returned to identifying and cleaning objects. They placed those too damaged to be of use in a separate pile. Jack wandered over to the heap. It was too large; years of Niels' work lost in a single night. He prodded a blackened cylinder with his foot: one of the tractor beams.

As always, Natalya led the villagers in group efforts. She spotted Jack and his friends and beckoned them to follow up a gently sloping gravel path, away from the burned area.

A narrow border of surviving trees separated the destruction from a grass-covered clearing overlooking a sheltered bay. Jack remembered this place; he and Ethan had climbed the rock wall below on their first visit to the island.

A simple wooden bench, cut from logs and showing years of weathering, faced the water. Behind the bench, a pile of dirt and gravel—a newly filled grave—rested atop a knoll the size of Niels' cabin.

"He used to come up here to watch the sunset," Natalya said. After a pause she added, "We'll have a proper service in a few days." She left them to return to her work.

Jack sat on the bench, not wanting to look at the grave behind him. Ethan and Sarah sat on either side.

It didn't seem right that the sky had cleared for the first time in days. The sun was high now but still at their backs, and it illuminated the rocky beach from where they'd first seen the burning cabin. Something was moving there; Victor had wired the trucks to the batteries they carried. The convoy would reach the village soon, but far too late.

The practical part of Jack's mind—the part not grieving— wanted life to return to normal and understood that there'd be no lights and no electricity for cooking without batteries. None of the vehicles would work, not even the tractor the community relied on.

As the convoy passed from view, Jack decided he'd had enough of sitting; he needed to be moving, to distract himself, to be far from the smell of smoke and freshly turned soil. He climbed the knoll, paused next to the grave, and said a silent goodbye.

Instead of heading back the way he'd come, he turned inland, where the trail that brought them to the clearing continued around the knoll. He walked that direction and passed through a sparse wall of trees into another clearing.

"What's wrong?" Sarah asked when she rejoined Jack, finding him standing before a vegetable patch.

"I … I know this place. When Ethan and I stayed here in August, I dreamed I flew over the island. I saw a garden. This garden. Right here."

"Was it a future memory?" Ethan asked. "Like Sarah has?"

"I was flying, so it definitely wasn't a memory."

"My memories don't come to me as dreams," Sarah said. "I don't *see* anything; I *remember* seeing it, as if it was something I always knew. Maybe you just figured out that there should be a garden here."

Jack considered the distance to the cabin. "That's probably it. Niels was more than ninety years old and lived alone for years before they built the lodge. It only makes sense to plant it near the cabin." He plucked at a wire on the pea fence. "It's just that … it looks exactly, and I mean *exactly*, as it did in my dream."

He continued along the path that passed through the center of the plot. Thanks to Cirrus' stable climate—and subtle genetic engineering—the garden still boasted a variety of ready-to-harvest vegetables.

The path forked. One branch led further inland, the other angled downhill towards the cabin. Several steps before the intersection, Jack froze.

"What?" Sarah asked.

"My wand. It's here. I can feel it."

"Where?" Ethan squatted to pick up a stone. "I don't see him." He searched the trees for Pieter.

"No, sorry. It's not my wand. But it's a portal. A big one."

"A portal out here?" Sarah looked around. The lake was visible through blackened trees over the cabin's remains, but there was only forest in every other direction. "Why would there be a portal here? And what's powering it? The generator was destroyed."

Jack started running. "The crystals. They must have survived the fire."

Ethan stood for a moment longer. "I doubt anything could have survived that." But then he hurried after Jack, anyway.

Until now, Jack hadn't even thought about the crystals. If he had, he'd have been even more upset; his grandfather's entire collection had been in the cabin. He stopped abruptly a few paces away. Ethan and Sarah had to stop short to avoid running into him.

"You're right. They couldn't have. They were never there." He slipped past them and rushed back uphill. At the intersection, he stopped, looked around, then jumped off the path. "Found it."

Ethan and Sarah caught up to him as he dropped to his knees and started digging with his hands into a pile of loose soil. Something had been buried there recently.

Ethan crouched on the other side and dug too. Within seconds they hit a hard, smooth surface that thumped like a drum. They cleared the dirt away and unearthed a bright red plastic toolbox. Jack found the handle and pulled it from the hole. He unlatched the lid and threw it open.

Inside, in an unorganized pile, were all the crystals Holden had brought to Cirrus. There were also batteries, handheld meters, two envelopes, and the tool needed to build coin portals from Holden's limited supply of crystal rods; someone had assembled the contents in a hurry. But it was the metal cylinder on top of the pile that held Jack's attention.

"A tractor beam?" The power light was blinking. "It's been rigged to cycle on and off."

"What's all this doing out here?" Ethan asked, then answered his own question. "Niels must have known Pieter was coming. He buried this for you to find. He knew you'd walk past and sense it."

"But why didn't he call for help from the village? This box weighs … forty pounds and he couldn't move very well anymore. This would have been incredibly difficult for him."

Sarah, who'd only ever spoken to Niels on the phone, was crying openly. "It's much more than that. He knew about this for a while."

One envelope had her family name written on it. She'd opened it and found a key attached to a green plastic tag. Jack read the number printed on it, "Twenty-eight." The last of the village's cabins, whose foundations had been laid months ago.

Jack's name was scrawled on the second envelope. He tore it

open and tipped the contents into his hand: a wooden rod with a circle of blue crystal showing at one end.

It wasn't the polished titanium of the original, but it was clearly a wand.

Chapter 13

Sarah took the canoe's middle seat for the return trip across the lake. As they passed the unseen threshold, she stopped paddling. Jack, at the front, didn't have to ask—he knew she felt the same sensation he did.

He'd hoped this time would be different, that the mysterious divide had suffered the loss of Niels and disappeared or diminished like a flag at half-mast. Instead, departing the island was like opening a door to an unfamiliar world.

The noise of power tools resumed while they were still offshore; the batteries had arrived. In the back of his mind, behind the grief, Jack understood the need to be practical—construction had to be finished before the start of the rainy season. Also, he'd be able to move out of the bunk room once his parents' cabin had a roof.

Ethan tied up the canoe while Jack and Sarah hurried to Holden's place to show what they had found.

"So," Holden said sadly when Jack explained where he'd dug up the box, "he knew." He examined the wand. "This would have taken at least a day to fabricate."

"I don't understand," Jack said. "Why didn't he call for help?"

Holden returned the wand. "I don't know. He said nothing to suggest he knew what was going to happen. However, if he had told anyone, there would certainly have been others on the island last night. We don't know what weapons Pieter brought. Many more people would have been hurt."

"Why did Pieter even come back?" Ethan asked. "And why show himself at the maintenance depot? If he'd waited until we left, we'd have never known he was there. Why come all this way for revenge?"

The toolkit contained more than just Holden's crystals. Jack started to rummage, hoping to find an answer, when Priya interrupted.

"Holden? What's happening? This isn't Sarah's place."

Jack spun to find Holden's portal frame resting on the wooden floor against the wall. Thousands of times bigger than a typical static crystal, the device was the largest ever created. As far as they knew, it was also the only remaining portal between Earth and Cirrus wide enough for a person to use—Jack had travelled through it dozens of times as an infant.

Priya sat on the floor on the other side of the wormhole, giving the appearance that she was looking through an opening in the cabin's wall. She was wearing a sleeveless top that showed off her well-defined arms. At five-foot-three, she was one of the shortest detectives in the UN's Off-world Police Division, but could easily take down a much larger opponent.

"Careful," Priya warned as Sarah kneeled beside the frame, "it's not charged enough yet to come through." She caught Sarah's expression. "What's wrong?"

"Pieter's back," Sarah cried. "He killed Niels."

Together, Jack and his friends explained everything that had happened since they arrived at the maintenance depot. He even described the link with Pieter; how he'd sensed what Pieter was thinking.

Priya considered the news for a moment, then asked, "Can you can get a drone up to the top of the sector wall?"

"That's too high for our mail carrier. Why?"

"We've been watching his offices around the world. There have been rumors, but no confirmed sightings. He couldn't have got into orbit on his own. If we find the ship he used, maybe we can work out where he's operating from and who's helping him."

"Even if we had a drone that could fly to that altitude, the winds over the wall are way too strong."

"I'll go up myself, then. How long until the portal is charged?"

"We still have only a limited amount of power here," Holden said. "You'll be able to come across later this afternoon."

"Can I send these now?" Priya set four gray objects on the

floor.

Jack confirmed the charge level and reached through to take the devices, which had only a tiny screen and two buttons on the side. "They look like little phones. What are they?"

"Radios. This is what we're stuck using right now. I found these in a storage room. They're older than I am, but I tested them and they still work."

Jack knew a little about radios, even if he'd never seen one. "How far apart do they work?"

"Not far enough. But your father should be able to adapt them to send the signal through a portal crystal instead of radio waves. That's what we're doing here. I'm supposed to turn these over to the department, but you need them just as badly."

"Can we come with you to the wall?" Sarah asked.

Jack prepared to argue why they should go, but Priya said, "Actually, yes. From what I've heard, it'll be safer to keep you three out of the village until we catch Pieter, or he returns to Earth."

"You think he's going back?" Ethan asked.

"Not necessarily, but he could. He'd have needed an enormous power source to get into orbit, and much more than that to make it to Cirrus. That'll be more than enough to run a man-sized portal. My guess is that he brought crystals to supply whatever power he needs there and to set up communications with whoever he's working with here."

"Either way," Sarah said, "he'll be at his mansion. All we have to do is watch that."

"*We* won't be doing anything. You three can come with me to help find his ship, then *I* will go into Caerton alone, to talk to Gutierrez."

"Why?" Everyone in Caerton knew that James Gutierrez was Pieter's business partner. He and Pieter jointly owned the city and surrounding lands. "I heard they hated each other."

"It's unlikely that Reynard will use his own equipment, but the rumors getting back to us can only come from Caerton.

Someone there has an active portal. If it's not him, Gutierrez might know who it is."

- - - - -

Priya couldn't leave Earth until the weekend. That was fine because there was so much work on the farm that Jack had no time for anything else. Not to grieve properly for Niels, or worry about Pieter, or experiment with new spells. He found only a few minutes to help Ethan practice ones he'd already seen, such as *shield* and *fire*. He and Sarah sat together at mealtimes, but Niels' death clouded their mood and stifled their conversation.

By the time Priya travelled to Cirrus, two days later, Victor had adapted the radios to use a wormhole instead of an antenna. He was still busy with farm work, so Emily delivered them.

"The batteries in these are awful, and we've been too busy to work on a power connection. We'll keep ours plugged in but yours won't last long. Leave it off unless you need to call us." Then she spoke directly to Jack. "Turn it on for a few minutes at the top of every hour in case we need to contact you."

Ethan whispered to Sarah, "You think she packed a lunch for him too?"

"No," Emily said, "but *your* mother packed one for you." She passed him a bag. Properly humbled, Ethan accepted the package while Jack and Sarah held back laughter.

"Okay," Priya said, "time to go."

"I *did* pack food for the rest of you," Emily said when she knew Ethan couldn't hear. "It's in the cargo box."

As there were four of them, they couldn't use Dave. Instead, Priya would drive Suresh's four-seater. On Cirrus, all personal vehicles shared a common platform; the only mechanical difference between Dave and Suresh's truck was the length of its cargo box and number of seats. Ethan joined Jack in the back seat and Sarah sat beside Priya.

"Who's this?" Priya asked as she drove. They'd reached the edge of the village when an electric motorcycle approached.

"That's Terrance," Jack said. "One of Niels' friends. He went back to Caerton yesterday."

Priya pulled to the side of the road and stopped. Terrance did the same, and Jack made the introductions after Terrance removed his helmet.

The first thing people noticed about Terrance was his movie-star good-looks. His flawless dark skin highlighted a rugged chin and pronounced cheekbones, and his very short hair was always perfectly trimmed. The first time Jack met him, he'd noted that Niels' assistant had a taste for expensive clothing and gold jewelry. As before, Terrance was wearing a gold watch, and three gold rings adorned the hand he extended to Priya.

"Detective Singh." Terrance smiled. "I've heard all about you. When did you get back to Cirrus?"

Priya shook his hand but dodged the question. "Jack tells me you were in Caerton recently. What's happening there?"

"There was some looting yesterday, but it was quiet when I left. Where are you all going?"

"We'll be back soon. I'm told you have useful contacts in Caerton. I might have questions for you later. Don't leave the village." As an afterthought, she added, "Please."

"Of course. Anything to help." He gave a friendly wave and continued into Icarus.

"What was *that* about?" Sarah asked.

"How well do you know Terrance?" Priya asked. "He's much younger than most of Niels' friends."

"He's runs a salon in Caerton," Jack said. "Anders thinks he'll do anything for money, but Niels trusted him."

"He's also a hacker," Ethan said. "He arranged the crash on the highway that helped us escape from Pieter the day before Newton."

"Why?" Jack asked. "Is something wrong?"

Priya shook her head and started driving. "I don't trust a person who wears that much gold."

Ethan zipped his jacket higher. Jack noticed the movement, and his portal sense told him that Ethan's lucky coin was around his neck again.

Chapter 14

Unlike Anders, Priya took no breaks for them to stop and stretch their legs. She made good time and they reached the elevator before noon. They were also better prepared this trip; Victor had assembled an adapter to power the lift directly from the truck. The vehicle, small by Earth standards, fit snugly into the oversized elevator with the seats raised. After Priya set the parking brake, Jack connected the cable and they settled in for the ride.

Ever cautious, Suresh had provided them with a checklist. Jack remembered the procedure for opening the doors, but Priya made them follow the written instructions anyway.

"Pressure is normal on the other side," Ethan confirmed. "Well, the new normal. A lot lower than it should be, but at least it's not vacuum."

They put on their winter coats—it would be very cold inside. The doors slid open and Priya drove into the foyer.

"Call Suresh and let him know we're here," Priya said.

Sarah held the radio awkwardly in front of her. "Hello. We're here. We're okay." She turned to Priya. "Do I hold it to my ear like a phone?"

Jack was sure there'd have been an eye-rolling emoji just then if the conversation were happening on a pre-Newton phone with an emotion detector.

They waited almost a minute for Suresh's response. "Roger. Remember to check in again before you leave. Over."

"Am I supposed to say 'over and out'?"

"*Goodbye* will do," Priya said.

"Oh, okay." Sarah pressed the *talk* button. "Thanks. Goodbye."

Priya hopped from the vehicle. "First order of business, let's get the power running. Jack, unspool that cable. Ethan, check the air pressure in the other rooms."

Jack worked on connecting the truck's power cable to a receiver in the foyer while Priya and Sarah unpacked extra winter gear. There would be a locker with snowshoes at the top of the stairwell, but they'd brought their own boots. Ethan went up to the control room.

"Pressure's good everywhere except the service bay," he called as the emergency lights came on throughout the complex. He leaned into the curved window overlooking the yard and yelled, *"What's that?"*

Jack ran upstairs to join his cousin. "It's the maintenance coach." Two hundred yards to the right, a pile of twisted metal and plastic appeared embedded in the stone on the opposite side of the tracks. "It's stuck in the airlock. I think it punctured the wall."

"I thought that was impossible," Sarah said from the doorway.

"It's impossible to leave the lock open or for it to fail. Come here." He pointed at the incoming airlock two hundred yards to the left. "See, it's just a rotating cylinder with a slot in one side. The slot always faces the tunnel, the bay, or the rock." He faced the outgoing airlock. "But Pieter ran the coach inside that one at full speed."

"Is the wand that powerful?" Ethan asked.

"It might be able to push something that heavy, but not very fast. He had to have used one of his own power cells."

"Why did he crash it?"

"Maybe it was an accident? He must have been trying to take it to Caerton. He'd have had to bypass a bunch of safety systems to make it run so fast in the yard."

"Well, there's nothing we can do about it now," Priya said. "If Suresh wants more batteries, he's got to come up with a plan for sealing off the tunnel first. Let's start climbing." She led the group downstairs and opened the door in the opposite wall.

Sarah peered into the darkness. "It's just steps." She angled her flashlight higher. "Lots of steps." A straight corridor with a curved ceiling extended over the top of the service bay, beyond the reach of their flashlights. The steps were gray concrete, but the smooth wall appeared to have been cut directly from the fused stone; its surfaced rippled with a ring pattern that resembled raindrops on water.

Priya slung her boots over her shoulder to free her hands for the railing. "According to Suresh, the north and southbound tunnels are separated by three hundred yards. The stairwells meet in the middle, below the tower. It's not far to the surface, but let's take it easy. Remember the elevation we're at."

Ethan paused after a few minutes of climbing in silence. "I've climbed Mt. Rainier. That was colder, but this is harder, even with reduced gravity."

"Rainer is what? Three miles?" Jack asked. "Without power to run the air compressors, we're closer to four."

They passed through an airlock at the top of the stairs to enter the chamber below the observation tower. As there was no difference in air pressure, the glass panels parted silently when Jack cranked them open.

The room was bare except for a bank of lockers, several sets of snowshoes and ski goggles, and shovels hanging from hooks on the concrete walls. An airlock on the east side of the room led to the northbound tunnel's service bay. Sunlight streamed through a square opening in the ceiling above a column of metal rungs embedded in the north wall.

Priya put on her winter boots and climbed the ladder to a landing thirty feet higher. She opened the hatch onto a brilliantly lit landscape. The sky had cleared for the first time in days, but the sun provided little warmth. A wave of freezing air flooded past her and settled in the locker room.

"We won't need snowshoes today," Priya shouted. "You can come up now. Watch the first step."

Jack climbed up next. It turned out that the square shaft was the inside of a slender, insulated tower, designed for access through significant amounts of snow. He stepped through the door and found himself on a narrow ledge twenty feet above the ground.

The rolling landscape was barren except where isolated pockets of compacted snow and ice had settled into depressions. Elsewhere, patches of solid gray rock poked through hills of gravel and boulders. Except for the color, the scene reminded Jack of photos he'd seen of the Martian polar cap.

"Good thing there's no snow." He had to speak loudly to make himself heard in the high wind. "His ship would be buried if it ever got this deep."

Priya scanned the horizon with binoculars. "Footprints would have made it easier to find, though. Any ideas, Miss Rogers?"

Sarah pointed. "North."

"That was easy," Ethan said as he came out the door behind her. "How far?"

"I don't mean I *remember* where it is, only that north makes the most sense. If he was trying to get to Caerton, he'd have been closer if something went wrong and he had to walk down the mountain."

"You're probably right," Priya said, "but try not to overthink these things. From what I know of Traveller's talents, they're easily confounded by logic. If it's a genuine memory, the first thing that comes into your head should be the correct answer. We're going north."

She descended to the surface using the rungs set into the outer wall and started walking. The others followed her toward a five-hundred-foot-tall mound, four miles away.

"Is this weather because of the hole in the roof," Ethan asked. Although it was sunny, the wind was vicious on the plateau and tore at their clothing.

Jack pulled his hood to cover more of his face. "I think this is normal for the wall."

Even though the slope was gentle, the group stopped several times to catch their breath. Priya scanned the terrain again when they reached the top of the stony hill. "There. Northwest. What does that look like to you?"

Jack took the binoculars. "Seems pretty small." He passed them to Ethan.

"Might be a patch of snow. It's only about the size of a minivan."

Sarah had the last look. "I think that's it. It looks brighter than snow to me."

Priya spent another minute evaluating other bright spots, then decided on her original target, six miles away. "We should reach it in two hours." She put on her goggles and signaled them to follow.

They'd gone less than a mile before it clouded over and began to snow. Ethan and Priya were unimpressed—they had plenty of experience with winter in Washington—but snow never fell anywhere on Cirrus except for the mountains. Jack and Sarah enjoyed the novelty until the fluffy flakes turned into tiny, wind-driven needles that stung their faces.

They walked together ten paces behind Ethan and Priya, who were discussing a shared interest in martial arts. Ethan had earned his black belt shortly before coming to Cirrus, but now had to practice on his own as there were no open dojos. Sarah was having difficulty moving into the wind and Jack caught her elbow when she stumbled.

"How are you doing?"

She leaned closer to avoid raising her voice. "It's tougher than I expected. I don't want Priya to think I can't keep up."

With the headwind, Jack knew Priya wouldn't hear anything unless they shouted. "Do you want to learn how to create a shield?"

The smile on her face warmed him more than the sun had. "Can I?"

"Sure." He took off a glove to reach inside his coat for the wand. "Ethan's been able to do it. I'm certain you can too."

She took the wand and held it in front of her. "How do I start?"

"All you have to do is say 'shield', but its size and strength will depend on how you visualize it."

She pointed the wand at the ground and said, "Shield." Instantly, a saucer-sized transparent disk formed at its tip, made visible by the circle of ice crystals bouncing away. Her fur-lined hood covered most of her face, but Jack saw pure delight in her eyes.

"Now imagine it growing larger."

The disk spread rapidly, a pulse of white that rippled before winking out.

"Oops."

"It's tricky. You have to think about its density at the same time. Try again."

"Shield." The disk reformed.

"Go as slow as you can. You might need to pause if it starts to evaporate."

The steady barrage of snow highlighted the shield's form, making it easy for Sarah to work with. In only a few minutes, she produced a barrier the size of an umbrella.

"Now think of someplace warm and say 'air'," Jack said.

"But this is blocking most of the wind. We can try that one later."

"Actually, we can do both. You don't need to connect to another portal for a shield. It's using an energy that's present in all wormholes. That means you can open a second one and allow whatever's pushing on the other side to come through."

"All right." Sarah thought for a minute and smiled. "Air."

Sheltered from the wind, a warm breeze flowed from the wand and reflected from the back of the shield. Jack breathed deeply. "Is that cinnamon?"

"It's Natalya's kitchen … I think. That's what I had in mind."

"I don't think there are any open portals there, but that's exactly the way to do it. It's more likely in a bakery somewhere on Earth."

For her first attempt, the results were amazing. The energy

field jumped around a lot, but she and Jack walked easily in a cone of warm air held in front of them like an umbrella. As a bonus, whenever her focus drifted, the shield surged forward, bouncing hail pellets over Ethan's head, where they were driven back at him by the wind.

"Aargh." Ethan batted at the onslaught with ice-crusted mittens. "This is insane. It's coating my goggles."

"Oh, yeah," Sarah shouted, "this is brutal." She was working hard to make her voice sound miserable. "How much farther?"

Priya stopped at the top of the next rise. "There it is." They'd done well in the limited visibility and were less than a hundred yards to the side of the white wreckage.

"He came in *that*?" Jack said when they finally reached the crash site. "It's so small."

Ethan had commented that the craft resembled a minivan from a distance; an apt description—if minivans flew. There wasn't much left of the wings, though. Tracks ran through the snow for hundreds of yards behind the shuttle. Deep furrows in the gravel contained bits of landing gear and shards of wing.

"This wasn't designed for spaceflight," Ethan said. "It's an executive mini-shuttle. They're only supposed to go into orbit, not fly across the solar system. One solar flare and Pieter would've been toast."

"I'll go in first." Priya removed a glove, drew her pistol, and opened the hatch slowly.

After she'd entered, Ethan turned to Jack. "Can you turn your wand into a heater when we get inside? I'm—" He stared at Sarah. "Hey, how come ice isn't building up on *your* coat?"

She drew her hood tighter to hide her expression. "It's a different type of material."

He examined Jack, whose winter gear was mostly free of ice.

Jack faked a shiver. "Brrr. I hope she lets us in soon."

Ethan's eyes narrowed, but Priya called to them. "It's safe."

Sarah pushed past him. "Finally. I don't think I can take any more of this cold."

Jack entered next, glad to be out of the wind where he could talk without shouting. There was space behind the cockpit to move around in, if he didn't want to stand up fully. The walls, ceiling, and floor were lined with bulky shielding panels, reducing an already confined cabin. The airbags had deployed, but otherwise the craft's interior was undamaged.

"What are we looking for?" Sarah asked.

"Anything that tells us where the shuttle came from. We need to figure out where his base on Earth is. Jack, can you sense a portal crystal in here?"

Jack paused for only a second. "There's no active portal. It'll take me longer to find one that's dormant." He sat in the pilot's seat and took a deep, meditative breath.

"I don't see anything written in Korean," Ethan said. "That's good, isn't it?" Danny Kou, Pieter's personal bodyguard, had ties to North Korean Extremists and may have escaped to Earth during Newton. "As far as I can see, it's all English."

"It's unlikely that Danny is working with Pieter again," Priya said. "Assuming he survived. And English doesn't narrow it down much; Pieter has offices around the world." She forced the lid off the garbage container. "I'll search the trash. You check the cargo boxes."

Jack stood. "There are no other portals. I can only sense the ones in Ethan's coin and the one in the radio."

"Oh, I guess we should check in." Sarah activated the radio. "Hello. We've found the ship."

This time, Jada was monitoring the radio. "Hey, how's it going?"

"Great. It's super cold up here, though. Um … Priya's warning me not to waste the battery. We'll call again when we're back at the depot."

Priya, having dumped the trash on the floor, read the food packages' labels. "There are several here from stores in Miami." She sat deep in thought.

"Is that important?" Sarah asked.

"Gutierrez is from Miami. And there are floating launch facilities in the gulf." She counted the packages. "It looks like the trip took ten days."

Jack opened the panels to the engine compartment. "He was thorough. He even removed the initiator crystals."

Ethan looked over Jack's shoulder. "He must have worked with gloves on. Look at those scratches."

Unlike smaller portals, where the entire crystal became the static wormhole, a dynamic portal used a crystal as an initiator only—the actual wormhole developed in an external frame. In this case, that frame was a thrust nozzle, and deep gouges from a sharp tool surrounded the crystals' housings.

"That's strange," Jack wondered aloud. "Why didn't he use his talent to remove the crystals?"

"He doesn't have the level of control you do," Sarah said. "Remember when we locked him in the booth in your grandfather's lab? He couldn't open the lock because he had to move two things at once."

"I guess. But I can't shake the feeling that we're overlooking something."

Chapter 15

Jack stamped snow from his boots. "No crystals outside." He'd taken a run through the shuttle's debris field to search for crystals that may have broken off as it slid through the snow and gravel. "But the nose is flattened, and there are scratches running across the top of the fuselage."

"That proves he came through the roof," Sarah said. "How fast do you think he was going?"

"Faster than he needed to," Ethan said. "He must have damaged sensors in the nose. Otherwise he'd have landed closer to the tower."

Priya dumped a handful of trash into the bin. "This isn't much to go on, but it suggests that James is involved."

Jack frowned. "You sound like you're trying to convince yourself."

"I am. He removed every crystal but didn't take his garbage? That's either a colossal blunder or he meant us to find it."

"He wants us to suspect James? Why?"

"I don't know. Either way, I've got to go to Caerton tomorrow to find out. Let's head back. It'll be dark by the time we reach Icarus."

"You can talk to James tonight," Sarah said, "if we go to Caerton with you."

Priya considered for a moment. "All right. I'll drop you at Holden's apartment first. Radio the village and let them know we've changed our plans."

- - - - -

Trouble, Priya thought as she approached the bridge.

With a pre-Newton population of nearly a million, Caerton was the largest city in the sector. Most of its food came from genetically engineered crops grown in thousands of multi-story steel and glass structures on the other side of the river.

"What's happened here?" Sarah asked.

A new town had sprung up around the greenhouses, except they weren't proper houses, only rough shelters assembled from tarps and leftover construction material.

Priya stopped short of the bridge and began a tactical assessment.

"What's wrong," Ethan asked.

She raised a hand, signaling him to be quiet. *Fifty yards to cross the bridge. Plenty of space to turn around. Thirty feet to the water. No place to hide.* The beam-style bridge had no support structure above its deck and only metals railings along the bike paths on either side of the roadway.

She crept forward, scanning for danger, until a group of twenty to thirty men emerged from the greenhouses and blocked the road. One of them shone a spotlight onto the bridge. Priya spun her head, looking for an escape. The road behind was clear.

Jack reached for the wand but she barred him. "Don't. They're not stopping us from leaving, only from entering the city."

"What do we do?" Sarah asked.

"Stay in the truck and keep your eyes open." Priya stepped out, wearing her UN Police jacket. The large lettering immediately drew the crowd's attention. "What's going on here?" she demanded as she strode forward.

A uniformed man pushed his way through the crowd. He spotted Priya and moved to intercept her, his expression a mix of caution and suspicion. "I'm Officer Reynolds. Who are you?"

"Detective Singh." She closed the distance between her and the CorpSec officer, who towered over her. "Why are these people out here?"

Reynolds hesitated when he noticed the lettering on her jacket and the holster under it. CorpSec was the generic term for private security on Cirrus. Priya was employed by the Washington State Patrol and seconded to the UN's Off-world Police Division. Reynolds may have taken charge of the situation, but Priya's authority was absolute.

"There was trouble during the night," he said. "One of the largest towers was damaged."

"What sort of trouble?"

He faltered. "We've got limited personnel and no communications. We've heard nothing from Earth in months. We're on our own out here." The last comment sounded like an accusation, as if the UN was responsible for Newton.

There's something he doesn't want to tell me. Priya softened her stance. "We're trying to help. Tell me what happened."

Reynolds waved the crowd away. "Clear the street. I'll handle this." As the mob dispersed, he lowered his voice. "The reports we've had are … they're unusual. They say a man broke in with a … they said it was a flamethrower, or a rocket launcher, or another type of weapon. We're not clear on that. Quite a few people said he was …"

"What?"

"Flying. Floating above the ground. Don't look at me like that, I'm just repeating what I heard. A lot of folks are telling the same story."

"Who was it?" Priya knew it could only have been Pieter, using Jack's wand. "Did anyone recognize him?"

"No. He went upstairs, trashed a single apartment, then got into the basement and … well, he blew up the building's power plant." Reynolds looked over his shoulder at the makeshift camp. "These people were residents. There are engineers checking the building now. If they give the OK, everyone can go home in a day or two. That's assuming they want to; there won't be any power."

"Which tower was damaged?" She knew the answer to this one, too.

"The Magnolia."

- - - - -

"He was after Grandpa?" Jack asked once they were driving again, and Priya had relayed the story.

"Relax," Priya said when she saw Jack's reaction. "He must have known your grandfather wasn't there. I'm certain he was looking for the portal. Reynolds said that Pieter broke into every room and storage closet in the basement after trashing the apartment. If he were after Holden, he'd have destroyed the building's power plant first to prevent him from escaping."

"What does he want Grandpa's portal for?" Jack sneered. Now that the initial fear for Holden had passed, he was just angry. "He must have his own by now."

"Well, besides the fact that it can transport radioactive material—something no other portal can do—there's you three."

"What about us?" Ethan asked.

"Travellers are incredibly rare. The three of you gained your talents by travelling through the same portal. Ethan, I don't think Pieter knows about your ability yet, but he must know that the odds against even two of you becoming Travellers are astronomical."

"But he's already a Traveller," Sarah said. "What more can he gain?"

"If someone offered you the chance to become a Traveller, how much would you be willing to pay?"

"Are you suggesting that *anyone* who uses Grandpa's portal will become a Traveller?" Jack asked. Then thinking about Priya's cautious approach to the empty bridge, asked, "Are you a Traveller now?"

"You are, aren't you?" Sarah was practically bouncing in her seat. "You're one of us."

"No." Priya looked embarrassed. "Nothing like that. But … since that first trip, I've felt more intuitive. It might have sharpened my senses a bit."

"Jack can tell when someone is lying."

"You can? Holden never told me that."

"I never told him. Or my parents. It had something to do with emotion detectors. Now that those don't work, I'm not sure I can do it anymore."

"Does that mean Grandpa is a Traveller?" Ethan asked. "What about Uncle Carl? They both used the portal as much as Jack."

Priya shook her head. "Most Travellers gain their talents as children, and each of you made your very first trip through Holden's portal. I'd been using a different one to get to Cirrus for years before I met him. He'd have taken many trips through other portals and been much older before he built his own. You might owe your abilities to the simple chance of how you made your first passage."

"That kind of makes sense," Jack said. "Remember, everyone experiences déjà vu their first time."

"Anyway, none of that's important now. You can't stay at Holden's place, so I'll leave you at my apartment while I interview Gutierrez."

Priya parked in front of a six-story brownstone on a tree-line boulevard. The building's façade wasn't actual stone. Like every other structure in the city, it had been printed from a blend of concrete, plastic, and steel. She got out of the vehicle and led them to the front door. As they approached, a man wearing a jacket like Priya's stepped onto the sidewalk and froze mid-step.

"*Priya*? What the hell are you doing here? Is the office portal working?"

She pushed past him. "Sorry, Davis. I can't go into it right now. Is the apartment empty?"

Davis, still too stunned to move, said. "Sure, why?"

"I need a safe place for these three while you and I talk to Gutierrez. Any idea where he is?"

"Most likely at his estate. He's been making public appearances downtown lately, appealing for calm, but doesn't hang around for long. Who are the kids?"

"I'll tell you on the way." She gave Sarah the codes to access the building and the apartment. "Don't leave until I get back." Her expression was stern and familiar.

Jack, Ethan, and Sarah entered the lobby and crossed to the elevator.

"Why does she always look like that when she tells us what to do?" Jack asked.

"Maybe because we rarely listen," Sarah said. "And with Pieter being in town somewhere, she doesn't want us wandering off."

Jack was about to argue when the elevator chimed, and Ethan yelled, "*Get down,*" then shoved him aside as the door opened.

Jack dove, rolled on the tile floor, and landed on his feet in a crouch. He'd drawn the wand before noticing that Ethan hadn't moved and was laughing uproariously. Sarah was also laughing but covering her mouth with her hand to hide it.

"*What was that for?*" Jack shouted.

Ethan stifled a laugh. "I just wanted to make the point that we can handle ourselves."

"Did you know he was going to do that?" Jack asked Sarah in a less angry tone.

"Sort of. I'm sorry, Jack. But you have to admit; it was funny."

Jack put the wand away with a shake of his head. But to himself he thought, *Yeah, it was funny.*

Chapter 16

"How did you get back to Cirrus?" Davis asked as Priya drove away from their apartment building. "What's happening on Earth?"

"I can't answer the first one yet. As for Earth; it's not going well. We've got inter-office communications again, but no phones in the field. Half of Olympia is without electricity or running water, and it's getting worse as more power stations fail. Believe me, you're better off where you are."

"You can't just show up and not tell me how you got here. I have family on Earth that I haven't heard from in months."

"And they're safer that way. Trust me. I can't even pass a message on for you. So don't ask."

Davis glowered at her. "Fine." He stared out the windshield as Priya drove. A pedestrian, who likely hadn't seen a working vehicle in days, lunged off the sidewalk to confront them, then backed off when he saw their jackets. "Why do we need to talk to Gutierrez?"

"He and Reynard might be working together. It was Reynard who attacked the Magnolia."

"Reynard's here? How?"

Priya merged onto Hillcrest, the road that climbed into the gently rolling plateau overlooking the city's north side. "He crashed an executive shuttle on sector wall a few days ago."

"Ah, the storm." Davis gestured at fallen trees. "It hit us like a wave. A large hole in the roof would have completely changed the air currents. Did it repair itself?"

"Yeah, I've just come from there. It's back to normal. Is this where Gutierrez lives?"

Even with the trees toppled in the recent winds, the rural neighborhood proclaimed wealth and power, a sharp contrast to the densely packed residences only a few hundred feet below. On the upper level, dozens of large estates were scattered among thousands of acres of orchards and vineyards. The one they were approaching was protected by a six-foot stone wall.

Davis pointed to a driveway ahead. "There's a gate up on the right."

Priya veered off the main road and approached the ornate steel barrier. A man dressed in camouflage emerged from the adjoining guardhouse and signaled her to stop. He was holding an assault rifle—something that shouldn't exist on Cirrus. Another armed guard watched from behind the gate.

Priya pulled up. "We're here to speak to James Gutierrez."

The guard looked her over and noticed the logos on both hers and Davis' jackets. "Wait here," he said tersely before returning to the guardhouse.

"We're seriously outgunned," Davis muttered.

"It won't come to that. If he's not working with Reynard, he has no reason not to talk to us. If he is, they'll be trying to hide that fact, not confirm it."

After an uncomfortably long delay, the gate slid open and the guard motioned them through onto a paved driveway that curved through an expanse of ornamental gardens. The house at the end of the drive was a sprawling, two-story Mediterranean-style mansion that wouldn't have looked out of place in Gutierrez's hometown of Miami. Here, with its manicured lawns and sculpted fountains, it was an outlandish cliché. An elegant, well-kept, and well-defended one, but still a cliché.

Priya parked at the foot of the stairs below the main entrance. Her vehicle seemed absurdly small next to a limousine and a CorpSec van. Another armed guard stood beside a marble column in front of tall glass doors, which bore an etched pattern that made it impossible to see what lay beyond. He opened the door without a word as they approached, then closed it behind them and resumed his post.

Left alone, Priya and Davis examined their surroundings. The oval foyer they stood in, beneath a forty-foot vaulted ceiling, divided the building into two wings. Stairs on either side of the room curved gracefully to the second floor, where they joined the ends of a wrought iron-railed balcony that overlooked the foyer on the near side, and a patio on the other. The windows bordering the patio were undecorated, revealing more lawns and well-kept gardens on the mansion's secluded north side.

"Cameras," Davis whispered.

At the top and bottom of the stairs, four sets of sturdy wooden double-doors protected the entrances to the west and east wings. The only asymmetrical features in the stylish foyer were the surveillance cameras mounted above the doors on the left. Also, only those two were shut. The lower doors on the right opened into an opulent lounge.

James entered the foyer through the open doors. "Good evening, Davis. A pleasure to see you again. How can I help you?"

He was dressed in a bespoke light blue blazer, tan slacks, and polished leather shoes. To Priya, the choice seemed too formal for wearing around his own home, but James seemed entirely comfortable. In fact, James fit his surroundings perfectly. He was handsome, fit for his age, with an amiable smile and gleaming white teeth. His silver-gray mustache was perfectly trimmed, his nails flawlessly manicured, and the gray streaks in his black hair could have been placed by an artist. It was hard to decide which was more refined: the man or the mansion.

Priya introduced herself, then said. "We have a few questions about your business partner."

"Certainly." James gestured to the lounge. "Please, take a seat." He turned away without waiting for a response.

Inside, an assortment of comfortable-looking chairs greeted them. Floor-to-ceiling windows provided pleasant garden views, and a gleaming bar with a dozen stools spanned one end of the room. James walked behind the counter. "Can I get you something to drink?"

Priya declined for both her and Davis. "Do you know where Pieter Reynard is?"

James poured a bourbon for himself. "I can only assume he's on Earth."

"When did you last time see him?"

"I believe the phrase is: *Before Newton*. Are you suggesting he's on Cirrus?"

"I'm not suggesting anything. I'm asking if you know where he is."

James set his glass on the counter and looked Priya straight in the eyes. "No. I haven't seen him. And I haven't seen Danny Kou either. I assume he's the one you're looking for."

"Why do you say that?" Her gaze was drawn to James' hands as he fidgeted with a ring. The movement wasn't subtle, indicating nervousness; the ring seemed to be irritating him.

"My people were checking into his criminal connections before the portals failed. How did you get back to Cirrus?"

"Who said I was on Earth?"

James appeared genuinely confused before laughing off his mistake. "No, I suppose you couldn't have been."

"Why do you think I'm looking for Danny?"

When James spoke again, it was with the confidence of the politician she'd seen in videos before Newton.

"Let's be honest, Detective. We've all heard the rumors about Pieter. You're here looking to tie him to Newton. But no one really knows what happened that night. Remember, his factories were sabotaged too."

"Sabotaged?" Davis asked.

James sipped his drink, aware that he'd said too much. "It was one of the final messages we received. A tip came in just before midnight, warning us that terrorists had mined both my own and his properties. My security team defused bombs in my facility in Texas, but we lost communications before we heard about the others. I can only hope they survived."

"And you believe Pieter's factories were also targeted?" Priya asked.

"The tip came from one of his aides. They'd found explosives at their sites as well. He was as much a victim as the rest of us. Anyway, once we've reestablished contact with Earth, we might find this was settled months ago. For all we know, Danny is in prison now."

"Have you heard any other rumors?"

James fidgeted again. "None that I put stock in." He wore rings on both hands but the one on the right, a plain gold band with a single clear stone set into it, seemed to be a recent acquisition. The skin underneath that one was tanned, but there was lighter skin showing at the edge of his wedding band. "Are you sure I can't get you something to drink?"

"No, thanks," Priya said. "That's all we need for now. We'll show ourselves out."

"Before you go …" James reached into a pocket. "Take these." He proffered two golden discs: coin portals. "They're attached to my fusion generator."

"No, thanks."

"Please, I insist. You never know when they'll come in handy."

Davis looked as if he might take one. After all, a working power cell would be more than handy. It could run anything from a phone to a car. But Priya's intuition warned against it. "No, thank you. We're not allowed to accept gifts."

- - - - -

James' house enjoyed a magnificent view of Caerton. But the panorama had transformed since Priya last saw it from the plateau, the day after Newton. Many buildings had already lost power, and more had failed since. The Magnolia created another darkened gap in the skyline.

"What do you think?" Davis asked as they drove into town.

"He's obviously lying."

"About?"

"Most everything. You've met him before?"

"A couple of days after Newton. I was following up on your investigation into Reynard." Davis rubbed the back of his head. "I still have a bump where one of his goons hit me. At that time, he had no problem accepting — even implicating — that Reynard was responsible."

"And now he's suggesting that it was Danny who was behind everything."

"What was that about the factories?"

"A slip-up. A lot of them *were* destroyed that night. I know that the one in Texas is still running. One of Reynard's in Everett too. Worldwide, there are perhaps a dozen smaller operations still producing."

"You think Reynard destroyed his own facilities as a cover?"

"Maybe."

"Where do we go from here?"

"Reynard is almost certainly in Caerton, and Gutierrez probably knows where he is. Those cameras above the doors looked like a recent addition. I think he's at the estate."

"Why would James support Reynard?"

"If Reynard wants — or needs — to be seen in public again, then he needs his reputation repaired. James is the only person who can do that. As for what's in it for him … I don't know."

"Then do we wait for him to show himself?"

"We can't." Priya paused, considering how much to tell him. "He might be planning another attack."

"What sort of attack?" he asked, but Priya gave him the same pained expression she'd given when he asked about Earth. "You're not gonna tell me, are you?"

"Not yet. But there's a good reason." She couldn't properly explain anything without revealing the connection to Holden and his portal. "And before you ask, I can't tell you that either."

Chapter 17

Jack was stretched out on Davis' faux-leather recliner when Priya returned to the apartment alone. Unlike everything else in the tiny two-bedroom suite, the chair had not been designed for efficiency but for comfort. Its thick cushions were a welcome change from the stiff seats of Suresh's truck.

Priya sank into an ergonomic black office chair by her desk. "Tell me about the wand."

Jack sat up. "What do you need to know?"

"Is it a weapon? Did Pieter use the one he took from you to destroy the power plant at the Magnolia?"

Sarah was sitting cross-legged on the sofa next to Ethan, giggling while he experimented with Davis' guitar. They both sat up and waited for Jack's answer.

"Yeah, I think so."

"So, it's a flamethrower and a rocket launcher rolled up into a pencil?"

"No, it's a crystal I can use to open a wormhole to any other portal crystal." He drew the wand, pointed it at his palm, and held it there for a second. "Here, let me see your hand."

Priya waved her fingers through the gentle breeze. "It's warm."

"The crystal on the other end is in a desert somewhere. It's the same one I used for air at the maintenance depot."

"But the air was blasting out then," Ethan said, "and there was a bright light."

"That's because we were at a higher elevation with lower air pressure. I can use the energy field on objects on my side of the portal, but I can't force it through the other side. Niels talked about the AI having security features, and I bet this is one of them. The only reason air is coming through at all is because the pressure is higher wherever the other end is. And there's no light because it's nighttime there now."

"Death Valley?" Sarah suggested.

"Maybe. I don't get a sense of *where* it is, only what's around it. Here's a different one." A high-pitched whistle rose from the wand. Jack set the tip near a fragment of leaf that had come in one of their shoes. It vanished into the wormhole. "That one's somewhere high, where it's cold and windy and the pressure is lower."

Ethan grinned. "So, you're saying there's a pile of garbage on a mountaintop from your own personal vacuum cleaner?"

"No. Well, maybe a few dead flies."

"Pieter used it as a flamethrower," Priya said. "How does that work?"

"If he knew of a crystal in an environment with a high-pressure flame, all he'd have to do is open the wormhole. Some fuel cells use plasma chambers. He could have opened a monitoring port into the Magnolia's power plant and used it against itself."

Ethan had been hunched over the coffee table while Jack was explaining. He nudged Jack's arm and showed him a scrap of paper he'd folded into a paper airplane. Jack obliged by opening the portal again, sucking the tiny craft into the wand.

Sarah laughed. "Are you two sure you aren't twins?"

Priya knocked on the table to get their attention. "Let's try to be serious. What about range? How far can he shoot something?"

"That depends on the pressure behind it," Jack said. "If he opened the wormhole to the end of a rifle, I suppose he could shoot a bullet."

"You realize you're talking about a dangerous weapon here, one that's virtually untraceable. Can he do that with any crystal?"

"No, the amount of energy a crystal can transfer depends on its volume. The water dispensers in phones could only handle a small flow without collapsing the field. I don't know if even a crystal as big as the wand could stand the energy of a bullet."

"That's a relief."

"Besides, there's something worse than a bullet."

The living room opened into the compact, efficient kitchen, without a dining room in between. Jack pointed the wand at a butter knife laying on the counter. He raised the utensil into the air and moved his arm in a slow arc. The blade followed his movement, drifting to the end of the counter.

"I can *move* objects up to around a hundred feet, but I don't have very good control beyond fifty or sixty. But the farther away an object is, the longer the lever …" He swung his forearm to show how a small movement resulted in a large effect. "and the faster it will go when I release it. Back in Fairview, I once threw a stone over a mile."

Sarah grasped the concept right away. "So, if you held that knife at the end of a sixty-foot *arm*, it would go supersonic."

"If I could hang on to it. Sixty feet may be farther than I can manage, but I've done thirty. Also, distance from the wand is a factor." He placed the rod on the coffee table and sat back in his chair. "The farther away I am, the weaker the bond. I need to be within arm's reach for proper control and I can't do much with it beyond six feet." He gestured at the wand, four feet away. A bright light shone from its tip.

"So, how do you find the portals?" Priya asked. "You sensed the ones in the radio and Ethan's coin. Can Pieter do the same?"

"I think so. Ethan could use the wand, but not very well. Pieter had no problem with it, so he must sense the energy field the way I do. Detecting a portal in the Magnolia's plasma cell wouldn't be hard if he was standing next to it. That's not the same as finding one in the *Cloud,* though."

"The Cloud?" Ethan asked. "You mean like the internet?"

"Yeah. It only just occurred to me that that's a good way to think of it. Once I discover a useful one, I can find it again easily. But I only learned how to do that during Newton, when they were merged."

"But how do you know if a portal will be useful?" Sarah asked. "Before Newton, there were billions of portals in phones."

"Niels described it as being controlled by an artificial intelligence. If the AI can record Traveller's memories, it could sense what I'm looking for and lead me in the right direction. There's some sort of organization of portals, based on function maybe, but I can't figure it out. For example, … well, I won't open it here because it might destroy your apartment, but I was wondering if I could use it as a fire extinguisher. I went looking for high-pressure carbon dioxide, and I think I found a portal on Venus."

"Why would there be portals on Venus?" Ethan asked.

"No, that makes sense," Sarah said. "The oxygen in Cirrus' atmosphere came from the carbon dioxide on Venus. It's under huge pressure. It's also really hot."

"Yeah, I forgot about that. It was a good thing I tried it outside of town that first time. It'd likely set more things on fire before it put them out."

Davis' voice filtered through the apartment door as he greeted a neighbor in the hallway. Priya glanced at the clock. "It's too late for driving to Icarus in the rain. Call Suresh and tell him we'll be staying here tonight." She got up and intercepted Davis at the door, leading him outside. "I need to talk with you in private."

- - - - -

Priya and Davis shared the apartment with Katherine—the third member of their detail—who was stuck on Earth. However, there were just two bedrooms because their overlapping work schedules had only two officers on Cirrus at any one time. That meant Jack, Sarah, and Ethan would sleep in the living room. Sarah was only two inches shorter than Jack, so the compact, thinly padded sofa was too short for either of them, and definitely too small for six-foot-tall Ethan.

Ethan prodded Davis' recliner. "Looks like one of us gets the comfy chair and the others get the floor. Who's it gonna be?" He sat on the arm of the chair with his arms crossed. Sarah's eyes narrowed. Jack grinned.

While Jack and Ethan rearranged furniture to create space for themselves on the floor, Sarah used the radio to call Suresh.

"No, it's Terrance," said the voice over the speaker. "It's my turn to monitor the radio."

"Oh, okay. Tell him we're staying at Priya's apartment tonight and coming home in the morning."

"I'll pass it on. Goodnight."

Sarah switched off the radio but didn't set it down.

"Is something wrong?" Jack asked, noticing her expression.

"No. It just surprised me that Terrance had the radio, that's all."

"Something you remember?"

"No. Or at least not very clearly."

- - - - -

Priya's apartment was stylish. The colors were tasteful, the oval rug under the coffee table suited the décor, and the faux-hardwood floor was a medieval torture.

Jack lay uncomfortably on a thin cushion of folded blankets. Sarah's comments about Terrance had him in a cautious frame of mind. Regardless, he eventually fell into a sleep deep enough to trigger a lucid dream: a state where he knew he was asleep yet had partial control over the dream's events.

The dream began as many lucid ones did—with flying. This time he was over Caerton. It was nighttime. His movements were quick and erratic as he darted through trees and alleys. He didn't understand what was going on until his view shifted to focus on a large moth. Suddenly, he sped towards the insect, lining up for a perfect intercept. In anticipation of the meal, he opened his mouth and …

Oh, gross.

He realized that his perspective was of a bird chasing its prey. The thought was enough to cause him to veer off and shoot upwards. He was about to force himself awake—something he could do easily—when it occurred to him how bizarre and novel the vision was. He let the dream continue.

In an earlier, similar dream, Jack had let the flight run its own course and land him in a tree. Could he could choose a landing spot this time? To his further amusement, he discovered he could, but he accidentally selected a branch that was too thin. The twig twisted and flipped him upside down. The grass was now above, as was the street in front of him. A group of people dressed in black hurried past, upside-down on the inverted sidewalk.

Jack's heart raced. He'd seen the men before: Pieter's guards.

He rotated his head and recognized the building: Priya's apartment block. The men, weapons drawn, paused briefly below the light at the main entrance before throwing the door open and rushing inside.

"*STOP.*" Jack sat up quickly and banged his head on the chair next to him. He didn't know whether he'd yelled in his dream or for real, but the crash was loud enough to wake everyone else.

Ethan was up in a flash, holding a wooden Bo staff. "What? What?" Before moving to Cirrus, he'd trained for years in the martial arts and was proficient with the staff. He'd been admiring Davis' weapon and borrowed it for a bit of practice before bed.

"They're coming," Jack said, loud enough for Priya to hear in her bedroom.

Davis burst out of his room. "Why are you shouting? Who's coming?"

"Pieter's men. They're downstairs."

Priya entered the living room, carrying her holster. She looked to the curtained window. "Are you sure? Maybe you were just dreaming."

Jack shook his head. "I saw them." Davis looked at him skeptically, so he turned to Sarah. "Tell them. They're downstairs." His wand was in his jacket, draped over the chair he'd banged his head on. He opened a portal for Sarah, who was sitting an arm's reach away.

She gasped. "There are three men. They're going to blow the door open."

"Into my bedroom." Priya drew her pistol. "*Now.*"

"Priya, what the hell?" Davis shouted as Jack and Sarah ran

for the open doorway.

Ethan had been sleeping near the front door. He moved towards Priya's bedroom, stopped abruptly, then reached back and hit the light switch. In the sudden darkness he said, "Too late."

The door burst open with a flash of light and a muffled boom. A man stepped into the doorway, raising a pistol.

For Jack, the incursion ran in slow motion. Had he been able to organize his thoughts, he'd have known that it passed in just under two seconds.

The intruder didn't get a chance to aim his pistol because Ethan's staff broke his arm first; a two-second prescience gave him enough time to apply the full force of the wooden rod.

The first attacker cried out in pain and fell back, slowing the second enough to allow Jack and Sarah to dive through the open door behind Priya. Sarah landed on the floor next to the bed. Jack followed, placing himself between her and the door.

Priya fired her weapon, striking the second man in the chest as he pulled the trigger. He was wearing a bulky bulletproof vest, and the impact caused his aim to go wild. His bullets struck the ceiling above Davis' head.

Priya took cover behind the kitchen counter. "*Ethan, get back.*"

Davis raced into his own bedroom to retrieve his weapon.

Unfortunately, Ethan was trapped in the space between the door and a chair. Moving away from the wall would leave him exposed. With multiple assailants, his gift for seeing the future might only let him foresee which bullet would hit him.

"*Ethan*," Jack shouted. "*Shield.*" He created a barrier in front of himself and Sarah, but was too far away to do anything with Ethan's coin.

Ethan's hand moved to his chest to expose the coin just as another man rushed into the doorway with an assault rifle. He pointed it directly at Ethan and fired. Ethan tumbled backwards across the chair. The staff fell from his hand. Sarah screamed.

"*NO.*" Instinctively, Jack jumped and ran towards the door.

The man with the rifle was turning his direction when Jack unleashed the wand's raw energy. It was unfocussed. It was unstructured, driven by his rage. It was a cannon blast.

The apartment's windows imploded as the attacker flew across the hall. The man whose vest had blocked Priya's bullets went with him, as did the door. And part of the wall next to the door. And most of the furniture between Jack and the hallway.

The first man—who'd been crouching in the hallway, cradling his broken arm—was buried under the remains of the printed concrete and steel wall.

Priya reacted first. "*Davis. Med kit. It's in your room.*" She ran to where Ethan lay on the floor beyond the toppled chair.

Davis had just re-entered the room with his pistol drawn and was staring open-mouthed at the apartment's new, roughly circular entrance. Priya kneeled beside Ethan and reached to pull his shirt open.

"What the …?" She pushed on the invisible barrier. "Why can't I touch you?"

Jack and Sarah were now at Ethan's side. It looked as if Priya was leaning against nothing at all. Her hands sank slowly towards Ethan's chest.

"Ethan …" Jack made a cut-off gesture to the coin. "*Shield off.*"

Ethan groaned and repeated, "Shield off." Priya's hands dropped without warning and landed on his chest. He yipped in pain, then grinned. "All right, you can touch me now."

"Oh, Dude," Jack said, "that is so inappropriate."

Priya's concern and professionalism allowed her to ignore Ethan's glib remark. She tore his shirt open. Four large welts marred his abdomen, but no blood. She looked to Jack for an explanation.

"Uh …" He flinched as shattered concrete crumbed into the hallway. "Sorry about your wall."

Chapter 18

Priya was relieved to find Ethan still alive. She helped him stand but he was in a lot of pain; he'd been right at the edge of the blast zone and was struck by the coffee table as it hurtled past.

A chunk of ceiling fell and landed by her foot. Jack cringed. "I … I can explain—"

"There'll be time for that later. We need to get moving. Help Ethan downstairs." Priya called to Davis, who was in the hallway checking on the unmoving assailants. "We have to evacuate the building, in case the walls come down."

She followed Jack into the hall. He stood frozen when he saw what he'd done. The man with the broken arm was stirring, but the other two were buried somewhere in the debris. The wall across the corridor had partially collapsed.

"Jack, *move*." Priya seized him by the elbow and hustled him away from the wreckage.

Ethan held an arm tight against his ribs and balanced on one foot. "Davis, can I borrow that staff?"

Davis looked at the Bo staff, which had survived its flight into the hallway. "Take it."

Ethan reached for the weapon, then grimaced in pain. Sarah picked it up for him and helped him to the elevator while he favored his right leg.

The truck's cargo bed was too short for Ethan to lie down in. Fortunately, the rear seats folded forward to make room for his legs. By the time Priya and Sarah made him comfortable, Davis had cleared out the building and was storming towards her.

"Priya. What the hell is going on here? What's that kid carrying?"

She intercepted Davis before he made it to the vehicle. She pushed him back and quietly asked, "Are they alive?"

"Does it matter?"

She pushed him farther. "Are they alive?"

Davis looked over Priya's head at Jack slumped in the truck's passenger seat. He calmed himself and answered quietly. "Yeah, but they're not going anywhere soon. What should I do with them?"

"Confiscate their weapons and let them go."

"*Are you crazy?*"

"If you don't, someone will come and get them. We don't have a facility to hold them in. And leaving them with CorpSec will only endanger innocent people."

"Fine. Tell me what's going on."

"Not yet." She handed him the radio. "Use this. Tell whoever answers who you are and that we'll be home in four hours. Don't tell them what happened. Don't ask questions. Find batteries for the radio and get yourself someplace safe. I promise I'll tell you everything in a few days." She strode away before he could argue.

- - - - -

No one spoke after they left Caerton, although Ethan moaned or grunted every time the truck hit a bump. Instead of taking the highway, Priya had chosen the shortcut to the grain roads. After an hour on the rough dirt track, she pulled over to allow Ethan a chance to rest.

As soon as the vehicle stopped a safe distance from the road, Jack hopped out and hurried away.

Sarah moved to follow him but Priya put a hand on her shoulder. "We'll be back. Help Ethan get covered up. We'll be on faster roads soon and it'll be windy."

"Hey, I'm fine. I can hardly feel them now." Ethan tried raising himself onto his elbows and winced again. The welts had blossomed into four massive bruises.

While Sarah helped Ethan, Priya went after Jack. She found him sitting on a rock out of sight of the truck.

"I'm sorry—" Jack began.

"You did what you had to. You're not entirely responsible for their injuries."

"I was only trying to stop them. I didn't know it would be that strong." He pulled the wand out of his jacket and looked as if he might throw it away.

"That you're concerned for *them*, not yourself, proves to me you won't use it irresponsibly. Most people I deal with are only worried about getting caught, not about the morality of their actions." She sat beside him and sighed. "If there were still passenger flights, I'd be required to take you to Earth until the investigation is over, but it's unlikely you'd ever be charged. I know you won't hurt anyone on purpose. But you've got to learn to control the wand better now that you understand how much damage it can do."

Jack nodded his head solemnly.

"And one more thing. How did you know they were coming?"

- - - - -

As they drove, Jack considered Priya's question.

"Sarah," he spoke quietly—Ethan looked like he'd fallen asleep, "when you saw Pieter's men coming, did it happen exactly as you saw it?"

"I didn't really *see* it. It's like your grandfather described it: a memory. It was as if I remembered what they had done."

"I saw them when they were outside. I mean, I actually *saw* them. And it's not the first time. When I was on the island in August, I dreamed I was flying and I saw myself through the window. When I woke up, there was an owl watching me. I think I was seeing myself through the owl's eyes."

"It's called streaming," Ethan said.

"Sorry," Jack said. "I thought you were asleep. Streaming? You mean like video?"

"You already explained to me that these are our own memories played back to us by an AI. I *remembered* the hand coming through the doorway with the gun and knew where to swing the staff. I didn't *see* anything, but it happened exactly as I remembered it."

"Then why do you only remember seconds when Niels had years of memories?"

"Maybe the computer gives each of us different amounts of storage."

"I think we're getting the same amount," Sarah said. "I remember many things, but I don't know the exact details. I only knew that there were three men. Wouldn't it take more memory to know exactly where the hand would be?"

Ethan was quiet for a moment. "Makes sense to me."

Jack raised an eyebrow. "I thought you said it was magic."

"You're right. That makes more sense. It *is* magic."

- - - - -

They reached Icarus at dawn. The lake was placid and it seemed they'd finally have a day with clear skies. There was no one about at the early hour and no lights on in the lodge, but Dusty was barking.

"She sounds happy," Ethan said, "but she knows she's not supposed to bark at night. We'd better find out what's happening before she wakes everyone."

Priya parked the truck, then she and Sarah helped Ethan hobble up the path.

Ander's voice roared from the far end of the village as Jack rounded the lodge. "*Caught you.*"

Two men wrestled in the yard in front of Holden's cabin. Ethan's dog, Dusty, was barking and jumping happily, thinking the fight was a game. It was still too dark to see clearly at that distance, but the larger combatant was clearly Anders. Priya reacted first. She drew her pistol and sprinted across the field. Jack drew his wand and followed.

By the time he reached the scene, Anders had the other man pinned to the ground. It wasn't a fair contest. Despite his age, Anders was still the strongest man in the village.

The noise brought many villagers out of their homes. Holden shuffled out of his cabin, dressed in a nightgown. "Terrance? What were you doing in my house?"

Anders tightened his grip on Terrance's arm. "Answer the question."

Terrance said nothing but looked at Jack, Ethan, Sarah, and Priya in turn, then grinned. He completely ignored Holden and Anders.

Priya pulled out a pair of handcuffs. "I'll take it from here." Anders flipped Terrance over roughly and Priya cuffed him. Together, they lifted him to his feet. "Is there a secure room in the lodge?"

"There's a storeroom with a locking door," Anders said. He led while Priya restrained Terrance as he struggled.

Ethan shouted, "He's got something in his hands."

Priya shoved Terrance to the ground, but not before he tossed that something away.

Terrance rolled onto his front and lifted his head. "What's wrong? Anders, why did you hit me? I only wanted to have a look. I didn't even wake him."

"Hold on to him," Priya said. "He threw something away." She hurried to where Terrance had pitched the object. A thin arc of gold reflected the first rays of morning sunlight from below the surface of a muddy puddle. "It's a ring." She reached for it.

"*Don't touch it.*" Jack sprang forward, pointing his wand at the ring. A fist-sized ball of air roiled at its glowing tip. "It's an active portal."

Chapter 19

"Jack." Sarah placed a hand on his tensed shoulder. "Relax."

Although they'd spent little time together in-person before Newton, when emotion detectors caused him so much anxiety, she'd seen how stress affected Jack countless times during video chats. His jaw was set and his muscles so rigid he was shaking.

She pushed his forearm down and the ball of turbulence at the wand's tip faded. He met her eyes briefly before casting his gaze to the ground at his feet.

"Sorry."

"It's fine." She could see that he was ashamed by his lack of self-control, so she moved closer to speak quietly. "We're all on edge because of what happened to Ethan. But he's okay now."

Jack nodded and pocketed the wand.

- - - - -

With Terrance locked up in the windowless storeroom, and Anders standing guard, everyone else returned to Holden's place. He'd already brewed a pot of tea.

Icarus's cabins had been designed for efficiency. The kitchen, dining, and living rooms were all one space. Jack sat alone on the edge of his grandfather's bed, watching the group through the open bedroom door.

Priya dropped heavily into a chair at the dining table. She seemed confused. "Terrance admits to coming into your cabin. He says he felt a strong urge to do it but doesn't know why or even what he was looking for. Anders said he'd been acting strangely since he returned from Caerton yesterday. He also says Terrance wanted to be the one to wait for our call last night."

"Anders has always had a problem with Terrance," Holden said. "But this behavior is strange, even for Terrance. As I understand it, he did many things for Niels which were … well—"

"Not entirely legal?" Priya suggested.

"Niels had his own agenda. I don't doubt that it was for the greater good, but he may have broken a few rules to get there."

"Why was Terrance so desperate to throw away the ring?" Sarah asked.

"Pieter was controlling him through it," Jack said.

"What do you mean, 'controlling'?" Holden asked.

Jack joined the group in the living room and described his dream at Priya's apartment, and the similar one from months ago. "It's as if I can control where the bird goes. As long as I'm asleep."

"You read Pieter's thoughts," Ethan said, "at the depot, after he attacked us. But he had your wand and you had my coin. How do you link with a bird?"

"Bats, owls, and many other birds are banded," Sarah said. "But the bands aren't just tags, they have portals in them for transmitting real-time data. Could those crystals have survived Newton?"

Jack tipped his head back and concentrated while staring at the blank ceiling. With practice, it had become easier to get into the meditative state he needed to search for portals. He got the impression of fleeting movements, sudden changes of direction, and of wind.

"You're right. Those crystals must have come from Earth, or else Pieter didn't think they were important enough to destroy. There are still … tens or hundreds of thousands of them."

He focused again, visualizing the network as a landscape of mountains and valleys. That wasn't their real-world arrangement, but when he found a particular type of portal, the neighboring ones often had something in common. The number of crystals that fit the leg band pattern was vast. But for every one that moved, there were several that felt cold, dark, and inert, as if they were buried in the soil.

"The bird outside the apartment last night might have been banded," Sarah said, "but how does that mean Pieter can control someone?"

Jack reached down to pet Dusty, who was sleeping beside the sofa. "Ethan, how did you teach your dog to behave on the streets of Seattle?"

"That was easy. There's a motivator in her collar. Whenever she got too far away, it dropped the 'happy' signal and she came back because she wanted to."

"Exactly. She *wanted* to. When I controlled the birds, I wasn't telling them where to go, it was where *I* wanted to go. You created a shield strong enough to stop bullets on your first try, but you couldn't skip a stone after several tries."

"I *really* wanted that shield."

"So, Pieter only has to *want* to control someone and it happens?" Sarah asked.

"I'm sure there's more to it," Holden said. "Pieter has been manipulating people his entire life. As with Jack's talent for visualizing machinery, he may have been practicing it for years without being aware of it."

"Wouldn't he still need a motivator?" Ethan stroked Dusty's neck. "Like the one in Dusty's collar?"

"Maybe Pieter built it into the ring," Sarah said.

Priya slapped the table. "The ring. I knew I'd seen it before. James Gutierrez was wearing one just like it. That's how Pieter's doing it."

Jack shook his head. "That can't be right. I connected to Pieter without one. The emotion detector and motivator must be part of the AI."

"Jack is right," Holden said. "A built-in emotion detector would make it easier, but the AI's motivator is more sophisticated than what we know how to build."

"Then what's the ring for?" Priya looked to both Holden and Jack for an answer.

"Uh …" Jack said, "it may have an antenna for a stronger bond, but I bet it's really more of a way for Pieter to make sure Terrance keeps the crystal nearby."

"And let's not forget that it's an active portal," Ethan said.

"Even if it's not for controlling Terrance, there could be a microphone and camera on the other side. Jack, can you trace the other end of it?"

"I'm not sure how. When I looked for the banding portals, I thought about the way birds fly. What would I look for to find Pieter? Evil?"

"It might not even be safe to try," Priya said. "If Terrance isn't faking, and Pieter can control someone through the portal, we can't risk him controlling you. You're far too dangerous."

"Am I supposed to be ashamed or proud of that?"

Priya didn't answer, but the look she gave led Jack to believe that the answer was *both*.

"How can we tell for sure if Pieter is controlling him?" Sarah asked. "Making a person do something can't be as simple as training a dog."

"Terrance remembers everything he did," Priya said. "He just remembers *wanting* to do things he normally wouldn't. But from what I've heard, sneaking around in someone's cabin isn't too much of a stretch for him. Pieter might not be able to force someone to do something they really don't want to."

"Then what was Terrance looking for?"

"It had to be that." Priya pointed at Holden's portal, leaning against the wall under a blanket. "Pieter attacked the Magnolia after Terrance left Caerton, so he knows it's no longer there, and he didn't find it on the island. Terrance was very interested in knowing when I arrived. If Pieter can figure out when I left Earth, and how long I took to get to Icarus, he'll know how far away the portal is."

- - - - -

That afternoon, Priya used Holden's portal to return to Olympia, to further investigate James Gutierrez.

"Keep Terrance locked up," she said from the other side. "And leave the ring where it is. If Pieter has a camera on it, he'll be blind for now."

After Newton, the apartment the UN leased for its officers in

124

Olympia was one of those left without power. The department had given her the option of relocating to a temporary barracks set up in a former high school—another casualty of Newton—but she chose to rent the basement of a private home instead. The suite was farther from the UN's office at the Capitol, but she needed privacy to use Holden's portal.

She could have driven to work—her personal vehicle was hydrogen-powered, not fully electric—but that would attract too much attention. So the car remained out of sight in her landlord's garage and she chose a walking route through Watershed Park.

Very few workers in her building had functioning phones, and the environment had become much louder, and more friendly, since Newton forced people to speak directly with each other. The computer that controlled the elevators hadn't been replaced either; Priya enjoyed several minutes of pleasant banter with colleagues as she climbed to the third floor.

Her office was a cubicle shared with Davis and Katherine. As only one partner would ever be on Earth at any time, the team needed just a single workstation. But Katherine had been transporting a suspect to a holding cell in Olympia during Newton, and the two women now used the space as they needed it.

Their shared computer had no active network connection, so the monitor had devolved into a bulletin board. However, all the sticky notes were gone except for one that asked Priya to come to the Chief's office. Katherine's personal effects were missing from the desk.

This can only be bad news.

Edmond Black had served with the UN for decades. Like Priya, he began his career as a police officer. Before the creation of the Off-world Police Division, he'd been seconded many times to the UN's Department of Peacekeeping Operations. He'd also worked at the colony on Mars. He was a gifted administrator and someone whom Priya respected a great deal.

She knocked on his door. "Good afternoon, Chief."

Edmond waved her into the room. "Please, sit down."

She closed the door behind her, took a seat, and waited patiently while he finished typing.

"I'll come right to it." Edmond pushed aside a stack of paper on his cluttered desk. "I'm disbanding your unit. Until we re-establish regular transport between Earth and Cirrus, there's nothing practical we can accomplish. You can re-apply for the posting then. I'll make sure you get it."

"There must be transportation somewhere," Priya said. "You told me yourself that some corporations might have working portals."

"If they do—and we have no proof of that—we have no jurisdiction over them. Even Customs and Immigration doesn't have the authority to seize them, only regulate what passes through them."

"What about Pieter Reynard? If he's gone to Cirrus, it's up to us to find him."

"Do you have information that he has? Or even that he ever returned to Earth. He's not been seen at his European offices."

"There were reports of water damage at his facility in Detroit."

"That suggests someone used the cargo portal with a water buffer. But it doesn't tell us when, who, or where they came from." Edmond paused for a moment. "The portal *you* used was addressed to Naef Dynamics."

Priya got the impression that Edmond doubted her. He had good reason to, of course. She'd reported that she swam through the portal in Holden's lab minutes before Newton, even though she made the trip the next day through his private portal at his house. Cargo portals weren't rated for human use; the only safe way to pass through the device was to flood the room it was in, to evenly spread the transfer of mass. A water-soaked portal chamber in the ruins of the Detroit factory was the only evidence of Pieter's return.

She had no way of knowing whether Danny had changed the portal's destination, or followed Pieter, or if his body was still submerged in the reservoir in Caerton. That tank—contaminated with nerve gas—would never be opened. But for her story to be true, Danny had to have escaped to Seattle.

Priya sat back and crossed her arms. "Reynard went first. He must have gone to Detroit. Danny changed the frame's address to Seattle before I followed him. There are reports of shuttle launches from a floating pad in the Gulf of Mexico. It's possible that Reynard made his way to Miami and used one that belonged to Gutierrez."

Edmond thought for a moment. "Unfortunately, even if that were true, we don't have concrete proof that Reynard was involved in Newton. What you've told us suggests there's a North Korean terrorist on the loose, one who attacked the US Navy from Doctor Marke's lab."

"Danny Kou betrayed Pieter in the end, but it was Pieter who made it possible. It was his equipment in Holden's lab. It was Pieter's company, Armenau Industries, that stood to gain the most from this."

Edmond shook his head. "Armenau has suffered as much as anyone. All but one of their factories was destroyed. On the other hand, only one of Gutierrez's was. He's now the world's largest producer of portal crystals. There's also fresh evidence he met with Danny weeks before Newton."

That's not true. From her meeting with him, she was certain that James didn't know he still had more operational factories than the one in Texas. *Pieter's setting him up to take the fall.*

"Priya, I've always supported you. You know that. I want to help you. But unless there's hard evidence showing that Reynard has a way to travel to Cirrus, this investigation is on hold. We've passed the file to the FBI and made arrangements for you to return to your original department in Seattle." He stood and extended his hand. "I can only give you to the weekend to bring me something I can work with. In case we don't get the chance to speak again, I want to say it's been a pleasure working with you."

Priya shook his hand, knowing he was sincere. He was

making the right decision based on the facts she'd given him. He was also wearing a gold ring on his right hand. A ring she'd seen twice already.

Chapter 20

"What will happen to Terrance?" Sarah asked.

She, Jack, and Ethan were sitting in the newly completed Rogers-family cabin. Her mother and Suresh had returned to Caerton yesterday and retrieved two boxes of their personal effects. Family photos, mostly of Sarah, now decorated the walls. A single photo of her father, whom she hadn't seen in many years, hung over the fireplace.

"Does it matter?" Ethan glowered. "He had the radio last night and knew where we were. He betrayed us."

"We don't know that. Pieter may have made him want to monitor the radio, and then listened in through the ring. We have to know for sure if Pieter was controlling him or if he did it willingly."

Ethan's expression was still angry. "Why?"

She lowered her gaze to the floor. "He stopped me from going up to Pieter's office. That's where he found the ring. If I'd have gone, it might have been me wearing it last night." She met Ethan's eyes. "We can't keep him locked up forever."

"She's right," Jack said. "Niels trusted him. There's no way he'd make a mistake like that."

Speaking Niels' name aloud paused the conversation, leaving Jack to wonder what the Traveller really knew. Then he realized these events were past Niels' time. If their AI theory was correct, he couldn't have foreseen the betrayal.

Eventually, Sarah asked, "So, how do we find out?"

Ethan leaned forward and grinned. "I'm thinking we try an experiment."

Her eyes narrowed. "I'm betting this isn't an experiment your grandfather will approve of."

"Probably not. Jack's bird-brain adventure proves—"

"*Hey,*" Jack said.

"Sorry. Your control of the bird's flight shows that the AI works in real-time. I want to see if it's possible to do the same thing with a person."

"You want me to control someone?" Anger and revulsion rose in Jack. He snapped, "Like Pieter does?" His breathing became ragged and he clenched his fists, fighting back the overwhelming anxiety he used to experience around emotion detectors.

"It's okay, Jack." Sarah touched his hand. "You don't have to do it. I don't think you *can*, even if it's possible. It's obviously something that's so offensive you can only manage it in your sleep."

Ethan waited until Jack calmed down. "Sorry, buddy. Sarah's right. But like Pieter, she can see the future. So maybe she can also learn to control someone."

Sarah appeared doubtful. "Who am I supposed to control?"

"Me," Ethan said to their surprise. "But we should first see if you can tell what I'm thinking, the way Jack did with Pieter."

"I really don't want to read *your* thoughts." When Ethan looked hurt, she added, "I'm kidding. Mostly."

"Well, you won't be reading my *thoughts*. At least I hope not. The AI can detect emotions; let's start with that."

"All right, so how do we do this?"

"Jack, you give Sarah your wand and link it to my coin. That'll be the same as Pieter using your original wand to control the ring."

The first part of Ethan's experiment was easy. Jack had accessed Ethan's coin before and could do it again instantly. "There, I've opened a wormhole between them."

Ethan faced Sarah. "I'm gonna flip the coin but I won't call it. Instead, I'll try to land it heads up. I'll be happy if I can do it and disappointed if I can't." He twirled his hand. "Turn around."

He and Sarah sat back-to-back on the floor and he began flipping his coin. Instead of predicting how it would land—something he could do easily—he tried controlling how many times it rotated, to force it to land heads up.

"Are you getting anything?" Jack asked after a few minutes.

Sarah shook her head. "Nothing at all."

"Priya said the first thing that comes to mind is usually correct. Just start making guesses."

They started again. Sarah relaxed and tried not to think about what Ethan was doing, only how he was feeling.

"Heads," she said at once.

Ethan held a finger to his lips and showed Jack the coin. It was heads.

"You two keep going," Jack said. "I'll keep score."

After a few minutes, Jack noticed several things. First, Ethan was landing the coin heads up twice as often as tails. However, there was no physical influence through the portal; he was changing the averages through nothing more than practice. Sarah was improving, too. Not only could she tell when Ethan was pleased with his result, she began to sense what side of the coin he was trying for.

"I've got it now," she said. "It's definitely not mind reading. It's closer to intuition."

"Then let's see if you can make him do something." Jack started for to the kitchen. "I'll be right back."

"What's he doing?"

"No idea."

Soon, Jack returned, hiding something in cupped hands. "Don't look."

With Sarah's back turned, he set a hot pepper and a slice of apple in front of Ethan. He choked back a laugh. "You have to commit to this. Remember, we're working with future memories. It may not work if she knows you didn't follow through."

"You want me to eat *that*?" Ethan pointed at the pale yellow pepper, one his parents used in small quantities when they prepared a spicy meal.

"No, but you'll have to eat one of them. That way, it *will* have happened and be something Sarah can remember. She can pick which one—right or left. She should be able to tell if it's the one you want, and then she'll try to make you eat the other."

"Is it a worm?" Sarah laughed. "Can we do this with a worm?"

"No," Ethan snapped, "it's not a worm." Then, to Jack, he said, "Fine, I'll commit. But if it's you know what, I'll only take a little bite." He settled himself on the rug again but didn't appear comfortable. "Can we get started before I change my mind?"

Sarah relaxed and recaptured her earlier frame of mind. She and Ethan did a few more coin flips to be sure they were communicating.

"How are you feeling, now?" Jack asked.

Ethan answered tersely, "You know how I'm feeling."

"Sarah? Left, or right?"

"Let's go with right."

Ethan scowled. It was the pepper.

Sarah giggled. She knew.

Ethan brought the pepper to his lips and prepared to take the tiniest bite possible. He hesitated, smiled, and popped the entire thing into his mouth. His expression changed quickly.

"*Water.*" He ran from the room while spitting the pepper into his hand.

Neither Jack nor Sarah could hold back their laughter. "Did you do that?" Jack asked. "Did you make him eat the pepper?"

"I'm not sure." Sarah got up and sat on the sofa. "I didn't *make* him eat it. I got the feeling that he didn't want to, and I thought it would be funny if he did. I only *wanted* him to do it."

"And then I thought it would be funny too." Ethan stumbled into the room. The front of his shirt was wet. "And I still do. Sort of. Does that mean you're still trying to control me?"

"No, I'm not. Honest."

"Could it be like the shield spell? Is it something you can turn on and leave on?"

"Maybe it's more like conditioning," Jack said. "And there's something else. He sensed that you thought it would be funny, and you sensed that he didn't want to eat it. That means it works both ways. If you can influence him, he can influence you."

Over the next couple of hours, the three friends devised more experiments to determine how the effect worked. Ethan and Sarah took turns holding a weight at arm's length, smelling a dirty shoe—things that were disagreeable but wouldn't hurt them. Eventually, they believed they had a solid understanding of how it worked and its limitations: it wasn't something they could activate and ignore, like a light switch; it was definitely a two-way effect, but not a permanent one; and both Ethan and Sarah developed a sense for knowing when the other was paying attention to their thoughts, even if they weren't trying to control.

"So," Sarah concluded, "Terrance *was* being controlled. Did you notice it got easier the longer we did it? If that's true for Terrance, then Pieter could make him do whatever he wanted."

Ethan agreed and asked, "What do we do with the ring, then?"

"We have to destroy it," Jack said.

Sarah shook her head. "We should wait until Priya gets back. She might need it for evidence. Also, there's something more important than the ring itself. Is there a way to stop Pieter from controlling someone? Priya said that James Gutierrez has the same ring. What if Pieter tries to control whoever picks it up?"

"*I* could force the wormhole to close," Jack said, "but that won't help anyone else."

"The shield spell?" Ethan suggested.

"It's worth a try."

Ethan already knew how to activate the shield, so they agreed that he'd use it while Sarah tried sensing his emotions.

"Just make sure you're not pointing it at her," Jack said. "Remember Marten? We want to block the link, not bounce her across the room."

Ethan stood two yards from Sarah and angled away for good measure. Jack opened the portal. Sarah held the wand loosely and concentrated on what Ethan was feeling.

"Aha," Ethan said, "there you are. *Shield*."

Sarah's eyes rolled back and she collapsed on the floor.

Chapter 21

Priya walked home to her rental. Instead of hiking through the park, she kept to the streets where she could see and be seen. She overshot by one block, then doubled back on the adjacent street. The place she was renting sat in the middle of an s-curve in the road, meaning there was limited visibility from a distance. She paid close attention to the parked vehicles as she approached. Grimy windshields confirmed that none had moved in two months.

"Is there someone staying with you?" an elderly woman asked.

Priya looked to the second-floor window. "Sorry, Mrs. Chen. What was that?"

"If you had extra keys cut, I need to know. There was a man here today." There was a hint of scandal in the way Priya's landlady said 'man'.

"Did he stay long?"

Mrs. Chen shrugged. "I only heard the door and saw him leaving."

"It was someone from the office. He was dropping off a package for me. I let him use my key." She shook her key ring to show that she still had it.

Priya had told the older lady she worked as a police officer. This seemed to be an acceptable vocation, and Mrs. Chen had been happy to rent the suite.

"Very well. But if you have someone living with you, I must charge more rent."

"I understand, Mrs. Chen. Thank you for keeping an eye out for me." She smiled and waited for her landlady to close the window and pull back the curtains, leaving the usual two-inch gap. Then she sidled to the basement entrance, which was under an overhang and hidden from Mrs. Chen's view.

The door had not been forced open. Priya knew from experience that Mrs. Chen had excellent hearing and little appreciation for music—she wouldn't have missed a loud noise. Whoever entered had not been troubled by the lock and lingered only a moment. The list of suspects and motives was very short.

She unzipped her jacket for easy access to her pistol before opening the door.

- - - - -

Jack ran to Sarah's side. "What happened?" She lay unmoving on the cabin floor.

Ethan stood immobile with his mouth hanging open. "I … I don't know. I just called for a shield."

"I didn't sense energy flowing from your coin. It must have backfired through the wand."

"Should we get her to a hospital?"

"And tell them what? We zapped her with a magic spell? Let's take her to Grandpa's cabin. If we have to, we can use the portal to go to Olympia."

Jack lifted her. Ethan limped ahead, opening the doors, but Sarah was coming around by the time they got to Holden's place. Jack set her gently on the sofa while Ethan activated the portal.

"What happened?" Sarah mumbled. "I have a *really* bad headache."

"Ethan used a shield to block your attempt to control him."

"We agreed to it." Ethan nodded rapidly, as if to convince her. "Remember? I was going next."

"I remember getting ready, then nothing after that." She tried sitting, winced halfway up, and lay down again. "Jack, Priya needs your help."

"Well it hasn't affected your ability to see the future."

"No, I mean, she wants to talk to you right now. Look."

Sarah pointed to the portal frame leaning against the wall. A cardboard box on the far side blocked the opening. A note taped to it read: *Jack. Need your help.*

Jack slid across the floor. There was more writing in smaller letters: *Room might be bugged. Portal nearby? Tap once for yes, twice for no.*

"Priya thinks she's being bugged. She wants me to check for a portal but I can't do that from here."

Ethan moved close enough to read the note. "Tap three times, then. She'll know something's wrong."

Jack could hear music playing through the wormhole. He confirmed that the frame had a full charge, reached through, and gave three light, distinct taps against the cardboard.

After a minute with no response, he prepared to tap again. Before he could, the box shifted and was repositioned at an angle. The new placement created a partially concealed area, and a pen and pad of paper dropped from above.

"I know what she wants," Jack said. The veiled space was large enough for his head.

With the recent practice, his skill for detecting portal crystals had improved. He passed his head through the frame and found one in seconds, even though it was small and relatively far away. He wrote: *One. Twenty feet from here, to my right*, then tapped once on the cardboard.

Shortly, the sound of moving furniture topped the music. The box lifted and Priya's hand whisked the pad away.

- - - - -

Priya had anticipated that her last move wouldn't be permanent and kept her shipping boxes. Under the pretense of packing, she placed one in front of the portal which, when dormant, appeared to be a normal mirror sitting on the carpeted floor in her bedroom. She turned on music, loud enough to mask sounds through the wormhole, but not enough to upset Mrs. Chen. She waited.

Three taps.

What does that mean? I've seen him detect portals before.

She cradled the back of her head in both hands and stretched her neck muscles, scanning the ceiling and walls without being obvious. Would the intruder have been so bold as to hide a camera in her bedroom?

The things Jack can do with the wand are almost magical. What's different this time? Does it only work on Cirrus? She thought back to her training before her first portal trip. *Of course … entanglement.*

Even when inactive, an entangled crystal was always part of a wormhole. One of the first things she'd learned was that a crystal couldn't pass through another wormhole without disconnecting. Jack had explained that he couldn't control the energy field on the far side of a wormhole. It seemed logical that he couldn't sense another portal through it either.

With a bit of shuffling of boxes, Priya made a space for Jack's head and soon had the pad with his response, which confirmed her theory.

She carried a box of clothing into the living room and dropped it on the sofa. It was bright outside, but the curtains were drawn. A glance towards the door was all she needed as she switched on a lamp. Above the frame, a three-inch square didn't quite match the surrounding wall.

While it was possible to capture video and sound through the aperture of a portal, law enforcement agencies preferred the *Patch*. The transparent, high-definition, lens-less camera not only provided better video quality, it was much easier to apply. Here, someone had simply opened the door and slapped the sticky square against the wall.

The surveillance device's weakness was that its reflectivity didn't always match the background. If you knew where to look, you might see it. Whoever placed this one had been more concerned about being seen than selecting the right spot.

Priya strolled to the fridge and poured a glass of water, then returned to her bedroom. The camera had an unobstructed view of the kitchen and living room, but only the doorway to her bedroom, not inside of it. She pulled the box aside and crouched by the portal. With music playing in the living room, she could speak freely.

"Thanks, Jack. What's wrong with Sarah?"

"Uh, we'll get to that." Sarah was sitting now, hunched over with her palms pressed to her temples. "Who's watching you?"

Priya explained her conversation with her boss, saying that he was shutting down her unit, and that Pieter might be controlling him through a ring.

"There's no way I can continue the investigation without revealing the existence of Holden's portal. If one of his spies sees me on Cirrus, he'll know that it's here." She slumped against the wall. "Tell me what happened to Sarah."

Jack explained Ethan's experiments. Priya was partly furious that they'd tried something so dangerous, but also impressed by how much they'd accomplished in such a short time.

"Just don't do anything like that again without consulting your grandfather first."

Holden had returned to his cabin partway through the story, carrying a pot of soil in which two tea plants had sprouted. He set his watering can aside and said, "I agree wholeheartedly. There may be safer ways to do this. There are certainly smaller, less powerful crystals. The tiny ones in leg bands are all you need."

Priya felt a cold rush of adrenaline. "You're right. There are plenty of crystals to work with. Jack, if you can create a wormhole to *any* crystal, can Pieter do the same? Can he use any portal to control anybody? Anywhere?"

She waited, hoping Jack would tell her it was impossible. But after an extended silence he said, "Maybe."

"This is … this is a nightmare."

Ethan held up an open palm. "Hold on. Priya, does your boss have a working cell phone?"

"Most department heads got replacements in the first week."

"Then the answer is *no*. If Pieter can search wormholes the way Jack does, he could have just hunted until he found the one he was looking for. He wouldn't have needed the ring."

"Jack?" Priya looked to him for confirmation.

"Ethan's right. I can find *a* phone crystal quickly, but that doesn't tell me whose phone it is or even where it is. Pieter can probably use any crystal, but he needs the ring to be certain he's working on the right person."

"And it's not possible to see or hear through a phone's wormhole anyway," Holden said. "The power and data connections are sealed. He'd have to disconnect the cable at the exchange."

Sarah was feeling well enough to join the discussion. "What about water portals? Pieter's company supplied drinking water. Wouldn't he know the identity of individual crystals through Armenau?"

"Actually, that's not a problem," Priya said. "Telephone exchanges are secure buildings, and police forces, governments, and the military have their own private exchanges anyway. When Danny attacked the Navy, he still needed physical access to a crystal from that production lot." She let out a deep breath. "I panicked there for a moment, but we're safe. Even if he can search crystals the way Jack does, it doesn't sound as if he could ever find the right one."

"I expect there will be another difficulty," Holden said. "Jack, how many connections can you hold open at once?"

"Lights and shields are things I don't have to think about. They'll keep running while I open a second portal, but I couldn't pay attention to them at the same time. It'd be like listening to two different conversations while juggling."

"That'll be the same for Pieter then," Priya said. "Reading someone's emotions will take concentration. We'll assume he can only *control* one person at a time, but we'll also assume that he's recording through every portal he has physical access to."

"There's another way to find a portal," Sarah said. "All he really needs to do is to broadcast a radio signal from somewhere in Olympia and listen for it on Cirrus. That's how we tracked birds at the aviary."

"That's easy to block." Holden stood and walked towards his workshop. "We'll put the frame inside a Faraday cage. I can have that done in an hour."

"What about the ring? He could do the same with that. Should we destroy it?"

"Let's use it to misdirect him," Priya said. "Tomorrow, I want you three to find a spot away from the village to stash the ring. It's got to be abandoned, but somewhere we could have been living."

Chapter 22

"Ow." Ethan winced. "Watch the bumps."

"Sorry." Jack slowed and steered around a puddle. It had rained overnight, making it difficult to tell the difference between shallow and deep potholes. "We'll be on smoother roads soon."

A day after being shot, Ethan's bruises had darkened to hues of purple and blue. He moved stiffly and claimed he was feeling better, though not well enough to drive.

Instead of driving Dave—Jack's preferred ride—they'd attached a trailer to Anders' four-seater. The only object on it was a metal box full of mud and Terrance's ring. They assumed the ring's range was equal to a phone's—an arm's length—and that Pieter would try to control anyone who got too close.

Following Priya's instructions, the villagers temporarily released Terrance and made him scoop the ring into the box along with a shovelful of mud. The box had to be metal in case Pieter was already using Sarah's idea of locating it through radio waves.

"Do you know where we're going?" Ethan asked when Jack turned at an unmarked intersection.

"We passed this road on our way to Icarus last week. Suresh told me they've visited every mill within a hundred miles and found them abandoned or looted. He says the one here also has an apartment block for the workers."

"Why pick one so close?"

"We can't go *too* far. Pieter may not have tracked the ring, but he knew how long Terrance had been driving for."

"I doubt Pieter knows about Icarus at all," Sarah said. "That might be why Niels never called for help. If Pieter crossed the lake near the cabin while it was raining, then he never saw the village."

Ethan peered at the hand-drawn map they were using. "What does 'Here be dragons' mean?"

"It's a joke," Jack said. "Something about sailing into the

unknown."

They drove in silence until Ethan spotted silos and grain elevators in an expanse of patchy forest. "I was expecting something more high-tech. It looks exactly like mills on Earth, except for the bridge. What's that for?"

"It's not a bridge." Jack pointed to a domed building that stood apart from the rest of the mill. "It's a walkway to the portal chamber."

"Why is it so far away?" Sarah asked. The elevated hallway was a half-mile long.

"The grain portal is huge. It's bigger than the thrusters on most spaceships. Anyone sensitive to portals wouldn't want to be much closer."

Jack sped past the mill, then slowed as he approached the apartment block. There was no sound, movement, or anything that suggested people had been around recently. He parked in front of the building and tapped the horn three times. There was no response. He shifted the wand under the fabric of his jacket. "Is it safe?"

"For the next two seconds anyway." Ethan handed his coin to Sarah. "How about you?"

Sarah shook her head and returned the coin. "I don't remember this place. But I don't like it. It's creepy."

"I agree," Jack said. "Let's get rid of the ring and get out of here."

Ethan eased himself from the car. "I'd be happier if I had my staff."

"You'll have one once we toss the ring." Anders had strapped the metal box to a sturdy wooden pole so the cousins could carry it without being near. He'd also attached a rope to the box's lid so they could open and dump it from a distance. "That pole is about the right size, isn't it?"

"Yeah. Until then, you're the muscle."

"Me?" Jack lifted one end of the pole. "You're the Black Belt."

"Right now, your wand is a better weapon than anything else.

Anyway, I can still barely move." He took the pole's other end and grimaced when he hoisted it to his shoulder.

As Sarah led the way into the forest, with Jack and Ethan in line behind her, Ethan said, "I guess I never thanked you for that shield. So … you know … thanks."

"No problem." Jack hoped he'd sounded casual. "How far should we take this?"

"I … I thought the thank you was enough, but I suppose we could shake hands."

Jack laughed. "I was talking to Sarah. How far should we take the box?"

"We want it to look as if we threw it away. But it's got to be somewhere we can find it if we ever need it again. And we can't bury it; Priya wants Pieter to detect it if he thinks of using a radio signal." She pointed to a towering tree with sprawling branches and leaves turning brown. "That's an oak. It looks like the only one around here."

Jack knew only a few tree species by name, but the one Sarah was pointing to was larger than its neighbors. "That'll work."

They hiked through tall grass to the base of the tree, where the recent rains had created a puddle. Jack maneuvered the box over the water while Ethan stood still, then Sarah pulled the rope. The mass of mud fell into the water with a plop—an undignified conclusion to their mission.

Jack untied the box and handed the pole to Ethan. He hefted it gingerly, testing its balance, and seemed satisfied.

"We should do something before we leave," Sarah said as they returned to the parking lot, "to make it look like people were living here recently."

"Footprints in the building should be good enough," Jack said. "The ground is still damp."

He drew his wand and turned the back door's handle. It was unlocked. Cautiously, he pushed the door open and flipped the light switch, even though he didn't expect the building to have power.

"Hello?" Jack called. No response. After a minute of silence, Ethan said, "Let's make tracks."

Ten minutes later, they'd visited each of the dozen vacant apartments several times, leaving muddy footprints. As long as no one looked closely at the prints, it would appear as if many people had moved out after the most recent rainfall.

"Should we check the mill too?" Sarah asked when they returned to the car.

"I'm sure anything useful has already been removed," Jack said.

Curiosity won out in the end. Jack had visited mills near Fairview before, but Ethan and Sarah had grown up in large cities and never seen one. He drove into the covered loading bay and parked on the pit grate.

Ethan leaned over his door to look through the steel grate, which was larger than Anders' car. "What's the hole for?"

"This is where the trucks dump the grain. Then conveyors under the floor carry it into the mill. There'd normally be a line of trucks waiting when this place was running."

Sarah asked a question that had been on Jack's mind for months. "How will Earth survive?" Apparently, Ethan shared the same concern because he joined them in silent contemplation.

Jack broke the silence. "Cirrus only ever provided a quarter of the grain Earth needed. Priya says there's rationing but no one's starving." He didn't add the word he was thinking: *yet*.

"Come on." Sarah hopped from the car and pushed open the double doors at the entrance. "Let's explore."

Ethan followed with his staff, still limping slightly. "Wow, it's clean."

"What were you expecting?" Jack asked.

"Not this. I thought there'd be, you know, flour everywhere. This is more like a hospital."

A dozen rows of squat, bulky machines occupied the main floor. The equipment in each row was different, depending on what grain it processed. Pipes ran up to a second level of machinery on scaffolding. Above that, a maze of larger pipes disappeared through the walls into other parts of the complex.

Jack wandered across the gleaming floor. He stopped by a milling machine and leaned forward to peer through the inspection window mounted in the front panel. "There's enough flour in these machines to feed the village for months. Should we take some home with us?" He poked his wand at the glass and created a mini-tornado of flour in the bin.

Sarah leaned to the window to see what he was doing. "We don't have a container to carry it in. We can always come back." She'd moved close enough to the wand to connect to the AI. "In fact, I remember this place now, except it was night time. We probably do return later."

Jack let the tornado fade. "Why hasn't anyone been here before us and cleaned the place out?"

Ethan shrugged. "Let's go to the transport chamber. That's what I really want to see."

They continued deeper into the mill, passing through empty storerooms filled with equipment they couldn't identify. The ceilings were three stories high in most rooms, and well-lit by skylights. The elevated walkway began at the top of a metal staircase and sloped gently towards the chamber.

"We need to go outside," Ethan said.

"Why?" Jack asked.

"I want to see where we are."

"Dude, you know where we are. You're the one who wanted to come here."

"Well now I want to go outside." Ethan gripped his staff firmly. "I *need* to go outside."

Sarah backed away from him. "Are you feeling okay?"

Ethan froze, swore, clasped his coin through his shirt and shouted, "*Shield*."

Jack whipped his wand out of his pocket and spun around, searching for whatever danger Ethan was shielding against.

"It was Pieter. He was trying to control me." The tension fled from Ethan's face. He grinned. "*I got him.*"

"Pieter? Are you sure?"

"Who else could it have been? It was just like when Sarah and I were practicing. But I got him." He pumped his fist. "I hit him *hard*."

"So now Pieter can find portals the same way you can?" Sarah asked as Ethan launched into a victory dance.

"Maybe not," Jack said. "He already had a bond with Ethan's coin. I used it to find him when we were leaving the maintenance depot." He shivered involuntarily. "He recognized me through it."

Ethan stopped his gyrations. "So now my lucky coin is cursed?"

"He wouldn't dare use it again," Sarah said. "If it's like what happened to me, he's unconscious right now. But you'd better get rid of it to be safe."

Ethan unhooked the coin from its chain and sneered. "I hope it's worse than that. I hit him a lot harder than I got you."

Jack didn't want to throw the coin away, but eventually agreed with his friends. They'd reached the end of the long hallway. The passage sloped gently from the mill so that the chamber itself was below ground, and a steep metal ladder with handrails led up to a ground-level emergency exit. Ethan, eager to be rid of the coin, sprinted up the steps.

From the outside, the portal chamber was large but unimpressive: a fifty-foot-wide, unadorned concrete dome surrounded by towering trees. It had suffered storm damage recently. A mangled tree lay against its roof.

Ethan swore again and threw the coin as far as he could into the forest.

Jack placed a hand on his shoulder. "Grandpa can make another for you."

"I guess." Ethan picked up and threw a clod of dirt after his lost coin. "Let's finish the tour and head home."

Back below ground, they entered the portal chamber: a round

mezzanine surrounding an open pit. Unlike the rest of the mill, this place had been looted. Someone had opened every cabinet, panel, and drawer, and dumped the contents on the floor. Every screen on the workstations and consoles that ringed the room was smashed or torn from the wall. Even the furniture was broken apart.

The windowless room reminded Jack of the converted water tank at the reservoir where his family had been held in August, except that the ceiling was flat. Or should have been. Instead of following the dome's curve, suspended panels created a hidden space under the concrete shell for ducts and cooling equipment. Sunlight was filtering into the room through a gaping hole in the center.

Ethan leaned over the pit's railing and looked up through a knot of twisted pipes. "That tree punched a hole in the roof." Then he looked down. "Where's the portal? At the bottom of the pit?"

"No." Jack tapped his foot at the pit's lip. "This *is* the portal. See the ring, right below the railing? That's the frame. The pit is there in case the wormhole collapses while flour is falling through. That way they don't have a blockage when they restart."

"It must be thirty feet across. Mom would barf if she even drove past this place." A quarter of people were sensitive to dynamic wormholes and suffered effects ranging from disorientation to nausea; Ethan's mother, Grace, was one of them.

Jack leaned over the railing. With no power, the lighting panels in the overflow pit were dark, but natural light from the opening in the roof partially illuminated the bottom, one hundred feet below.

"What's that?" Sarah asked. "There's something shiny down there."

"I see it too. Let's have a closer look."

Two sets of metal stairways descended to a scaffold encircling the cylindrical pit. Below, more debris-covered scaffolding divided the pit into eight levels. The staircases doubled back on themselves—fire escape style—so that each landing was directly below the one above. Jack chose the set on the north wall as it appeared to be free of rubble.

The pit itself was wider than the portal ring, at least forty feet across, and much darker at the bottom than expected. He activated his wand as a flashlight.

"Where did this mess come from?" Sarah asked as she began the final flight of steps.

"It looks like the tree knocked the fan out of the ceiling," Ethan said.

The fan blades were obvious, but there were also piles of branches, twisted metal panels, plastic tubes, electrical wiring, and other debris from the mezzanine spread across the floor. A wheeled vehicle that resembled a miniature Zamboni squatted in the center of the space, partially buried. Bristled brushes lined all sides of the machine, which appeared sturdy enough to withstand the pressure of the tons of flour that must fall on it.

"Over here." Sarah beckoned them to one side of the pit. "This is what we saw from up top."

Jack shone his light where Sarah stood near a pile of glittering objects. The mound was a mix of machine parts, coin portals, and even a few real coins.

"It looks like a cache," Ethan said. "Don't birds collect shiny things? Maybe it's a bird's nest." He considered the pile's size. "Or the nest of a lot of birds."

"That's actually a myth," Sarah said. "Some birds and mammals collect all sorts of things. It's either people that notice the shiny ones, or the natural materials break down and only the metal remains. Besides ..." She picked up a threaded metal cylinder and offered it to Jack. "This is much too heavy for a bird. What is it?"

"It's an inspection bolt." Jack turned it around. "It has a portal in one end. You can screw it into an engine or furnace and measure temperature and pressure while it's running."

Ethan picked up a handful of shiny strips.

"Those are leg bands and animal tracking tags," Sarah said.

"We used them at the aviary."

"Then what made the pile?" Jack asked. "A mammal maybe? A pack rat?" Ethan dropped the bands and jumped back when he heard the word 'rat'.

"I don't know. But there's a pit in the center of the pile. Whatever made this has been sleeping on it."

"You guys remember anything about this place?" Jack looked around at the scaffolding. "I feel like we're being watched."

"My coin was cursed, remember," Ethan said.

Sarah showed her empty hands. "And I don't have a portal."

"There's something here." Jack flashed his light around the room, stopping at the stairs on the south wall.

A massive branch leaned against the railing, creating a sheltered space below the scaffold. From the darkness, two glowing disks reflected the wand's light.

"It's a dog." Ethan placed his staff in front of him and squatted. "Here, boy. Come here."

A low growl answered.

Jack felt something similar to when he'd linked with Pieter: another mind, and a sense of recognition. *"That's not a dog."*

A large and sinuous creature slunk from the shadows.

Chapter 23

Pieter awoke on the antique Persian rug beside the rosewood desk with a mighty headache and no memory of how he got there. His chair was tipped over too. He recalled only that he'd been trying to control Jack's cousin, Ethan, to make him think of his location.

"Simon," he called.

"Sir?" The reply came from nearby.

Pieter raised his head, wincing against the pain, and spotted the engineer standing obediently on the opposite side of the desk.

"What happened?"

Simon smiled. "You fell off your chair, sir."

"*I know that*. Why did I black out?"

"I don't know."

Pieter stood and righted his high-backed leather chair, then glared at Simon, wondering how much free-will the younger man still possessed. He'd been controlling Simon for long enough that his loyalty was beyond question. He no longer had a choice; he *wanted* to be loyal.

"Play back cameras one and seven," Pieter said as he sat facing a wall-mounted array of a dozen monitors. He checked the clock. "The last ten minutes."

Number seven monitor still showed a black screen, as it had ever since Pieter willed Terrance to throw the ring away. He raised the volume but heard only static.

Four of the remaining screens were also dark—those rings had not been deployed yet—and the video on five others depicted blurred movements or hands in pockets. Camera Two showed the inside of a glass, where an ice cube spun lazily in a shallow pool of bourbon. Pieter spared a moment to cause the wearer to fidget and rotate the ring. Camera one showed Pieter himself, sitting at his desk, from the viewpoint of Simon's right hand.

"Fast forward."

His image disappeared from monitor one as Simon returned to the kitchen. Ten minutes sped past on seven. Nothing changed.

The boy knew where the ring landed.

He'd recognized Ethan's voice that morning as the one shouting a warning just before Terrance tossed it. Ten minutes ago, he'd been willing Ethan to retrieve the ring—to reveal the hiding spot of Holden and his portal—when he lost consciousness.

This is your doing, isn't it, Jack?

As the pain in his head subsided, Pieter reflected on the events that had brought him here.

The ability to control others through wormholes was his greatest and most unexpected discovery. He had Jack to thank for that. In their final encounter before Newton, Jack had shown a knack for knowing when someone was lying. Logically, if the boy shared the skill of manipulating the energy field, and had gained a second portal-derived talent, Pieter assumed he could learn it too. His experiments on Simon proved that not only could he detect a lie, he could influence the man's thoughts.

Pieter considered that Jack might also have a Traveller's ability to remember the future, but that gift was unpredictable. He attributed his own skill to his frequent passages through portals as a child, something not possible for Jack.

It's just you, me, and the girl now.

For years, another Traveller had been working behind the scenes, protecting Jack, deliberately removing traces of him and his family from all records. They'd also intervened during the abduction attempts on Jack's family. That required a level of foresight even greater than his own. Only one person could do that.

Pieter knew of Niels, of course. He'd heard rumors of the man's lifelong success in a range of endeavors; always picking and financing market-leading companies and technologies. Pieter's own investing experience told him that Niels was using more than just research and analysis.

What he didn't know—what no one did—was when and how Niels had come to Cirrus. And why had he changed his name and lived in isolation on his own private island? Was it possible that his foresight spanned so many decades? Had he moved to Cirrus only to protect Jack?

That was all moot now; the island hadn't been hard to find. Pieter had followed a dirt track that ended at a sheltered cove on the southern shore of the tree-lined lake. A two-seat fishing boat tied there—an illegal hobby—provided the means to get to the island. It even had a battery for its electric motor, almost as if it was waiting for him.

The worst of the storm had passed, but it was still raining that night, forcing Pieter to hug the shoreline as he circled halfway around the island. The lights from the cabin didn't reach the water; his talent guided him the final steps.

Niels had not appeared surprised to see Pieter walking through his door unannounced, and hadn't moved to defend himself. Pieter took no pleasure in killing him; it was just something that had to be done.

Before leaving, he'd searched the cabin and discovered the high-tech workshop. He'd found the right man. The crystallization tanks confirmed that Niels was still very much involved in current research. Pieter set fire to the building and was halfway around the island when the fusion plant exploded, obliterating the cabin.

He then returned to Caerton, intending to find Jack's grandfather and his portal. That wasn't part of his original plan, but neither was finding Jack at the maintenance depot—the boy should have been stuck on Earth. Clearly, Holden's undetectable portal had survived Newton.

There had been an odd change in the vacant apartment. On his first visit, Pieter had seen a painting above the fireplace. It stuck in his memory not because of the wall safe behind it, but because the painting—a cheap reproduction—was less valuable than the Art Deco frame that held it.

Holden had apparently abandoned his home and taken everything of value, then replaced the frame with another. *Why would he go to the trouble?* In hindsight, the answer was obvious: the painting's frame was the missing portal.

"Normal speed." With only thirty seconds to go, nothing had changed on seven.

The scene on monitor one moved from the kitchen, along the hall, into Pieter's office, then dropped to the desk. Pieter glanced at the coffee cup resting there, then returned his attention to the screen and saw himself fall.

"Play back that last bit."

Simon pointed the remote. "Gladly." He smiled as he slowed the video and zoomed in on Pieter's face.

There was nothing unusual until the moment he collapsed. Before that, he'd been alert and concentrating, wearing a determined grin. He didn't fade out or drift off. The change was sudden, as if he'd been struck.

Pieter scowled, noting that Simon hadn't moved to help or even investigate his fall. "What could have caused that?"

"I don't have sufficient data to support a hypothesis."

"You know enough. Take a guess."

"Very well. I have reasoned that the rings you had me build are for a form of mind control. As I have no desire to remove the one I am forced to wear, I assume they are effective. However, they're nothing more than standard data portals and there's no reason they should affect your health.

"This other device, though—the rod you won't let me examine—I can't say how it might affect you. Your interaction with the rings seems to require a great deal of concentration. It appears you're trying to use the rod the same way. Is it also a portal crystal?"

Pieter glared at Simon but the man held his mechanical smile, an unexpected consequence of the control Pieter exercised over him, making him *want* to stay loyal, *want* to keep Pieter's secrets.

He briefly thought it was better when his employee did those things out of fear and intimidation, but knew he needed Simon's complete obedience at this stage. Also, he had to acknowledge Simon's brilliance; the engineer had worked out what was happening with so few clues.

"Assume it is," Pieter said.

"Very well. The ring you wear has a dozen crystals in it, one for each of the secondary rings. However, I'm certain that's just for convenience. You convinced me to wear this ring, so you must be able to exercise control through any pair of crystals, and therefore, the rod. The problem must be at the other end. What's different about that one?"

"As far as I know, it's a standard coin portal."

"That narrows it down, then. Each secondary ring is entangled with a crystal in yours. Is the rod bound to the coin or are you still using the merging technology?"

Pieter hesitated. "I've encountered it before. It's a direct connection."

"Was the subject aware that he was being controlled?"

Simon's question was alarming. Pieter reacted quickly. "Possibly. But you *want* to be controlled, don't you?" Pieter allowed his own desire to flow through the portal and saw it reflected in Simon's smile.

"That's right. I want to be controlled. But maybe the subject doesn't. Maybe he's found a way to resist."

Simon continued smiling.

- - - - -

Pieter dismissed Simon and replayed the video, hoping he'd overlooked a detail.

He'd held back one very important fact, even though Simon could never repeat it. He wasn't about to disclose how the rod was different, that it allowed him to connect to other crystals as if they were still merged.

He also knew that Ethan carried a coin portal, or wore it around his neck as a lucky charm. Jack had used it to create a shield at the maintenance depot. Later, Pieter sensed Jack's probing and realized there was a bond between the coin and the rod. That led him to discover the hundreds of links it held to other portals.

While Pieter still didn't properly understand the technology, that hadn't stopped him from exploiting it. He'd already learned to reproduce the shield and other functions.

Jack's ability to detect a lie had been the inspiration for the rings, and controlling a person was a taxing job, but he'd never lost consciousness using his own devices. His intuition told him that Jack was involved somehow.

He turned his attention back to monitor seven.

The boy has more secrets yet.

Chapter 24

Sarah screamed. Ethan fell over backwards.

A beast, large as a jaguar, shot from the pile of debris and leapt directly to the first level of scaffolding. It surged over the railing, darted to the staircase, and faded into the higher levels, moving fluidly over the stairs.

As one, Jack, Sarah, and Ethan ran to the opposite stairs and began climbing. Ethan yelled, "*Shield. Shield. Shield.*" Whether that was a reflex or he was pleading for one, Jack didn't know. The creature flowed over the railing onto the upper level, leapt into the air, caught the edge of the ragged breach in the ceiling, and disappeared.

When they reached the mezzanine, Jack said, "I saw it leave through the dome."

"What was that thing?" Ethan leaned against the railing to catch his breath. "A lion? An armored lion?"

"No way," Sarah said. "Did you see the tail? It was longer than a cat's and much thicker at the base. More like a lizard."

"Do lizards have forward-facing eyes?" Jack asked.

"Some do. Why?"

"Because it's looking at us right now."

Jack pointed to the crumbling hole in the ceiling. The creature was invisible in the shadows except for the twin reflections from its eyes.

Ethan raised his staff. Jack opened a portal with his wand.

Sarah crept backwards. "Move slowly. It's probably just as scared of us."

Ethan shifted his staff to a blocking position. "I doubt it."

Jack sidestepped to avoid a block of concrete on the floor. The creature's eyes followed him, even though Ethan's staff was a more obvious threat. "Wait."

"For what?"

"It has a portal. No … two portals." Jack created a soft beam of light with his wand and pointed it into the opening. "There's a second one."

"More reason to go."

"It's hurt."

"How do you know?" Sarah asked.

"I just do." Jack stepped forward cautiously. The creature growled. "It's okay. I won't hurt you."

Ethan whispered, "That's not what you should be worried about."

The beast growled louder as Jack brightened the beam. Sure enough, a second, smaller creature lay partially hidden behind the first. A tangle of wires prevented him from seeing either animal clearly, although they resembled reptiles, and the second one was the size of a large dog.

"It's wearing a collar. Or a chain. It's caught on a rebar sticking out of the concrete." Scratches and gouges exposed bare metal, as if the larger creature had tried chewing the twisted bar apart.

Sarah grabbed the back of Jack's coat. "Don't get too close."

"It's trapped. I'm going to cut its collar off."

"You sure you want to do that?" Ethan asked.

"It's suffering. There's blood on its neck."

Jack canceled the light and focused a tight beam of energy on the collar. The first creature tensed, raised itself into a pouncing stance, and growled louder.

"*Jack*," Sarah tugged on his sleeve.

"Don't worry, this won't take long." As he was prying a link apart, Jack noticed the same collar around the first creature's neck. "They're both wearing portal crystals. Like larger versions of animal tracking tags."

The weakened link shattered and the smaller creature snapped its head back, then leapt upwards through the gap. The other followed, knocking chunks of concrete loose with its tail as it whipped around.

Ethan moved almost as fast as the beast had. "*Run*."

Jack sprinted from the chamber, following Sarah. Ethan slammed the door behind them and they raced up the inclined corridor. They held that pace all the way to the car.

As Jack sprang into the driver's seat, he sensed they were being watched from above. He scanned the roofline and saw a beast silhouetted against the sky. He locked eyes with it and—

[…]

Adrenaline coursed through Jack's veins, creating a surge of anxiety as strong as the one he'd felt at the maintenance depot when he'd touched Pieter's mind. The sense of connection was the same, but there weren't any words.

"*Jack.*" Ethan shoved him. "*Go.*"

Jack snapped his attention away from the creature and stomped on the accelerator.

"What was that thing?" Ethan asked as they sped out of the loading bay.

"I don't know," Jack said, "but we have *got* to get you two your own portal crystals."

- - - - -

Upon returning to Icarus, Jack and his friends ran straight to Holden's cabin. They wanted to learn about the creature they'd discovered at the mill, but more pressing was regaining the ability to see the future. For that, they needed portals.

Holden was out, but Jack found the plastic toolbox in the spare bedroom in a pile of equipment salvaged from the island. He opened it on the workbench. Now that his parents' cabin was complete, Jack's grandfather was transforming the second room into a workshop.

"Niels left me another wand. He obviously knew I'd need one. Maybe he left something for both of you."

"There are hundreds of rods here," Sarah said as she poked through the pile. "What's the other stuff?"

Ethan removed a complex device with multiple chambers, connectors, and ports. "This is a nano-programmer. Why would he include that? The equipment to build nanobots was destroyed."

"There are more envelopes underneath," Sarah said.

Jack tipped the box to shift the rods out of the way, then dug out and opened an envelope with his name on it.

"Jewelry?" He picked out a ring that appeared to be made of steel, or possibly silver. It was broad, masculine, and decorated with a line of four amber gemstones. "Those are portal crystals. I can feel them."

"That's meant for me, then." Ethan took the ring and tried it on several fingers. He decided it fit best on the index finger of his left hand.

"Then these must be yours." Jack held out a pair of diamond-stud earrings.

Sarah lowered her gaze and accepted them. "Thank you, Jack."

He was glad that her head was still down as she worked the clasps—he felt his face warming. There was also a scrap of paper in the envelope. The words '*deal with it*' were scrawled in Niels' unsteady script. He crumpled the sheet before anyone else saw.

He tried to think of something clever and casual to say as she replaced her silver studs with the larger crystals, but failed. Fortunately, Ethan spared him further discomfort by repeating '*Shield*' several times.

"It's not working." Ethan jabbed his hand forward and repeated the command. "What's wrong?"

"Let me try," Jack said. "No, don't bother." He signaled Ethan not to remove the ring. "I can sense them from here. Just hold your hand steady." He concentrated and forged a weak shield—a wise precaution considering Ethan was pointing the ring at him. "Try again."

Ethan thrust his fist towards the center of the room. "Shield. *Whoa*. I can *see* it."

They all saw the shield. The overlapping fields generated by multiple portals formed a scintillating wall an arm's reach beyond his hand.

Jack reached out and pressed against it. "That's as strong as any I've ever created." The shield was hemispherical, partially wrapping above and around Ethan.

Ethan tightened and relaxed his fist. The barrier expanded and contracted. "*I can control it too*. Why couldn't I do it the first time?"

Sarah finished adjusting her new earrings. "Could you create a shield with your coin without Jack's help?"

He let the shield fade. "I never got the chance. Jack used it against Pieter before me."

"I wonder if I can do it." Sarah frowned in concentration and stopped at once. "No. Jack has to teach the crystals first."

"How do you know? You barely tried."

"There's no … connection."

"Then let's try something different," Jack said. "Ethan could do a half-sphere. I want to see if I can create a full one around you."

Sarah stood and brushed her hair away from her ears. She faced him and smiled. "I'm ready."

Jack was glad that her talent was seeing the future, not reading minds. He closed his eyes—not because he needed to—and concentrated. "I'll make it really weak. I don't know what'll happen when it closes you in."

"It's working." Her voice was full of awe as Jack shaped the barrier. "I've got it now."

He felt her taking over, but not like when Pieter seized control of his first wand. This was a gentle but firm handing over of power, although he sensed he couldn't have stopped her. Distance was a factor and Sarah's link to the AI through the earrings was stronger than his.

When he opened his eyes, she was standing in the center of the room, shrouded in a milky, pearlescent sphere. She stretched out her arms and pressed her hands to its inner wall. "Stand back."

Jack backed away and the sphere became more cloudy, as if Sarah was standing in a thick fog. His adrenaline spiked. "Are you all right?"

Sarah laughed. "I'm okay." She spread her arms and twirled in place. The sphere spun with her. She took a few steps and it followed, flowing around the furniture like a silk scarf.

"How are you keeping it from dragging through the floor?"

"I didn't even notice." Her voice was muffled behind the shield. "The AI must do that."

"So, do you have to teach the portals every spell?" Ethan asked.

"I don't know. Try skipping something. You've done that before."

Ethan opened the cabin door, pointed his ring at a rock on the gravel path, and said 'skip.' The stone rolled and bounced away.

"That was your best so far."

"Yeah." Ethan appeared troubled. "But something's not right. Let's try another experiment."

Sarah's shield turned opaque.

"Oh, come on. No one's gonna get hurt. I promise. I just want to understand the rules."

She allowed the shield to collapse so they could hear her clearly. "Rules? What rules?"

"Jack taught me how to use *skip*, but not *shield*. Later, I used *shield* on my own with a crystal he'd already used. But neither of us could use *shield* with these new crystals until Jack taught them. So, is he teaching *us*, or the crystals?"

This brought blank stares from both Jack and Sarah.

"Jack …" Ethan held his hand out. "Teach my ring a spell but don't tell me how it's done."

"Sure. Let's try something simple." He produced a bright light from the ring, then extinguished it.

"Now I'll try." Ethan raised his hand. "Light." The same light shone.

"I'm still confused," Sarah said.

Ethan devised several safe experiments involving water, wind, and fog. His process was slow and methodical but made sense. Eventually, they arrived at a definitive conclusion.

"Either we have to know the spell first," Ethan said, "or the portal has to know the spell. Also, Jack has to *enable* a crystal to make it work in the first place."

"I'm not sure about that one," Jack said. "My guess is that anyone who can sense portal crystals could activate them."

Ethan looked disappointed. "I was hoping we could learn new spells without Jack's help."

Sarah seemed relieved. "Don't you see? This is great news. If he has to teach the portals, then Pieter can't do anything with the stolen wand other than what Jack already taught it."

"So, what does Pieter's wand know how to do?"

Now it was Jack's turn to look depressed. "Unfortunately, quite a lot."

Chapter 25

James, Pieter typed, *please come see me when you have a moment.* He sent the text, then watched for James' reaction on Camera Two.

The message was unnecessary. Pieter's sway over his business partner was so great that he only had to imagine meeting and the man would respond. But he had to be careful how much direct control he exerted; he needed James to retain enough free will to make his own decisions.

The image on the monitor shifted and went dark as James reached into his suit jacket, then brightened and focused on the hardwood floor of his office.

As James read the text, Pieter sensed uncertainty, suspicion, and fading patience. He'd been staying at James' place for a week and refused every request to explain how he'd returned to Cirrus. He waited almost a minute before overriding the negative emotions with a more powerful one: curiosity.

James yielded and crossed the elegant foyer that separated the two halves of his mansion. The screen flashed marble and mahogany, leather and lead crystal, then a close-up of the polished door handle. Pieter blanked the wall of monitors.

"Are you all right?" James asked. "You look ill."

"Fine, thanks," Pieter said, although he hadn't fully recovered from the effects of Ethan's shield. "I've just received unpleasant news, that's all." He pushed an emotion through the portal: *'Sympathy.'*

"We've both had too much of that." James strolled to the window and gazed at his manicured gardens. "I'm always glad to help you, you know that." Then he faced Pieter. "Will you let me use your portal?"

Pieter suppressed a grin. He'd known where James was headed without the aid of the ring. James Gutierrez had always been the wealthier of the two, and therefore in the stronger bargaining position. Now, Pieter had something James wanted dearly.

Pieter pushed *regret*. "You don't want to go to Earth. I've only got a single working connection to my factory in Everett. Apparently, it's being raided as we speak." He sent, *'Newton.'*

James' suspicion flared. "What's going on? Does this have to do with Newton?"

"There's something I haven't told you." He projected a memory of that night: a machine wired to thousands of crystals.

"The destruction of the portals. You know what happened."

'Caught.' He allowed James to savor the minor victory before confirming. "That's right. And it might happen again." *'Fear. Loss.'*

"How?"

"Danny Kou."

"Your head of security?"

"A North Korean extremist, actually."

James leaned on Pieter's desk. "You're not making sense. How could a terrorist group have destroyed virtually every portal in a single night?"

Pieter pushed a stack of papers across the desk and tapped the name in the header.

James spun the stack to face him. "Holden Marke? What's he got to do with it?"

"This is a paper he wrote thirty years ago. It suggests a method for combining multiple wormholes, to create a single input with many outputs. It relies on the principle that portal crystals are identical."

"I'm familiar with his work, but he abandoned that study. He thought it would never be stable. What does that have to do with terrorists?"

"Marke was working with Danny." Pieter projected a little *'doubt'*—just enough to lead James to the next subject.

"That doesn't seem likely. Have you told anybody about this?"

"How could I? Danny was working for me." *'Suspicion.'*

"You think you'll be blamed. Why?"

'Guilt.' "Some years ago, Simon came to me with an idea for expanding on Doctor Marke's research. I gave him the funding to try."

"Did he get anywhere with it?

"In the end, he failed. But he made several important discoveries. That's when I realized how dangerous it could be if someone else succeeded."

"Dangerous?" James' face lit up. "It would revolutionize communications. *Again*. Instead of needing a matching portal for every phone at the switchboard end, we could create something like the older cellular network. It would be so much more efficient."

"And less secure."

James tossed that concern with a flip of his hand. "No less than before there were portals. True, it might be possible to eavesdrop on communications, but anyone who needs a secure channel orders a custom batch anyway."

"Danny attacked the US Navy with a custom batch. All he needed was access to a single crystal in Marke's lab to send poison gas through thousands of wormholes. Now that people know that cloned crystals can be merged, it could happen again." *'Fear.'*

James shuddered under Pieter's influence and his own memory of that night. "So, what's the solution? It's impossible to make every single pair unique."

Pieter said nothing but sent, *'Wrong'*, along with a touch of smugness.

"Unless … Ah, you've already figured it out, haven't you? But you can't tell anyone because it'll look as if you're part of the scheme, that Danny was still working for you. Why are you telling me this?"

"You're right. I know how to make unique pairs efficiently. Obviously I don't want a repeat of Newton, but I can't just pop up with a solution to a problem it looks like I created."

James stepped back from the desk. "You want *me* to pretend

that Aetherton developed the technique? Is that it? How long does it take to grow these crystals?"

"Same as any other. Six months."

"Six months for the first batch. Another two years to produce enough to repair our communications. Hmm." He began pacing the room.

Pieter was silent. *'I've got a secret.'*

James stopped. "Except that you've already built them. How many?"

"Enough to supply all government, military, and emergency service needs. I've moved them to a secure location." *'Opportunity.'*

James stroked his silver-gray mustache as he thought, then said, "No. I can't do what you're suggesting." He leaned on Pieter's desk again with both hands. "Whoever shows up with those crystals will be blamed for Newton."

"Or become a national hero." Pieter smiled and pushed his own desire through the portal. *'Praise. Fame.'*

"No way. It needs to be you. You're already involved."

"If I come forward, they'll arrest me and seize those crystals. All that'll do is delay the recovery until someone analyzes and copies my process. That'll take a year, and whoever works it out will gain a six-month lead on the market." Pieter stood and faced James. "The only question is who that will be."

James paced the room again. Pieter did too, circling the desk opposite James, sensing his internal conflict and countering every negative emotion: risk with *'reward'*, doubt with *'confidence'*.

"Okay," James said, "I can make this work. We've always had an interest in secure communications, and Marke's research wasn't a secret. But I expect something in return."

'Trapped.' "Name your price."

- - - - -

James' price—a recorded confession—was trivial in the grand scheme. It gave him the security he wanted, but by day's end he'd delete that video himself and forget about it. He also gained a controlling interest in Armenau Industries, but that control was an illusion. Eventually, Pieter himself intended to be recognized as the driving force behind the recovery.

He'd have given James anything he asked for; his plan relied on having those crystals shipped. He pressed the intercom button. "Simon. Come to my office. You have another delivery to make."

Chapter 26

The service for Niels was scheduled for the weekend. That gave Jack, Sarah, and Ethan several days to experiment with the portals. They were kept busy during daylight hours with a range of chores, everything from construction to gardening, but had free time in the evenings to gain a better understanding of how 'spells' worked.

They also finally sorted through the envelopes Niels hid in the toolbox. Jack delivered the sealed and addressed ones to grateful villagers, and they found an unlabeled packet containing two more wands. Sarah selected the slim, pencil-length one with a yellow crystal, but Ethan rejected a shorter, thicker one, saying the only wooden rod he'd carry was a Bo staff.

Jack helped Sarah learn to move objects and access portals he'd already identified. She discovered a method for creating fireballs by tapping into a fuel source with her wand and then using her earrings to ignite and throw the flaming material. They practiced that only when they had time to row a canoe to the far side of the island. It was fun for Sarah, who could soon hit a floating branch from fifty feet, and he got to spend almost every evening alone with her.

Holden worked with Ethan to refine the experiments, which confirmed their earlier results: if they knew how to do a spell, they could repeat it on another portal. But if Jack performed the spell first, then anyone could duplicate it using that same portal. There was a difference, though. They couldn't do a spell as well as Jack unless they worked with their own crystals.

"My theory," Ethan said one evening as they sat by the fireplace in Holden's cabin, "is that the AI thinks of Jack as a System Administrator, who can assign rights and privileges."

Sarah waved her wand, creating two wisps of white smoke that rose in a double-helix spiral. "Why do spells work better with our own crystals?"

"It might be like how the emoji selectors used to behave on our phones; they got to know our individual quirks."

They learned little about the creatures in the mill. Several of the villagers had heard rumors of genetically engineered predators, but no one had first-hand information. Anders, who'd taught microbiology at Reykjavik University, recalled a conversation with a colleague who was trying to isolate the genes responsible for obsessive behavior.

"He never told me where he was working," Anders said, "but he claimed to have made a major breakthrough during Cirrus' construction, one that would be important for its future."

"I met someone on the trip from Earth who said something similar," Ethan said. "She called them 'dragons' and said they ate only one type of prey until they starved to death."

"Maybe that's what the obsessive gene is for," Sarah said. "It'd be impossible to create a trap for just one kind of pest. But if they designed a predator that hunted a single prey, they could release it wherever there was a problem and not worry about it wiping out everything else; the creature in the mill was *fast*."

"So," Jack said, "Cirrus has dragons now? What's next? Unicorns?"

- - - - -

There weren't enough boats for the villagers to cross to the island at the same time, so Jack, Ethan, and Marten were employed as ferrymen. By late morning, everyone had assembled around the knoll overlooking the bay. They'd even freed Terrance. After hearing how Pieter used the ring to control him, no one still believed he'd acted on his own. Even Anders, who was always suspicious of Terrance, had forgiven him.

"My friends," Suresh began, "we are gathered here not to mourn, but to celebrate a remarkable life."

Suresh spoke at length about Niels, then invited others to do the same. As each of Niels' friends recalled their memories, there were tears, but as many laughs; Niels had been well respected and loved. Jack was left wishing he'd gotten to know the man better. All told, he'd spent less than three full days on Icarus Island. Sarah, who'd never met Niels in person, was as upset as Jack. She sat with him and held his hand for the duration of the service.

After the funeral, Jack and Ethan manned the boats again. Sarah took over Marten's job and made several trips herself. Eventually, only Natalya and a few others remained to harvest the remaining vegetables from Niels' garden.

"You can return to the village now," she said while digging a row of carrots. "We'll be a while yet."

"Thank you," Sarah replied before Jack could, "but we want to explore the island first. Where does that path go?"

Natalya, younger than Anders but still in her late sixties, stood and pressed her hands to her lower back to straighten her spine. "It leads to a hill. It's not very tall, but you can see the village from the top. Niels used to go there to relax before his knees gave him trouble. Keep an eye on the weather, though; it changes quickly at this time of year."

"We'll be home before dark."

The friends followed the narrow dirt path deeper into the pine forest. After an initial short climb, the ground leveled again. Jack had seen the island from the Vault and knew it spanned four miles, but Sarah wasn't interested in its geography. She strode ahead as if she remembered the route well—which she probably did.

Jack hurried to catch up to her. "Where are we going?"

"To the center of the island. There's something important there."

He pulled alongside her. "You can sense it too, can't you?"

"What is it? Why is it centered here?"

"What are you two talking about?" Ethan asked.

"It's hard to explain," Sarah said. "Whenever I paddled back to the island, it was almost like reconnecting to a portal. Like when we were experimenting with mind control and I sensed your emotions. Is it the same for you, Jack?"

"For me, it just feels familiar. As If I'm going home."

"I felt nothing at all," Ethan said.

"But then you didn't sense the connection through the portals as strongly as Sarah did, either."

"Could Niels have built another portal here?" Sarah asked. "A big one?"

"If he did, it wouldn't be working," Ethan said. "Pieter destroyed his fusion generator. Only the crystals cut from Grandpa's rods work without a power source."

Jack stopped walking abruptly. "He *did* build a portal here. The biggest one of all. Remember when Anders told us how they created this island."

"Yeah, they dropped an asteroid. What does that have to do with portals?"

"He said the impact disrupted the artificial gravity lines. Grandpa said that his brother was searching for those lines where construction forced them to the surface." He paused to let Ethan and Sarah work it out on their own. "Gravity generators are portals."

"They are?"

"Close enough. They're solid; so nothing passes through except gravity. But there are billions of lines of cells, stacked and layered like the steel wires in a tire. They focus the gravity from Cirrus' crust so it only pulls in two directions."

"Aren't those over a mile deep?" Sarah asked. "I thought you couldn't sense a portal from more than a few yards."

"Even if they were a *hundred* yards away, that'd be billions of them a hundred yards away. When we were in Grandpa's lab in Seattle, I sensed the portals in the Archive through the shielding, and there were only thousands there, not billions."

"That means the island is one big portal," Ethan said, "except it's solid. Do you think Niels knew?"

"I think Niels knew *before* the island was built. Anders said the impact was larger than expected and that Terrance was involved. I bet Niels planned to disrupt the lines when he created the island."

"Why? If the portals are solid, there's nothing he could do with them."

Jack hesitated.

"What's wrong?" Sarah asked.

Jack had only described everything that happened during Newton to his grandfather. If there was anything to make people think he was insane, this would be it. "I spoke to Uncle Carl."

"Carl? You mean your grandfather's half-brother?"

"When?" Ethan asked. "I thought he was dead."

"He is. Maybe. It was during the final moments of Newton. I was in the impactor room, trying to figure out how to destroy the portal network. I had a dream, or something like a dream, and Uncle Carl was there. He told me there are hundreds of places on Cirrus where the gravity lines are broken and buried near the surface, and that Niels hired him to find them. I've had that same dream hundreds of times. I didn't know it then, but Uncle Carl was always there. He explained that he experienced the same dream—the one I was having, except from his point of view—every time he stayed near one of these places."

"When was the last time?" Sarah asked. "How old was he? If it was something other than a dream, he might still be alive."

"He said it didn't work that way." Jack was relieved that his friends believed him. "For him, I was a different age each time he saw me. And not always older. He said we were sharing the dream, and even though it seemed to be the same time for us, we could have been decades apart."

"Yeah," Ethan said, "that makes sense."

"*What?* It hardly makes sense to me, and I'm the one who was having those dreams."

"Look, I can remember things two seconds into the future. We've proven that. I don't have long-term future memories the way Sarah does, but mine are clearer. That makes sense to me because I'm getting those memories back from the AI in the same context I create them. Sarah gets them in a context that's hours or weeks after th—"

"Months," Sarah said.

"Months," Ethan continued, "after they were created. Why is it so hard to accept that you're getting them years apart? And if you've had a similar dream hundreds of times, it'll stitch itself together from fragments and seem like the same one."

They resumed their hike, silently considering the implications of what they'd figured out. The hill at the island's center came into view before Sarah spoke again.

"Niels' gift wasn't just in getting memories, but in interpreting them. For him, the island might have been a sort of collector, or antenna, that allowed him to make lots of links. Maybe that's why he never left. He used the memories he collected over time to predict the future."

"So," Ethan said, "Niels built the island and created the massive portal, because the portal gave him the clarity to pick the winning lottery numbers, which made him enough money to build the island in the first place. Paradox, anyone?"

"We've dealt with paradoxes before," Jack said. "It's plausible."

"Jack," Sarah asked, "if this place is as connected as we think, why aren't you going nuts detecting other people's emotions?"

"If these places create links across time, then what Ethan says makes sense–there's no context for me to match them up with. I don't have future memories. My talent—moving the energy field—works in real-time. My bird dreams happened in real-time too."

"But those dreams of your uncle suggest you *can* see the future, even if only in one of these places. That means you should be able to learn how to remember things the way we've learned to control the field."

- - - - -

Jack closed his eyes, already certain that the attempt would fail. "I've spent my entire life blocking the AI."

"But that was from the feedback of emotion detectors," Sarah said. "You've always allowed the connection for the energy field. And there are no local detectors anymore. Just keep your eyes closed. We'll join you."

"We will?" Ethan asked.

"Yes." She glared at him. "We will."

"Oh, right. I'm here for you, buddy." He sat down and closed his eyes.

They'd found a carved, rustic log bench in a clearing at the summit of the hill, where Niels used to come to relax. Sarah decided it was the best place for Jack to try to remember the future, but just the idea was making him anxious. And the fear of linking to Pieter again had his heart pounding.

"Start with something simple," Sarah said, "like what's for dinner tonight."

Jack breathed deeply, forcing himself to relax. The sun was warm against his back in the chilly air, which reminded him of his recurring dream, so he chose the Vault as his focus. This was the first step in the visualization technique his therapist had taught him. Picturing a calm and safe location was supposed to reduce his anxiety, but he always found it hard to remove himself from the present. Even now, he couldn't stop imagining how they must look, sitting on a log bench with their eyes closed.

Ethan sat at the opposite end of the bench, with Sarah between them. Her hand rested near his and he was tempted to hold it, as they'd done during the service, but wondered what his cousin would say. He imagined Ethan looking at him from above with a confused expression.

Jack tilted his head back. *From above?*

"Uh, Jack?" Ethan mumbled.

Jack jerked his hand away from Sarah's and opened his eyes. "What?"

"That."

Ethan pointed to the ground in front of the bench where two ravens stood watching them.

174

Chapter 27

"Why are those birds staring at us?" Ethan asked.

The ravens reacted as if they were following the conversation. They looked at Ethan as he spoke, then focused on Jack. If birds had expressions, theirs would be 'expectant'.

"I don't know." Jack waved his hands. "Shoo." The ravens, one entirely black and the other black with a dull brown chest, took off and landed in a nearby tree.

"*You can talk to birds.* How?"

"*What?* That's ridiculous. I just scared them away. I wasn't …" Then he remembered imagining Ethan looking down at him, as if he were on the ground. He stood, gestured to the birds, and said quietly, "Come here."

The larger black bird cocked its head at him. Its smaller companion pecked at the tree trunk.

Jack palmed his face. "Yeah, that was foolish. I don't know why I thought—" The larger raven cawed, dropped from its perch, and landed where Jack had pointed.

Ethan jumped to his feet. "You *can* talk to them."

The raven recoiled from Ethan with a two-footed hop, then focused again on Jack.

Sarah leaned forward. "Look at its leg. It's still banded. You're controlling it through a portal."

Jack faced the second bird. "You too." He gestured to a spot on the ground near the first.

It plunged to land beside the other.

"That is *so* cool." Ethan tapered his reaction to a whisper so as not to scare the ravens, but they didn't seem bothered. "This one doesn't have a leg band, though. Why is it listening to you?"

"But it *has* a portal," Jack said. "I can sense it."

"I don't see one."

"It's inside. Maybe it bit its band off and swallowed it

accidentally."

"No," Sarah said, "this one is much younger. It might never have been banded. But ravens are corvids, and they swallow stones to help with digestion. It must have swallowed an object with a portal crystal. Like that bolt you found at the mill."

"Make them do something," Ethan said.

Jack frowned. "They're not toys."

"Better yet," Sarah said, "send them off and see if you can tell what they're seeing."

Jack looked at her dubiously. "I know what you're getting at. You're thinking that we're using the AI the same way, that we're accessing memories; in my case, other people's memories. But I've only ever done that in dreams. Also, these are birds, not people."

"They might not be as sophisticated as people, but they still have thoughts and memories."

"Can you tell what they're thinking?" Ethan asked. "Like you did with Pieter?"

Jack considered the birds as they watched him silently. "I get the sense that they're curious about us."

"Was it the same with the dragon?" Sarah asked. "When you knew it was hurt?"

He bobbled his head. "Kind of. I felt that it was in pain, not what it was actually thinking."

"With my memories, the first thing that comes to mind is usually correct. Priya says don't overthink. Give them a simple task. Have them look at something you can't see but one we can check later."

Jack heaved a sigh. "Fine." Then he said to the ravens, "Fly to the village."

Ethan laughed as they flew away. "See, you can control them."

Jack glared at him. "We don't know that. They seem to understand me, but they might just like hanging around people."

"Let's try something different, then." The birds were approaching the island's north shore. "Imagine the garden. Is

Natalya still there?"

Jack closed his eyes. "I don't think so."

"Can you *see* the garden?" Sarah asked. "Through their eyes?"

"Sort of. But I know what it looks like, so it's easy to picture it from above. I'm probably just imagining it."

"Make them go closer," Ethan said.

Jack sat on the bench and wrung his hands. "I really don't want to do this."

"What? Why?"

Sarah shushed him and sat beside Jack. "I'm sorry. I get it." She rested a hand on his knee. "But this isn't the same as Pieter controlling Terrance, and Ethan and I aren't controlling anyone when we remember things. Do you feel they'd do anything you wanted them to? Even if it hurt them?"

That was easy. "No. No way."

"So you're not really forcing them, are you?"

Jack sighed. "No. It's more like they're listening."

"Then *ask* them to go closer. Let them decide."

Jack didn't know how to ask the ravens to go closer. However, as with calling them to him, he merely imagined doing it and it happened.

"They just dove into the trees." Ethan laughed, then whispered to Sarah, "This is better than flying a drone." She gave him a dirty look.

"I think the garden's empty," Jack said, "but that doesn't prove anything. Natalya may have left by the time we get there."

"Ask them to go to the dock," Sarah said, "and see which boat Natalya left for us."

Two black specks rose into the sky and headed towards the water.

"I'm thinking the green canoe is still there. But I've got a one-in-three chance of being right. We need something more difficult." Recalling Sarah's earlier suggestion, he said, "Let's see what's for dinner."

The ravens soared over the lake, but by this time they were

over three miles away and nearly invisible.

"They're gone," Jack said.

Ethan squinted. "I can still see them."

"No, I mean, I can't sense them anymore. They're beyond range of the island." He drew his wand and concentrated. "I can open a wormhole to crystal in the leg band, but it's just wind and movement."

Ethan shrugged. "Well, that was an interesting experiment. But if it only works on the island, it's not that useful."

"And the sun's going down," Sarah said. "We should head back."

"Maybe it's useful after all," Jack said as they walked down the hill. "Niels must have had a good reason for hiring Uncle Carl to find zones where the gravity lines were broken. The place I met him in my dream is one of them. And it's real; Ethan and I were there in August. It's a lake in the Spine on a mountain called the Vault. I had the same feeling of familiarity there as I do here. What if they're connected the same way a regular wormhole is? Maybe I could see what's happening there."

"So," Ethan said, "we need to find another bird to send to the Vault."

"We'd still have to go there to confirm whatever Jack saw," Sarah said.

Jack pointed to the distant peak. "It's only a few hours away."

The garden came into view. Sarah searched for Natalya. "She's gone."

"That was a fifty-fifty thing. We've got two more tests to pass."

"Look." She pointed to the sky. "They came back."

Jack's own curiosity was enough to call the ravens down. They landed directly in front of him and stood attentively, like soldiers waiting for new orders.

"Well?" Ethan asked.

"My first thought was of tomatoes. And fish. My guess is … stew?"

"You know. If you're right, you've got an entire world of spies. We could find Pieter easily. Once we have a plan for getting the wand away from him, we can use the birds to search."

Jack's stomach knotted. Hunting Pieter wasn't something he was looking forward to, though he was starting to think it would eventually come to that.

"Thanks, guys." He dismissed the ravens. "I'll see you later."

- - - - -

When they reached the dock, they found that Natalya had left the green canoe for them. Ethan grinned and was about to speak when Jack cut him off. "It could still be chance."

Halfway across the lake, he sensed the fading familiarity. It was melancholic, like leaving home for the last time, except now he understood its source and knew it would be waiting for him whenever he returned.

They completed the journey, tied up the canoe, and walked to the village. Ethan took a deep breath and smirked. "Smells like fish stew to me."

"I smell it too," Jack said as they climbed the stone walkway to the lodge.

The front door burst open and Natalya stormed out. "*Thieves*." She thundered down the stairs brandishing a wooden ladle. "Go on. Off with you."

"It wasn't—" Jack started to protest their innocence, but Natalya barged through the group.

She picked up a stone and threw it at a raven. "That one stole one of my trout. And the other stole a tomato."

The ravens had followed Jack to the village and were perched on a nearby driftwood log. They darted into the trees before Natalya got close enough to swing her spoon.

"They came right through the kitchen window." She shook her ladle when one cawed, then strode furiously back to the lodge.

Ethan covered his mouth to suppress a laugh. Natalya, a former Russian Air Force pilot, was not someone he wanted to upset. He turned to the ravens, perched high in a fir tree. "Guys, you were only supposed to see what was for dinner, not bring it back."

"That proves it," Sarah said. "The bond was real."

"I'll be more careful next time," Jack said. But he was fighting back laughter, too.

Chapter 28

Priya missed Niels' funeral. She apologized when she showed up later that evening, even though she had an excellent reason. She sat cross-legged on her bedroom floor in front of the portal, but didn't seem very relaxed. "Pieter's thugs were following me today."

Sarah gasped. "Are you sure?"

"They weren't hiding. They drove right past the house. I think your idea of using a radio signal to locate the wormhole was actually a Traveller-memory."

Jack's father had expanded on the Faraday cage concept. Instead of enclosing the portal frame in wire mesh, he'd built a closet-sized mesh box in the corner of Holden's living room, and placed a second wire box for the frame inside. Together, the two worked as an airlock for radio waves.

Ethan smirked. "Good luck finding us now. They—"

Priya interrupted with a raised hand. "There's more. When I logged on to the department's servers this morning, I found that my files are locked. The authorization for that—and for bugging my suite—could only have come from a very high level." Her shoulders slumped. "Pieter is using Edmond to spy on me. Officially, I'm still working for the UN and the case is open, but only for another day. After that … well, I'm sure they'll break in and find the frame."

"What can we do?" Jack asked.

"Can you destroy the crystal in Edmond's ring the way did during Newton?"

"Not from here. I'd have to be near it."

Priya sighed. "Then you'll have to come to the capitol with me."

"When?"

"Tomorrow. I told him I have new information and he's

agreed to meet me. Pieter won't try anything before then if he thinks I have real evidence."

"Okay, but I'll need a working portal crystal. I can't bring my wand."

She thought for a moment before nodding. "I'll get you something."

- - - - -

In the morning, Jack and Sarah were waiting in Holden's cabin when Priya opened the wormhole. She tipped a cardboard box, tumbling six identical devices onto the carpet. "I found these."

"Are those phones?" Sarah asked.

"Our IT department has boxes of them that missed being recycled. The techs have been configuring them to work with the existing networks, but these are too old and don't have the right encryption firmware, so they're being tossed. Will you be able to use one to break Edmond's ring?"

Jack entered the large cage and closed the mesh door behind him. Then he opened the smaller cage that held Holden's portal frame and leaned through the wormhole.

"I can feel them, but the energy field is really weak."

"Is that a problem?"

"It shouldn't be. Let me come through and try a shield."

Priya scooted backwards to make room. She also cranked the music to mask their voices; they had to assume someone was monitoring the surveillance device in the living room.

Jack stood, pointed the phone to a clear spot in the center of the room. "Shield." He held the phone steady for a few seconds, then wrinkled his nose and repeated the command.

"What's wrong?"

He thumped the invisible barrier against the bed, leaving a depression in the blanket. "It's working, but these old data crystals are very thin."

"Can you draw enough power to break Edmond's ring?"

He flicked the phone at a pillow and bounced it against the

ceiling. "Yeah, that should be plenty. But too strong of a shield might shatter the phone's crystal."

"Let's hope we aren't forced to use that function then. We only need them to disconnect the ring and for Sarah and Ethan to access their AI memories. You can come across now," she said to Sarah. "Where's Ethan?"

Jack snickered. "Last I saw him, he was showing off his bullet wounds to the younger kids." Priya rolled her eyes.

"He's coming," Sarah said. "He was feeling paranoid about leaving his ring behind and went to double-check that his father put it in the truck with our wands."

Ethan returned to Holden's cabin and scrambled through the portal after Sarah. Then Nathan arrived to help Victor move it. Everyone had agreed that keeping it in the village was too dangerous. While Jack was disabling Edmond's ring, his father would move Holden's portal to the Spine.

Priya passed three of the phones through the wormhole to Victor, then handed Ethan a coin. "I want ten accurate predictions. If you miss one, you both go back."

Ethan obliged by taking a phone and putting it in his pocket. He flipped the coin. "Tails."

"What do you mean, we *both* go?" Sarah asked.

"If Ethan can't predict a coin toss, we've got to assume that you can't remember reliably either."

Ethan stretched out his hand. The others leaned forward. He uncovered the coin, revealing tails. "See, no problem."

"Nine to go," Priya said. Ethan's smug expression faded.

To Jack's great relief, Ethan correctly guessed the remaining tosses, otherwise he'd have to work alone.

"You all know the plan?" Priya asked. "Do you need to see the map again?"

"I think I have it memorized," Jack said, "but let's have another look to be sure."

She spread the map on her bed and pointed to a bend in the road. "We're here. Wait until the next power outage at nine-thirty, then follow this street to Capitol Boulevard. Then take Capitol Way up to Fourteenth. Edmond takes a fifteen-minute walk at ten-thirty. That gives you an hour to get there. I'll try to guide him to the Tivoli fountains, but pay attention because he might go anywhere. Got it?"

They agreed and Priya left, closing the bedroom door behind her to block the surveillance camera's view.

"I'd be happier if I could create a shield without trashing the phone," Ethan said. "Should we try while we're waiting?"

"That's not a good idea," Sarah said. "Neither of us can sense the stress on a crystal the way Jack can. If we wreck the portals, we lose access to our future memories too."

"What about creating a new spell for it? One that cuts off before overloading."

"That may be possible," Jack said. "Let me try something."

He created a shield several times until he was satisfied that it could take a hit without overloading the matrix. "I've assigned the word Block as the trigger." He passed the phone to Ethan.

Holding the phone in his right hand, Ethan said, "Block." He reached with his left but his fingers met no barrier.

Jack frowned. "That's not good."

Sarah held out her hand. "Let me try." Ethan passed her the phone and she told it to 'Block'. Then she pushed it against the wall with no resistance.

Ethan began pacing the floor. "We're in trouble."

"No," Jack said, "you predicted a coin toss, so you still have your two-second warning. But there's something different with the connection here. It's weaker."

"Why should that make a difference? Isn't it the same AI?"

"Yeah, but the portals you've been using at home don't need electricity, they're entangled with a common power source. These phones need batteries. Also, they're at least twenty years old— people used to select emojis manually."

"That's it," Sarah exclaimed. "They don't have emotion detectors. We can receive through them, but the link is too weak to send. We can't tell the AI what we want."

"But Jack can. Why him and not us?"

"Jack's different. Sorry, Jack. You know what I mean. The same rules don't apply."

"It's okay. I get it." Jack took the phone back and started dialing.

"Who are you calling?"

"Nobody. I've got an idea."

He dialed a string of numbers and pressed *send*. Then he pressed the phone against the bed to make a curved indentation in the blankets. He passed the phone to Ethan. "Just hit redial."

Ethan pressed the button, forming the same shield.

"It works." He disconnected the call and the shield faded. "What did you do?"

"It's an old phone, so it stores its contacts onboard instead of in the cloud. That means when you dial a number, it tries to send that data through its portal. The one I dialed doesn't work anymore, but the AI still knows what I *want* it to do. All I've done is associate that number with a shield."

"Whose number did you use?"

"A pizza place in Fairview." He shrugged. "It was the first thing that came to mind."

"So, if someone calls for a pizza, they'll get a shield." Ethan mimed an explosion coming from the phone. "Do you not see a problem with that?"

"Jack still has to enable the portal," Sarah said. "Don't you?"

"Um ... I'm not actually sure. Try entering the number on your phone and see what happens."

Sarah dialed the number Jack gave her. Instantly, a shield sprang from her phone.

"Oops."

"That's gonna be a hell of a surprise to anyone who calls for a pizza." Ethan's shock faded and he began laughing.

"It's a Cirrus number. No one will be ordering takeout for a long time."

"Maybe not," Sarah said, "but you'd better use extra digits if you create more spells. Anyway, we've got to get moving."

Ethan climbed on Priya's bed and gently slid the window open, careful not to alert Mrs. Chen upstairs. As if on cue, the scheduled rolling blackout hit and the house became silent.

Jack climbed onto the windowsill and breathed the mid-October morning air; Earth smelled so different from Cirrus. A blanket of red, orange, and yellow leaves covered the lawn, although most of the foliage was still on the trees. That was different from Cirrus, too; genetically engineered trees dropped their leaves over a period of months, not weeks.

"Is it clear?" Jack asked.

"Only if you can be out of sight in two seconds. Get ready to run when I say so."

After a brief wait, Ethan tapped him on the shoulder and whispered, "Go".

Jack dropped to the ground as quietly as possible and sprinted around the corner of the garage, out of sight of the upstairs windows.

Mrs. Chen's yard had many trees, and a tall hedge between the neighboring properties. The sheltered spot beside the garage blocked every viewing angle except the one from the street, but he kept checking all directions until Sarah slid in beside him with a huge grin. She looked as excited about their new adventure as he felt nervous. He was glad for her company, but wished he shared her confidence—she'd have gone through with the plan even without her ability to see the future.

It was a full minute before Ethan joined them. "Had to close the window. Are we good to go, Jack?"

"Oh. Yeah." Jack was surprised that they automatically assumed he was their leader. He reached out with his talent, lifted the gate's latch, and pushed it open. It was only a minor gesture, but he wanted to show that their faith in him wasn't groundless. "Let's go."

They passed through the gate and veered onto the sidewalk

without looking back. If Mrs. Chen was watching, she'd have had only the briefest moment to spot them before they were under the cover of the trees again.

Sarah admired the well-kept yards as they walked. "This is a nice neighborhood. It's so quiet."

"Not having cars makes a big difference," Jack said. "The last time we were on Earth we could hardly talk on the streets for the noise."

"Ethan." Sarah sounded peeved. "What are you doing?" His head was in the familiar texting-while-walking position.

"I'm putting the shield phone number as a contact on my home screen so I don't have to remember it. You should too."

"Oh. Good idea." She drew her phone to do the same. "But don't let anyone see you."

"Why not? The shield is invisible."

"That's not what I mean. Few people on Earth have phones anymore. If someone sees you using one, they'll get suspicious."

Jack stopped next to a large hedge and watched the houses while Sarah and Ethan finished creating shield shortcuts.

Once they got out of Priya's neighborhood, the streets were no longer entirely empty. A light but steady stream of traffic—mostly buses—passed them on Capitol Boulevard. The growl of their motors was unexpected; open rear panels exposed oversized hydrogen plants, squeezed into cavities that previously held batteries.

"What's all this?" Ethan stopped walking when they reached an overpass. For as far as they could see in either direction, a solid mass of cars—parked end-to-end—filled half of the six lanes on each side of the highway.

Sarah stopped, too. "Priya told me they've been clearing the streets for months. Vehicles that aren't running get towed to the freeway. She says it's the same everywhere."

But it wasn't just derelict cars. The city's troubles were fully revealed by acres of mismatched tarps stretched between vehicles, and small groups of pedestrians milling about in the narrow gaps.

"There are people living there," Jack said. He had to push feelings of guilt aside to continue walking. On Cirrus, it seemed inevitable that more power plants would fail, but they'd always have enough food. Earth, however, hadn't produced sufficient crops to feed itself for decades. Sarah and Ethan recognized this too, and no one spoke for the rest of the trip.

Jack forced himself to focus on their task as they entered the capitol campus. "We've got fifteen minutes to spare. We should keep walking so we don't look suspicious."

The buildings that made up the campus surrounded several blocks of gardens and memorials. With a mobile cell tower set up to service the capitol, it was a popular place; hundreds of people strolled along its walkways.

Ethan pointed to a bench. "I'll sit over there where I can see everything. If I pull my hoodie over my head, it'll mean I've spotted trouble."

"We'll keep walking in a loop until we spot Priya," Sarah said.

Her intuition had told her that the encounter would happen near the Attorney General's office, so that's where they started. Jack kept checking on Ethan while she watched for Priya.

Sarah nodded just as she and Jack completed their first loop. "There they are. He's on his phone. Hopefully he'll be distracted and we can get close without being seen."

"Then let's go this way so we can come up from behind." With all the intersecting paths through the gardens, it wasn't difficult to find one that crossed Priya and Edmond's.

Jack adjusted his pace so Edmond wouldn't notice them approaching from an angle. At fifty feet, his portal sense let him visualize the ring's crystal as a bright pinpoint of light set into the gold band. He reached out, made the connection, and prepared to shatter it the moment he was close enough. Then he saw Priya's face. Although he was too far away to hear what Edmond was saying, her expression said that something was seriously wrong.

Chapter 29

"Excellent news." Edmond was smiling as he disconnected. "It seems we'll have you back sooner than we thought."

"How's that?" Priya could hardly believe what she'd overheard. "You said we're dropping the investigation into Armenau Industries."

"We've just learned that there are now enough crystals for all government needs. And this isn't a temporary patch. These are unique pairs. This will be a permanent solution."

"Unique? That's the evidence we've been looking for. It proves Reynard knew about Newton. He had to have started growing those crystals months before—"

Edmond stopped walking. "Hold on, Priya. I didn't say it was Armenau. The supplier is Aetherton."

"James Gutierrez? That's Reynard's business partner. They're working together. Why else would he have grown millions of crystals before they were needed?"

"Aetherton is one of the world's largest suppliers of communications crystals. They've had government contracts for decades. It's certainly in their best interests to develop more-secure technologies. As I understand it, their process is no more expensive than cloning. There's no reason they wouldn't have switched their production."

"Then why didn't they announce it six months ago?"

Edmond shrugged. "A simple advantage in the marketplace."

"But that doesn't—"

"Priya, I know you've been working hard on this, but it's no longer our case. The FBI has shifted their focus to Gutierrez, and the only connection between him and Pieter is their shared ownership of assets on Cirrus. There's no evidence of wrong-doing. And even if there were, it's unlikely they'll pursue him with much vigor; he's shortened this crisis by at least a year. I'm taking the train to DC tomorrow. They're drawing up a plan for distributing the new crystals and I want our department near the top of the list." Edmond resumed his stroll. "With any luck, we'll have communications and transport to Cirrus in a few months."

- - - - -

Jack and Sarah were too far away to follow the conversation, but could tell that Priya wasn't happy. She'd stopped walking and was arguing fiercely, naming *Reynard* and *Gutierrez*.

Jack quickened his pace. "This is our best chance." After passing within an arm's reach, he motioned for Sarah to take the next fork in the path. He shook his head at Ethan.

Ethan saw the signal and hurried over. "What's wrong?"

"I made a mistake. When I tested the phone in Priya's room, there was extra energy nearby from Grandpa's portal. But the phone's crystal is too small and there's not enough now. I can't break it."

"Does that mean our shields won't work either?"

"It means they'll never be as strong as they'd be on Cirrus."

"Doesn't Edmond take a walk every day? We can find more portals and try again."

"We won't have another chance," Sarah said. "He's leaving tomorrow."

"So, what do we do?" Ethan asked. "We can't just knock him down and steal his ring." He looked over at Edmond, as if considering his chances. "Can we?"

"*No,*" Sarah snapped. "*We can't*. But what *are* we going to do?"

"I've got to get closer," Jack said.

"*Stop that.*" Sarah slapped Ethan's chest because he was still sizing up Edmond. "How much closer?"

"A lot. I need to touch the ring. I'll have to shake his hand."

"If you get too close, Pieter might recognize you."

"We have to take that chance. I'll only need a second, but we've got to go now. They're heading to his office."

Ethan resumed his position as observer. Jack and Sarah hurried along a different path to get ahead of Priya and Edmond, then doubled back to intercept.

"Oh, man." Jack fidgeted with the phone in his pocket. "How should we do this?"

"Relax. I have an idea. Just play along." Sarah waved, then veered directly in front of the very surprised detective and extended her arms for a hug. "Priya, I didn't expect to see you here." Then she stepped back and slid an arm around Jack's shoulders. "This is my boyfriend, David. David, this is my cousin, Priya."

Priya's mouth hung open and Jack's anxiety vanished. He'd always viewed Priya as confident and in control, even intimidating. But Sarah had baffled her and defused his nerves in one stroke. Instead of panicking, he grinned and extended his hand. "Hi."

"Um … hello." Priya shook his hand. "David? It's nice to meet you." She paused again and raised her eyebrows at Sarah. "Boyfriend? That's new."

Jack understood that Sarah was making things up as they went along, but wished she'd given him a warning. She began telling Priya a story of how they'd met, leaving him and Edmond to themselves.

He offered his hand to Edmond. "Hi."

Edmond reached to shake Jack's hand, then pointed a finger. "Have we met? I know you from somewhere."

"No, sir." Jack kept his hand out and forced a smile. "I'm new in town."

Edmond's accusatory finger didn't budge. "I'm certain we've met. Where are you from?"

Jack sensed another presence; Pieter was watching. His hand had only been on offer for seconds but it was turning into a lifetime. Sarah and Priya had stopped talking and were staring at Edmond.

"Seattle," Jack said. "My class took a tour of the capitol buildings in June. Maybe you saw me then?"

"No." Edmond's brow furrowed. "That's not it."

... I see you ...

Jack's heart raced. *He'll arrest me if I run. I need a distraction.* He looked over Edmond's shoulder, hoping Ethan was near.

... grab him ...

Edmond, reacting to Pieter's command, noticed Jack's extended hand and grasped it firmly. That was all Jack needed.

The combination of energy field and dark matter was nowhere near as strong as on Cirrus, but there's no substitute for proximity. In the fraction of a second before he severed the tiny wire to the ring's battery, Jack felt Pieter's rage rising.

Edmond reacted to the change in mood, too. He inhaled sharply, as if he'd received an electric shock, and squeezed Jack's hand harder. It happened so fast that Jack had no time to pull away from the crushing grip.

"Ow."

Edmond noticed Jack's pained expression. "Sorry." He visibly relaxed as Pieter's influence faded. "My mistake. I must have been thinking of someone else." He released Jack's hand. "Priya, I didn't know you had family here?"

As Jack calmed, Priya picked up the thread. "My sister-in-law's cousin, actually."

"It was nice to finally meet you, Priya," Jack said. "But we've really got to go. We've got company coming." *And they'll be armed.* He hoped she'd picked up on the hint.

"Take care," Priya said as he and Sarah wandered away. "Even on foot, the street is a *hazardous place.*" She turned to Edmond. "I'll walk with you to your office."

As soon as they were far enough away, Sarah said, "Pieter saw you, didn't he?"

"Yeah, and he's furious."

Ethan rushed over. "Did you get it?"

"I broke the ring, but Pieter was watching. We've got to get out of here."

"We can't go back to the house," Sarah said. "It'll take too long."

"We don't need to. Priya said the street is a 'hazardous place'."

Ethan glanced around. "Yeah, especially if Pieter's goons are on their way."

"That's not what she meant. Remember the map? There's a park on the other side of the highway, and a pond at one end called Hazard Lake. Priya's lived here for a couple of months and usually walks through the park to work. I'm betting one of the neighboring streets is called Hazard Place, and she wants us to meet there."

"Maybe," Sarah said. "But let's at least get off the street before we're spotted. We can wait for her in the park."

Jack resisted the urge to run and attract more attention as they hurried away from the memorials. Watershed Park was beyond the Fourteenth Avenue overpass, only two blocks ahead, but it seemed like hours before they reached the highway.

At the crest of the overpass, Sarah started running. "Let's go. They'll be here in a minute."

"Where are they coming from?" Jack asked.

"That's them." She pointed north, to where the highway curved out of sight three hundred yards away. A few buses and semis moved in the free lanes beside the permanently parked cars, but no private vehicles.

Jack watched the highway while he ran. A single, loud engine thundered above the rest of the traffic. Then a black SUV rounded the corner, passing other vehicles as if they were standing still.

"Faster," he shouted.

It was a cool morning and would have been a pleasant one for running if they were doing it willingly. But the SUV was flying. It swerved past a bus and flung itself onto the exit ramp.

The ramp merged into westbound traffic, heading towards the capitol. That didn't deter the driver, though. He attempted a U-turn onto the overpass, but his speed was too great. The black Chevy slid and bounced over a dirt strip at the intersection, creating a swirling dust cloud before colliding with an oncoming bus.

Please be wrecked, Jack thought, but the Chevy's engine roared as the driver sped away from the scene. The collision had caught the bus at a glancing angle and the only damage was shattered windows.

"We're out of time," Jack called. "Into the trees."

Sarah and Ethan were several paces ahead. They leapt over the low guardrail and plunged into the park. Jack followed without checking on their pursuers; a stumble now would be the end of the chase.

Horns sounded from the roadway, followed by squealing tires on pavement; the Chevy had encountered oncoming traffic from the northbound off-ramp. A staccato volley of gravel against the metal guardrail told Jack exactly where they'd stopped. Despite being in the forest, he was still close enough to hear the vehicle's doors slam and men shout.

Ethan was leading their charge through the brush, using his two-second warning to avoid obstacles. "Which way?"

Jack pictured Priya's map. "There should be a creek straight ahead with a path on the other side."

The SUV's engine revved again.

"They're splitting up and heading to the far end of the park," Sarah said.

"Jump," Ethan warned.

The creek was too wide to leap across where they emerged from the trees, but the water was low in the fall and he'd picked a route with patches of exposed gravel and solid footing. They made it across without even getting their shoes wet. A scramble up the short bank on the other side and another quick dash through the trees led them to a hard-packed gravel path.

Ethan stopped and waited until Jack and Sarah caught up. He was about to say something when two loud splashes and an angry shout interrupted him; they had only a thirty-second lead. He turned south and sprinted away.

The path under Jack's feet was solid, with a thick covering of dry, fallen leaves. He ran without worrying about how much noise he made, but had gone only a hundred yards when Ethan reached a fork.

"Which way?"

"It doesn't matter," Sarah said. "It's a loop. They meet up at the far end and there's more than one person following us. They'll split up."

Ethan chose left. "You got any magic tricks that'll slow them down?"

"I can't dig a pit for them to fall into, if that's what you're hoping for," Jack said. "The crystals in these phones are too small."

"We can't keep running," Sarah said. "The ones who drove off will come at us from the other end."

"I know, I know." Jack realized his friends were trusting him to decide. *I wish I could see the future too.*

Ethan glanced to his left. "I hear traffic."

"We're right at the northern edge of the park. But we need to go south to find Priya." Though they'd been on the path for less than a minute, they'd already reached another fork. A signpost at the intersection pictured a left-branching path leading to an exit. "Go straight."

Ethan sped past the sign, pulled out his phone, and prepared to dial up a shield. Sarah did the same.

Jack estimated they'd been running for less than two minutes, but they were already nearing the far end of the park and the second group of pursuers. He also realized that the forest was so dense that they needed to get just thirty feet off the trail to be completely hidden. He was about to shout directions to Ethan to leave the path when another fork came into view.

"Right," Jack shouted. "Go right."

Ethan rounded corner at full speed and slipped, leaving a long, shallow gouge in the dirt. Without even concentrating, Jack drew on his phone's energy field to pick up and scatter wads of fallen leaves over the mark.

"That loops back to the start," Sarah said when she reached the intersection.

She was right. A brief glimpse at the signpost map told Jack that the other half of the loop twisted through the woods and met up at this intersection. They had less than a minute to hide.

The trail dipped and crossed the creek at a bridge, then climbed again and headed south.

"Here," Jack called at a sharp bend. "This is as close as we'll get to the road. Take cover."

Ethan ducked into the trees. Sarah followed. The undergrowth was thick, and they struggled to move into the denser bush.

Sarah stopped and looked back. There was fear in her voice. "They're coming."

Chapter 30

Ethan braced his phone and prepared for a fight.

"Wait." Jack placed his hand in front of his cousin. "I need your portals."

"What are you going to do?" Sarah asked.

"This." He made a sweeping motion with his phone, causing thousands of leaves to leap into the air.

Knowing the AI could read and interpret his thoughts, Jack gathered the energy from the three portals and swirled the leaves into columns, then willed the AI to finish the task. Seconds later, three ugly trees stood in the gap between himself and the trail.

"Oh, Jack." Sarah's voice melded pity and mirth. "They look like Christmas trees."

Ethan choked back laughter.

"That's not … I tried … it's the best I can do."

Footfalls. Someone was running towards them.

Sarah raised her phone. "Let me fix it."

Jack felt her trying to take control of the fields and softened his mental grip.

She waved her hand and the leaves flowed like paint. It took only seconds for her to create a more natural arrangement. The trees wouldn't pass close inspection, but her finishing touches made them more realistic.

Jack held his breath as the runner passed, unseen behind the wall of leaves. He'd come from the west, from the loop's other side. Had they continued, they'd have certainly run into him. Now he was moving north, towards the bridge.

"C'mon," Ethan whispered.

"You two go," Jack said. "I'll hold the trees up."

Sarah started to protest, then angry voices shouted from the intersection.

"It's okay." Jack waved her away. "You can't go far. Your

phone is holding the better part of this illusion. But you can at least get out of sight."

Sarah went first, picking her way through fallen branches, trying not to make noise.

A third voice joined the argument as the two chasers who'd followed through the park met up with the driving group.

"Go," Jack whispered when he could no longer hear Sarah.

Ethan nodded, then moved quickly, making almost no sound. His talent let him place his feet where no branches hid under the leaves.

Jack moved slowly when his cousin caught up to Sarah. His caution wasn't just for stealth; he had to keep part of his attention on the illusion. Now wasn't the time to experiment with the AI, to see if it would hold three separate fields when he turned away. He'd covered half the distance when Ethan whistled softly, signaling him to stop.

Gravel crunched underfoot as someone approached the corner. Jack froze. The footsteps stopped. He held his breath.

"What the ..." A confused voice filtered through the wall of foliage, followed by snapping branches as the runner stepped off the path.

Caught. Jack abandoned the illusion and launched the leaves. The trees dissolved and wrapped themselves around Pieter's thug. There was a muffled shout as the man—now with a giant, autumn-colored beach ball for a head—staggered and swatted the churning debris.

"Hurry," Sarah shouted.

Jack directed the field to cocoon the man in a thick, full-body coat of leaves, then gave him a shove and tumbled him off the path.

"Run." He bounded after his friends.

His grip on the leaves was slipping away, so he released them and shook the surrounding trees with as much force as the small phone crystals could muster. Thousands more dry, colorful leaves drifted to the forest floor, masking their escape route.

Fifty feet into the woods, a gunshot echoed from the path.

"*Duck.*" Jack scurried behind a tree.

"I think he's just calling the others," Ethan said. But he sheltered behind a trunk, too.

Jack checked the sun filtering through the forest's thinning canopy. "South is that way."

Ethan angled away, walking quietly now. Jack and Sarah followed in his footsteps to avoid snapping hidden branches. A stream, barely an inch deep, meandered south. Ethan followed it to a culvert, then climbed a bank and stopped near the road, being careful to remain hidden between trees. Traffic was sporadic but passing at high speed.

"You're not doing what I think you're doing," Jack said as Ethan ground his shoes into the dirt for better grip. "Are you?"

Ethan looked over his shoulder and grinned. Without bothering to look, he sprinted onto the roadway just as a bus passed.

Jack swore and climbed the bank with Sarah. They spotted Ethan across the road, waiting on a narrow path a dozen feet above the road.

He lifted a broken branch and held it out like a starting flag. "Get ready."

"You're nuts," Jack yelled. The slope on the far side of the road was densely treed, but a searcher in an approaching car would see them before they reached it. "This isn't a coin toss."

"Listen," Sarah said, and Jack heard voices in the forest. "Pieter's men will be here in less than a minute. We have to trust Ethan." She twisted her shoes into the road's shoulder.

Ethan straightened his arm. Sarah braced.

No, no, no, Jack thought, but the pursuing voices were growing louder. He crouched beside Sarah, listening to the unseen traffic. A large vehicle was approaching.

Ethan dropped his arm. "*Now.*"

Sarah reacted first, leaping into the street at Ethan's signal. A car sped past and she landed right behind it. Jack sprang after her as a bus loomed in the far lane, then passed a fraction of a second before she reached it. The bus's wake nearly spun him off his feet, and he skidded in the loose gravel on the road's shoulder. It had all happened so fast that neither driver saw them.

Jack leapt off the road, following Sarah and Ethan over the rise and through a hundred yards of forest. The twisting path connected to a dead-end street in a quiet neighborhood with manicured lawns and cedar fences.

"Where's the lake?" Ethan asked.

"It should be another block away." Jack leaned against a fence post and took several deep breaths. "We need to get off this road fast. If they followed us from the park, they'll end up right here too."

Sarah, who'd been competing in Caerton's marathons for the past three years, began jogging, followed by Ethan. Jack was in good shape but he lagged behind—until he heard horns and screeching tires.

Wordlessly, the three friends sprinted for the next intersection, knowing that Pieter's men were crossing the road behind them. They maintained that pace until they turned the corner.

"That's it." Jack stumbled and collapsed on the sidewalk. "I'm done. I can't take another step. We have to hide."

Ethan hauled Jack to his feet and pointed into an open garage at the end of the closest driveway. "There."

"Wait," Sarah said. A car was rounding a corner half a mile away. "It's Priya."

Jack wiped the sweat from his eyes. "Are you sure?"

"I've driven that car, remember."

"Yeah," Ethan said. "How could we forget?"

Ethan loved cars but had never driven a full-sized one; the driving age in Washington had risen to twenty-one a decade before he got the chance. Sarah, despite being years too young, drove Priya's classic seventy-fifth anniversary Mustang through Seattle hours before Newton. Her first and only driving experience had been instrumental in their escape from Pieter Reynard.

Priya spotted them. The growl of her hydrogen-fueled V8 swamped every noise in the neighborhood as she sped up abruptly. In seconds, she was sliding to a stop beside them. The convertible top was down. Ethan took the passenger seat, and Jack and Sarah hopped over the side and tumbled into the tiny rear seats. Priya was already moving before they twisted themselves into sitting positions.

"Where are we going?" Sarah asked.

"I'm going to Everett. You're all going back to Cirrus. The portal is under that blanket."

As Priya careened onto Henderson Boulevard, Jack turned and lifted a corner of the fabric covering a flat, square panel wedged under the trunk-mounted spoiler. He recognized Holden's portal lying face-up, inactive.

Sarah ducked low in her seat. "Get down."

When either Sarah or Ethan gave a warning, Jack knew better than to ask questions. He scrunched as low as he could. "Ow. Ethan, move your seat."

Ethan pulled the front passenger seat forward to give him more room, then slid below the dashboard.

The car's engine thundered as four-hundred and fifty horsepower shoved its passengers backwards. Jack couldn't see what was happening, but Priya had apparently decided that they needed to be going very fast. Then she down-shifted and threw the Mustang into a turning circle.

"You can get up now, but hang on. We're taking a shortcut."

With no northbound freeway access, Henderson Boulevard led straight into the Capitol. Instead of taking the overpass, Priya cut across the oncoming lane and made a sharp U-turn onto the off-ramp. In pre-Newton times, the maneuver would have been suicidal. Now, there wasn't enough traffic to worry about. The car's tail end swung furiously and its tires smoked as she drifted onto the ramp, then accelerated onto the highway.

"Victor," Jack's father shouted, "turn that frame away, quick." The voice came from under the blanket.

"Dad?" Jack spun in his seat, pulled off the portal's covering, and experienced an immediate surge of vertigo. He swayed and grabbed the back of his seat. Sarah jumped to support him, but he said, "Stay back. The portals are coupled." He leaned away from the frame and the dizziness faded.

A few more seconds of confused scuffling sounded from the Cirrus side while Priya pushed the Mustang to its cruising speed. A cloud of Cirran dust that drifted through the wormhole was stripped away in the car's slipstream.

"That's better," Nathan said. "Jack, what direction is your frame pointing?"

"Straight up. It's hooked to the trunk of Priya's car."

"Oh, that explains things. Give me a minute."

"What do you mean the portals are *coupled*," Sarah asked.

"It means we have to hold on to the frame. Grab that side but don't get too close. Uncle Nathan is going to rotate his frame and this one will try to follow."

Sarah copied Jack, pushing on her side of the frame as it lifted by itself. "Why is that happening?"

"You can move a wormhole as much as you want, but you can't change the relative angle of a portal without causing the other side to follow."

"That doesn't make sense. We've always been able to turn our phones around."

"Those crystals are too small to feel the effect. This one's big enough that even the air passing through creates a drag."

"That should do it," Nathan said.

Jack leaned over the opening. The wormhole caused no more vertigo, but the view was unsettling. Nathan had fastened the frame upside-down to the truck's roof rack. From Jack's perspective, it looked as if his father and his uncle were sitting inside Priya's trunk. From their point of view, he was peering through a hole in their roof. The frame on Cirrus was still in its wire cage, to block radio signals.

"Where are you?" Jack asked.

"We stopped at the mill. What's happening?"

"I disconnected Edmond's crystal, but not before Pieter saw me. He sent his thugs after us."

Priya raised her voice to make herself heard over the wind. "I'm heading to Armenau's facility in Everett. As soon as I find a place to pull over, I'm sending them back."

"There's no time." Sarah pointed to an overpass. "*Look*."

Two black SUVs crossed above them and veered onto the ramp. Their engines rumbled as they descended to the highway.

Chapter 31

Priya pushed the accelerator pedal to the floor. Post-Newton, fewer than one percent of cars were still functioning. But this was the I-5—the main corridor between Olympia and Seattle—and there was relatively heavy traffic. With an uninterrupted line of parked vehicles and temporary shelters taking up the inside lanes, she couldn't drive safely above fifty miles per hour. The two black Chevy Suburbans swiftly closed the gap.

"Tell Priya to pull over now," Victor said. "It'll only take a few seconds for all of you to jump through."

"Mr. Scatter." Sarah leaned over the portal. "Keep moving. Get away from the mill."

"Why?" Jack asked. "What's going to happen?"

"Pieter's men will be on the mill road."

"How many?" Victor asked. "Are they ahead of us or behind?"

"Four, I think. Behind you." She shook her head. "I'm not sure. I only know that they'll be on that road soon."

Victor and Nathan conferred while Priya struggled to maintain a safe distance from the pursuers. Her car—older than herself—was powerful and agile, but the vehicles following were forty years newer and gaining ground. Pieter owned the same type of full-size SUV on Cirrus and those would completely outclass Nathan's and Victor's smaller All-Terrain-Vehicles. They had to plan quickly.

"Nathan and I will start driving again," Victor said. "You three will have to come across while we're moving. If Pieter's mercenaries show up, we'll go off-road."

Victor ran to the second truck as Nathan sped off on the gravel road, vacuuming more dust from Cirrus through the wormhole.

Jack checked the portal frame's indicators. "The matrix is eighty percent charged."

"Plug it in anyway," Priya said. "We're not taking chances."

Jack found the charging cable and plugged it into the Mustang's power port. *There's no point hiding it now.* He opened the Faraday cage. "Sarah, you go first."

Sarah hopped up, dropped her legs through the opening, and landed in the truck's back seat. Jack was looking down, ready to help, and didn't spot the passenger in the closest SUV leaning out the window with a pistol.

"Jack," Ethan shouted. "*Shield.*"

Ethan's two-second warning was more than enough, and Jack had the full resources of Holden's portal. Sparks appeared in mid-air as his shield obliterated the bullets. Inside the pursuing vehicle, the driver bellowed and smacked the foolish gunman, who lowered his weapon and ducked inside.

"They've stopped shooting," Jack said.

"They're after the portal," Priya said. "Pieter won't risk damaging it."

She slowed and swerved around a taxi, but the driver of the lead Chevy charged ahead and shouldered the unfortunate car aside. Side mirrors flew and windows shattered as the taxi ground to a halt against the string of parked vehicles. The Suburban advanced to within five yards.

Jack gathered the energy field and pushed against the SUV's bumper. The Chevy shuddered and wobbled dangerously close to another car. He swore and released the pressure. "I can stop their bullets, but I can't stop their vehicles without causing them to crash. And there are too many cars on the road."

"They'll have reinforcements soon," Priya said. "Don't drain the matrix."

Jack glanced at the indicator. She was right, he'd used too much energy already. He dropped through the opening and landed beside Sarah.

"You too," Priya said to Ethan.

"What about you? How will you get away?"

"I'll destroy the frame if I have to. *Now go.*"

Ethan crawled into the back seat, then stopped before reaching the portal. "Here they come. *Drive faster.*"

"They're going to jump on Priya's car," Sarah said.

As soon as Jack had dropped through the wormhole, the lead Chevy sped up. The passenger—dressed in combat gear—had climbed through the sunroof and was easing himself onto the hood. Jack grabbed the lip of the portal but Sarah put a hand on his shoulder.

"Wait." Her grin was mischievous; she'd just recovered and put on one of her earrings. "Pieter's men will be on the mill road. Remember?" She clambered into the front passenger seat.

"Really?" When Sarah nodded, Jack smiled and said, "Okay." Then he shouted, "Ethan, hold down the frame."

He unhooked one side of the portal frame from the overhead rack and hung his weight on it to overcome the coupling force. Ethan kept the matching frame on Priya's car secure under the spoiler as the wormhole resisted the rotation. With the Cirrus-side portal now hanging vertically, facing outwards, Ethan's view was of Victor following in Dave.

The Suburban closed to within a yard of the Mustang's rear bumper. The man on the hood prepared to jump. Ethan shouted, "Go left."

Priya reacted at the same moment the man committed to his leap. She swerved, shifting the would-be-assailant's landing zone to the side. He dropped smoothly through the wormhole.

On Cirrus, the unfortunate thug's scream ended with an abrupt thud. Jack looked around the frame and saw a black-clad figure tumbling in the dust. Victor swerved to avoid running over him.

"Here comes another," Ethan shouted.

The SUVs—which each held only a driver and a single passenger—had swapped places when the first jumper disappeared. Priya swerved again when Ethan told her to, but the mercenary landed with his feet wide apart and only one leg dropped through the wormhole. He grunted as he crashed against the frame with half his body in the Mustang's trunk.

Ethan may have known what was coming, but he didn't have room to do anything about it. The attacker grasped his arm as he tried escaping into the front passenger seat. "Jack, *help*."

Jack reached around the frame to grab the protruding leg, which was thrashing in the wind.

There is nothing a parent won't do when their child is in danger. Through the rearview mirror, Nathan saw what was happening. "Sarah, take the wheel. Jack, spin that frame. *I'm coming, Ethan*."

While the frame was pointing out the rear of the truck, Pieter's hireling had nothing to stand on. As Nathan and Sarah traded places, Jack hauled on the coupled frame, rotating it back to horizontal while keeping the mercenary's leg hooked. Now that it was inside the vehicle, the man kicked and found footing on the back seat. But before he could push himself up, Nathan surged over the seats and wrapped his arms around the man's waist.

Nathan—whose profession was computer security—had the physique that came from long days at the keyboard. Regardless, while the mercenary struggled to pin Ethan, Nathan reached through the wormhole and seized him by the collar. This unexpected attack caused the man to release Ethan and grab Nathan's wrist. Had they been on solid ground, he could have easily flipped Nathan over his shoulder. But with Jack holding his lower half on Cirrus, he had fewer choices. Releasing Ethan was a poor one.

Ethan twisted himself into a sitting position and landed a solid elbow strike against the man's temple. That was enough to turn to tide. With a final effort, Nathan dragged the attacker backwards while Jack pulled down. Together, they tumbled the mercenary out of the truck. He joined his partner on the dusty mill road.

Nathan stood and offered his hand to his son. "Let's go."

"Stop," Jack shouted. "You can't come back. The matrix is almost discharged. Uncle Nathan, you have to go all the way through."

Because of the difference in their masses, less energy was needed to travel from Cirrus to Earth than from Earth to Cirrus. "How long to recharge?" Nathan asked as he eased himself into the Mustang.

Jack connected the charger to the truck's power port and checked the frame. "It'll be at least ten minutes."

Priya changed lanes to avoid a bus. "I can buy us another five. The inside lanes are only used for storing cars for a few more miles. Once we're past that section, they'll be able to get around."

"Then we'll get off the road sooner," Nathan said. "There's a commercial zone ahead. We can lose them in there."

It had begun to rain and the roads were slick, so Priya slowed for the exit. Even so, her nimble car slid around the corners. The heavier SUVs had to slow even more. By the time Priya reached the cluster of warehouses and empty shops, she'd gained a ten-second lead.

She veered into a parking lot, darted between two windowless concrete buildings, and turned again at the end of the structures. Transport trucks that hadn't moved in months partially blocked the alleys between warehouses, and Priya used them for cover. After a few more turns, she lost sight of their pursuers.

"Stop over there," Ethan said. "By the ladder."

Priya pulled over. "Where are they coming from?"

"They're not. I have an idea."

He jumped from the car and wiggled the portal frame out from under the spoiler. Then he sprinted to a stack of wooden pallets under a sliding ladder mounted to the side of the steel walled building. After climbing onto the pallets, he placed the frame directly below the ladder.

"That won't work a third time," Nathan said.

"It's better than fighting our way out."

Ethan jumped and caught the ladder, then pulled it down through the open portal. He picked up a piece of cardboard the size of the frame and climbed to the first landing. When he stepped off, counter-balanced weights raised the ladder to its starting position with a loud clang.

"Cover it with the blanket," he said. "Jack, prepare for incoming."

Priya shook her head, but the squeal of rubber on pavement stopped her protest. "Get up to roof and stay out of sight. We'll be inside."

Ethan rushed up the ladder with what he hoped appeared to be Holden's portal under his arm. Priya and Nathan slipped into the warehouse through the open door before the SUVs came into view.

On Cirrus, Jack rotated the rack-mounted frame to point rearwards.

"Flip it all the way up," Sarah said.

"Huh? The portal will face the sky. Are you sure?"

She laughed. That was good enough for him.

He rotated the frame until it stuck out the back, horizontal with the ground but level with the roof rack. Victor, following twenty yards behind in Dave, waved his hand in a questioning gesture and mouthed, "What are you doing?" Jack shrugged.

He'd just finished aligning the portal when the pair of Chevys slid to a stop near Priya's car. He couldn't see what was happening on Earth, but a door slammed nearby.

"Angel," one of the mercenaries called, "I'm going around the other side." The second SUV's tires smoked as the driver peeled away.

The mercenary nicknamed Angel spotted Ethan scrambling to the warehouse roof. In a single motion, he leapt onto the pallet stack and snagged the ladder's bottom rung. The steel ladder plunged into the wormhole. But Angel was fast. He climbed hand-over-hand as he descended and his knees touched the bottom rung before the ladder completed its journey.

From Ethan's perspective, Angel appeared to drop into a pit of blue sky. From Victor's viewpoint, Nathan's truck sprouted a mast; six feet of blanket-covered ladder shot into the air. Beneath the fabric, unable to see, a now-terrified mercenary was getting his first lesson in portal physics.

Atop the pallets, the upward-facing portal blocked gravity from below. However, Earth pulled from every angle around the frame and Angel wouldn't have noticed a difference while he was there. But artificial gravity on Cirrus worked differently: it only pulled vertically to its surface.

As he fell through the wormhole, Angel rose into a gravity shadow. From his perspective, he was in constant freefall, pinned by the slipstream against the ladder. He tore the blanket away and froze. He was staring directly at a startled Victor, who looked to be driving upside down on an inverted road. Victor swerved to avoid the drifting blanket.

Angel looked *up* at Earth's cloudy sky. He looked *down* at Cirrus' blue sky. His knuckles turned white as he clenched the ladder harder.

Fortunately, he was an experienced combat veteran and it only took him seconds to suppress his panic. He raised a foot onto the lowest rung and assessed the situation. Realizing that he only had to pull himself through the wormhole, he started climbing. Unfortunately, Priya and Nathan returned to give him his second physics lesson.

Priya climbed onto the pallets. "Spin it."

Nathan seized the opposite side of the frame and they both lifted, pushing the ladder further through the wormhole. The coupling effect kept the frame level—the metal ladder would have to bend to change that—but they could still rotate it.

As Angel fought to haul himself through, Priya and Nathan twisted the frame, straining to overcome the coupling resistance. The portion of ladder protruding into Cirrus spun slowly. The wind—which had been pinning Angel against the steel—now pushed him sideways. He struggled to hook a foot on a rung as the ladder turned. Now facing forwards, he gazed *up* at Sarah in the driver's seat. She looked over her shoulder, smiled and waved, then stepped on the accelerator.

Angel's feet lost their grip against the oncoming wind. He

pivoted away, leaving the portal's shadow. His reflexes were excellent but gravity and wind combined were more than he could handle and they yanked his hands off the rung. Angel fell to Cirrus, twisting and curling himself into a ball. He landed safely, but painfully, in a paratrooper's roll.

"Ethan," Priya shouted as Victor carried the frame into the warehouse, "there's still one left. Stay out of sight. I'll try to lead him away."

"Wait." Ethan tried to warn Priya that the other driver was only going around the building, but she drove off too quickly.

- - - - -

Ethan hurried to the far side of the roof and crouched just as the second SUV stopped directly below. He listened for the sound of Priya's V8. *She's heading the wrong way.* He peered over the edge.

There was no ladder on this side, so the driver didn't look up as he headed to the door. He drew his pistol, though. And Nathan was somewhere in the warehouse. *Gotta warn Dad.*

Ethan started running to the ladder, then noticed a flat bulkhead door in the center of the roof and went there instead. He leaned down and yanked the handle, but the door didn't budge. *Locked.*

He was about to head for the ladder again when he recalled how noisy the metal contraption had been on the climb up; his two-second warning would be useless if he was caught halfway down. Instead, he dug his fingers into the gap under the bulkhead door and heaved. The metal panel twisted but held, then sprang back to its original shape when Ethan let go.

I'm going to be making noise one way or another. Maybe I can lure him up here so Dad can escape.

Without knowing how effective it would be, Ethan placed his phone against the door panel next to the handle. Turning his face away in case it rebounded, he held the phone down with one hand and tapped the shield shortcut with the other.

The result was disappointing. Instead of a loud bang, the phone twitched and there was a thin, metallic clink from below.

He threw the panel open and found an enclosed, fire-resistant stairwell: one he could use to reach the ground floor unseen. There hadn't been a lock securing the door, only a rusted latch.

He dashed down the concrete steps without concern for how much noise he was making, paused at the lower door, positioned his thumb over the shield icon, and eased the door open.

The warehouse was unlit, but enough sunlight reflected through the open bay doors to reveal a cavernous space filled with tall racks of shelves. The orange-painted steel structures ran parallel to a wide corridor that connected opposing bays—a truck could enter through one side of the building, be loaded, then exit through the other.

The stairwell opened to the ground floor beside an office. Ethan crept along the wall and glanced through the window facing the loading lane. *Empty. Where are you, Dad?*

Metallic creaks and pops echoed through the building as it cooled from the earlier shower. The sounds drew Ethan's attention but were vague and impossible to pinpoint.

He peeked around the corner of the office, into an aisle wide enough for two forklifts. An identical aisle separated the racks on the far side of the loading lane. Together, these passages divided the warehouse into four blocks.

He's either got to walk the entire perimeter or use the forklift aisle and check both sides.

Ethan realized he'd have only seconds to get out of sight if the man chose the second option. He dashed across the forklift aisle and veered into the corridor between the first two racks, which ran parallel to the loading lane. The door Nathan had used was straight ahead. Ethan ran quietly towards it, hoping his father had stayed nearby.

The shelves throughout the warehouse were only partially filled, so Ethan kept himself as low as possible to avoid being seen from a distance. With just seconds to go, he sensed danger. He thumbed the shield icon and sprinted the final steps to the door.

As he leapt across the gap, a bright flash lit the perimeter aisle and his phone jerked. The gunshot would have been deafening without the shield to muffle it. And the bullet would have been fatal.

Instead, the projectile ricocheted a second time off the metal door and cratered the gravel parking lot. Ethan slid on the loose surface and spun to face his attacker, who'd been only yards away.

The man stepping out of the warehouse was as fearsome as any Ethan had ever faced at his dojo. Tattoos covered his arms and neck, and his left wrist bore multiple scars that looked like knife wounds. He pointed his weapon. "Where's the portal?"

"She's taken it." Ethan held up the phone defensively and backed away. "You'll never find her."

A light rain was falling, and the gesture he made to indicate Priya's direction scattered drops against the shield. For a moment, the invisible barrier's size and shape were revealed. The mercenary grinned.

"Boss-man wants the portal, but I'll have that toy." He returned his pistol to its holster, then reached back and pulled a hunting knife from his belt.

Ethan retreated a step. His assailant followed and—with a quick hop—launched himself at the shield, kicking it hard at chest height. The force of the impact drove it back six inches, but the phone only twitched in Ethan's hand, as if there'd been an invisible shock absorber between the two.

How much can it take? Jack had warned them to be careful not to overload the crystals, but he had no way of knowing how fast they recovered between attacks.

The mercenary waved the knife. "You got nowhere to run. I'm takin' it off you one way or another."

Nathan leapt through the open doorway. "I don't think so." He swung the frame over the man's head.

The force of the wind on Cirrus sucked the thug off his feet when the portal was only halfway down his body.

- - - - -

On Cirrus, Jack poked his head through the roof rack,

straining to hear what was happening on Earth. A very surprised tattooed man popped straight up in front of him and rotated backwards in the forty mile per hour slipstream. It happened so quickly that he gained no forward momentum, but rose and fell vertically. Despite the swift departure, his landing was the gentlest of all those dumped on the mill road that day.

Chapter 32

Jack tucked his wand into a pocket. "Why are you going to Everett?"

"After you destroyed his ring," Priya said, "I asked Edmond where he got it from. He told me that Simon gave it to him. If Simon is still on Earth, he'll be at Armenau's last remaining factory in Everett."

Priya had returned shortly after the last of Pieter's men landed on Cirrus. She'd decided it was too risky to drive her own car, which was more recognizable, and moved it to another parking lot. The Earth-side portal frame was now strung up in the cargo area of a 'borrowed' Suburban. Nathan paced the asphalt, waiting for the matrix to recharge, but Ethan had already gone back, eager for his ring.

Priya continued. "Whatever's going on has something to do with the portal crystals. Edmond was told that Aetherton grew them and that they're unique pairs, but I'm certain they were produced by Armenau. We need Simon to talk, or to get a set for Holden to examine before they're distributed." She then asked Sarah, "Will Pieter's security team be back before tonight?"

"Any communication device they carried would have been disconnected when they fell through ..." Sarah paused when Priya shook her head. "Oh, sorry. That was logic. Okay, my first impression was that they're stuck on Cirrus for a while. But logically, there'll be regular security in Everett. You can't just walk in."

"Then I'll sneak in."

"That won't be easy."

Nathan beamed. "I've broken into that building before."

Victor, leaning against his truck on Cirrus, crossed his arms and said, "*We've* done it before. And you'd have got caught if it hadn't been for me."

That grabbed Jack's attention. "You broke into Armenau?

When was this?"

"Oops." Victor's expression turned sheepish. "That's not good parenting—admitting to a crime in front of your kid. It … it was a long time ago."

"Is that what Grandpa was referring to when he said you and Mom had to go into hiding? You got caught, but Uncle Nathan got away?"

Victor noticed the frown forming on Jack's face. "It's not that simple. Don't blame Nathan. One of us had to take the blame or they'd have kept looking for us. I couldn't have stayed hidden without his help and he wouldn't have had the computer access he needed if he was on the run."

"And now it's time for me to pay you back," Nathan said. "I'm going with Priya. You're staying on Cirrus."

Nathan stepped towards the portal. "You're not going without me and having all the fun."

"Hold on." Priya stood between the two and raised a hand to each. "Who says either of you are coming?"

"You can't get into the facility without our help," Victor said. "Do you even know where the tunnels are?"

"And what about the security systems?" Nathan asked. "Do you know how to disable them?"

Priya eventually admitted she could use help, and Victor made the passage to Earth.

"We'll wait until you three get up the Spine," Priya said. "Once we've got Simon, I'll send him through and take this half of the portal to a safe place."

- - - - -

Without a GPS-style map, Jack had to rely on his memory, navigating by landmarks he'd seen only once before. The first part was easy: head south to the serrated wall of four-mile tall peaks poking through the clouds. But then he had to find a dirt track he'd only driven once, when it was dark.

On the north side of the seventeen-thousand-mile long mountain range, the transition from plains to mountains was abrupt. Barely two miles of foothills separated the grasslands from the Spine. He and Sarah traversed a network of roads through sloping orchards and vineyards for half an hour before stumbling onto a familiar grove of willows.

"This is it. Ethan and I hid under these trees from Pieter's drones."

"Should we let him go first?" Sarah asked. "You said the road is rough."

"Good idea." Ethan had been following in Dave. If everything went to plan, they'd need both vehicles to bring everyone down from the Vault. He waved Ethan past. "He'll be able to avoid anything that might blow out a tire."

Jack followed through ravines and over ridges that climbed steadily higher. Sometimes the route was obvious. At others, Ethan traversed rocky stretches, not knowing if he'd pick up the trail on the far side. After bumping up a particularly brutal incline, during which Jack smacked his head on the padded roof rack, Ethan stopped at a level stretch of crushed gravel. He craned his neck to look up the mountain on his right.

"What's wrong?" Sarah asked. "That's clearly the road in front of him."

"It can't be. We never hit a single flat section on the way down."

Ethan cranked the wheel hard and raced up a slope of solid rock, towards a wide belt of pine trees.

"Where's he going?"

Jack didn't answer. If Ethan didn't act soon, he'd smash into the trees. But Ethan didn't turn, and he didn't crash either. Instead, Dave disappeared into the woods without a sound.

"That was … different," Jack said. He spun the steering wheel and crawled up the slope. At the top, a truck-width gap opened into a hundred-yard long S-shaped path that completely hid whatever lay beyond. Ethan was waiting for them on the far side. He grinned when they came into view, then resumed climbing.

It was late afternoon when they reached the pass. Ethan

pulled off the road and parked beside the creek where he had on their first trip. Their ultimate destination was a short hike away: the cave where Jack had found the power cell before Newton. If his theory about connections between broken gravity lines was correct, he could monitor the portal remotely with the raven's aid.

He hopped from the truck and beckoned Sarah. "Come with me. The view is incredible."

All three of them trekked downstream to the cliff's edge and marveled at the nearly smooth surface of the mountain beyond a forested saddle. For Jack, the scene was hauntingly familiar.

"That peak is the Mirror. The one we're on is the Vault." He stuck his hands in his pockets and sighed. "I dreamed of this place hundreds of times before I knew it was real. This is the exact spot where I always met Uncle Carl."

Snow and ice capped the Mirror. Beyond that solitary peak, the Spine continued in a meandering line that was never greater than twenty miles across. In some places, as with the Vault, only a single massif separated the north and south halves of Cirrus.

"Where's Icarus?" Sarah asked.

Jack pointed north. "It's too cloudy now, but you'd normally see it over there, sixty miles away." He walked towards a rocky crag. "Climb up with me."

"I'm gonna get the power connections ready to set up in the cave," Ethan said. "You guys go ahead."

Jack led Sarah up a thirty-foot-tall tower of rock that perched at the cliff's edge. The natural lookout rose above most of the surrounding trees, giving them a majestic panorama. In his dream, the trees in the broad saddle fifteen-hundred feet below were immature. Now, the forest was lush, fed by water flowing from both the Vault and the Mirror. A hawk—little more than a speck at this distance—dove silently into the woods after an unseen prey.

"I think that gravel road we didn't take goes through the saddle." He pointed southwest. "Port Isaac is that way." Then he rotated slowly, naming places Sarah was familiar with. "Port

Nelson, the maintenance depot, Caerton." He faced southwest again. "Fairview's over there." He was quiet for a moment before he sat facing the Mirror, with his legs dangling off the crag.

Sarah joined him. "You're worried about your dad, aren't you?"

He nodded and idly tossed a pebble into the void. "Do you have any memories of what's going to happen?"

"It's all so confusing. I'm remembering … sounds, flashes of light, weird things that don't make sense. I can't put them together."

"What about Pieter? Will he be there? Will Priya stop him?"

"No. You're the one who eventually faces him."

"Great." Her answer came too quickly, too certain for his liking.

"Sorry. If I remember something useful, I'll let you know." She turned to face the Vault. "Where do we hide the portal?"

Jack shuffled around. "We're in the mouth of a hanging valley. The cave is at the far end of the trees. We should go before Ethan gets lonely."

Ethan was testing the connections for the remote power cell when they returned. The plan was to stash the frame along with a radio, so Priya could communicate with the village when she visited from Earth. If anyone else discovered and used the portal, they'd find themselves trapped atop an isolated mountain.

"I'm going to show Sarah where the cave is."

"Okay, I was talking to Dad. They stopped at Grandpa's house, but there's no food there and we've got nothing here. They'll go buy dinner before the break-in. What do you want?"

"You know, I've been to Earth twice now and still haven't been to a restaurant. Do you think Priya will let us go back for a while?"

"Sorry, I already asked. Rolling blackouts. Everett will be running at forty percent power. It's takeout tonight."

"Fine. How about a *real* hamburger? I've never had one of those, either."

"That's what I'm getting. I haven't had a proper burger in months. Sarah, do you want the same?"

"Sure, I'll try one."

Ethan mimed writing an order slip. "Three burgers and fries. They're waiting until dark before they leave the house. It'll be an hour."

"We'll be back before then."

Jack led Sarah to the cave, observing her as they approached the invisible threshold.

"Oh …" She spread her arms and twirled around as she felt the transition. "It's like the island, except it comes on quicker, as if the lines are closer."

"I guess that sort of makes sense. Icarus Island was created in one big blast that reached to the core. The asteroid would have broken many lines, but the Spine would have swept along any loose ones it encountered when it was still molten."

They reached the dam of packed boulders over which the stream ran. Jack hiked to the top, drew his wand, and shone it into the darkness below a lintel of gray stone.

"It's deeper than I thought. I can see at least forty feet." He crouched and shuffled through the narrow opening. "It's taller inside, too. I can stand without hitting my head."

Sarah scuttled into the cave. "It must go farther than we can see; I feel a breeze. There has to be another entrance."

"Do you want to explore?"

"Not right now. It'll be dark soon." She stooped and walked outside.

"This is where Uncle Carl left the power cell that got us to Caerton," Jack said as he followed. "This is where we'll leave the portal. If anyone comes through it, the birds will let me know."

"You're sure of that?"

In response, a black shape dropped from a pine branch and landed at Jack's feet. "I am now."

"Is that the same raven from the island?"

"Yeah, I was thinking of asking him before we left. He must

have picked up on that and came on his own. He's been waiting for us."

"Be careful what you think of. I know you wouldn't do it on purpose, but if he's listening to you, he might accidentally go somewhere dangerous."

"I think he likes it here." The raven croaked noisily. "Should I ask someone to come keep you company?" The bird sounded off again, provoking a response from high in the nearby trees. "Oh, you've already got a friend."

"Are you … talking to him?"

Jack laughed. "No, not talking. I'm just guessing. But I get the sense I'm not too far off the truth."

Sarah raised onto her toes and looked at the lake beyond the rock wall. "What's over here?"

"We didn't have time to explore the last time we were here."

She rounded a car-sized boulder to the side of a circular tarn, a hundred feet across. An irregular ledge encircled the pond except for a gap at the far end. There, a thin sheet of glacial water spilled over a featureless stone slab and flowed silently into the pool.

Sarah removed her shoes, sat on the rock shelf, and dangled her toes in the clear water. "That is *so* cold." After a pause, she said, "Can you feel it?"

Jack thought for only a second that she was referring to the water, then understood that she meant the energy field and how close it was. The field was powerful here, as strong as near any active portal frame. "Yeah. It's just at the bottom of the pool."

"You want to go for a swim?"

"You're the one with her feet in the water. You tell me."

"No way. It's like ice. Which is too bad because it's so peaceful here."

Jack sat beside Sarah and stared through the V-shaped opening over the dam. It was almost sunset, so the view was of the brilliantly lit tips of the Spine. "It's like a miniature version of Niels' island, in the sense that it's isolated and has a strong connection to a natural portal." There was even enough room above the ledges to build a cabin or two around the lake. In pre-Newton days, this was exactly the sort of secluded location he'd have sought to get away from the sensory overload created by emotion detectors.

"What are you thinking?"

"Uncle Carl said he shared our dream whenever he was near one of these places. I wonder if that works the other way around. If I sleep here, will we share the dream regardless of where—or when—he is?"

"But you weren't asleep during Newton. You were meditating. And there were only thousands of crystals in the Archive. The line at the bottom of the pool is farther away, but it could be the equivalent of millions of portals."

Jack thought for a while, then said, "I want to try."

"Are you sure?"

"Uncle Carl knew things about the future; facts I apparently told him. Dad and Uncle Nathan are planning something dangerous. Maybe there's something he knows, a detail I'll eventually tell him, that can help them."

"All right, what do you want me to do? Do you need privacy?"

"No, stay. I don't even know if this will work. If it does, I don't know what'll happen."

Ordinarily, he'd have felt awkward closing his eyes with someone watching. But he and Sarah had become so close in recent days that it might be easier with her around. He shuffled away from the water's edge and found a comfortable rock to recline against.

Meditation wasn't something he practiced. During Newton, he'd merely been concentrating on a portal crystal, trying to find a weakness he could exploit to destroy it. This would be much different.

He began by imagining the natural portal hidden under the water. His sense of the field lines told him that the pond was much deeper than it was wide: funnel-shaped with a long, drawn-out spout at the bottom. Recalling how his recurring dream always opened at the edge of the cliff overlooking the saddle, he allowed his imagination to drift there. That was easy; he'd been standing in that exact spot only minutes ago.

The transition was seamless. One moment he was imagining the scene and the next he was no longer alone.

"Uncle Carl?" Jack asked, surprised and elated by his success.

The man looked at him quizzically. "Do I know you?"

Chapter 33

The man standing beside Jack was definitely his uncle, but was much younger than he'd been in their previous encounter. Carl stared for a few moments before recognition dawned.

"Jack? It *is* you. You look so much like your father." He scanned his surroundings, then rubbed his arms, as if surprised to find them solid. "This is the strangest dream."

"It's not a dream," Jack said. "Well, not really."

"Now that's something only a dream would say. Your voice is the same as Victor's, too. Is this what you'll sound like when you're older, I wonder. You're always so quiet. You hardly made a peep when I brought you through the portal last week." Carl leaned to look down on the saddle between the Vault and the Mirror. "Where are we?"

"Don't you recognize it?"

Carl shook his head.

"We're in the Spine." Jack gestured to the snow-capped Mirror and the line of peaks beyond. "I guess you haven't been here before, but you will. You showed me this place."

"Did I? Well, thank you for returning the favor. I've always loved the mountains. What a gorgeous sunrise."

In Jack's time, the sun was setting. Now, it was rising over the Mirror, as it always did in his recurring dream. The surrounding trees had reverted to an earlier era too; they were barely waist high. Above the young forest, with its many spires and smooth surfaces, the Vault gleamed like a golden cathedral in the morning sun.

"This really is a magical place, isn't it?" Carl laughed. "Sorry. An inside joke. I asked Niels the other day why he was looking for *Ley Lines*."

"What are ley lines?"

Carl lowered the pitch of his voice to parody a movie trailer.

"Lines of power. In ancient times, folks believed they criss-crossed the Earth, creating special places wherever they met. Everyone from shaman to Druids were drawn to them. They built henges, temples, centers of worship. Or darker places." His voice returned to normal. "Niels hired me to find locations on Cirrus where the artificial gravity lines have been disrupted. He's an interesting character. Bit of an eccentric, though. He may actually believe in magic."

"It's not magic he was looking for. But this *is* one of those places. You told me about it."

"Now how could I have told you? I've never been on the Spine before. I may never get the chance."

"What do you mean?"

"This job I'm doing for Niels ..." Carl shook his head. "It doesn't seem to have a point. The only reason I agreed was to give me something to do between trips bringing you back and forth. I'm taking you—" He chuckled. "*Little you*, to Nathan and Grace tomorrow. I might not return."

"No, you can't quit. I know you won't believe this until you come here on your own, but it's important." Jack pointed. "Look, there's Icarus Island. When you come back, you'll see it. That'll prove it's real."

"I don't know about that. I can see the Spine from the island when I visit Niels. This *is* a spectacular location, though I can easily imagine how it would look from above. Seeing the island won't prove anything."

"Then let me show you something you can't possibly know." Jack backed away from the cliff. "This way."

He led Carl up-slope, along the stream, knowing he had to convince his uncle to return to Cirrus. When he'd first seen the cave himself, after dreaming of it for so many years, there was no room for doubt.

"You have to make one more trip." Jack crouched below the overhanging slab of rock. "If you find this cave, in this spot, will you believe it's real?"

Carl took a moment to look around. "All right, I'll come up here. if I find this cave, then I'll believe it. Why is it so important?"

Jack told Carl how he'd dreamed of this place his entire life, then relayed the events of the past few months: how he'd fought Pieter, Niels' involvement, and the destruction of the portal network.

Carl's mouth was hanging open for the last half of the story. He didn't respond right away after Jack finished, but finally said, "This is easily the most complicated and detailed dream I've ever had."

"There's something else. Something I need you to do for me. I'll need a power cell someday. You carry a spare, don't you? One that's connected to the apartment in Caerton? Can you leave it in the cave for me?"

Carl shrugged. "Sure, why not? Anything else?"

"Yes. We're going to meet in this same dream over and over. But some of those will be in my past, and I won't remember any of this. Someday you'll have to tell *me* what's going on." Jack extended his hand. "Do we have a deal?"

Carl shook Jack's hand. "Deal. So, if all this *is* real, what are you doing here?"

"Hiding Grandpa's portal. Pieter Reynard is searching for it. Also, I came here to see if you know anything that could help Dad and Uncle Nathan. They're breaking into Armenau tonight."

"*Again?*"

- - - - -

Dinner ranked as one of the most unusual events any of them had ever experienced.

The portal frame on Earth hung in the back of the Suburban, parked a block from Armenau's factory in Everett. The Cirrus-side frame was hanging vertically from the truck's roof rack again, facing inwards. Jack, Sarah, and Ethan sat in the truck on Cirrus while Priya, Victor, and Nathan dined on the Chevy's tailgate. Together, they shared a meal across one-hundred and ninety million miles.

"This is great," Jack mumbled with a mouthful of hamburger. "Much better than cricket-burger."

"Ugh." Ethan shuddered. "Don't remind me. I ate one of those last month."

Before dinner, Jack described his conversation with Carl to Sarah and Ethan, but decided not to share the story with their fathers or Priya. Carl didn't know the details of the first break-in, only that it had happened and led to Victor and Emily fleeing to Cirrus.

"How did you two break in last time?" Priya asked.

Jack and Ethan reached for the portal frame at the same time. The question was for their fathers, but—due to the difference in elevation—the portal was running in a filtered mode that restricted passage. This created a cloudy threshold that prevented air from rushing through and also muffled sound.

Sarah placed her hand over the switch. "*Stop.* Remember what happened to the food?" They'd learned the hard way that they had to close the Chevy's doors before fully opening the wormhole, to prevent a torrent from blasting through.

"Well …" Nathan exchanged guilty looks with Victor. "We didn't break in so much as use my pass card."

"*What?*" Priya lowered her salad abruptly. "That's not a break-in. It's just trespassing."

"That doesn't mean we don't know *how*. We only need to get to a tunnel and we can go anywhere we want."

"And how do we do that?"

"The loading bay," Victor said. "It's not a secure zone. Once we're inside, we only have to bypass one alarm to get downstairs. And even if they see us, they'll be in the security offices on the far side of the campus. We'll be gone before they get there."

"The goal of a successful break-in is to be *not* seen."

"There are cameras everywhere. Sorry, Priya, there was never a chance of not being seen. The security system's AI will know where we are, but all we really have to do is keep moving—same as last time."

Priya fumed. The planned, stealthy infiltration was turning into a smash-and-grab. But there wasn't time for anything else, and definitely not enough time to get a warrant to search legally. Whatever Pieter was planning would happen in the next few days. "Fine. We'll stick to the current *plan*." She made air quotes around the word 'plan'.

After dinner, Jack demonstrated the phone's shield function and warned that he didn't know how long it would last. Ethan had already used one to stop a bullet, although that was a single round from a small-caliber handgun.

"There's one more thing before we go." Priya nodded at Victor, picked up the portal, and carried it outside the vehicle.

"Wait," Jack said when it became obvious what she was doing. "What if you need our help?"

"There's nothing you can do here if we're caught." She leaned the open side of the frame against a cinder-block wall and said to Victor, "Back it up. A few more inches. That's it." The SUV's bumper pinned the frame to the wall. Only a sliver of light leaked around the edges.

"What if I remember something?" Sarah called.

"Anders sent one of Icarus' radios to Davis. If we're not back in two hours, call him and tell him what happened. He'll know what to do."

"That'll take hours," Ethan said. "We could be there in minutes."

"Call. Davis," Priya repeated.

- - - - -

Ethan activated the portal and pressed a hand against the cold, concrete wall while air whistled through gaps around the frame. "You could break it down if you wanted, couldn't you?"

Jack shook his head. "I can't direct the energy field past a wormhole unless I get my head through."

"So, we're stuck." Ethan slapped the wall. "Unless we make a hole?"

"Looks that way."

Sarah waggled her wand. "I could try a fireball."

Jack grinned, imagining people's reaction to seeing a wall melt. "Unfortunately, we don't know what's on the other side. Even a hammer would attract too much attention."

"We could be sitting here for hours." Sarah detached one of the removable seats that had been mounted in Dave's cargo bed that morning. She set it on the ground behind the truck and dropped into it. "We should at least try to do something productive. What other spells can you create that we might need later."

"They're not sp—. Fine, we'll call them spells until we come up with a better term."

"And ley lines," Ethan said.

Jack sighed. "Ley lines too. But it's not magic. It's science."

"Jack has a point," Sarah said. "If we want to create new spells, we should approach this scientifically. Let's start with the basics. How about a spell for water?"

Jack lifted a phone Priya had sent from Olympia and tapped its keypad. Victor had swapped out the disentangled crystals with one of Holden's new coin portals. The devices couldn't make phone calls—they'd need to pair the crystal with another at the telephone exchange for that—but they hoped to build their own mini-network at Icarus someday.

"There's no mystery there," he said after adding a new contact number to the list. "We've been using the equivalent of that spell most of our lives. The water is under pressure, so it flows as soon as the portal is opened." He pressed *Send*. A stream shot from the phone's dispensing port.

"Maybe we can come up with spells to *do* things." Sarah pointed her wand at a stone and made it hover.

"You mean like this?" Jack set the phone on a log and made a stone fly a circle around Sarah's stationary one, then used his wand to make a second rock orbit in the opposite direction. "The AI can keep those going as long as the wormhole is open."

"I meant something more complex. Something that relies on

our recorded memories."

"How about opening a lock?" Ethan asked. "*You* can do that by sensing the insides in real-time, but could the AI be programmed from your memories so that *anyone* could do it with the phone?"

While Sarah and Ethan discussed ideas for spells, Jack entered contact numbers for resources he already knew, things that would pass through a wormhole on their own. It was getting chilly, so he set the phone down to gather wood for a campfire. Ethan raised it to read the list, then selected the one labeled 'Light'. A bright white beam shone from the phone.

He scrolled the directory. "It's too bad we didn't think of doing this earlier. We could have added more spells to our dads' phones. What's this one? RBL?" Without waiting for an answer, he pressed the icon. The entire forest lit up with a dazzling light.

"*Aaah,*" Jack screamed. "*Turn it off, turn it off.* That's the *Really Bright Light.*"

Even though the aperture had been facing the ground, the light was so bright and unexpected that Ethan fumbled the phone. Fortunately, Jack was close enough to connect to its portal and close it.

"*Ow.*" Sarah uncovered her face. "That actually hurt."

"Sorry, I thought it might come in handy."

"For what?" Ethan rubbed his eyes. "Signaling Icarus? I'll bet they saw it too."

"I didn't have a plan for it." Jack recovered the phone and started tapping the screen. "But I just thought of more things to test in case Priya comes back and I get to add them to their phones. I wonder how they're doing."

Chapter 34

Victor gestured at an inclined ramp that sloped down to two sets of roll shutter doors. "I still say the loading dock will be easiest."

After circling Armenau's facility for ten minutes, Priya had no better plan. The campus occupied two city blocks, and she knew nothing of the underground maintenance tunnels that linked its dozen buildings. Also, with its own fusion plant, it was well lit in an otherwise darkened neighborhood; they'd be attracting unwanted attention if they kept driving.

"He's right," Nathan said. "Those bays were made for self-driving trucks, but everything's being done manually now. I'm betting they're short-staffed. We'll listen at the door. If it's quiet, we pull the truck ahead and slip through the gap."

They'd parked directly across from the dock. A semi-trailer truck backed up against the left bay blocked views of the loading zone from the windows on that side of the building. On the right, a smaller five-ton straight truck hid the dock from an access road that looped around the three-story parking garage.

Priya shook her head. It was a terrible plan. But she'd investigated enough break-ins to know that getting into a building was easy. What mattered was how quickly they found Simon and got out.

"We'll check it out. But if there's anyone there, we'll do it my way." She clipped her badge to her belt. "You two will go around the front and create a distraction while I bluff my way in."

Victor and Nathan agreed and started across the rain-slicked street, approaching the building from the only spot where there were no cameras: between the two trucks. Priya waited until they reached the wall before following casually.

Victor tugged the flexible foam barrier that kept cold air from leaking between truck and wall, and whispered, "I'll make a gap.

Give me a light. I can't see what I'm doing."

Nathan already had his phone out in case they needed a shield. "What's all this? Where did these icons come from?"

"What's wrong?" Priya asked.

He angled the phone to show her the contact list. "Who are Smoke, Fog, and Ink?"

She frowned. "Just find the light."

"Hurry," Victor said.

"Hold on." Nathan scrolled the list. "I found a lightbulb icon."

"Wait." Victor placed a finger to his lips after forcing an opening. "There's a security guard."

Priya leaned closer to listen to the muffled voices.

"Hey, Brian. I didn't know you were back. How was Nevada?"

"Lot drier than this."

"What are you picking up?"

"Nothing. Just dropped off one pallet."

"They sent you all the way back for one crate? What was in it?"

"Don't know."

"Hector," the guard called, *"let me see that manifest."*

A third man joined the conversation but Priya missed what he said. "Did either of you get that?"

Victor leaned away from the opening. "Something about moving it to the lab building. I don't think they know what it was." He dragged the seal to widen the gap.

"I heard you had a passenger on the trip out last week," the guard said.

"Yeah, one of them scientists. Strange fella. Didn't say a word the entire trip. Awful edgy about the cargo, though."

"How's that?"

"Wouldn't leave the truck. Not even when I stopped for the night. He slept in the cab."

A passing car honked, muddying the guard's response. The other men laughed.

"Where you headed now?"

"Nowhere. Got an empty truck and two weeks off."

Victor released the foam barrier, sealing the gap. "He says he took a scientist to Nevada. Simon?"

"The spaceport is in Nevada," Nathan said. "Could he be on his way back to Cirrus?"

"They've got a working portal. What do they need to get into orbit for?"

"It has something to do with the crystals," Priya said. "I'm sure of it."

The truck's electric motor gave no warning that the driver was pulling away from the dock. Priya was caught off guard as light from the open bay illuminated her formerly secluded shelter.

"*Hey*," the surprised security guard shouted. "What are you doin' down there?"

Nathan—still holding up his phone—swiveled to face the guard and accidentally brushed an icon.

Lightning flashed on the loading dock. Or something close to it. The guard, who'd been reaching for his weapon, screamed, covered his eyes, stumbled, and fell to the floor. A dock worker standing beside him did the same. Priya was safely behind the phone with Nathan and Victor. Even so, her vision swam with afterimages and blotches from the Really Bright Light.

She moved instinctively, vaulting onto the chest-height platform where she sprang to her feet and seized the guard's weapon. Victor and Nathan were only just climbing onto the raised deck as she removed the radio from his belt.

The guard's screams faded to a loud moan. Priya leaned down and—with as much reassurance as she could muster—said, "You'll be okay in a few days. It's called *welder's flash*. But see a doctor tonight just to be safe." She then used his own handcuffs to shackle him to his co-worker before moving deeper into the building.

As Nathan passed, he added, "Oh, and don't move for an hour or you'll go blind."

"What was that?" Victor asked when they were out of hearing range.

"I don't know. There's a bunch of new contacts on my screen."

Victor checked his phone. "Mine too."

Priya scanned the room. "We don't have time." A set of tall double-doors opened to the warehouse, and a hallway was visible through a barred glass window in an adjacent door. "Which way?"

Nathan pointed the phone at a cluster of security cameras. "Cover your eyes." He activated a flash that was blinding even through closed eyelids. "If that didn't burn them out permanently, it should have at least overloaded them for a while." He strode to a second, unmarked steel door and said, "This way."

Victor, who'd brought an assortment of tools in his jacket, used a screwdriver to pry the cover off the basement door's card reader. It took him only a few seconds to identify and cut the correct wires. The door unlocked and they ran down the stairs.

- - - - -

"So ..." Jack scrolled the contact list. "Besides the basics, I've added what I think are: freon, carbon dioxide, liquid nitrogen, liquid—"

"Liquid nitrogen?" Sarah said. "Some of those things are dangerous. Shouldn't you be more careful?"

"I'll label them properly when we have time to test them. For now, I'll call them all *gas*."

- - - - -

"That's the last one, all right?" Priya leaned against the door she'd just slammed. "We've been lucky so far, but who knows what might happen next."

"Okay," Nathan gasped, "but you have to admit the nitrous oxide was funny."

Victor doubled over with laughter.

Priya was not happy. The plan had been weak to begin with and was crumbling the farther they went. Campus security had spotted them the moment they reached the basement, and Nathan went for the light blaster again. But the icons had shifted. Instead of a blinding light, the phone spewed an enormous quantity of expanding foam. While not as instantly disabling as the flash, it had been useful. That hallway was completely sealed now, maybe permanently.

Next, they'd almost been caught when Nathan led their group into a dead-end, until he filled that corridor with helium, forcing the guards to flee in chipmunk-voiced panic. Since then, they'd dissuaded anyone from following by randomly selecting from the growing number of similar icons. They left hallways filled with a range of deterrents: great patches of ice, clouds of fog, and what was almost certainly maple syrup.

With the radio Priya had borrowed from the guard, she knew that Armenau's security forces were maintaining a cautious distance.

"*Where are they?*" The voice was one Priya had identified as the security supervisor. "*We called a code black fifteen minutes ago.*"

"*Still no response,*" a woman Priya believed to be a senior administrator answered.

"*Should we call the police?*"

"*We've got our orders. Keep them confined to the campus until backup arrives.*"

"*Backup* must be Pieter's men we sent to Cirrus." Nathan started jogging to the next intersection. "Why aren't they calling the police?"

"There are things going on here they don't want anyone to know about," Priya said.

- - - - -

"We need to try something else," Sarah said. "Opening links to other portals isn't telling us how to create spells that *do* anything."

"How would I even begin to create a spell that will open *any* lock?" Jack asked. "The few I've tried were easy because I could see inside them."

"That's because you're getting direct feedback from the energy field. But Ethan and I can't sense that; we only get memories."

"So," Ethan said, "we need to figure out if the AI can deliver feedback to us as a memory."

"I have an idea." Jack pointed his wand into the trees, illuminating a large section of the woods. He sat quietly, concentrating. Slowly, the light dimmed until it was feeble as a candle.

Ethan squinted into the darkness. "I don't what you're trying, but it's not working."

Jack's expression became triumphant as the light disappeared. "Actually, that tells me it's working perfectly." He added a number to the contact list, focused for a moment, then waved the phone in front of himself. "Try that." He handed the device to Sarah.

Sarah pressed the icon. "Isn't that just another light?" She panned the phone across the trees. "No, wait. I get it. Everything I point it at stays lit up for a while."

Ethan frowned. "What are you talking about? It's completely dark."

"No, it's not." She passed him the phone. "Try it."

"Okaaay. I understand. It's bright, but it doesn't seem that useful."

"What are you seeing?"

"It lights up the area right around me." He extended his arm. "It's like sunlight, but what good is a flashlight that only works for a yard?"

"Try walking," Jack said.

Ethan stood and lurched back in surprise. "It just got wider." He took a step forward. And another. "*This is amazing*."

"What's going on?" Sarah asked. "It's not as bright as sunlight for me."

"That's because it's a memory. The AI gives each of you a memory of everything in the beam's path. Ethan gets his usual two seconds, and you—"

"And I get a longer memory with less detail."

Ethan ran through the trees, laughing and hollering.

"Right," Jack said. "Anything Ethan can reach in two seconds is lit up in perfect detail."

"And everything *I* point it at seems to stay lit for longer. What do you see?"

"For me, it's a normal flashlight." He shrugged. "Real-time."

Ethan ran to the truck and jumped over the door. Despite the near total darkness, he landed perfectly in his seat. "This would be perfect for a burglar."

"So," Sarah said, "we've proved we can create spells that combine the energy field and AI memories. Now we need to work out what to do with that."

Ethan grinned broadly. "This is gonna be so much fun."

- - - - -

Priya bobbed her head around a corner, then stepped into the empty corridor.

"This place was running twenty-four hours a day last month. With hundreds of workers. Something's changed." Before Newton, the facility employed more than a thousand people. Now it was virtually deserted. "Let's get over to the production building."

"The tunnels converge ahead," Nathan said. "We need to get back to the surface before they box us in."

Victor disabled another camera and they backtracked to the nearest stairwell. They emerged next to an open courtyard with an unobstructed view of Production and its glass-walled vestibule, directly across the square. It would take only seconds to run to the doors, but they'd be completely exposed until they got inside.

"Will you be able to open that door?" Priya asked.

"The outside set will be unlocked," Nathan said. "It's the inner ones that'll be a problem."

Victor scrolled through his contact list again. "How are they adding these things?"

Priya checked the growing list on her screen. "If they're like the UN's new phones, they automatically synchronize contacts from the server. Jack might not even be aware of what's happening."

"Well, this icon is definitely a lock. They must be listening to us somehow." He raised the phone to his mouth. "Keep up the good work, guys."

Given the unexpected results from the earlier tries, Priya had good reason to avoid experimenting. She looked at the icon and sighed. "Yeah, that's a lock. All right, we'll try it."

They dashed across the courtyard. Victor placed his phone against the inner door's locking panel and pressed the screen. Priya waited nervously, knowing they could be seen from a distance.

"*They're at the south entrance to Production,*" a guard announced on the radio.

"*Don't let them get in,*" the supervisor replied.

"Too late." Victor swung the door open after its lock emitted a sharp click. They hurried inside.

Priya crept forward with her pistol drawn, pointed to the floor. She peeked into every window along the corridor. "There's something very wrong here. Even if there's no one working, there should have been at least one guard in the lobby."

Nathan pointed to a sign hanging from the ceiling. "Here's the laboratory."

The actual manufacturing of crystals took place in a controlled, sterile, and airless environment. They couldn't enter the lab, but its control room on the other side of the window was dark and quiet.

Nathan read a wall-mounted monitor beside the door. "This is their production schedule. There's no activity at all."

Priya peered into another windowed room across the hall. "We have to get out of here. *Now.*"

"Why?"

"You don't shutter a billion-dollar enterprise." She pointed to a large crate in the center of the room, strapped to a wooden pallet. "Pieter knew we were coming."

The radio sounded again. *"Evacuate the campus. These are the terrorists we were warned about. They've planted a bomb."*

Chapter 35

"Bomb?" Victor shouted as he ran, following Priya. "What are they talking about?"

"Pieter's going to destroy the factory and blame it on terrorists," Priya said. "*Us.*"

In their haste to catch the intruders, the guards had left the doors open. Priya navigated back to the warehouse in under a minute. The loading dock was empty and Nathan sprinted through the bay door, then jumped to the pavement below.

Victor was about to join him when Priya veered behind the counter. "What are you doing?"

"Shipping manifests," she said. "I need to know for sure what's going on."

Victor wavered at the platform's edge, scanning the wads of paper tacked to the walls. "We don't have time."

Priya ducked under a shelf. "Got 'em." She stood up holding two clipboards.

By then, Nathan had reached the road. "I'll stop traffic," he shouted.

He activated the light spell and began flashing oncoming vehicles. Except for the nearest car—which swerved around him and nearly lost control when its wheels hit the curb—the intense light had the desired effect: all traffic stopped immediately for up to two blocks away.

Victor found the *shield* listing. He slowed enough to let Priya pass, then activated the spell, holding the phone behind him as they ran.

Priya lunged around the corner. "Take cover."

Nathan, still in direct line of sight of the loading dock, quit warning traffic and bolted for the far side of the road just as a deafening explosion ripped the night.

The trees lining the zone between the buildings and the street suffered the brunt of the blast; fragmented safety glass stripped them bare. Victor's shield partially protected him and Priya, but Nathan—who was even farther away—was knocked off his feet by the pressure wave. He tumbled over the sidewalk and landed in the grass. Victor ran to him and found him covered in leaves and wood chips.

"You all right?"

Nathan groaned. "I feel like I've been run over by a wood chipper." He was stung but not seriously wounded. "But I don't think anything's broken."

"Let's go," Priya said. "The police will be here in minutes."

"You're the police," Victor said as he helped Nathan to his feet.

"I won't be if they find us here."

"Where are we going?"

"Nevada." She held up the handful of manifests. "If I'm right, we've got to stop a shuttle."

- - - - -

More than an hour had passed since Priya pinned the portal against the wall. Jack and his friends had kept themselves busy learning about the AI and spells, but after so long with no contact, he was spending as much time checking the portal as he was focusing on his work.

He slapped his wand on the truck's hood and sagged against its bumper. Besides being concerned with what was happening on Earth, he was frustrated by his lack of success in producing a lock-opening spell. Ethan's hope that creating new spells would be fun was way off the mark.

With only a pair of locking toolboxes to experiment with, Jack found that each time he got the spell working on one, it no longer worked on the other. When he got it to unlock both, it couldn't open the truck's cargo latches, and so on. After an hour of wrestling, he was exhausted and had no way of knowing if the spell would work on another type of lock.

Ethan and Sarah were sitting quietly by the fire when Priya

shouted. He glanced at the portal just as the cinder block wall brightened and tilted away, but even his two-second foresight failed to stop him from tumbling sideways as a cone of Earth's gravity passed through the forest. The disorientation lasted only a second, though; the abrupt change triggered the portal's safeguards and closed the wormhole.

"What was that?" he asked. "Are they back?"

Jack ran to Holden's frame, which they'd removed from the truck and leaned against a tree. "I don't know. The portal shut down." He angled the frame away and reopened the wormhole.

"What's that?" Sarah asked. A black, rubber-like wall filled the frame. Branches on nearby trees bent towards it.

"A cargo mat," Ethan said. "The frame's lying face-down in the back of the Chevy."

Jack leaned away from the opening to avoid the disorienting effects of mixed gravity. "What's happening over there?" The portal was consuming a lot of power by facing Earth's gravity well, but after so long without news, he was reluctant to close it.

Priya replied, but her voice was too muffled to understand. Another minute of loud engine noises, squealing tires, and anxious conversation followed before the vehicle stopped and Victor realigned the frames.

"Sorry, Priya," he said. "The matrix is discharged. Looks like you're stuck with us for a while."

"What's happening?" Jack repeated.

Nathan shook bark and leaves from his hair. "We had a few problems. Nothing we couldn't handle. Those functions you added were a big help."

Amid Ethan's laughter, Victor summarized how they'd used the new spells, then asked. "How did you do that from Cirrus?"

"The AI must be *distributed*," Jack said. "Like *Little Brother*."

"I know what Little Brother was," Sarah said—everyone on Cirrus was familiar with the pre-Newton network of public surveillance cameras, "but what do you mean by *distributed*?"

"Its actual name was DAIGON, which stood for *Distributed*

Artificial Intelligence Global Observation Network. Most AI systems split their processing across hundreds of nodes as a safeguard to prevent hackers from getting complete files from a single server, and the 'Magic' AI must be the same. Somehow, it's tied-in to Earth's phone network. The phones are just synchronizing their contact lists the way they always have."

Priya had been reviewing the shipping manifests. "Jack, get your grandfather on the radio. I know what Pieter is planning."

Jack called the village. The radio was in Holden's cabin, so he answered right away. Jack held his handset near the portal and pressed *Talk*.

"Holden," Priya said, "Armenau shipped eight containers of coin-mounted crystals to DC, and a second truck left the same day for Nevada. It doesn't say what it was carrying, but the weight is exactly half. Is it possible that Pieter created a third identical crystal in each set?"

Jack released the talk button. There was a lengthy delay as Holden thought it over.

"Yes, it's possible. What makes you think he did that?"

"It makes no sense for him to destroy his own factory unless he's trying to cover something up. When I met with Simon before Newton, he had paperwork that proved Armenau's fabrication process was using fifty percent *more* raw materials than their competition. But Simon was very focused on efficiency; what if that fifty percent wasn't wasted?"

"Why would Pieter create a third crystal?" Ethan asked.

"There are five million portals in that shipment. They'll end up in high-priority communication systems: government, military, police. Some will go to corporations: those who have government contracts and need secure network channels. That extra crystal would be like a third eye for Pieter. We know he can merge portals. With a third crystal in each set, he could tap into any network without being detected."

Sarah paled. "Oh, no. It's so much worse than that. A lot of those crystals will be used in phones. Not only could he listen in, he'll be able to control the people on the other end."

No one spoke. They'd seen Pieter's power firsthand; Terrance had no idea he was being manipulated. The possibility of the same thing happening millions of times over was a nightmare scenario.

Eventually, Priya broke the silence. "I think Simon went to Nevada to take the crystals to Cirrus."

Jack began pacing, tapping his wand against the side of his leg. "How long has it been since he left?"

Priya checked the manifest. "Six days. The spaceport is more than seven-hundred miles from here, so the driver would have had to stop for one night. Simon might still be days from Cirrus, even under constant acceleration."

"We could disable the airlock above Caerton the way Pieter did at the maintenance depot," Ethan said. "If Simon can't get through, Pieter doesn't get his crystals."

"He could take them anywhere. It doesn't have to be Caerton."

Jack spun abruptly to the portal and raised his voice. "Yes, it does." He waved the wand in the general direction of Caerton. "If he could set up his operation in another city, he wouldn't need to control James." The wand's tip glowed. "He'd never even have come back to this sector, or have killed …" He noticed the glow, lowered the wand, and slunk away to slump into Dave's passenger seat.

Sarah moved to follow, but Priya waved her back. "He's right. For whatever reason, Pieter wants those crystals in Caerton. But Simon could land at any port and put them on a truck. The smartest thing we can do is stop them from getting to the surface."

"Then we need to find out what port he's heading for," Sarah said. "Ethan can do that in Nevada."

"Hold on. None of you are coming with me."

Ethan looked suspiciously at Sarah. "Well … the ship will have a telemetry connection to the launch facility. I could track it from there."

"I can do that myself. There's no need for you to tag along."

"But he will," Sarah mumbled.

"But," Ethan realized, "the only way you can let us know where Simon is headed is to send a message through the portal. It's not really practical to carry it around."

"It's going to be Ethan," Sarah sang.

"We've got phones that work here now," Priya said. "I'll leave the portal in a safe place. Nathan or Victor can stay with it and the other can wait in the Spine to relay a message by radio."

Sarah said nothing, but looked to Ethan expectantly.

"Hold on," he said. "That's not necessary. If Jack can create a flashlight that works from memories, he can make a radio that works the same way. Jack?"

Jack, calmer now, stood and faced his friends. "I guess that makes sense. And it'll have to be me or Ethan that uses it Earth-side. Otherwise, Sarah would need to remember months of conversation. It should be immediate for me and only two seconds for Ethan."

Priya looked at Sarah with exasperation. She shrugged with an *I told you so* expression.

With the decision made that Ethan would accompany Priya to Nevada, Nathan and Victor returned to Cirrus.

"We'll leave one of the trucks here for you," Victor said, "so you don't have to call for a ride. And we'd better get going; it'll be a long trek down the mountain."

"You should camp in the Spine," Priya said. "It's too risky to drive past the mill at night."

Jack tapped his wand against his temple. "We've got night driving covered. If Pieter's men are on the road, they won't even see us coming."

- - - - -

The cave twisted and descended deep into the Vault, but Jack stashed the portal frame just forty feet from the entrance.

"It feels weird leaving it behind," he said. "We could do good things with it. We could bring tools, supplies, or medicine to Cirrus. It's going to waste here."

Sarah placed a hand on his shoulder. "You know Priya's right. Pieter will never stop looking for it. If he finds it, none of those things will ever happen anyway."

Jack nodded and set Ethan's ring on a nearby shelf so his cousin could call for a light as soon as he returned.

- - - - -

The two-hour descent passed in total darkness for Nathan and Victor. Jack would have driven using headlights except that Sarah discovered an unexpected aspect of her night-vision: not only could she see clearly, her long-term memory highlighted the actual route. Where Jack and Ethan had struggled to find the path across stony ground, Sarah drove as if under streetlights.

"We're approaching the crossroad," Victor said after the foothills merged into the plain. "We need to take precautions."

"Could they have made it this far on foot?" Jack asked.

"If they knew where they were, they'd have gone east. That would have been the fastest way to Caerton. If they didn't know, the smartest choice would have been to split up and go both ways. What do you think, Sarah? Do you remember anything?"

"No, but I understand what Priya means about listening to your instincts. It makes sense for them to split up, so that's all I can picture now. I have to learn to rely on intuition."

"We'll assume they're waiting at the crossroads," Jack said. "I'll prepare a surprise for them."

Nathan and Victor could do nothing to help, so they sat back and watched as Jack moved his wand in a circular motion. A dust-devil formed in front of the truck. The faster Sarah drove, the faster it swirled, keeping the same distance ahead.

"We're close," Jack said. "Put a shield around us."

Sarah used her earrings to fashion a barrier around the truck. Jack raised his wand through the roof rack and twirled it in a larger circle. Ahead, the swirling wind became a tornado that spanned the road. It picked up small rocks up and flung them into the fields.

"Here we go." Sarah raised her own wand. "Let's make this

more impressive."

She pointed at the twister and cast the Really Bright Light. In the back seat, Nathan and Victor shielded their eyes. The towering column of dirt and gravel was painfully bright for Jack and Sarah as well, but their night-vision spells helped them see the road ahead.

The spark of anger Jack had been harboring flared when he spotted two of Pieter's men standing in the intersection. He recognized one from Priya's apartment. *You shot my friend.*

The AI maintained the tornado while Jack modified Sarah's spell. He wanted the thugs to suffer the same fear they had inflicted. With only a thought, he cast another light, and the twister blazed fiery-red.

One man froze in place as the hellish storm bore down on him. The other was awestruck but retained enough sense to grab his companion and pull him off the road at the last moment. They both tumbled over the rocky shoulder, adding to the bruises they'd collected from their earlier rough landings.

Jack canceled the light and allowed the whirlwind to fade. "Sorry, I should have asked before I used your wand. One of them was the man who shot Ethan."

Sarah laughed. "That's all right. He would have appreciated it."

Chapter 36

Priya rubbed her bloodshot eyes. "I should have taken the Chevy."

"I can drive," Ethan said. "It's not a problem."

"It *is* a problem. The driving age here is nineteen."

Instead of leaving Everett in the newer, self-driving Suburban, Priya had detoured to Olympia for her Mustang, which was old enough that its automated navigation features relied on a non-existent GPS. With three hundred miles to go, she had no choice but to let Ethan take over; it was no longer safe for her to be behind the wheel.

She pulled over and unfolded a map for Ethan, who'd fallen asleep after midnight but was wide awake now. "Turn here, here, and here."

The sun was rising as Ethan buckled himself into the driver's seat. "I'll be really careful. I'll stick to the speed limit and everything." He grinned.

Priya looked at him with narrowed eyes. "Just wake me in four hours." She reclined her seat and draped her jacket over her face to block the sun.

- - - - -

Jack awoke to the sound of static and Ethan's voice. "Jack? Are you there?"

"What? Where are you?" He glanced around the empty room.

"Four hours from the spaceport."

Jack rolled over and spotted the phone on the table next to his bed. Before leaving the Spine, he'd created a spell to allow the devices to transmit memories. They worked as two-way radios on Cirrus—anyone could use them—but only he, Sarah, and Ethan could *remember* what was sent between Earth and Cirrus. To everyone else, it sounded like white noise.

"Spaceport? Oh, yeah. Okay, I'll let the others know. Are you whispering?"

"Can't you tell?"

"Sort of. Remember, we aren't actually *hearing* each other. I just got the impression you were trying to be quiet."

"I am. Priya's asleep and I'm driving her car." Jack sensed joy in Ethan's words, then *heard* the engine's roar as his attention shifted to the powerful rumble. "Sarah was right, this thing is incredible."

"She'll be upset that she can't tease you about it anymore."

"Tell her I hit one-twenty. Oops." Ethan focused on Priya, and Jack sensed that she had shifted in her sleep. "Sorry, I meant, *fifty-five*. I'll call you when we get to Nevada."

Jack dressed and wandered to the lodge to see if Sarah was there. She had another of the phones, so he could have called her, but he didn't want to risk waking her. They'd returned to Icarus before midnight, then spent several hours discussing Priya's plans with the villagers. He found her sitting in the dining hall with Marten and Jada, who sat with her arms crossed and a scowl directed at her father.

"What did I miss?" Jack asked as he joined them.

"Not much has changed since last night," Sarah said. "We're still going to Caerton, but Marten and I won't go up with everyone else to disable the airlock. We'll be meeting up with Davis at James' mansion."

"Where will you be, Jada?"

Jada stormed out of the room.

Bewildered, Jack asked, "What did I say?"

Sarah lowered her voice. "Suresh won't let her come with us. She's upset that *we* get to go."

"She knows that Pieter's homicidal, right?"

"That's what I tried to—" Her answer was interrupted by Anders calling from the door. "Time to go."

Jack, Sarah, and Marten gathered below the lodge. Anders and Natalya had loaded the village's six vehicles with enough food, water, and cold-weather and rain gear for the eighteen people making the trek.

"Davis," Suresh spoke into his radio, "we're leaving now."

"Okay. Tomas and I have been at James' mansion for an hour. There's no sign of Pieter."

With that assurance, Suresh directed everyone to the vehicles. He instructed Jack to join him and Anders in the lead car. Anders carried a Cirrus-only radio for communicating with Davis, and Jack's Earth-Cirrus memory-phone would relay updates from Priya.

Before taking his assigned place, Jack pulled Sarah aside. "Be careful. Pieter might be at the mansion."

"He might be at the port too."

"I know." He fidgeted with the radio. "It's just that … you know, I—"

She leaned over and kissed him on the cheek, then hurried to her own vehicle before he could respond.

- - - - -

Terrance was waiting in Suresh's truck when Jack arrived. He seemed uncomfortable, and Jack didn't need an emotion detector to recognize what he was feeling. It wasn't until they reached the highway that Terrance finally spoke.

"Jack, I … I've never really apologized for what happened."

"It's okay. You were under Pieter's influence. As I understand it, I owe you my thanks too."

"Oh?"

"In August, during our escape from Pieter. It was you that blocked the highways, wasn't it? You made one of Pieter's trucks overturn right in front of us."

Terrance nodded. "I guess we both owe Niels a lot. He knew exactly when and where you needed help."

"How did you meet him?"

"He approached me out-of-the-blue after I landed myself in trouble with the police in Dallas. He bailed me out and told me to apply for a job on the bombardment team. I had no chance. I was only eighteen—no skills, no experience—yet somehow I got the job. And when I screwed *that* up, he was there to bail me out again."

"Screwed up?" Terrance seemed reluctant to continue, so Jack said, "I heard you tried to spell your name in nickel under the sector wall."

Terrance laughed. "You heard right. A lot of us were doing it. I was the one who got caught."

"How did that work? Spelling your name, I mean, not getting caught."

"It was right before the roof was grown. You know how portals were used to break up the asteroids and separate the ore?" Jack nodded and Terrance continued. "My division was building the sector walls. What we were sending down was mostly gravel. We had to keep the flow high enough so the rock fused but didn't completely melt; the rest of Cirrus had cooled years before. The computer told us what particle streams to direct through which portal to make the walls grow evenly, but I wrote a subroutine that misidentified the occasional shipment of nickel. I didn't think anyone would notice. As it turned out, others had the same idea, except they did it with gold and silver. Someone noticed."

"There's gold buried in the walls?"

"Not just the sector walls, this had been going on from the beginning; most of the precious metals will be in the rim mountains. Niels convinced the authorities that I'd helped him discover the identity of those people. In return, he asked for a favor. A *big* favor."

"Icarus Island?"

"Yep. I'd already learned how to trick the computer into mis-grading an asteroid. It wasn't hard to make sure the one the committee selected was more dense than expected."

"It's amazing how much he foresaw—that he knew it would create the island and not punch a hole through the ring."

"I wish he'd told me more. The day before Pieter showed up, he asked me to keep an eye on you, to stay close in case you needed help. That's why I kept track of you when you went to

Caerton with Priya. I don't think Niels knew what Pieter could do."

"Maybe not," Jack said, though he was certain Niels had known more than anyone guessed.

Chapter 37

Ethan had intended to let Priya sleep the entire way, but woke her when he got lost.

The Nevada spaceport wasn't like the larger one in New Mexico. All passenger flights departed from there, but the Nevada complex was set up to launch cargo ships for hundreds of corporations, from dozens of pads spread over four hundred square miles. Priya checked the manifests and identified the correct site. Ethan had the speedometer pegged at exactly fifty-five, so she let him keep driving.

He continued another fifteen miles on a laser-straight road that veered just twice, and only by a few degrees, as if the surveyors had been unsure of their target. They passed circles of withered alfalfa, half a mile across. Once irrigated by giant sprinklers that pivoted around a central water supply, the fields were being reclaimed by the desert.

Ethan pointed to a sign mounted above the open door of a hangar, one in a line of eight. "That's Armenau's logo." He parked next to the Command and Control Center: a steel Quonset hut five-hundred yards from the launchpad, from where they could see into the hangar. "It's empty."

"Wait here," Priya said as she left the car, even though theirs was the only vehicle they'd seen since bluffing their way through the security checkpoint. She rattled the hut's door handle before walking to the back to climb the chain link fence. After a minute, she reappeared on the other side of the hut and peered through its only window. Returning to the door, she signaled to Ethan. "Bring the phone."

As he walked, Ethan scrolled the phone's contact list to find the unlocking spell. "Can I try it?"

Priya frowned. "This is technically break-and-enter."

"But …. we're gonna do it anyway. So, why not me?"

She heaved a sigh and stepped away from the door. "Fine."

Ethan pressed the phone near the door's handle and touched the icon. The locked clicked. He chuckled.

Priya shook her head and held him back as she pushed open the door. "You're enjoying this *way* too much."

The hut was more modern than it appeared from the outside. A dozen office chairs surrounded a boardroom table on one side of the building. Another group of deep-seated leather recliners were arranged on the opposite side—theater-style—in front of a giant screen for executives to watch launches in safety. Kitchen and dining facilities crowded the near end of the hut, but Ethan's attention was drawn to the cluster of workstations at the far end.

He crossed the room. "They left everything on." An eight-foot screen on the wall above the command console flashed numbers and diagrams. Three smaller panels on either side displayed grainy video.

"I think Simon had to do everything on his own," Priya said. Two of the screens pictured the empty launchpad. "There was no one here to turn it off."

"Uh, oh. I'd better call Jack."

"Why?"

He traced a diagram on the larger central screen. "This is a depiction of the shuttle's flight path relative to Cirrus." He raised the phone and touched the icon for the conference spell. "Hello, Jack? Sarah? Where are you?"

"We're already past Caerton," Jack said. "We should hit the airlock in an hour."

Sarah, who'd split off the main group at the city, said, "Marten and I will be meeting up with Davis and Tomas in fifteen minutes. Where are you, Ethan?"

"At the Command Center."

"Did Simon make it to Cirrus?" Jack asked.

"Yeah. And he's a lot closer than we thought; just two hours away."

- - - - -

The tunnel access to Caerton's spaceport was similar to the one at the maintenance depot in that it required an initial climb up a mountain. But unlike the Spine—formed by the violent collision of opposing masses—the rim mountains had been shaped by the steady collapse of a thirty-mile-thick band of semi-molten rock.

In many places, the mountains shielded the rim wall to its full interior height: six miles, creating ice-covered plateaus that melted year-round in spectacular waterfalls. But the tunnel Suresh sought was at the base of a four-mile-tall treeless slope. Crowning that gray and black stone, two miles of bright, exposed metal guided the group through the forest, which had been dusted by a recent snowfall.

He waited until all the vehicles arrived before cranking open the tunnel doors. "Put on your winter gear now. The base of the mountain is only two miles thick, and the rim wall has been out of the sun for six weeks. It will be *very* cold inside."

A blast of freezing air rolled over the line of vehicles. Jack hurried to open the duffel bag that held his heavy coat and gloves.

"What are you doing here?" Natalya exclaimed, two cars back. Jada tumbled out of her truck from under a blanket in the cargo bed.

Suresh gaped as—without a word—Jada zipped her winter coat, pulled on a pair of gloves, and dropped into the empty seat beside Isabel. He wagged a finger and prepared to tell her off, until she tilted her head to crack a joint in her neck, crossed her arms, and stared straight ahead. Isabel covered her mouth to stifle a laugh.

- - - - -

Jack tucked his gloved hands under his armpits as they drove. "Is that as high as the heaters go?"

After Suresh aborted the attempt to scold Jada, they'd gathered in the tunnel and sealed the doors to prevent ice from forming and Pieter from following. Jack's coat was designed for winter on Cirrus' surface, but the heat stored in the wall during the six months of constant sunlight before the equinox had already dissipated; the inside temperature was minus forty.

Anders, who'd been driving silently while Suresh brooded, cleared his throat and set his jaw to wipe any trace of a smile. "We'll be at the elevator soon."

Unlike the maintenance depot, the rim elevator shafts were vertical and contained entirely within the metal wall. Its cars were also insulated and designed for people, not heavy cargo, so they were smaller, faster, and warmed up quicker. In less than three minutes, they'd ascended two miles and reached the elevation where gravity was only one-half gee.

The doors opened into an airlock. From there, Suresh led the party into the control room where he connected a power cell to the emergency lighting system, revealing a cavernous landing bay through a four-inch-thick glass window.

Jack recognized several Earth-to-Cirrus passenger liners parked below two-mile-tall docking tubes. These craft weren't streamlined like the one Pieter crashed on the sector wall, but tubular frames that stacked eight passenger cabins: flattened cylinders one-hundred-eighty feet long and forty feet wide, connected by escape hatches at each corner. They also didn't have rocket nozzles, only fixed maneuvering thrusters. The main engines, with dynamic portals spanning twenty feet, detached from the cabin frame and remained outside during docking.

"The transfer station is below us," Suresh said. "We can't stop Simon from landing, but we can prevent him from getting into the station. Let's go down to the observation deck and see what we've got to work with."

The observation room's window overlooked a space with the same footprint as the bay above. With forty-foot ceilings and six rows of tracks, it resembled the maintenance depot. In addition to two coach-sized airlocks—one on each side of the station—a central elevator, which also functioned as an airlock, connected to the landing bay.

Suresh described the facility for the group. "The merging lanes for the high-speed tunnels are outside those airlocks. The elevator moves shuttles between here and the landing pad. All we have to do to stop Simon at any port is block its elevator."

"What's that tunnel?" Jack pointed to a wide rectangular opening at the far end of the station.

"The trunk line to Caerton," Anders said. "We'll weld the breach doors shut to stop anyone from opening them from the other side."

Suresh gestured at the single coach parked near the passenger airlock. "I was hoping there would be more than one. We brought plenty of power cells, but if we send this coach out, we won't have one to park in the elevator until it returns."

Preventing Simon from unloading the crystals would be easy once they learned which port he was landing at. It would have been even easier with several coaches; they could have spread them around the sector and reached any destination more quickly.

Jack considered the assortment of equipment parked at the near end of the yard. Tools, carts, and other gear lay scattered around. "What's that one?" He pointed to a much smaller vehicle in the corner. "It looks like it has a rocket engine."

"It's a *crawler*," Natalya said. "They're used for inspecting the roof. They can land on the surface to make repairs. That was my job. I've flown that same machine a thousand times."

"Can it crawl into the airlock?"

"Not on its own. We can drag it, though."

Suresh organized everyone into teams and reviewed the safety protocols, reminding them that the outside pressure was equal to its actual elevation: four miles. In the event of a breach, air would rush up through the trunk line. They wouldn't suffocate in the bay, but there was a danger of being blown through a large enough hole.

As expected, the batteries had been pilfered from every vehicle in the station, even those in the bathtub-sized tractor needed to shift the crawler. Isabel removed its engine panel and poked around for a few minutes, then gave Suresh a thumbs-up; they could power it with a module from one of their own trucks.

Jack's job was to wait for a call from Priya while the others worked in the transfer station. He and Jada watched from the heated observation deck as one group repaired the coach, another dragged the crawler, and a third welded the breach doors.

"Something's wrong," Jack said into his phone. "This is too easy. Do you think this was part of Pieter's plan?"

"What's that?" Sarah asked.

"Did Pieter know we'd be here? Once the tunnel door is welded, there's no chance of him getting between here and the city. Why isn't he trying to stop us?"

"Maybe Pieter is planning on showing up later. Or maybe Simon's landing at another port."

"I don't know. Suresh will have the coach running soon, and then we can block any port. If he doesn't stop us now, he won't have another chance. How are you doing, Ethan?"

"I'm still trying to take over the shuttle from here."

"How close is Simon?"

"An hour."

Sarah said, "He's not going to Caerton, is he?"

"If I'm reading this correctly, he's headed for your sector, but not Caerton."

"Where, then?" Jack asked. "We may still have time to get there first."

"He's not headed for a port yet. He's approaching from outside the ring."

"What does that mean?" Sarah asked.

"Spacecraft normally fly to the center of the ring to avoid the asteroid defense jets, then loop around to a port. But he's halfway between Caerton and Port Nelson. He could go either way."

"That doesn't make sense. Why Port Nelson? It's too close. If Pieter knows we're here and only have one coach, he'd send Simon to the far side of the sector and have him unload crystals before we got there."

"Then he must not know where any of us are," Sarah said. "He'd need a spy to be sure."

"Oh, no," Ethan said. "Where's Terrance?"

Chapter 38

"Terrance is Pieter's spy," Ethan said.

Jack leaned on the observation window and spotted him working with the team repairing the coach. "No way. He was under Pieter's control then."

"Maybe he still is. There are crystals in the power cells. Is he near one?"

"Yeah, but Pieter would need to find that portal to make the link. It has to be a crystal he's used before."

"He had to send someone to the mill to pick up his men," Sarah said. "Maybe they used the radio trick to locate the ring."

"They'd still have to force Terrance to take it." Jack tried to recall everyone's movements since then. "When would they have had the chance?"

"I don't know," Ethan said. "You can check if he's carrying it, right?"

"He's too far away. And Suresh won't let me into the bay without a good reason."

"Can you link to the ring and see if it's still buried?"

"That's too risky," Sarah said. "If Pieter has it, he might be able to control Jack."

"There's another way," Jack said, "but it'll take longer. The mill is half an hour from Icarus … as the crow flies." He used his wand to portal-search for the ravens. A shared sense of recognition told him he'd found the older member of the pair on the island. As before, he let the AI push his own desire to the bird. He thought of the oak tree and the pile of mud beside it. *I need to know if the ring is still there.*

With the combined focus of billions of crystals beneath the island, Jack sensed the raven's curiosity peak and felt him take flight. "He's on his way. I can't communicate with him once he's out of range of the ley lines, so it'll be an hour before he returns and we get an answer. How long before Simon gets to Cirrus?"

"It's gonna be tight," Ethan said. "We'd have a lot more time to plan if you checked whether Terrance has the ring."

Jack paced the observation room. "If he sees me while Pieter's controlling him, Pieter will sense that and become suspicious."

"Give me a minute," Ethan said. "I have to tell Priya what you said."

"That shouldn't be a problem," Priya said after Ethan's update. "It won't matter If Pieter knows we're watching Terrance; he won't decide until the last second. Sarah, tell Davis to enter the mansion. We need to know if Pieter is there or not."

Jack paused at the window. "Then we just need to get past Suresh."

Jada, who'd heard mostly white noise from the radio, had pieced together the conversation from the parts she could hear. She zipped up her coat and headed for the airlock. "I can handle my dad."

- - - - -

Sarah and Marten had parked behind a low hill in an orchard opposite James' mansion. Davis and Tomas were lying in the tall, dry grass near the top of the rise, observing the gatehouse. Sarah left the truck and crept up the hill to relay Priya's instructions.

"How do you plan to get in?" she asked, crouching to stay below the hill's summit.

Tomas slunk backwards, being careful not to disturb the grass. "Through the gate. Anything else will provoke an armed response."

Tomas, a member of Caerton's CorpSec, had served in the army for years before coming to Cirrus. He had no actual combat experience but was well trained and carried one of the confiscated assault rifles from the night Pieter's men attacked Priya's apartment.

"I didn't think CorpSec carried weapons," Sarah said. "Won't *that* provoke an armed response?"

"It'll stay out of sight unless needed," Davis said. "The UN still has jurisdiction here."

She shook her head. "It won't be that simple."

Davis glared. "You two stay hidden. Tell Priya we'll be at the gate in ten minutes."

Sarah returned to the truck and sat next to Marten with her arms crossed. Davis and Tomas drove downhill, away from the mansion, so they could approach it again from the road. After sitting quietly for a minute, Sarah jumped out of her seat and jogged towards the hill.

"Where are you going?" Marten asked.

"Don't worry. I'm just getting closer."

"Pieter's men are armed."

"I'll be all right." She drew her wand and activated her shield. To make her point, she allowed it to push aside the grass as she ran. "Move the car closer to the road when you smell smoke."

- - - - -

From the observation deck, Jack watched Jada approach her father outside the airlock. He couldn't hear what was being said, but the conversation was heated.

Jada gestured wildly as she spoke, attracting the attention of others, while Suresh made calming motions with his hands. She counted on her fingers, possibly listing the ways he was being too restrictive or protective. But Suresh held his ground. He was known to be a stickler for rules, though that was based on decades of experience working in these conditions.

The argument calmed, and the two spoke for another few minutes before Jada wrapped her arms around Suresh and he kissed the top of her head. As she turned away, she grinned and flashed Jack a thumbs-up.

He dashed downstairs and met her at the airlock. "How did it go?"

"We're on garbage duty. That's my punishment for sneaking away from Icarus."

"Sorry. I didn't want you to get in trouble."

"I'm not. This is his way of letting me get what I want."

As Jack left the airlock, he scanned the station and spotted Terrance working on the coach with the others. Jada dragged a bin to a pile of debris and stooped to collect it. Whoever had taken the batteries from the station had done so with no regard for others — they'd left garbage everywhere. Jack didn't mind; some of the trash was in the airlock, where he'd have to go to check on Terrance.

- - - - -

While Ethan familiarized himself with the telemetry systems, Priya spun the dial that selected which of the shuttle's many functions to monitor. She scrolled through hundreds of readings: temperature, pressure, voltage, radiation, and more. With a huff, she shoved her chair away from the console, stood, and pointed to the wall of giant screens. "How can we see the last time he flushed the toilet yet not know where he's going to land?"

Ethan brought up a data-heavy graphic that showed the position of the shuttle relative to Cirrus. "At the rate he's slowing, he's still got twenty minutes to decide."

Priya began pacing. "And then?"

"Thirty minutes to reach Caerton or Port Nelson."

"And it'll take the coach forty-five to reach Port Nelson." She slammed her hand on the console. "Pieter's forcing *us* to decide where he goes. If we send the team to Port Nelson, he goes to Caerton. If they stay in Caerton, he goes to Port Nelson. But why these ports? Jack's right, Simon could get to any other city in the sector before us."

"Then it can't be the port. It's got to be about *Jack*. Simon could land anywhere, but Jack can only be in one spot. Pieter wants Jack out of the way and needs Terrance to let him know where he is."

Priya stopped pacing. "Maybe."

"And there's no way he could predict we'd create memory-phones for communicating with Jack from here; you said that Pieter doesn't know about my ability. Why don't we have Jack get on the coach and head for Port Nelson? That'll force Pieter to decide. We can turn the coach around if we have to."

"All right." Priya leaned against the console and rested her head on her folded arms. "Tell him to board the coach and then ask Sarah which port Simon will be landing at."

- - - - -

Sarah reached the road shortly after Davis and Tomas, on the opposite side of the gate. She stepped from the orchard, unseen, and *remembered* what Ethan was saying in Nevada.

"Sarah. Priya wants you to predict—"

The guard swung his rifle to bear on Davis.

"Can't talk now," Sarah shouted, then launched a fireball at the guardhouse.

Tomas—still in the truck—was holding his pistol in his lap, out of sight. He rolled from the vehicle and fired a single shot as Davis stumbled backwards. The guard's body armor saved his life, and he wisely retreated into the guardhouse. Seconds later, he was bolting from that same shelter as it burst into flame.

Davis spotted Sarah approaching while he crouched behind a stone wall. "Get out here," he shouted.

She ignored him and sent another fireball after the fleeing guard. "We've got to get into the house." She strode to the gate. "I'm not sure why yet, but we only have a few minutes. Are you coming?"

Davis, unaccustomed to taking orders from a sixteen-year-old, started to argue, but then thick smoke from the flaming guardhouse flowed smoothly around her invisible shield. She caused the barrier to become slightly opaque and created a gap large enough to walk through.

Tomas didn't wait for an invitation. He collected his rifle from the back seat, sprinted to the gate, and leapt through the opening.

- - - - -

Jack could hear everything happening in Caerton: the creaking gate, footsteps running on pavement, intermittent gunfire, and the whoosh of fireballs—lots of fireballs.

"Jack," Ethan shouted, "Sarah's under attack. She's not answering."

"I know." *Come on, Sarah. Answer.*

[Not now.]

A pulse of anxiety slammed into Jack. *Were those Sarah's thoughts?* He hadn't spoken aloud, and the answer wasn't embedded in white noise. In fact, there hadn't been a voice at all. Could he have imagined the exchange?

"Jack," Ethan called, "can you hear me?"

"Yeah, I … there's nothing we can do to help her right now." He struggled to fight down a rising wave of vertigo. "She'll need concentration to defend and attack at the same time. It'll be easier for her if we don't distract her."

"What about Terrance?"

Jack calmed himself. Why had a single thought affected him so badly? Was that even her? He'd touched the minds of birds and dragons recently. What was different this time?

"Jack," Ethan repeated, "what about Terrance?"

"He's—" Jack had only experienced such a strong reaction twice before. Most recently, he'd felt it at the mill with the dragons. Before that was the connection from Ethan's coin to … *Pieter.* He spun, searching the bay, then shouted, "Where's Terrance?"

The group working in the airlock only then noticed that Terrance wasn't among them. The crawler's door was open. Jack sprinted to the smaller vehicle and jumped onboard. Terrance was lying on his back with his hand in an open access panel.

Jack drew his wand. *"What are you doing?"*

"Hey, Jack. I'll be with you in a minute. As soon as I finish disabling the navigation system."

As he reached into the opening with a pair of wire cutters, Jack directed a blast of energy to pin his arms to his side. Terrance had only a moment to protest before Anders barged in, seized him by the collar, and dragged him outside. In the reduced gravity, Anders could have thrown the younger man halfway across the yard, but tossed him to the ground instead.

"How did this happen?" Suresh asked when he joined the

group. "Is he being controlled again?"

"No." Jack scanned Terrance a second time. "How could I have been so wrong? He doesn't have the ring. He's doing this on his own."

Chapter 39

Bullets hammered Sarah's shield from several directions the moment she passed through the gate.

Got to save the shield, she thought, knowing she couldn't perceive the toll the gunfire was taking. If her crystals overloaded, they'd fail without warning.

She made the barrier opaque and used her wand to gather the dirt along the driveway into a whirlwind. It wasn't nearly as dense as the one Jack created on the grain road, but it had the desired effect. The cloud grew denser and the number of impacts diminished as she climbed the hundred-yard driveway, guided by the lawn's edge beneath her feet.

The green grass and black asphalt gave way to a block of polished marble. "Steps," Davis said.

Sarah edged forward. A second step emerged. The rate of gunfire abruptly increased, confirming they'd reached the stairs.

"There's no point in hiding anymore." She allowed the shield to become transparent again, revealing two men guarding the main entrance at the top of the steps.

Tomas spun. "There's two more behind us."

"I'll take care of them."

With a flick of her wand, the rotating wall of dirt peeled away and surged towards the mansion's grand entrance. The guards howled in pain as hundreds of pounds of gravel, sand, and sod pelted them. She created an opening in the shield facing the steps.

"Stay out of sight," Davis ordered as he leapt through the hole. Tomas followed.

After sealing her shield, she turned to face the other guards. They'd stopped firing and were crouched behind a fountain, awestruck by the force that had swept over their cohorts. Sarah guessed they were ready to flee and launched another fireball at them to make sure. The glowing plasma blasted a head off one of the marble lions. The men recoiled and ran for the gate.

By the time she got to the top of the steps, Davis and Tomas had disarmed the two assailants and handcuffed them to a railing. They hadn't put up much of a fight; they were battered, bloody, and partially buried. The foyer itself suffered as badly with broken windows, scratched tiles, and pitted walls.

"Pieter had six men in his guard," Davis said. "The four here worked for James. Some of Pieter's men may be here as well."

"They're not," Sarah said.

"Priya told me about your talent, but we'll still assume they are."

She pointed to the doors on the left side of the foyer. "I remember that hallway."

The corridor was empty, as was each room Davis and Tomas checked, except for the one at the far end. Flickering light and intermingled voices sounded through the partially open door.

Davis approached cautiously, pushed the heavy wooden door fully open with the barrel of his borrowed rifle, and entered the office. Pieter wasn't there; the noise was coming from a bank of wall-mounted monitors that displayed bewildering scenes recorded at strange angles. He moved closer, trying to make sense of the images. "These must be from ring-mounted cameras."

Eight of the twelve screens were blank. The view on remaining four only made sense if they were shot from a finger: the stem of a wineglass in a fancy restaurant, helicopter blades seen from below, an extreme closeup of a pistol's trigger.

"Someone's coming," Sarah said.

Tomas spun to face the door and the empty hallway. "Where are they?" He looked out the windows.

She pointed at the swinging image on Monitor Two. "He's crossing the foyer."

- - - - -

Ethan pushed away from the console. "This is insane. I need to *do* something."

He'd been relaying events on Cirrus to Priya as they unfolded.

268

She remained calm as she listened, but he couldn't stop thinking that his two-second precognition was being wasted as a messenger.

"The best thing you can do for them is keep working on the shuttle," Priya said.

He reached forward and spun the function selector, causing the central screen to scroll wildly. "It could take days to hack into the control system."

Priya paced to the boardroom table and rested her forearms on the top of a high-backed office chair. She noticed the omnidirectional voice conferencing microphone mounted in the center of the table.

"Is there any way to talk with Simon?"

Ethan rolled his chair back to the console. "Sure. There are several voice channels through the communications portal. But they won't work while the main thruster is running."

"And Pieter would hear everything we say, right?"

"Well, there's a data-only channel. You can type messages to show up on Simon's heads-up display."

A tone sounded. The central screen flashed new data: approach vectors, g-forces, and nozzle pressures.

"What's happening?" Priya asked.

"The main thruster is down. He's made a decision."

"Which port?"

Ethan studied the screen for a moment and shook his head in disbelief. "Neither. He's still heading straight for the middle."

- - - - -

Jack checked a third time but Terrance wasn't wearing the ring, didn't have it in a pocket, didn't have a portal on him at all.

"I trusted you," Jack cried as Anders dragged Terrance to his feet. "Niels trusted you."

"What's happening?" Terrance asked. "How did I get over here?"

"You're not getting away with that again." Anders squeezed his arm. "You don't have the ring to blame this time."

Suresh appeared at the crawler's door. "He's done a fair bit of damage. Lucky for us it wasn't the coach."

Terrance seemed confused. "Me? It wasn't me. I would never betray Niels."

"Jack," Ethan called, "we know where Simon is going."

"Hold on." Jack held up the phone to show the others that he was listening. "Which port?"

"Neither. He's coming through the roof again. He's headed for the maintenance depot."

Jack was silent for a moment as everything came together.

"Are you there?" Ethan asked.

Jack swore. "How could I have been so stupid? Suresh, how long would it take the crawler to reach the roof directly above the maintenance depot?"

"It's fast. Once it's outside, it could get there in fifteen minutes. I'll see how much damage he did." Suresh leapt into the crawler.

"Ethan?"

"I heard. It'll take twenty minutes for Simon to reach the wall."

"That gives us five minutes to spare. We can still beat him."

"No." Suresh stepped out of the crawler with his shoulders slumped. "We can't. Terrance destroyed the terrain sensor array."

"Terrain? We'll be in space. How does that affect us?"

"In this case, *terrain* means the roof. It rises and falls with the weather below. We can't fly too high or we'll be out of its magnetic field and exposed to radiation. And we can't go fast enough at low altitude without automatic guidance."

"That's why Pieter destroyed the airlock at the maintenance yard. He wasn't trying to escape. He was blocking us from getting to him while he's bringing the coins down from the observation tower."

"And it wasn't him who crashed on the wall, either," Ethan said. "He sent Simon with crystals to repair a portal."

"That's it. That's what was bugging me. Pieter was in the

southbound tunnel. He wasn't trying to get to Caerton. We should have figured this out long ago."

"He saw this coming. He knew everything."

Jack swore and kicked the tractor, dislodging a panel. He picked it up and flung it away. At one-half gee, in thin atmosphere, the metal cover soared like an airplane.

Anders put a hand on Jack's shoulder. "I'm sorry, Jack. I should have been watching him."

"It's okay." Jack grinned as the panel glided the length of the station, only inches above the tracks. "Pieter didn't predict everything. He doesn't know we have a pilot."

- - - - -

Tomas knocked the pistol from James' hand the moment he entered the room, and Davis threw him roughly to the floor. "Where's Reynard?"

"Take his rings," Sarah said.

James seemed confused, much like Terrance had been when released from the ring's hold. "I don't know what you're talking about. What was all the shooting? Why is my foyer filled with dirt?" He tried to stand.

Davis placed a foot on his back and shoved him down. "Where's Reynard?"

"That won't work," Sarah said. "He can't answer truthfully if he was being controlled. And there's something wrong here. Look at the monitors." She picked up James' ring, shifting the image on the second panel. "This is where Pieter watched what was happening through the rings."

Davis tapped a screen. "I'm sure that one is on Earth; it looks like New York. What are these monitors connected to?"

"That's the problem. If the wormhole to James' ring connects to that monitor, then the other end must be in this room. How is Pieter controlling him?"

"Controlling me?" James asked.

"Quiet," Davis ordered. "Search the room," he said to Tomas. Sarah was drawn to a black lacquered box on the wooden desk. She flipped open the lid. Inside, a coil of sensors surrounded another ring. The images vanished from the monitors as she lifted it out.

"There are a dozen crystals on this ring." She peered into the box. "There must be cameras and microphones in here. This is bad news."

"Why?" Tomas asked. "If we've got the command ring, Pieter can't use it on anyone."

"Or else it means he doesn't need it anymore, that he's found another way to control people. It also means Terrance isn't acting on his own after all." She raised her phone. "Jack, what's happening there? Is Terrance with you?"

"We're taking a maintenance ship out to intercept Simon. You were right; he isn't heading for a port. He's planning to crash through the roof again. Natalya can fly the ship without the terrain sensor, and we're bringing Terrance with us because we don't know what else to do with him."

"Pieter is still controlling him." She regarded James, who was watching her intensely. "And he might still be using James too."

"How? Terrance didn't have a portal that Pieter would recognize."

Sarah gestured to the phone. Davis nodded to show that he understood, and she stepped out onto the patio to speak with Jack privately. "Were there crystals anywhere in the port?"

"Just the ones we brought with us. Are you suggesting that Pieter found Terrance through one of those? That's not possible. He'd have had to search through millions. If he could do that, he'd try to control any of us."

"What if there's another way? What's different with Terrance?"

"Well ... he'd recognize Terrance. I recognized Pieter. But he still has to find the right crystal."

"We're missing something. What's the connection between Terrance and Pieter?"

"That's it." Ethan joined the conversation. "The *connection*.

The ring is still the connection."

"How?" Jack asked.

"The AI recognizes us, and the bond with our crystals got stronger the more we used them. If Pieter found Terrance's ring, maybe he can use it to find Terrance wherever he is."

"That's … possible. And certainly less scary than Pieter being able to find anyone, anywhere. But why did he leave the command ring?"

"If he developed a strong bond to it, then all you'd have to do is find one of the control rings and reverse the link to locate him."

"All right, that explains why he didn't take it with him. But why leave it behind? Pieter wouldn't make a mistake like that."

"Half these monitors are blank," Sarah said. "We don't know where or who they were connected to. Pieter could have had James reporting what he saw and ordered the wearers to throw the rings away to hide the evidence."

"What about James? Does he still have his ring?"

"He did, but Pieter spent days in the mansion and would know where all the crystals are. He could control James through any of them."

"Jack," Ethan said, "you have to find out if Pieter has Terrance's ring. We need to know if Terrance is innocent."

"You're right. If Niels was wrong about that, then he could have been wrong about so much more."

Chapter 40

The crawler was an odd, bulbous vehicle with robotic arms and manipulators protruding from its nose and sides. It resembled a deep-sea diving vessel more than a spacecraft. It had not been designed for comfort.

Natalya piloted the craft while Terrance was tied up in the single passenger seat. Jack had to find a spot on the metal floor next to Suresh to sit and meditate. He missed the entire passage through the port, never got to marvel at Cirrus' eight-mile-tall vertical rim, or the icy arc of its inner surface fifty-five-hundred miles away as the crawler made its ascent over the wall.

His bond with the ravens strengthened as they flew closer to Icarus Island. They'd understood his request and found a hole next to the oak tree. The combined impression from their thoughts and memories created a clear image in Jack's mind: the hole had been dug by a shovel, not an animal.

He stood between the two seats. "The ring is gone. Pieter's men must have found it. I'm sorry for not trusting you, Terrance."

Terrance gave Suresh an accusing look. "Can you untie me now?" Then he read Jack's expression. "Oh. I guess you can't."

Jack shook his head solemnly. "As long as Pieter has that ring, he can control you wherever there are crystals."

"Does that mean he knows what we're doing, or where we are?" Suresh asked.

"No, he still needs a camera and microphone to watch us. He's relying on the AI to locate a portal near Terrance, but there's no way for him to know where that crystal is."

"Then how does he know what to tell Terrance to do?"

Jack met Terrance's eyes. "He can feel your emotions. He wanted the crawler disabled and sensed your happiness when the job was done. He'd have felt the opposite when you got caught."

Terrance hung his head. "I hope he feels the way I do now."

The crawler soared over the undulating roof like a seabird skimming the surface of an ocean. Natalya ignored house-sized crests and troughs that rippled the transparent fabric, and guided the craft through thousand-foot-deep twisting valleys created by larger swells. Her experience showed in the way she read the clouds and predicted updrafts.

In the distance, a shimmering bubble marked the sector wall. The prevailing winds kept this section of roof permanently stretched into a shape that mirrored the eight-hundred-mile long berm two miles below.

"Ethan says that Simon is approaching from the far side," Jack said, "but he doesn't know how fast he'll be going."

"If he goes too slow, he'll get stuck in the roof," Suresh said. "If he goes too fast, he could destroy the ship and save us the trouble. My guess is somewhere between thirty and forty miles per hour."

"They'd have learned a lot from Simon's first attempt. I'm betting he'll be landing this one right by the tower."

- - - - -

"Press this button to talk to Simon," Ethan said, explaining the controls to Priya, "or just type and it'll show up on his heads-up display."

"Can you make it so I can speak to him without Pieter hearing?"

"I can, but if Pieter sees, he'll not only know what's happening, he'll force Simon to fix it."

Priya typed, <Simon, this is Priya. Please respond.>

They waited.

"Can you alert him somehow? To make sure he sees the message?"

"It should be in front of his face. It's up to him now."

They waited.

<Hello, Priya,> the response finally came. <It's good to hear from you again.>

- - - - -

The ridge loomed ahead. It no longer resembled a bubble, but a cloudy, mile-tall tunnel that stretched from rim to rim. Natalya rolled the crawler to fly parallel to the slope, then side-slipped up the incline at an angle, keeping the vessel within the roof's protective magnetic field.

"Jack," Ethan said, "Priya's made contact with Simon. She's trying to convince him to turn around or dump the cargo."

"We're coming over the top of the ridge now. We should see him soon. If we can get close enough, I can disable his thrusters."

"What if Pieter predicted this," Sarah said. "Is there a way he can stop us?"

"He doesn't know everything," Ethan said. "He didn't expect Jack to show up at the maintenance depot."

The bump on the back of Jack's head had disappeared, but he rubbed the spot anyway. "It sure felt like he did."

"I don't think so. I'm certain that Simon crash-landed the shuttle and brought a crystal to repair a portal frame in Caerton. Pieter would have come through there and taken a coach to the depot."

"That makes more sense. I can't see Pieter risking his own life. But if his plan was just to bring the crystals to Cirrus, why did he kill Niels?"

"Something changed," Sarah said.

"What?"

"It …" Sarah faltered. "It was you."

"Me?"

"Pieter wasn't expecting you. As far as he knew, we were stuck on Earth. When you showed up, he must have thought you were sent to look for him. He said he was after the 'other Traveller'. He'd have assumed that someone knew his plans."

"I thought he meant you." Jack's throat tightened. "I made a mistake that got Niels killed."

"Oh, Jack. It wasn't your fault. He must have been aware of Niels. He'd have thought Niels was the reason you were there."

"But that was Suresh's decision," Ethan said. "Wasn't it?"

Jack turned to Suresh, who'd been following his and Sarah's half of the conversation. "Why did we go to the maintenance yard for batteries? I mean … why there? And why that day?"

Suresh hesitated before answering. "It was Niels' decision. He warned us that his fusion plant was failing. That's why he asked your parents to come early."

"See," Ethan said. "Niels knew."

Jack shook his head. "You think he sent us to the depot knowing we'd run into Pieter? That doesn't make sense. He nearly killed us when he stole my wand. Wouldn't that also mean Niels knew that finding us there would make Pieter come after him? Why would he do something to get himself killed?"

"Pieter might have pursued him anyway," Sarah said. "The only thing that happened is Niels forced him to do it sooner rather than later. As for the wand … if Niels knew about Pieter, then he knew you'd escape. He wanted Pieter to have the wand."

"Why?" Jack felt the weight of his new wand in his pocket. "It's a powerful weapon."

"Didn't you say Ethan's coin was made from a slice of that wand?"

"Yeah."

"Don't you see? Niels understood the bond between the two."

Jack considered this for a moment. "So, if we had the coin, we could find Pieter."

"And he could find us," Ethan said.

"*If* we had the coin," Sarah said. "Which we don't. Although we know where it is."

"*Here be dragons*," Jack said.

"What are you talking about?"

"Here be dragons. Remember? Niels wrote that on his map. We thought the phrase referred to the future, the unknown. What if he literally meant dragons? What if he was talking about the creatures at the mill?"

"Here be genetically engineered lizard-hybrids?" Ethan asked.

"*Intelligent* lizard-hybrids," Sarah added.

"Here be intelligent, *obsessive* lizard-hybrids, then. Remember all the crystals that thing was sitting on? It's hunting portals now, not pests. But what does that mean? What was he trying to tell us?"

"I don't know," Jack said, "but it's too accurate to call it a coincidence." Suresh tapped his shoulder and motioned for him to look out the window. "I can see Simon's ship now. He's almost at the wall. We're not gonna make it."

"*Don't slow down.*" Sarah's voice was urgent.

"Why not? We'll overshoot if we don't."

"You need to put distance between you and Simon's ship. *Trust me.*"

"Jack," Ethan said, "you'll have to work fast. Make a close pass by the shuttle. Priya, keep working on Simon. I know how to distract Pieter."

Jack told Natalya to buzz the other spacecraft. On Earth, before Priya realized what was happening, Ethan pressed the microphone switch.

"I know you can hear me, Pieter. You're going to fail."

"*What are you doing?*" Jack shouted.

There was a moment of silence before Pieter laughed. His voice, heard by Ethan, was relayed to Jack and Sarah with the cruel confidence they'd come to expect. "I've already succeeded. You can't stop me now."

"You're not the only one who can see the future. I've seen a very different ending. I'm offering you an exchange."

"What could you possibly have of value to me?"

"A coin. One you've been looking for. I know where it is."

Pieter hesitated. "I'll find it without your help."

"I'll destroy it long before you do. I told you, I've seen the future. I'll prove it. A solar flare is about to scramble your communications. Ten … nine …"

"You're stalling. But it makes no difference."

Jack understood Ethan's plan and hated it. The scheme

required split-second timing. They'd be passing the shuttle at hundreds of miles per hour. Finding the correct crystal would be like catching a fly ball by reaching through the window of a moving car.

He drew his wand. "Natalya, get as close as you can." He began counting aloud with Ethan to allow her to time the pass.

Pieter was still talking. "I'll complete my plans and then find that coin. Once I have it, you'll tell me where Jack is."

"… two … one."

Natalya was far more skilled than Jack expected. She rolled the crawler over so that its flat bottom missed the underside of the other vessel by inches. Jack sensed the millions of crystals in the cargo bay, which guided him to the cockpit where there were only a few. Even so, they were passing out of range when he found the one he wanted.

"Got it," he said as they sped away. Now that he recognized that crystal, he could locate it in the virtual world with his wand. He didn't close the portal, though; Pieter had millions of crystals nearby to use on Simon. Instead, he pinched it off, distorting sounds passing through the wormhole.

- - - - -

Ethan turned up the volume to make sense of Pieter's garbled words. What he said wasn't clear, but it sounded like he was calling Simon's name.

"What happened?" Priya asked.

Ethan spoke rapidly. "Jack's blocking the channel, but data is sent with error correction codes—it repeats bits that get lost. That's how telemetry works through the thruster's interference. You can still communicate with Simon through the console."

Priya wasted no time. <*Pieter can't control you now. You can stop the shuttle.*>

<*How is Terrance?*>

"Why does he want to know about Terrance?" Priya asked. Ethan shrugged.

She typed, <*He's fine.*>

<It's my fault. I discovered how to use the portals for mind control.>
<Pieter made you do that. You can stop him.>

"Jack," Sarah said, "Pieter will switch to another crystal if you don't let him speak to Simon."

"She's right, Ethan." Jack allowed the connection to return to normal.

Ethan forced a laugh. "That flare left the sun days ago and I timed it to the second. You didn't see it coming at all, did you? Are you ready to make a deal?"

Pieter was silent. *He's not going for it*, Jack thought.

Finally, Pieter said, "I've underestimated you. Your grandfather's portal has properties I never expected. Tell me where it is and I might reconsider."

Ethan signaled for Priya to keep working on Simon. "No chance. I'm only offering the coin."

"If you can see the future, you know I won't abandon my plans. Those crystals will be on Cirrus within the hour. I'm not leaving to chase a coin that I'll have in a week."

"I don't expect you to. You'll fail either way. I'm just making it more interesting."

"Then tell me."

Sarah shouted for Ethan to stop, but he said, "It's at the mill."

- - - - -

The crawler was already miles away from the shuttle when Jack shouted, *"Why did you do that?"*

"What happened?" Suresh asked.

"Ethan told Pieter where the coin is." He raised the phone and yelled, *"Why did you tell him?"*

"Because," Ethan said, "you just told Terrance. And now Pieter will know it's true. Sorry, Jack. There's no other way. Now block Simon's portal again."

- - - - -

Priya pushed Ethan's hand off the microphone switch. "Why did you tell him the truth?"

"Pieter will concentrate on Terrance now. This is your last

chance to convince Simon." He flipped the switch again and gestured for Priya to continue.

"Simon," Priya said, "we know everything. We know Pieter is controlling you. Destroy your console. We'll take over and land your shuttle at the port."

"How is Terrance?"

"He's fine, he's—"

"He's not fine, is he?"

"No, he's … Pieter is still controlling him. But we know how that works now. We can help him. We can help you too."

"You don't understand how deep it goes. Once he's controlled someone for long enough, they lose their free will. He wants me to deliver the coins to Cirrus. I *want* to do that. That's what I'm going to do. I'm sorry, Priya. Goodbye."

Simon closed the connection.

The speaker came alive with the sound of Pieter's laughter. "Oh, that's brilliant. You hid it in plain sight, thinking we wouldn't go there a second time. But I won't abandon my plans to chase that coin. I'll have my portals *and* your coin. Don't be upset. You'll enjoy working for me. Simon does. Isn't that right, Simon?" There was a moment of silence, then an angry, "*SIMON*."

- - - - -

The shuttle disintegrated in a golden bloom.

Natalya had slowed the crawler and turned to face Simon's ship. From a distance, the sunlight reflecting from the cloud of coins made it appear like a fireball. When Simon opened the cargo door, the air trapped in the individual coin packages expanded. Layer upon layer magnified the slight difference until the outermost coins were traveling at the speed of bullets.

Many coins pierced the roof and tumbled to the sector wall. Others impacted too slowly, and either bounced or embedded themselves within the roof. The majority followed the shuttle's original path, drifting into a diffuse cloud that would orbit in Cirrus' weak gravity for years, eventually spreading themselves across every sector.

Simon had delivered the coins.

Chapter 41

No one spoke inside the crawler until Suresh—ever practical—warned Natalya of coins heading their way at high speed. She turned west and sped over the ridge, then dropped below the crest to place the transparent barrier between her ship and the projectiles.

"What happened?" Ethan asked. "We've lost telemetry."

Jack, the only one in the crawler who could perceive Ethan's question, was too horror-struck to reply. Sarah already knew. "It's over," she said.

Natalya turned the ship north, to return to Caerton, but also to fly past the shuttle's last position. A ragged tear in the opposite slope was blasting atmosphere into space. Below the hole, an unidentifiable piece of the shuttle tumbled in the chaotic air currents, looking as if it might be pushed back outside. But even the paltry gravity at this elevation was constant and soon overpowered the random gusts. Mercifully, swelling clouds obscured the fragment as it began its lengthy dive to the sector wall.

Jack fought back tears. "It's not over. Pieter's right below us. We know where he's going. We can stop him. We have to go through that hole."

Natalya deliberately angled her ship away from the scene. "No, Jack. The crawler isn't aerodynamic. And the holes are already sealing themselves. Even if we could make our own opening, we'd fall straight down."

He wanted to argue, to confront Pieter immediately, but Natalya was right. "We have to do *something*. Pieter is driving to the mill to get the coin. If he finds it, he'll be able to control Ethan and Sarah."

"Priya and I can be there in three hours," Ethan said.

"No way." Priya couldn't hear Jack or Sarah's part of the

conversation, but knew they could hear her. "I'll take you to Icarus, but not to the mill."

"Pieter's at the observation tower. It'll take him four hours to get there. That gives us almost an hour to search."

"It's too risky. We need Davis and Tomas for backup."

"That'll take six hours. Pieter might have found the coin and left by then. Sarah, what do you see?"

"I'm not sure," Sarah said. "It's … It's so confusing. I remember fire."

"Does the mill burn down?" Ethan asked optimistically. "With him inside?"

"No, it's something different, I can't make sense of it."

"Jack can have the ravens warn us. They can fly high enough to spot a vehicle half an hour away."

"I didn't know you could do that," Priya said.

"He can," Ethan said at the same time Jack said, "I can't."

"Fine," Priya said, "but I want proof. Jack, if you can prove that you can warn us, we'll stop for the coin." She then asked Sarah to relay further instructions to Davis and Suresh; the two groups would meet up outside Caerton and travel home together.

"I can't communicate with the ravens once they're away from the island," Jack said. "You know that."

"I've got an idea," Sarah said, "but it'll have to wait until we're together. Start by asking them to fly back to the crossroads."

- - - - -

"How far should we go?" Ethan asked as Priya drove into the mountains, following an ever-narrowing series of tracks.

"Far enough that no one can find the portal while we're gone." She pulled off the road and parked behind a patch of creosote bushes that were taller than the car. "This should work."

Ethan dropped the memory-phone into the glove compartment, then helped Priya move dead brush to better camouflage the Mustang. She moved the portal frame a short distance away, piled more branches around it, then crossed over to Cirrus.

284

Warm, dry air flowing from Nevada warmed the rocks as they made the passage, but the cave reverted to cool and murky after closing the wormhole. Ethan groped above the frame to locate the hidden shelf Jack had described. His ring was there, along with a radio. He passed the radio to Priya and spelled a light from the ring.

When they reached the truck, Ethan went for the driver's seat automatically, earning a raised eyebrow from Priya. He was so accustomed to driving on Cirrus that he forgot sixteen-year-olds didn't drive where she was from.

He gestured with his ring. "I can get us down the mountain faster. You can take over then, if you want."

"That's fine. But when we get to the mill, you *will* listen to my instructions or I'll handcuff you to the roof rack, two-second warning or not."

Ethan grinned but let the opportunity to make another inappropriate comment pass. He silently guided the vehicle out of the trees.

- - - - -

Jack and Sarah switched vehicles to ride together in Suresh's truck when the two groups met. He wanted to talk but had difficulty starting.

"Don't worry," Sarah said, "we'll find the coin before he does."

"It's not just Ethan. If Pieter gets his hands on it, he'll control you too."

"That won't happen."

"Is that your memory or what you *want*?"

She didn't answer. Instead, she reached over and held his hand—she wasn't going to discuss it anymore.

"What's your plan for communicating with the ravens? So far I've only been able to do that when they're near the island."

"You've controlled birds in your sleep, and seen *exactly* what they see, *and* told them where to go. And you figured out how to connect with your uncle while meditating. You *can* use that

285

control while you're awake. We know it's possible. Pieter does it to people."

Jack's gut churned and he felt the familiar tightening of his throat that signaled an anxiety attack.

Sarah squeezed his hand. "It's okay. They're just birds, not people."

"I know, I know. But it's still so … so wrong." He couldn't help but think of Simon.

"What Pieter does is wrong because he doesn't care what happens to his victims. All you're doing is asking them to watch the road."

She was right, of course. He'd never make them do something dangerous. He held his wand loosely, extended his senses, and found the ravens' crystals. As with any other portal, he got a sense of what was on the other side: rustling leaves, bird sounds, a cool breeze.

"I think they're at the crossroads. They're not flying anymore, and I hear the same noises from both."

"Good. Now start with their feelings." She let go of his hand and mimed taking a deep breath. "You're not going to control them yet. Take your time."

Jack leaned back into his seat and wondered what emotions any bird would have, not the ravens in particular. Even if they differed from humans, they had to have certain drives. Something made them behave the way they did: hunger, the need for shelter, a desire for companionship. He waited for anything like that to filter through. Nothing.

There's got to be something else. Even if I sense what they're feeling, how does that make them respond? Controlling another mind has to be an active process, not a passive one. I can't just wait for feedback. I've got to take it. He breathed deeply, committed himself to the act, and slammed into a familiar wall.

Wrong. Memories of a thousand experiments flooded back to him. *I can't affect anything on the other side of a portal. No one can do that. Not me. Not Pieter.*

"I'm the problem," Jack said.

"No, you're … what do you mean?"

"I've been thinking that Pieter was connecting directly to Terrance the way we grab an object through a portal, or send a radio signal through it. But it doesn't work like that."

"Ethan and I could do it."

Jack shook his head. "It only seemed that way. We forgot why emoji sensors were built into modern phones when they didn't even have processors or memory. It's because the electrical signals in the brain are so weak they can't be sensed through the same connection that carries power or data."

Sarah drew her wand and examined the smooth crystal surface at its business end. "But we already figured out that the AI must have its own emotion detector and motivator that works through a portal."

"True, but it still wouldn't work with a single connection. When you and Ethan were experimenting, I opened a direct wormhole between you. That means there had to be a third link to the AI to detect and guide your thoughts."

"Like Pieter's third-eye crystals." Sarah considered her wand warily. "You think someone else has done the same thing?"

"Not yet. But Traveller's memories can only come from a future AI, so it'll eventually happen, and they'll work across time."

"That means it could even be Pieter's crystals. Could he recover them and use them as planned?"

Jack gestured at the sky. "There are millions of them and most are still in orbit. Eventually, they'll hit the roof, though it may take decades for them to fall through. One person could never collect them all."

"If there's a third link, why are you the problem?"

"Because I'm blocking the AI. I thought I was *sending*, that I was in control. What I'm really doing is *allowing* the AI to read and control my thoughts. That's why it only works when I'm asleep; I'm not blocking then."

"So, what's the solution?"

"I've got to find the AI's connection and let it in." He fidgeted with the wand. "I've got to … trust it."

Sarah gripped his hand firmly again, forcing him to focus on staying calm. He took several deep breaths to steady his nerves, then thought about the ravens while knowing the AI would soon make its own link to his mind. His hands trembled.

Why is this always so difficult? I'm still missing something.

With Sarah still holding his hand, Jack opened a wormhole without a destination in mind. He visualized the network of portal crystals as an abstract landscape, something he'd learned to do during Newton. With that framework, he could usually find a crystal in a given environment, although it told him nothing about where it was on Earth or Cirrus.

What am I looking for? If he imagined heat, he'd be drawn to crystals where a flame, or molten metal, or white-hot plasma burned on the other side. If he pictured cold, something similar happened. But a sensor? He needed a link guaranteed to create a reaction strong enough to uncover a single crystal among billions.

Pieter.

With that thought, tens of thousands of wormholes flared, blasting him into the real world.

"What happened?" Sarah exclaimed as Jack lurched in his seat and drew a sharp breath.

He leaned forward and rested his head on the back of Suresh's seat. "I found it." His hands were shaking and he felt queasy. "But it's not just one; there are thousands of links to the AI."

"I'm sorry, Jack. I shouldn't have pushed you." She slumped. "We'll find another way."

"No, this is the right way." He tightened his seatbelt and shifted into a reclining posture. "I was caught off-guard. I was looking for one portal, but there's so many. They're weak, but they're all trying to work at once. It's like …"

"Drinking from a fire hose?"

"Yeah. It's got to be the same for everyone, but I'm just more sensitive to them. I can do this on the island because the portals are so distant and tiny. But when they come through my wand or a phone, it's too much."

"Can you isolate a single detector?"

"Maybe. The last thing Niels told me was to make my anxiety a strength, not a weakness. I'm extra-sensitive to the portals, which also means I should be able to use them better. I've got to try again."

Sarah said nothing, just squeezed his hand.

He relaxed and dropped into the imagined landscape again. *I can do this. I need to think of something that will create a strong bond, but without fear.*

Sarah.

Countless portals jetted like geysers in an endless volcanic caldera, but Jack didn't shy away. Each flare was a crystal through which the AI could find Sarah and transmit her feelings to him. He waved his imagined hand over the erupting surface and calmed it. Then he selected a single crystal and zoomed closer.

[Jack.]

A disembodied voice acknowledged his presence, except there weren't any words. He felt the sense of recognition he'd experienced with the dragons: something not quite human, but intelligent and aware. It was the same voice he'd been hearing his entire life, repeated as many times as there were nearby phones, and the voice he'd associated with Pieter's thoughts below the maintenance depot, and Sarah's at James' mansion.

So, this is the AI.

[Yes, we are.]

Finally, he understood. He wasn't imagining the voices, wasn't hallucinating. It was the AI. It had always been the AI. On its own, the single link he'd isolated wasn't invasive, and he knew he could work with it transparently, the same way anyone else did.

He found the older raven's leg band crystal. Knowing the AI enabled their partnership, he reached out and touched the creature's mind.

    Fly, Jack thought, and took to the sky.

Chapter 42

"We're at the crossroad." Ethan looked to the sky. "I see a raven."

"Hold on," Sarah said. "Go ahead, Jack."

With Ethan and Priya on Cirrus, radio communication became much easier. The antique devices still needed the user to press the transmit button, but everyone could hear what the others said. After an hour of practice, Jack had also mastered his own form of AI-mediated broadcast. A raven swooped low and glided ahead of the truck.

"I'm impressed," Priya said. "All right, we're heading for the mill now. Give us as much warning as you can. As far as we know, Pieter never learned that there's a village near the island, and we want to keep it that way. Don't let him get close enough to follow us, and tell everyone to meet at the bridge on the main road, just to be safe."

"Got it," Sarah said. The raven flapped its wings and climbed.

"We have less than an hour," Priya said to Ethan.

"I know where I threw it. It shouldn't take that long."

He parked in the trees two hundred yards before the mill complex. If Pieter showed up without warning, they'd run through the forest and sneak back to the road.

Instead of walking through the front doors, they skirted the buildings through thick brush to make sure the escape route was clear. It took fifteen minutes to hike to the forested location near the elevated hallway.

Ethan stopped beside the dome. "I was right here." He picked up a coin-sized pebble and threw it into the trees. "It should be around there."

The underbrush in the area where the stone fell was dense, and Priya struggled through the branches. "I don't think we can even find the rock, and we saw where that landed. Is there a way to make the coin more visible?"

Ethan keyed the radio. "Jack? Any ideas?"

- - - - -

Jack was relaxed now and could divide his attention between two tasks. "I could shine a light through my wand."

"You can't do that," Sarah said.

"If it's lying face-up, they might see it."

"That's not what I meant. There's never been a link between your new wand and the coin. If you create one, there's a risk of Pieter following it back to you."

"Then what do we do?"

"Make a link through my earrings. I'll listen for Priya and Ethan to come closer."

"But then he'll …" Jack stopped when he remembered that Pieter would already have a way to find Sarah through any crystal if he gained the coin. He focused his attention on Sarah's earring while maintaining a weak hold on the ravens through his wand. Ethan's coin contained a crystal he knew very well, and it took only moments to connect. "Do you hear anything?"

Sarah cupped her hands around her ears. "Make some noise, Ethan."

- - - - -

Ethan walked a standard line-search pattern, following Priya's instructions. They stopped every few paces to shout. After several passes with no results, she reduced the gap between them and repeated the search from a different angle. Only once did Sarah stop them and ask them to recheck a spot, saying she heard scraping, but the sound didn't repeat when they retraced their steps.

After they'd covered an area twice the size of a baseball diamond, Priya said, "We're running out of time. Sarah, do you hear anything at all?"

"Nothing that corresponds to what you're doing. I've heard scratching noises, but they keep going even when you're not moving."

"It's got to be here," Ethan said. "I was standing beside the dome when I threw it. I remember this tree."

"Sorry." Priya sounded defeated. "We're out of time."

Arguing was pointless. They'd covered the entire zone four times. Besides shouting, he tried invoking the *skip* spell, something both he and the coin were familiar with. He'd have to be almost on top of the portal for that to work, but they must have been close enough at some point.

"Pieter's coming," Jack said. "I see … *we* see clouds of dust. From the east. Maybe fifteen minutes away."

"We're already on our way out," Priya said.

"Maybe it's buried." Ethan slumped back to the car. "Or maybe somebody other than Pieter was here looking for salvage and found it."

"I hope you're right, but we can't take chances. Give me your ring."

"My ring? What if we need a shield spell?"

"It's *your* ring or these ones." She dangled a pair of handcuffs.

Ethan laughed before realizing she was serious. "I can block him. I've done it before."

"And neither of us can take the risk that he's learned how to defend against that."

Ethan reluctantly handed over his ring.

"Jack," Priya said, "we're heading back to Icarus. How much distance do we need to keep between Ethan and the ring?"

"Pieter won't be able to control him as easily as Terrance or Simon. As long as he's not actually wearing it, you should be okay. But be prepared to toss it. The phone and radio too."

"Got it. Sarah, you know what you have to do."

- - - - -

Sarah set the radio down. "I know what I have to do. But I don't have to like it." She passed her wand to Jack. "You'd let me keep it if I asked, wouldn't you?"

"Of course. It's …" For Jack, the wand wasn't a weapon. It was a tool that gave him a sense of connection, more so than he'd ever had with texting or video chat on a phone.

"I won't make you decide." She removed her earrings and handed them over, too.

He placed Sarah's items in the door panel's pocket, then dropped his own wand there as well.

- - - - -

By the time the convoy from Caerton reached the bridge, most of the remaining villagers were gathered there. They'd done a fine job of camouflaging the road; the lake access would be difficult to spot, even in the daytime. Now that it was dusk, the path to Icarus was essentially invisible.

Sarah's mother practically dragged her from the car the moment they stopped. Jack's parents were also there, but happy enough to see him safe that they let him go to Priya first.

Priya updated Davis with what they'd learned. She and Ethan had hidden in the trees a safe distance from the intersection and seen three black vans turning towards the mill. "Assuming there were two men in each vehicle, we have six armed opponents to deal with, plus Pieter."

"That's what we expected," Davis said. "I've never seen more than that in his personal guard."

Priya had changed into combat fatigues and body armor and was quick with her orders. "Tomas, I'll take the lead with Davis. You bring the second car."

"Which car do you want me in?" Jack asked.

"*You* are not going," Emily said tersely.

"Of course I am." He strode to the vehicles.

"No." Victor blocked him. "You've helped enough. This job is for the police."

Jack clenched his hands into fists. "*I am going.*" His volume matched his rage. "You can come with me, but *I'm* the only one who can detect that portal, and *I'm* the only one who can stop Pieter. It's *my* fault he has that wand. It's *my* fault he used it to kill Niels. *I'M TAKING IT BACK.*"

"Jack," Priya said, "calm down."

Her tone caught his attention in a way that no shout or order could. There was fear in her voice, something Jack never expected to hear from the woman who took on armed mercenaries twice her size. He looked down, wondering what scared her. She was looking at him. She feared *him*.

That's when it hit him that he was looking down at everyone, even Anders. He was hovering a foot off the ground. He hadn't even realized he'd picked up his wand, but it was in his hand, glowing an angry red.

He recalled the night Pieter torched the Magnolia. Witnesses had described him as floating and carrying a flaming weapon. Now, the villagers' faces reflected the same fear Pieter had caused. He dropped the wand and collapsed on the road.

"I'm sorry." He held his face in his hands. "I'm not like him. I don't want to hurt anyone. I just want this to end."

Sarah rushed over and put her arms around him. "No, you're not like him. None of what happened was your fault."

Jack's parents moved to comfort him, but Priya intercepted them and ushered them to the bridge, where Davis and Tomas stood.

Ethan helped Jack to his feet. "Sarah's right. This was all Pieter. He'd have come after Niels sooner or later. If we hadn't been there, we'd have never learned his plans. He'd have an army by now. He'd have gotten to all of us."

They were right. All the evidence proved that Niels had predicted these events a long time ago. This was part of his plan.

Ethan leaned closer to Jack and spoke quietly. "We'll swipe a truck after they've left and find the coin while they're taking care of Pieter."

"No chance." Priya had come up behind Ethan. "Jack, you're coming with us. But there are very strict rules. I've seen your shield in action. You will put it up and not take it down under any circumstance. And if I say leave, you leave. Is that understood?"

Jack stooped and recovered his wand. "I understand."

"And you two are not coming." Priya pointed a warning

finger at Sarah and Ethan. "I know you can defend yourselves, but if Pieter finds that coin, you'll put us all in danger."

"She's right," Jack said. "You have to sit this one out."

"It's okay." Sarah hugged him tightly. "You'll find the coin first. I've seen it happen."

"You're sure?" Jack whispered in her ear.

"Positive." She kissed him. On the lips this time.

Despite being their first true kiss, Jack retained the presence of mind to slip Sarah's earrings into her jacket pocket. He stepped back, not wanting the moment to end. She passed her hand over the pocket and smiled.

"Good luck, Jack." Ethan covered his closed fist with his left hand in a martial arts salute. "Kick his ass."

"Thanks, I will."

"Wait." Sarah ran over to Anders, who was holding her wand and Ethan's ring. "Can I have my wand for a second?"

Anders looked nervously to Priya for approval.

As soon as Sarah touched the wand, she said, "There are two men waiting in the trees a mile before the mill, on the left. And Pieter knows you're coming." She smiled coyly at Jack. Her prediction had come too quickly; she'd received future memories through her earrings.

"I can take care of that," Jack said. "But get in first." He gathered four radios and clipped one to each car's front and rear bumper, then sat beside Tomas. "Shields up."

The air shimmered around each car.

"Ooh." Jack winced. "That really does sound geeky when I say it out loud. I'll re-train that spell to work silently."

Chapter 43

The Eye, Cirrus' artificial moon, was behind clouds as Priya and Tomas swung their vehicles onto the mill road. It was impossible to hide their approach, so they drove without lights to present as poor a target as possible. Jack, certain that Sarah's prediction would prove true, kept the invisible flashlight trained on the road's left shoulder.

"There they are."

His warning was redundant. The two men hidden in the grass opened fire. Dozens of sparks ignited directly in front of the car.

Jack flinched, alarmed by the number of bullets. This was no longer about intimidation or control; Pieter had ordered his guards to kill. Without the shield, they wouldn't have survived more than a few seconds.

The crystal in the front radio, taking the brunt of the assault, was too far away for him to sense accurately, but he knew it couldn't take much more abuse. He had to stop the gunfire.

"*Close your eyes.*" He set off the Really Bright Light.

Even through closed lids, the flare was overwhelming. Both vehicles swerved as their drivers reacted with surprise. Jack flicked off the intense light, opened his eyes, and switched back to the invisible beam.

He spotted a van in the trees, out of range. "That should buy us some time. I couldn't disable their vehicle, but I doubt they'll even be able to walk a straight line for a while."

The assault had so far taken only a few seconds, and the mill was less than a minute away. Unfortunately, the bright light defense had ruined everyone's night vision. Priya turned on her headlights.

"There's a covered, drive-thru loading bay on the front of the building," Jack said. "If we pull in there, I can reconfigure the shields."

Priya angled towards the bay as soon as it came into view. Designed for full-sized grain transporters, it would fit dozens of their own cars. "Too much chance of an ambush. *Hang on.*"

She jerked the wheel hard to the left and rammed straight through the metal double-doors. The sudden impact was too intense for the overheated radio crystal. It shattered as the heavy doors flew off their hinges, then spun and rebounded against the sides of her car, smashing its windows.

Directly ahead, another set of doors led further into the mill. Jack recognized a distant hammering as gunfire and prepared to create a replacement shield. However, Priya had already figured out that her front shield had collapsed. She veered into the nearest aisle, sideswiping two milling machines, and slid to a stop with the car's nose touching the far wall. Tomas followed through a swirling cloud of flour.

Before the car had even come to a complete stop, Priya and Davis tumbled out and took cover behind the bulk of the machinery.

"Stay down." Priya motioned to Jack. Tomas hopped from his seat and crouched beside the car.

Another burst of gunfire rattled the ceiling ducts.

"Who are they shooting at?" Davis asked.

Priya stood as the rifles sounded again. "I don't know, but this room is clear. That sounds like it's indoors, far away."

Tomas joined Priya. His military training was evident in the way he moved stealthily along the aisle while covering both sets of doors.

"Jack," Davis said, "stay here until we've assessed the situation. We don't know who they're shooting at, but they're probably not friendly."

"Wait." Jack unclipped a radio from the car's rear bumper. "I can adjust the shields so you can carry them." After concentrating for a moment, he handed the device to Davis, then crouched to gather and lob handfuls of flour in the air.

Davis swung the radio experimentally through the drifting

cloud. "It's a riot shield."

The repelled flour swirled in front of the shield, revealing its dimensions. Davis thumped the invisible barrier against a milling machine and seemed satisfied that it was real.

Jack retrieved another radio from the front of Tomas' car and gave it to Priya. She'd seen the shield in action and didn't need proof it was there. He offered the last one to Tomas.

"I can't hold that and my rifle. It'll be in the way. You need it more than I do."

Jack waggled the wand. "I have my own and it's a lot stronger. I can clip it to your belt so you don't need to carry it."

"Sure. But put it behind me. I need to move freely."

Jack clipped the radio to Tomas' belt and activated the shield. He struggled to shape the field but eventually produced something that fit close to Tomas' body, protecting his head and torso without restricting his movements.

Tomas shook himself, banging the shield against a steel column. "I feel like a turtle."

"Sorry. If Sarah was here, she could mold it into body armor." He then used Ethan's ring to shield himself. "I want my hands free too."

"Damn," Priya said. "I just thought of something. Can Pieter create a shield?"

"He's seen it done. I created one at the depot. I don't know if he can do it on his own … unless he gets the coin. That's what I used to create it."

"Best to assume he can." She faced Davis and Tomas. "You got that? If you see Pieter, assume he can't be hit. Jack, what about his guards?"

"I didn't sense portals on the men we drove past. My guess is, no, he can't train crystals on his own. And even if he can, he's only ever shown brute force. Sarah can shape the field in ways I can't. If Pieter's goons have shields, they'll be simple, like the ones I created for you."

"How do we get to Pieter if he's invulnerable?" Davis asked.

"He's not, but that wand will absorb a lot of damage. It took smashing through steel doors to break the smaller crystal in the radio." Jack breathed deep and exhaled slowly. "I have to face him. He'll try to force my shield down while I try to force his. We'll be evenly matched. If we can get rid of the mercenaries, we can overload his wand. Also, he won't be able to attack effectively while holding a shield."

"How powerful is this wand thing?" Tomas asked.

"I've seen Jack throw a man bigger than you through a wall," Davis said.

Distant gunfire, mingled with the screams of men, echoed again. Jack recognized another sound in the battle chorus—familiar and terrifying. "I know where Pieter is."

Tomas led the group to the second set of doors. Jack pushed them open slowly before he got there. Cloud-filtered moonlight illuminated the room only dimly through the skylights, so he also used his wand to create an invisible beam for himself.

"Turn out that light," Priya hissed.

Startled, Jack asked, "You can see this?"

"What light?" Tomas asked. "What are you talking about?"

"Uh, don't worry. Only Priya and I can see it. It must have something to do with going through Grandpa's portal."

"I guess I'm taking point then." Priya swapped positions with Tomas.

"What do you see?" Davis whispered.

Priya advanced. "It's a dim flashlight."

"It's a spotlight for me," Jack said. "But now that I know you can see it, we can improve it later."

A sustained burst of automatic gunfire followed more screaming. Flashes of light leaked through gaps in the doors ahead. Jack pointed the wand and swung them open from a safe distance.

Priya edged cautiously into the next room—the mill's main warehouse—which was partially lit by the eerie green shine of discarded chemical glow sticks. Tall rows of steel shelving reached to the forty-foot ceiling. The next set of doors was at the end of the nearest aisle, a hundred yards away.

As Jack scanned the warehouse with the memory-light, a sustained red flare erupted from somewhere near the middle of the vast space, followed by another scream, punctuated by gunfire.

"Everybody out." Priya motioned them backwards as she retreated. "They're using flamethrowers. We'll let them sort themselves out."

"Wait." Jack switched to a visible light, gradually increased the intensity, and pointed it at the top of the nearest rack. "Don't move. There's something here."

A pair of bright, gold-hued disks stared back at him. As the beam brightened, it illuminated an animal the size of a large dog watching from the highest shelf. Tomas raised his rifle.

Jack raised his hand and stepped forward. "Stop." The creature had a portal crystal on a chain around its neck. Jack felt a sense of recognition.

"What is that?" Tomas didn't lower his rifle. "It looks likes a cross between a dog and a dinosaur."

"It's … well … it's a dragon. It won't hurt us." *I hope.*

Footsteps pounded in an adjacent aisle; the runners were getting closer. The creature jerked its head away and disappeared. Jack dimmed the light, and Priya and Davis crouched and faced the aisle's entrance. Tomas spun to cover the rear.

Two men burst from the aisle. The first looked as if he'd rolled through a furnace; his camouflaged clothes were torn and singed. The second, with a deep gash running the length of his thigh, was leaning on him for support. Both were pointing assault rifles down the lane they'd come from.

"Drop your weapons," Priya ordered. She planted the invisible shield in front of herself and aimed her pistol alongside. Davis did the same.

The first man faltered. He looked into the aisle, then at Priya and Davis, who were in his path. He made a decision and swung his rifle toward Priya.

Before Jack could react, something flashed through the scene. The first man screamed, dropped his partner, and clutched his arm. A deep wound appeared on his forearm where the dragon slashed him as it passed, impossibly fast. Jack got a strong sense of a portal but no feeling of recognition as the beast leapt away, landing on a nearby shelf.

The second man had fallen to his knees and was trying to raise his own rifle when another blur knocked him backwards. The new dragon rebounded from the wall and landed on his chest.

Jack knew this dragon. This was the one he'd cut free of its chain recently, the one that had watched them enter the room from the top shelf, the one he told everyone wouldn't hurt them. It hunched low on the body of the second mercenary, pinning him to the ground.

"*Stop,*" Jack shouted as the dragon clenched a jaw full of razor-sharp teeth around the man's neck. "Please. Let him go."

The dragon paused but didn't release its grip.

The first man regained his feet and ran for the door. He managed only three steps before he was struck from behind. A third dragon had joined the fight. It was impossible to tell where it came from; it leapt from so far away that it had appeared to be flying.

The man's body armor had protected him from the claws, not the force of the blow. He bounced off the wall next to the door and fell in a heap. His rifle tumbled away, spraying bullets wildly around the room. A bright spark appeared in front of Davis, where a bullet ricocheted from his shield.

Until then, Jack had kept his personal shield tight around his body. Now he extended it to cover his companions. The effect was immediate. All three dragons turned on him.

Chapter 44

Jack strengthened his shield. It was impressive: a dome of frosted glass; a thick, powerful barrier that shimmered in the dim moonlight.

The dragon's shields were equally impressive.

"What's happening?" Priya said. "Why do those creatures have shields?"

Jack could think of only one answer. "Ethan's coin. They've found it and learned how to use it."

"How could they—" Priya began, then the dragons fanned out and advanced in unison. One of their shields touched Jack's with a discharge of sparks. The creature recoiled, then returned and pressed more forcefully, testing.

Davis hunkered behind his personal shield as sparks flew. "Can they get through?"

"Not yet. I'm using Ethan's ring. It'll take a while to overload."

"How many are there?" Priya asked.

"I didn't even know there were three. No, wait. Four. We saw a bigger one last time."

Two dragons circled Jack's shield. Their iridescent, snake-like hide glistened as they slunk with their heads low to the ground. The one facing Jack had a bluish tinge. Those to the sides were mottled greens and grays.

"We're trapped here, aren't we?" Davis asked.

The animals snarled as they probed the shield.

"Don't panic," Jack said. "I'm going to try something." He lowered his hand.

"Stop," Priya said as the dome faded. "Raise that shield again." She waved her personal shield, alternating between the two closest dragons.

"Pieter must have attacked them and used a shield. Now they think we're attacking too." Jack spoke directly to the one in the center. "It's okay, Blue. I won't hurt you." *Remember me?*

"Blue?" Tomas's voice was tinged with panic. "It has a name?"

"Gotta call it something."

As Jack lowered his shield, the beasts crouched into leaping postures, but he allowed the dome to weaken even more. Blue stood unmoving, with its eyes fixed on Jack's until the barrier was gone.

"What are they doing?" Priya whispered.

"Just wait." Jack exhaled slowly to calm his nerves. Could he regain the animal's trust now that people had attacked it? *We're here to help. The man in the transport chamber is not our friend.* "Tomas, lower your rifle. It's the same as what Pieter's thugs are using."

Tomas, crouched behind Jack while trying to cover both green dragons at once, hesitated.

"Please," Jack said. "It's the only way."

Reluctantly, Tomas lowered his weapon.

The barrier surrounding Blue winked out. The dragon glanced at its companions and their shields did the same.

Jack relaxed. "We seem to have reached a truce."

"Are they communicating?" Priya asked.

"See the chains around their necks? There are portal crystals there. They were originally used for tracking, but now the dragons must share a link to the AI through them."

"Can they understand you? The way the ravens do?"

Jack didn't know how to answer. It had felt natural; communicating with them as he had with the ravens, but he couldn't say if they were responding to his thoughts or actions.

A thunderous rumble shook the building. The beasts sprang towards the sound and disappeared into the gloomy aisles.

"What was that?" Priya asked.

"Pieter. I know where the coin is and why you couldn't find it. Pieter knows too." Jack started running after the dragons. "He's in the transport chamber."

The entrance to the half-mile tunnel was at the warehouse's far end, at the top of a metal staircase. A bloody handprint on the exit door near the base of the stairs showed that at least one of Pieter's guards had escaped that way.

Jack scrambled up the short flight of steps to the tunnel's entrance with his wand in flashlight mode so the others could follow more easily. He stepped into the corridor, expecting to see the dragons far ahead, but found one crouched facing him with fangs bared, ready to attack.

He backed up a step. The creature made an odd rattling growl but didn't move. Farther down the sloping tunnel, at the limit of Jack's light, Blue waited like an agitated cat with its tail snapping side-to-side.

"Okay, okay." Jack retreated to the stairs. "I'm stopping."

The tunnel floor trembled with another crash from the chamber. A screech that resembled an eagle's resonated through the corridor. Blue responded with a similar call. The dragon barring the tunnel twisted that way, then quickly returned its glare to Jack.

Jack shuffled towards the green dragon. "It's Pieter. I know what he's after. I can stop him." *I think you can sense my feelings. We're trying to help.* He inched to the side to walk past. To his immense relief, the beast allowed this.

Priya and the others moved to follow, but the dragon countered with an aggressive yowl and lashed its tail against the floor.

"This has to be just me," Jack said. "There's an opening in the dome's roof. That's where Pieter will try to escape." He sprinted towards Blue.

Priya motioned for the others to back up. "All right. We'll go around."

The green dragon watched Priya and the others until they left through the bloodstained door, then whipped its long body around and dashed towards the chamber.

- - - - -

305

Jack dimmed the plight and raised a shield again as he crept the final yards to the transport chamber. Blue and the other dragon had outpaced him and vanished long before he reached the end of the tunnel. Wherever they were now, they were staying quiet.

As he approached, he kept his wand trained on the gap in the ceiling, which was illuminated by a flickering red glow from deep in the overflow pit. An acrid stench of burning plastic rose from there in a column of black smoke.

He stopped several paces from the railing and extended his senses, searching for portals. *They've been busy*.

On his first visit, the dragon had seemed to be caching metallic objects, many of which contained a crystal. Now, he sensed hundreds of them scattered at different levels throughout the pit.

The hole in the roof was larger than he remembered, too. That was a good thing, because it allowed most of the smoke to escape. He leaned over the railing cautiously, but couldn't see beyond five yards.

He felt a sudden change in the energy field, the way he might have heard an unexpected gust of wind. It rose too quickly for him to raise a new defense. Part of an industrial air conditioning unit slammed into the scaffolding he stood upon. His shield absorbed the brunt of the blow and saved him from injury, but the force ripped the metal grate apart and he fell headfirst into the pit.

The shield spell was instinctive now. His existing barrier transformed into a sphere as he tumbled past dozens of small fires. Seconds seemed to stretch into minutes while he dropped blindly, unable to tell which way was up.

My original wand. Jack sensed it amid the disordered collection of crystals.

The flow of time returned abruptly to normal when Jack landed on his back. Thanks to the shield, he'd survived a hundred-foot fall without breaking anything, although he was dazed and winded. Ethan's ring burned his finger; its crystals were close to shattering.

He didn't have time to take it off, though. The air conditioning unit, momentarily caught up in the scaffolding, plummeted towards him. He used his wand to create a new, nearly opaque shield a moment before impact.

The machinery exploded with a deafening crash and a shock wave traveled through his body. Debris bounced and scattered on the surrounding floor. Smoke swirled in the eddies created by the falling mass.

Pieter's voice boomed from above. "Is this your doing? Did you teach these scavengers how to use a shield?"

Jack was too breathless to reply. He tried to sense where Pieter was standing, but there were so many portals scattered around that it was impossible to isolate just one. He crawled to the side of the pit and sheltered beneath the scaffold.

"I thought you of all people knew the difference between predators and scavengers," Jack groaned. *Got to keep him talking.*

Pieter laughed. "It doesn't have to end this way. It's your grandfather's portal I want."

That was enough for Jack to think he'd located Pieter. He scanned the room. A tire from the robotic vacuum—snapped off its axle—lay nearby. He captured it with his wand and flung it where he believed Pieter was standing. A grunt of surprised effort told him he'd guessed correctly. Pieter's wand flared and the tire rebounded at a much higher speed, but missed Jack by ten feet.

Our shields, Jack realized as the signature from Pieter's wand faded. *They hide the wormhole. He can't find me, and I can't find him as long as they're active.*

"Throw down your weapon and tell me where the frame is," Pieter said. "If you don't, I'll eventually find the coin and force the answer from your friends." Footsteps echoed softly around the chamber as he moved to a new position.

"Is that how you think of the wand?" Jack asked, keeping his voice low. "As a weapon?" He flung a handful of crystal-embedded debris into the air and rolled away. A jet of white flame struck the spot he'd just vacated. *There he is, above the first set of stairs*.

"And what would you do with it?" Pieter laughed. "Feed the poor?"

Jack netted two warped metal panels and flicked them towards Pieter's voice. He put a spin on them to make them fly without tumbling. Another surprised shout followed two loud crashes.

"*Enough*," Pieter thundered. "Tell me where the frame is now or I'll bring the entire roof down on you."

"That won't work. Your crystal is overloaded." He hoped Pieter didn't have the ability to sense the stress on the crystal; it was possible that Pieter's wand would outlast his own. "Go ahead and try. I've got hundreds of portals now."

Pieter laughed. "That's not all you've got."

A jet of fire speared the large branch on the pit floor as Pieter climbed the stairs. Jack scrambled behind the vacuum and hid while a dozen more lances ignited scattered debris. When he popped his head up, the spark of energy from Pieter's wand had already faded into the background clutter.

He coughed. The smoke was getting thicker, and it was harder to breathe. He couldn't risk turning off the shield, and Ethan's ring needed time to recover, but he had to have fresh air or he'd suffocate. He needed another portal; a large one.

Most of the crystals in the pit came from leg bands or animal tracking tags, too small to draw air from. He sensed the location of the nesting cache and started crawling, hoping to find something larger. Halfway there, he spotted a gold coin on the floor, but it wasn't Ethan's.

How did this get here? The coin's central crystal was smaller than Ethan's. *It's one of Pieter's spy-coins.* But they'd only sliced through the roof a few hours ago.

Jack reached for the coin but a warning growl made him freeze. At the same time, he sensed Ethan's coin. It was moving closer.

A dragon appeared from the haze with its head lowered and

fangs bared.

Chapter 45

The dragon lumbered towards Jack through the black smoke, a fusion of myth and Mesozoic.

The creature was more fearsome, more heavy-bodied than it had seemed the first time he encountered it. Then, its long sinuous tail created the illusion of a slim, lithe animal. But the beast menacing him now weighed at least three-hundred pounds. And the graceful way it had flowed over the railings belied its power and heavily muscled frame.

Still on hands and knees, Jack drew back from the red-hued dragon and noticed more spy-coins scattered on the floor. "You're collecting them?"

The dragon snatched the nearest coin away with a wicked claw.

Jack held his ground, but only just. "I wasn't going to use it to hurt you. We need air. Let me show you." Keeping his eyes on the beast, he opened the coin's portal. "Here—" *Something's wrong.*

Air hissed from the wormhole immediately. The dragon tensed and growled, reacting not to the coin but to Jack's surprise.

Why is there an airflow? I didn't create a link to another crystal. Cautiously, with the dragon watching him, Jack concentrated on the coin and realized his error. *The spy-coins aren't part of the regular network.* Instead of the virtual landscape he'd expected, he sensed just two connections: the other crystals in the set of three. *Of course, these crystals were still growing during Newton. The only reason there's air flowing is that the other two haven't been sealed in a communication device yet.*

As Jack relaxed, so did the dragon. It pressed its scaly nose to the coin, inhaled deeply, then curled its massive tail to its head and sunk to its belly. A noise somewhere between a cat's purr and the rumble of Priya's Mustang issued from its throat as it exhaled.

How long would a shield have held under those claws?

Movement in Jack's peripheral vision caught his attention. He glanced to his right as the blue dragon slunk up to the coin and dropped its head to breathe the clean air. Despite the heat, he shivered; he hadn't known Blue was in the pit. Then the green dragons emerged from the smoke and huddled near the portal.

Each beast wore a chain collar with a coin-style portal crystal mounted in a circular steel receptacle that joined two links. Even Blue, whose collar Jack had removed recently, had one again. The two ends—ragged where he'd cut them—were crudely fastened with wire.

He eased away from the cluster of dragons and stifled a cough. They seemed content, but he still needed fresh air—a lot of fresh air. He linked his wand to a low-elevation portal he knew of: a weather station on the Atlantic coast. The ocean-scented wind delivered many times more air than the breeze rising from the spy-coin.

The red dragon had been watching Jack. Its nictitating membranes closed, clouding its eyes. Seconds later, its coin portal whistled a jet of dry, desert air. The creature nodded to its smaller companions and clean air flowed from their portals too.

Jack gaped. *You learned a new spell.* But how? Then he remembered Pieter accusing him of teaching the dragons to create shields. He peered closely at the portal on the red dragon's chain: *Ethan's coin.* "*You* taught them the shield spell."

A small amount of fresh air made a big difference. His thoughts cleared as he inhaled deeply. *They're not caching shiny objects. Everything they collect has a portal in it. Or looks like a portal.* That's why Sarah knew *he'd* find the coin, not Pieter. It was because he didn't actually *want* it. Like the ravens, the dragons shared their memories with the AI through their portals. They must have been doing the same with Pieter and understood that he wanted not only Ethan's coin, but all the spy-coins. They'd only been defending their hoard. *I know how to defeat Pieter.*

"I've got the coin," Jack shouted. "But you'll have to come down here and get it yourself."

Pieter responded with a barrage of flame through the thick smoke, causing the dragons to activate their shields. His attack revealed his position on the third level of scaffolding, but Jack didn't act against him. Pieter's intentions would be his downfall.

As he descended the stairs, Blue leapt into the smoke clouding the first level while the red dragon dashed to the bottom of the stairwell. Pieter pressed on, spewing flames at every shadowy movement. Jack surrounded himself with a spherical shield from his wand and used Ethan's ring to produce a stream of cold air.

Pieter spotted Blue slinking towards him and sprayed fire, causing the small dragon to hunker down and intensify its shield. Seeing this, the red dragon flung its head back and screeched. Pieter was caught off guard when a jet of flame expanded from the coin around its neck and lit his jacket and one pant leg. He slapped at the flames in panic before remembering he could produce water from the wand. It took only a second to extinguish the fire, but he'd already suffered burns before he countered, tossing Blue—shield and all—over the railing.

Blue landed nimbly but Jack realized the dragons faced real danger. "I can help." He stooped and picked up a spy-coin.

The trio of entangled crystals that made up a third-eye connection would only ever create an entwined wormhole to the AI and each other. They'd never be useful for passing matter, but that's not what he had in mind. He could access the AI through any crystal. Pieter's wand could access any crystal. All the two needed was an introduction.

Can you handle more dragons?

Jack studied a green dragon creeping along the scaffolding and imagined how it might look from Pieter's perspective. Then he pictured the same beast approaching from the other side, and from above, and from below. His years of experience with lucid dreaming provided the focus he needed to envision a dozen creatures in intricate detail. He let the AI into his thoughts and pushed the images to Pieter the same way he sent instructions to the ravens.

Pieter staggered as the AI presented a memory of a horde crawling towards him. He jetted flames in every direction. The dragons, real and imagined, advanced.

"How are you doing this?" Pieter screamed as his blasts passed through the illusions. He abandoned his attack, enclosed himself in a shield, and started climbing.

One of the real green dragons swept up and over the railings and reached the top scaffold first. It then proved Jack's theory that it could learn from its larger cousin by jetting its own flame.

Pieter's shield held, but he couldn't lower it to counter-attack. He backed up the stairs, favoring his burned leg. One of his hands was red and blistered.

Jack dropped the illusion and followed the procession as Pieter crawled onto the mezzanine. The dragons stopped there and let him withdraw into the tunnel while Jack waited one level below. After Pieter fled into the darkness, they scurried back to the pit.

Jack plodded up the final steps, then slumped, exhausted, into a chair in front of a control station. He was dirty, sweaty, scratched, and bruised. But he'd defeated Pieter and found the coin, although he'd never get his hands on it.

The fires in the pit had nearly burned themselves out, and stars were again visible through the hole in the roof. Beams of light played in the leaves of trees surrounding the dome—Priya, Davis, and Tomas had missed all the excitement.

"I'm in here," Jack shouted. "Pieter's gone."

He was looking through the open ceiling, listening for an answer, when an invisible force swatted him from his chair. Pain lanced through his leg as it struck the corner of a metal console. His wand—which he'd been holding loosely—flew into the darkness.

"You didn't think it would end so easily, did you?" Pieter floated down the inclined hallway, as Jack had when rage overwhelmed him at the bridge. His single remaining guard, Angel, followed, nervous yet well-armed. "I will have that frame."

313

He sent another blast of pure energy from his wand.

The attack slammed Jack against the wall. He bounced and tumbled towards the pit, scrabbling for a handhold in the floor grating. For a dizzying moment, he tipped unsupported into the void until his wrist dragged over a jagged piece of metal. He caught the broken edge of the transport ring as he fell and felt it bite into his fingers.

A trickle of blood ran down Jack's forearm as he hung by one hand. He heard Pieter approaching. Without his wand, he had only Ethan's ring to work with, and it was at the point of failure. He'd have only one chance to use it.

But as Pieter stepped into view, he wasn't aiming the wand at Jack. Instead, he pointed it at the damaged ceiling, making it tremble and crack. Below, the dragons screeched in unison as bits of insulation and plastic fell on them.

Jack looked down, understanding that Pieter intended to bury the dragons. The red one was crouched on the upper level of scaffolding, but the others were at the bottom. Quick as they were, they wouldn't make it out in time.

Ignoring the pain, Jack raised his free hand and focused on the roof girder that Pieter was trying to dislodge. The wand crystal was far larger than the five in Ethan's ring combined, but Jack had a lifetime of experience with machines. To him, the steel beam was a simple lever. While Pieter used brute force, Jack countered with finesse. Even so, Ethan's ring began to burn. He dropped his gaze to the dragons and said, "*Climb.*"

Ethan's ring was now so hot that Jack could barely focus; the energy fields wavered and the roof groaned. It no longer mattered that the crystals were about to fail. If they didn't, he would. He closed his eyes, expecting a deafening crash as the roof fell. And then … nothing.

Jack opened his eyes. The red dragon had not escaped. Instead, it had climbed into the ceiling and wrapped its muscular tail around the trembling steel. It had stabilized the structure, but now it was vulnerable. Pieter, seeing that his efforts had failed, took aim at the creature.

An intense flash illuminated the chamber and a thunderous bang shook more insulation from the ceiling. Pieter tumbled up the inclined hallway and Sarah shouted, "*Leave them alone.*"

Ethan called from above, "You all right, Jack?"

[…]

Jack *heard* the dragon growl, but sensed something more through the AI: a warning. "It's okay. They're my friends."

The dragon calmed and Sarah jumped from the split in the ceiling, still pointing her wand at Pieter. She drifted far too slowly and landed far too lightly; she was wearing her earrings again.

Pieter's guard finally reacted. He raised his rifle and pulled the trigger.

This time, it was Ethan who dropped from the ceiling—fast. Sparks appeared ahead of him as he leapt, spinning his staff. His shield was invisible but Jack sensed it emanating from a crystal embedded in the wooden rod. He blocked the bullets easily, swatted the rifle away, and flipped the shooter's legs out from under him. He pressed one end of the staff against Angel's chest and shouted, "*Stay down.*"

Finally, the smaller dragons swarmed onto the mezzanine. Ethan saw them coming and jumped back, but the beasts ignored him and Angel as they launched themselves down the hallway, followed by the red dragon. Pieter ran but they were on him in seconds. Four jets of flame played across his shield. He stumbled and fell to the floor.

With Sarah's help, Jack scrambled onto the mezzanine. He staggered towards Pieter. "*Lower your shield.*"

If Pieter heard, he didn't listen. He tried crawling away, but the dragons surrounded him. Jets of fire from each of their portals coated his shield, which was becoming increasingly transparent.

Jack, knowing he could talk to the dragons through the AI, reached out to them. *Stop.* Blue glanced at him, then growled and fired another jet. *Please. He's done.*

Blue slashed once more at Pieter's shield, but stepped back.

The other dragons did, too.

Jack limped up the hall. "Lower your shield and drop the wand. They'll let you go."

Pieter said nothing.

"Your call." Jack shrugged and ambled away. The dragons focused on Pieter.

"Wait." He glowered at Jack, then allowed his shield to fade. Slowly. The dragons tensed.

"The wand," Jack said. "They won't let you leave with it."

Pieter tossed the wand aside. Blue slapped a taloned foot on it and the other dragons parted to create a path, watching Pieter closely as he stood and shuffled backwards. Voices sounded from the dome; Priya and the others had found their way to the top. Then a rope dropped from the opening, and Pieter turned and hobbled up the hall with Angel scrambling after him.

Jack felt no fear as he joined the dragons, and they showed no aggression at his approach. He crouched beside Blue. "Pieter can sense that wand. He'll come back for it."

Blue backed away from the rod and Jack picked it up, then inserted one end into a gap in the floor panels. He set his foot against it and looked to the dragons to be sure they understood. Their tails lashed, signaling their agitation, but they made no move to stop him. He pushed against the titanium case, felt it resist, and leaned his entire weight into it. A spray of fine particles jetted from the open end as the crystal shattered.

To Jack, the destruction felt like the creation of a void, a miniature black hole opening and disappearing. It brought a sense of loss, but also of closure.

The smaller dragons turned to leave, but the red one met Jack's eyes and *spoke*.

[...]

Once again, the sound was only a growl, but the extra push from the AI made its meaning clear: *Thank you.*

Then the dragons glided to the pit as one.

Chapter 46

"Why did you come back?" Jack asked as Sarah and Ethan rushed over to him. "I'm not complaining, but how did you convince the others you wouldn't be controlled?"

"We didn't exactly ask permission," Sarah said. "After you left, I listened through the portal again and realized I'd been hearing breathing. That's when I remembered the dragons were hoarding metal. But it wasn't metal, it was portals."

"I figured that out too. The hard way."

"So ..." A worried and confused look crossed Ethan's face. "Dragons can breathe fire now?"

"I'm guessing they can do anything you could do with your coin. They can also draw fresh air, so I won't be surprised if they learn to breathe underwater. Oh, and skip stones too."

Ethan leaned over the railing. "Is it safe to go down and get the coin?"

"*No.*" Jack raised an arm to bar Ethan from the stairs. "Don't even think about it. I mean that literally; don't *think* about it. Trust me, it's much safer where it is."

- - - - -

The mood that night was festive; Icarus was livelier than it had ever been. Everyone had returned safely, they'd defeated Pieter, and his coins were scattered across millions of square miles.

Suresh drove Priya onto the Vault, so she could return to Earth. She called Jack before hiding the radio in the cave and returning to Nevada.

"Your grandfather had the right idea but the wrong place. The portal has to be hidden, and it's best done in plain sight. I know someone who collects antique frames."

After she'd disconnected, Jack described for his friends how the dragons had communicated with each other and learned to use spells the coin had already performed.

"I think something went wrong with their obsessive gene." He flipped the spy-coin he'd picked up in the overflow pit. "The portals seem to allow them to communicate with each other, but it's like they're hoarding them."

"What I don't understand," Ethan said, "is how they came to be wearing chains with portal crystals in the first place."

"They must have needed constant conditioning and instructions," Sarah said. "I bet there was a motivator circuit built into their collars. And now that it's dead, they're obsessing over the coin portals that used to guide them. They must be able to link with the AI the way we can."

"Does that mean they could use the coin to control us?"

Jack laughed. "I really doubt it. I'm sure their minds don't work the same way as ours. But if you ever have the urge to chase squirrels, let me know."

"Are the dragons safe?" Sarah asked. "Pieter must sense that his wand was destroyed, but he knows the coin is there. He might go back for it."

"I suggested they move. I gave Blue an image of a place where I can keep an eye on them."

"A ley line? Which one?" Ethan faced the island and shuddered.

Sarah looked towards the Spine. "I know which one."

- - - - -

Most visitors to Fairweather Castle describe it as elegant, luxurious, and traditionally Gothic. Some say it's haunted.

Imported from England, the fifteenth century Tudor inn was reassembled stone by stone in a quiet, wooded valley near Puget Sound. Preoccupied guests will stroll its Hall of Mirrors without even glancing at their reflections in the diverse collection. Others will take a few minutes to appreciate the Renaissance craftmanship or the Baroque flourishes. But there is one mirror that captures the attention of some in a way no other can.

Guests have reported coming upon a friend or family member standing mesmerized, or speaking in confidential tones before a square, Art Deco frame. When questioned, the affected person has no recollection of how long they've been there or what they've said. Others feel as if they're being watched, or hear the breathing of a huge animal, or feel a moist draft. Some claim to have followed a hooded figure, then found the hall empty when they turned the corner. Guests near the passageway report opening their doors to investigate late-night footfalls or voices, only to find a vacant corridor.

The fortunes of the inn, and of Earth itself, shifted over the years. Fairweather stood empty for decades after the first portal crystals reached the distant world known as Dawn, sparking *the Great Migration*. Cirrus faded into legend as most of Earth's population made the one-way trip deeper into the galaxy's gravity well. The inn changed hands many times, survived many trials, and much of its history was forgotten. No one recalled when or where the name came from, but the mirror's reputation lived on.

It became known as, *The Blue*.

ABOUT THE AUTHOR

John Harvey lives in British Columba. He trained as an Electronic Engineering Technologist and worked for decades in Information Technology and Healthcare Support Services before turning to writing and freelance editing. He writes mostly science-fiction and fantasy, but occasionally delves into humor.

Manufactured by Amazon.ca
Bolton, ON

20726958R00189